Margaret Skea was born in Ulster, growing up there through the 'Troubles' but now lives with her husband in the Scottish Borders. An Hawthornden fellow and award-winning short story writer - credits include Neil Gunn, Winchester, *Mslexia* and Fish - her first novel, *Turn of the Tide*, set in 16th century Scotland, won both the Beryl Bainbridge Award for Best First Time Novelist 2014 and the historical fiction section in the Harper Collins / Alan Titchmarsh People's Novelist Competition. The sequel, *A House Divided*, was long-listed for the Historical Novel Society New Novel Award 2016. *Katharina: Deliverance*, the first of the Katharina novels, was runner-up in the Historical Novel Society Novel Award 2018.

For more information about Margaret Skea, or to contact her, please visit her website
www.margaretskea.com

sanderling

Also by Margaret Skea

Katharina: Deliverance

Munro Series (Scottish Historical Fiction)
Turn of the Tide
A House Divided
By Sword and Storm

Short Story collection
Dust Blowing and Other Stories

KATHARINA:
FORTITUDE

Margaret Skea

sanderling

Published by Sanderling Books in 2019

Cover design by www.hayesdesign.co.uk
Layout by www.ebook-format.com

Cover image: Katharina von Bora / Martin Luther by Lucas Cranach the Elder. National museum (Stockholm) Photographer: Erik Cornelius (Public Domain) Wittenberg: 1546 engraving, photo: petervick 167/ 123RF

ISBN: 978-0-9933331-5-6
Sanderling Books
28 Riverside Drive
Kelso
TD5 7RH

Main Characters

The von Bora Family
Katharina von Bora, 1499–1552
Hans von Bora (father), died before 1523
Anna von Haugwitz (mother), died 1504
Hans and Klement, Katharina's brothers (also Franz, died in infancy)
Frau Seidewitz, Hans von Bora's second wife, (Johannes and Emil, sons)
Magdalene von Bora, (later known as Muhme Lena) sister to Hans senior, a nun in the Marienthron convent at Nimbschen
Anna, a servant

The Luther Household at Mansfeld
Hans Luder, father, 1459-1530
Margarete Lindemann, mother, 1463-1531
Martin Luther, born Luder, 1484–1546
Barbara, Dorothy and Margaret, Martin's sisters
Jacob, Martin's brother
Cyriac, Martin's nephew

Colleagues and Friends
Eberhard Brisger, last prior of the Black Cloister
Johannes Bugenhagen, pastor of Town Church, Wittenberg
Walpurga, his wife
Georg Rörer, deacon of Town Church, Wittenberg

Lucas Cranach, painter, printer and apothecary, Wittenberg
Barbara, his wife
Justus Jonas, dean at Castle Church, Wittenberg
Katherine (Kath), his wife
Andreas Karlstadt, professor, dissenter
Anna, his wife
Philipp Melanchthon, Luther's chief co-reformer.
Katharina, his wife
Johann Agricola, co-reformer, professor
Else, his wife
Caspar Cruciger
Elizabeth, his wife
Jerome Schurf, physician
Hanna, his wife
Eva Axt (von Schonfeld) Katharina's closest friend from
    Nimbschen days
Basilius, her husband
George Spalatin, secretary and chaplain to Elector
    Frederick
Herr Köppe, merchant at Torgau
Dorothea, housekeeper at Lutherhaus
Jerome Baumgartner, student and early suitor of Katharina

Other Notable Characters
Chancellor Brück
Albert, Archbishop of Mainz, elevated to Cardinal of
    Magdeburg in 1518
William Tyndale, Bible translator

House of Wettin – Ernestine Line

Frederick 'the Wise', Elector of Saxony, 1486–1525
(Catholic)

John 'the Steadfast', Elector of Saxony, 1525–1532
(Lutheran)

Johann Frederick 'the Magnanimous' Elector of Saxony,
1532–1547 (Lutheran)

Prince John Ernest

House of Wettin – Albertine Line

George, Duke of Saxony, 1500–1539 (Catholic)

Henry, Duke of Saxony, 1539–1541 (Lutheran)

Maurice, Duke of Saxony, 1541– and Elector of Saxony
1547–1553 (Lutheran)

Other Nobility

Charles V, Holy Roman Emperor, 1519–1558 (Catholic)

Duke Albrecht of Konigsberg (Lutheran)

Count Philip of Hesse, leader of the Schmalkaldic League
(Lutheran)

Duke Franz of Lüneburg

Henry VIII of England

10 ml. Magdeburg

N

Mansfeld •

Eisleben •

Frankenhausen • • Allstedt

• Mühlhausen

Eisenach

The Wartburg

• Erfurt

R. Werre

Worms 125 ml.

Jena •

• Schmalkald

Thuringian
Forest

• Coburg

Map of Saxony and Surroundings

The Wife of Noble Character

'A wife of noble character, who can find?
She is worth far more than rubies.
Her husband has full confidence in her
and lacks nothing of value.
She brings him good, not harm, all the days of her life.
…She gets up while it is still dark;
she provides food for her family
and portions for her servant girls.
She considers a field and buys it;
out of her earnings she plants a vineyard.
She sets about her work vigorously;
her arms are strong for her tasks.
She sees that her trading is profitable
and her lamp does not go out at night.
She opens her arms to the poor
and extends her hands to the needy.
…Her husband is respected at the city gate.
Where he takes his seat among the elders of the land.
…She watches over the affairs of her household and
does not eat the bread of idleness.
…Her children arise and call her blessed;
her husband also and he praises her:
'Many women do noble things,
but you surpass them all.'
Charm is deceptive and beauty is fleeting;
but a woman who fears the Lord is to be praised.

Proverbs, Chapter 31
The Bible

Torgau: September 1552

They say autumn is coming. And I well believe it, for though Frau Karsdorfer has lit the stove and Margarethe has placed an extra coverlet on the bed, the air is chill, my fingers white-tipped. I turn my head towards the window and see the diagonal line stretching from corner to corner of the small upper pane, the two halves creaking in the draught slipping between them. I told Frau Karsdorfer, when the bird flew against the glass causing the first star-shaped crack, 'That pane should be replaced. Else when next there is a gale it may break altogether.'

It seems she didn't listen, or perhaps, if I am to be charitable, didn't properly hear. I worry her hearing is increasingly faulty, for though I am sure my voice is strong enough, oft-times of late I have to shout to make myself heard. And when she comes to bend over me, I see concern in her eyes, as if it is I who have a problem. Frau Karsdorfer I can understand, for she shows her age, the skin of her neck wrinkled like an over-ripe plum. But Margarethe and Paul are young. If they are also struggling to hear, we must find the money for them to be examined.

I slip my hands back under the blankets and rub them together, seeking for a warmth to spread through them, as it once did, as surely as if they rested on a warming pan. Anna could not tell me the how or why of it, despite my plaguing, but when Hans, taking pity on her, sought to explain, he used words I didn't understand, and I wished I hadn't asked, for listening to him made my head sore.

Father, appearing halfway through the lengthy explanation,

13

said, the corner of his mouth lifting, 'Well, well, Hans. It seems we must send you to the university, if your bent is for the scientific.'

Klement smothered a guffaw and Hans flushed, and I felt sorry to be the cause of his discomfort. But when Father had gone, Anna, with a smile for Hans and a glare for Klement, put her arm around me and squeezed me against her side.

'It doesn't matter, Liebchen, how it works, only that we are grateful to the good God who planned it that way for our comfort.'

Now, however hard I rub, my hands remain as cold as if I were in my grave, as others are. Father, Mother, Anna. Even baby Franz.

Muhme Lena once said, when we were still at Nimbschen, and word came my father had died, 'No one is truly gone while they are remembered.'

My memory of him then consisted of little more than the scratch of a beard against my cheek and the roughness of his palm as he pulled his hand from mine and his final gruff 'Be good, Katchen.' I can picture him now, as clear as if he is standing at the end of my bed; as he sometimes does, my mother at his side, the scent of lavender surrounding her like a cloud.

A cart rattles over the cobbles, vibrating the broken pane and blowing a gust of air across my face, nipping my cheeks. I shall ask Paul, when next he comes, to sort it. In the meantime, perhaps the shutters should be closed, though it would be a shame to shut out what little sun penetrates this chamber. It is slanting across the floor and touching the bed frame, and I edge my toes sideways in the hope of catching its warmth, but it isn't strong enough to penetrate the covers. If only I could be at home, where

14

the sunlight pools on the floor of our bedroom and sets aflame the gold threads in the embroidered bedspread Barbara gave as a wedding present, the pipes and drums adding a splash of cheer to an otherwise dull room.

'Something beautiful to bring you joy,' she said. 'For your love of music.'

How well she knew me.

CHAPTER ONE

WITTENBERG, JUNE–JULY 1525

The music stops, the sound of the fiddle dying away, the piper trailing a fraction behind, as he has done all evening. I cannot help but smile as I curtsy to Justus Jonas, his answering twinkle suggesting he shares my amusement.

'Thank you, Frau Luther.' And then, his smile wider, so that even before he continues I suspicion it isn't the piping amuses him, 'For a renegade nun, you dance well.'

It is on the tip of my tongue to respond with 'For a cleric, so do you', but I stop myself, aware that should I be overheard it would likely be considered inappropriate for any woman, far less a newly married one, to speak so to an older man, however good a friend he has been. And on this day of all days, I do not wish to invite censure. Instead I say, 'I have been well taught. Barbara saw to that. She did not wish me to disgrace myself or her, and there is a pair of slippers with the soles worn through to testify to the hours of practice she insisted upon.'

'She succeeded admirably then.'

All around us there is the buzz of laughter and chatter, an air of goodwill evident in every flushed face. Martin is waiting at the foot of the dais, and as we turn towards him, his smile of thanks to Justus is evidence he too is grateful for the seal of approval, of me and of the marriage, our shared dance a tangible sign to the whole town that Justus Jonas at least has no reservations regarding our union. Over his shoulder I catch Barbara's eye and she nods also. I nod back but am unable to suppress altogether the inner voice, *Tonight there is drink taken, tomorrow some may feel differently.*

As if he can read my mind, Justus says, a new seriousness in his tone, 'You have not made a mistake, either of you.' He waves his hand at the folk clustered in groups along the length of the room. 'Look around. When the difficult times come, as no doubt they will, remember tonight and the number of those who came to wish you well.'

The first challenge is not long in coming. We stroll home in the moonlight, accompanied by those guests who will spend the night in the cloister with us, adding their acceptance to our union. Among them are Martin's parents and three councillors from Mansfeld, snatches of their conversation penetrating my thoughts.

Hans Luder's tone, though gruff, cannot mask his satisfaction. 'It is a good day's work, and glad I am to see it, however long the wait.'

Martin's mother's voice is sweet and low, but bubbles with amusement, like a sparkling wine as it is poured into a glass. 'Old you may be, but I trust your end is not yet nigh.'

There is an answering chuckle from one of the councillors. 'Indeed, Frau Luder, so do we all.'

Hearing him, I tuck my arm into Martin's, the momentary disagreement regarding Cardinal Albert's gift forgotten, and look up at the myriad stars – pinpricks of light in an ink-flooded sky – and my heart swells. *Frau Luther* – the spelling may be different, but the status is the same, and a title to be proud of, and though our marriage is already two weeks old, it is the first time I have felt it truly mine. The music still rings in my ears, the memory of the dancing, the coin in the chest: all symbols of the regard in which the doctor is held and in which I now share, spreading a warmth through me from the top of my head to the tip of my toes. Justus is right. This is not a mistake, or not on my part at least. And, pray God, he is right about Martin also. We part from the company at the door of our chamber, and the light from the oil lamp flickers on the bedspread Barbara Cranach gifted to us. It is the last thing I see before sleep, the first when I wake, a talisman-harbinger of good things to come.

At first I think the insistent rat-a-tat rain, and shiver. Despite the triumph of the previous day, despite Justus' encouraging words, it is hard not to think of omens and portents, however much I wish to be free of such superstitions. I do not want our marriage to be heralded by ill weather; for even if I take no heed to it, there are others who will, and some with the power to sway more credulous folk. I think of Philipp Melanchthon, poring over his astrology texts, his gloomy predictions a blight

18

on our decision. Would he have felt differently had Martin chosen someone else? Likely, yes. I am too forthright, too willing to share my opinions on matters best left to those who, by diligent study, have earned the right to pontificate. If the weather turns foul there may be many to think Melanchthon right.

I trace the bold pattern on the coverlet with my fingertip, the music it represents a flowing counterpoint, rising above the steady drip, dripping of the rain. I turn my head towards the shuttered window, thinking of the chipped overhang – another job in the long line of repairs required before winter. Perhaps it will be a passing shower, long gone before daybreak. The noise increases, and belatedly I recognise it is someone pounding on the cloister door. I slip from the covers wrapping a shawl around my shoulders, my toes feeling in the darkness for slippers, thankful Martin is a heavy sleeper, for I do not wish him disturbed. I catch my foot against the leg of the bed and collapse back onto the mattress, the bed frame creaking, and he stirs.

He pulls himself upright, unease clear in his bunched shoulders. There is a roughness in his voice, as if there is sand on his tongue. 'Who demands entrance on this night of all nights? And where is Brisger?'

'Asleep, perhaps? And with the amount he drank last night, hardly surprising.' I regret the criticism instantly, for with all his faults, of which I have become only too aware in the last fortnight, Brisger's loyalty to Martin cannot be questioned. And loyalty is to be prized. And this is, after all, his last night in the cloister, a fact he might have wished to dull with beer. And who could blame him, for it has long been his home.

We are part way down the stairs when I realise I have maligned him, for he has beaten us to it and is already hauling back the bolt, the sound clearly audible from outside, for the knocking stops. As the key grates in the lock I mentally add a locksmith to my list of tradesmen that must be engaged, lest one day it fail altogether. There is a murmur of voices, the first one unknown to me, but even without being able to make out the words it is clear it is refuge they seek. The tension in my shoulders and neck drains away. Not trouble then, or not directed at us at least. I turn to look up at Martin following close behind, my relief countered by the firm set of his mouth and the mounting colour in his face. I know his glare is not for me, but in that first instant it still has power to wound and I forget the manner in which I have determined to address him in front of others. 'Martin?'

He brushes me aside as if he doesn't see me and takes the stairs two at a time. Apprehension mounting, I follow. As he reaches the bottom Brisger turns, his face ashen, his hands trembling. Over his shoulder I see he has pushed the door to again, and fear solidifies like a lump of lard in my stomach. His glance slides past me and he rubs his tongue across his upper lip, taking a deep breath. 'It is…'

'I know *who* it is,' Martin says, his harshness reinforcing my fear. 'What I do not know is why that spawn of Satan should come here now.'

I have heard the phrase before, in the Cranach's Stube, Martin spewing invective like vomit, Melanchthon seeking in vain to moderate his outburst, Barbara holding herself stiff as a board, her knuckles white. There is only one person he can be referring to, for the other man he once described in that manner is dead. I share Martin's surprise

20

that Andreas Karlstadt should arrive on our doorstep, and in this manner, but I cannot share his feelings. For whatever has happened since, I owe my salvation to him and thus my marriage.

The knocking begins again, punctuated by a whimpering, as of a child. I move towards the door. 'We must let them in.'

'Must nothing.' Martin grasps my arm to halt me. 'He has forfeited the right to our hospitality.'

It is our second disagreement here, and though I am less sure of my ground, for this is not a matter of household cleanliness, which any reasonable person might consider my domain, I surprise myself by the firmness in my voice. 'We are told to forgive seventy times seven. I do not think any wrong he did to you can amount to that.' This time the glare *is* for me, and for the first time I see why caricaturists sometimes depict him as a turkey-cock, for he puffs up, his hair an unruly tangle around his face. 'And besides' – I look to Brisger for confirmation – 'it is the middle of the night and his family are with him. You will surely not turn a wife and child away?'

There is a moment of silence before Martin capitulates, though his words and voice remain stiff. 'I am not an ogre, they can stay for tonight, but as for longer, that will depend.' He glances at my nightgown and my slippered feet peeping from beneath the hem. 'You should return to bed, lest you are embarrassed in the company of strangers. If I need you I will send. Either the Karlstadts are come belatedly to wish us well, which I very much doubt, or, as is more likely, they are in some trouble, though why Andreas should expect me to clean up a mess of his making after all that has passed between us is anyone's guess.'

The knocking begins for the third time, the child's whimper become a thin wail. Martin's irritation resurfaces momentarily before he nods to Brisger, who scurries back to pull the door wide.

Ignoring his injunction, I draw my shawl more tightly across my chest and tie the ends together to stop it falling open, and strive for a reasonable tone. 'I cannot judge the rights and wrongs of it, but I am the hostess here and it will be easier for the children if they see a woman.' I meet his eyes, risk, 'They will not think *me* an ogre.'

Martin tenses, then bows, an ironic gesture, a fencer acknowledging a strike. Despite that he uses their Christian names, there is no warmth in his voice. 'Andreas, Anna. This is unexpected.'

Anna Karlstadt is clearly aware of his reluctance, and I feel sympathy for her and anger on my own account, for this is not how we should treat guests, however unwelcome. There is a fractional pause before he draws me forward, a telltale throb in the muscle under his right eye and more than a hint of sarcasm as he says, 'Lest you think I have fallen further from grace, let me introduce my wife, Katharina. You will not have heard of my recent good fortune, as the Wirtschaft was but today.'

Karlstadt steps forward. 'Martin…'

Without his support Anna sways, her weariness apparent, and I take her arm. 'Come. You must be tired, and the children also.' And to Brisger, who is hovering in the background, 'Attend to the stove in the Stube. It should not take much to stir it into a blaze. And bring some food and drink. Late as the hour is, our guests are no doubt in need of some sustenance.' I meet Martin's eye, dare him to contradict me. 'And whatever the day, or hour, or circumstance, our home is always open for those who are in need.'

The younger child, whom I take to be perhaps three, and whose face is buried in Anna's skirts, lifts her head and stares at me, causing my stomach to lurch. Her eyes are red-rimmed, as if dust has been ground into them, her pupils enlarged – no wonder Barbara feared for them when Karlstadt broke with Martin. But whatever the theological differences it is not right his family should suffer. 'Come,' I say again. 'Time enough for explanations when your physical needs are dealt with.'

'You are indeed fortunate, Martin.' Andreas attempts a smile with the quotation. 'The worth of a good wife is beyond rubies.'

Whether it is calculated or not, it is a fitting commentary on the day just past, and though there is no answering smile from Martin, there is a relaxation of his shoulders, the veins of his neck no longer standing out like taut cord. I seize the opportunity. 'If you will see them to the fire, I will go to supervise Brisger, for I fear he is not well practised as regards hospitality.'

I am rewarded by a tremulous smile from the older child and a sound halfway between a sob and a cough from Anna.

Andreas bows. 'Thank you.' He draws in a deep breath, exhales again. 'We are in your debt.'

Martin waves away Andreas' thanks. 'Katharina is right. We will talk tomorrow. For now, let us see to the children, and' – he inclines his head to Anna – 'to your wife.'

23

There is no further sleep for us, though the Karlstadts, for whom we prepare two makeshift beds in a spare chamber, do not surface until noon, which gives us time to see off the wedding guests without having to offer any explanations. I try not to allow thoughts of our midnight arrivals to cloud my face as we bid the others goodbye.

Martin's mother hugs me as they depart, her genuine affection cheering my heart. His father also has a smile for me, and a word of encouragement.

'It is a good thing you have done, Katharina von Bora' – there is a twinkle in his eye – 'and one I shall pray daily you have no cause to regret.'

'Hush, Hans!' Margarete shakes her head. 'Do not listen to him, Katharina. We will surely pray for you both, but our prayer will be that God will grant you joy in each other' – she glances at her husband – 'as he has us.'

The guests trickle away, the last to go, Herr Köppe and his wife. 'Will you,' I begin, feeling a constriction in my throat, 'Will you…'

Frau Köppe nods. 'I will tell Eva she was much missed.' She places her hand on my arm. 'She would have been here if she could, for she talks of you constantly. It is her one regret, in moving to Torgau, that there is distance between you, but it is not so far and I'm sure she will seek to visit you soon.' She smiles. 'I shall tell her you have done wonders with the Black Cloister and then she won't be able to stay away, for curiosity's sake.' She casts a glance at Martin. 'Or perhaps you may be able to find an excuse to visit Torgau. You will both be equally welcome there.'

We return to the Stube, which I have established as our temporary living space; serving as a place to work, eat, or as now, simply to sit. Martin alternately pokes at the stove and peers out of the window, and I know his thoughts are also with the Karlstadts. I am unsure whether to risk opening a discussion of them before they wake, or whether it is better left until we have heard Andreas' story, and likewise cannot settle to anything productive. I spy some crumbs, fallen from the bread and cheese with which we fed Andreas and his family, and unwilling to leave Martin alone long enough to retreat to the kitchen to find a brush, I go down on my knees under the table to pick them up. It is as the bells ring for the quarter hour that we hear the front door opening again, and this time there is no hesitation in Brisger's voice as he welcomes the Cranachs. They blow in, the door swinging behind them, Barbara shaking off her cloak and tossing it onto the settle.

'You may be glad it wasn't so windy yesterday. We walked part of the way by the riverside and were nearly blown into the Elbe twice. But wind or no, we could not let today pass without coming to compliment you on how the day went. It is all the gossip in the square, and I suspect those who did not attend now wish they had.' She pauses for breath and glances at me and then at Martin and then back to me again, and raises her eyebrows.

I jump in before Martin can. 'We had unexpected visitors last night…'

'We still have,' Martin cuts in, 'but have not yet had an explanation for their coming.'

'Not entirely welcome, then,' Lucas says. 'Who…'

'Would you welcome Andreas Karlstadt after all that

25

has passed?' Martin has begun to pace, his face to flush, a sure sign he is working up to an outburst.

Barbara, ever the pacifist, says, 'If he has come to offer an apology, to return to the fold, what then? Will you receive him as the prodigal, or act the older brother?'

The barb strikes home, and when Martin doesn't reply, she continues, 'We are none of us faultless, nor able to cast the first stone, and I for one would be happy to kill the fatted calf for them.'

Behind her the door opens, Anna Karlstadt framed in the entrance, and with her the two children, their faces scrubbed clean, their hair neatly braided, though the edges of their caps are in shreds, the cloth tinged grey. Anna's face is flushed and I wonder how long she stood outside, how much she heard.

She steps towards me, drops a curtsey. 'My apologies, Frau Luther, I did not intend we should sleep so long. I hope it has not inconvenienced you.' She looks at the Cranachs. 'Or forced you to change your plans for the day.'

I begin, 'No, not at all…' But Barbara is on her feet, bridging the distance between them in a couple of strides and enveloping Anna in a hug.

'How good to see you… You have suffered much, I know, but I trust you are in good health nonetheless?'

There is a slight hesitation before she answers, 'Yes … thank you.'

Barbara smiles at the children peeping shyly from behind Anna's skirts. 'These are your girls?'

'Gerda and Marta.' A shadow flickers across Anna's face. 'We had a son.' Her glance at Martin is shy. 'We called him for you, but he survived only three months.

Perhaps' – she touches her stomach again – 'next time it may be different.'

There is an awkward silence, broken by Lucas. 'Where is Andreas?'

'Here.' He is hesitating at the door, as if uncertain of his welcome, as well he might be after Martin's reception of him last evening. I will Martin to go to him, and clasp his hand and draw him into the circle, but it is Lucas who makes the first move.

'A pity you had not come a day earlier, you would have approved of the Wirtschaft. The town was out in force to wish Martin and Katharina well.'

His eyes are on me and his expression is kind, not that of a zealot; and I determine to do all in my power to heal the breach between him and Martin, for they are both good men, despite their theological differences.

He slides his tongue around his lips, looks over at Anna. 'I'm afraid we do not wish to be so public. In fact, yourselves aside, we would prefer...'

'If no one knows you are here?' I see the effort it is for Martin to keep the edge out of his voice.

Andreas nods. There is a simplicity and a hopelessness in his voice. 'I did not know where else to go.'

'With Müntzer gone?'

'Martin.' There is warning in Lucas' voice. 'It does no good to rake over old ills.'

Andreas raises his head, and for the first time I catch a glimpse of the steel once his watchword. 'It will not be an old ill if it is not addressed.' He meets Martin's eye, his gaze steady. 'I did not advocate violence, nor lend credence to it, any more than you did, but like you I must acknowledge some small part in it all.'

27

Martin flushes, and opens his mouth to respond, Barbara jumping in.

'How long will you stay, Andreas?'

It is the question in all our minds, but she is the only one with the courage to voice it.

'As long as they wish,' I say. 'And in more comfortable conditions than we were able to offer last night.' My smile is for Anna. 'Now that our wedding guests have departed we have chambers to spare; all that is required is to change the sheets. Since' – I risk a touch of humour, in an attempt to lighten the atmosphere – 'I have managed to convince Dr Luther of the need of such things.'

'And not before time.' Barbara follows my lead. 'You wouldn't believe it, but when Martin married, the straw of his mattress had not been changed in two years! It's a wonder it didn't walk out of the cloister itself.'

Lucas guffaws, and Martin has the grace to look shamefaced, and for the first time I hear Anna's silvery laugh.

They have been with us a month, the thaw between Martin and Andreas almost complete. The first week was awkward and strained, the past enveloping them in a fog I feared couldn't be dissipated. But, as is often the case, it is the children who are the catalyst. It is my first experience of seeing Martin with children and I cannot but feel a warm glow as I watch him dandle the younger girl on his knee and sing to her. If God gifts us children he will be a good father. And once having begun to love the children, it is impossible to maintain his distance from their parents.

Especially when Bugenhagen and Justus Jonas call often, as if as a bridge, to spend the evenings reminiscing about the early days, when Andreas was a lecturer and Martin a student.

We sit around the table after supper, the conversation lively, the laughter frequent, the need that drove the Karlstadts to seek refuge and their continuing reluctance to be seen about the town little more than a shadow in the background. Anna too has relaxed, no longer startling at every knock on the door, her innate sense of fun allied to common sense more apparent with every passing day. Her face is filling out, becoming rounded, the suspicion I had when I first saw her solidifying into near certainty, though I am not yet sufficiently confident in our friendship to risk it by direct questioning.

Barbara, calling in to renew acquaintance with Anna, also avoids any conversation that might be considered probing.

We three are outside, sitting in the shade of a pear tree in what will become our garden, once I have opportunity to tackle it. I stretch and yawn, and Barbara, with a lift of one eyebrow, says, 'Tired, Kat?'

'A little. I took a notion last night to make an inventory of all the rooms and their condition and it took rather longer than I anticipated.'

'You have plans for them?'

'We cannot sustain this house on Martin's salary alone, despite the generosity of the duke in both cash and kind.'

'What then?'

'Students.' I am thinking aloud, my ideas crystallising as I share them. 'There was always so much going on when I stayed with you I hadn't thought what it would be like to rattle around in such a large house.' I look at Anna. 'It has been so good to have you all here; it has brought the place alive. And when you go, I will miss you sorely.'

Barbara looks surprised. 'Are you leaving, Anna?'

She nods. 'In a week or two, I think. Oh, don't worry, this won't be another moonlight flit. We think to take a house of our own.'

'Here? In Wittenberg? Is it safe?'

'Andreas and Doctor Luther think so, at least once Andreas' retraction is published. For now we remain in hiding, but once the reconciliation is public knowledge we should be able to go about without fear.'

Barbara is direct, as usual, but her words are spoken in such a pleasant tone it is impossible to take offence. 'How will you live? Will Andreas return to the university?'

Anna smothers a sigh, faint colour staining her cheeks, though her voice is steady. 'He says not. Returned to the fold he may be, but he clings to his belief that honest toil is his true vocation. Once it is safe to be seen about he will look for employment in the town.' She speaks with confidence, but her eyes betray a lingering uncertainty.

I remember, when Barbara first talked of the Karlstadts, how she spoke of the need of a wife to be loyal to her husband. From everything I have heard, then and since, Anna Karlstadt has proved her loyalty tenfold, but I cannot help wondering what the cost has been, what it might still be.

Barbara offers a reassurance. 'There is plenty of honest toil to go around, for anyone willing to soil their hands. If he isn't overly fussy he will find employment … perhaps Lucas could make use of him…'

This time Anna is definite. 'He will not accept anything he might think of as patronage, so we must let him search out his own work. He has found it hard enough here' – she gives me an apologetic smile – 'to stay without being able to contribute to the household purse, and is determined he will repay you so soon as he is able.' She hesitates. 'He has always been able to give and give, even to the point of almost penury for his own family, but to be on the receiving end of the generosity of others is a different matter altogether.'

'There is no need of repayment.'

Barbara cuts in, 'He is not alone in that. It is a failing of many good people, but one they should be helped to overcome. When you find a house, and if furnishing it is necessary, we will help.' She forestalls any protest. 'Just to begin with, until you can find your feet. I have an attic full of unneeded items. And if Andreas is minded to object, leave him to me. I will convince him it is a temporary measure only, until you have a chance to choose your own things.'

The sun is dipping towards the west, the shadows lengthening. Anna stretches out her feet to find the last sliver of sunshine, and says, 'There is another reason why I want to be in my own place. I want…' – she takes a deep breath – 'when our son was born we were constantly on the move and in fear of our lives, and though in my calmer moments I do not think it the reason he died, yet I do not want this babe to be born a refugee.' She hesitates, then in a rush, her face flushed, continues, 'I would like … I would be honoured if you would both agree to be

31

godmothers to the child.'

'Of course.' I reach out to grasp her hand.

'The honour is ours,' Barbara says.

I expect her to smile, but instead she toys with her nuptial ring, and I sense there is something else troubling her, some deeper reason for her fear for this child. She is studying her feet, her voice a whisper. 'If word was to get out, it might spoil everything.'

Barbara is gentle. 'Whatever it is, Anna, rest assured you may share it with us and we promise it will go no further.'

Our heads are bent together, almost touching, and she swallows. 'Our son … he died unbaptised. It is Andreas' belief the only baptism that counts is one done when a person has made their own choice.'

My mouth is dry, but I tell myself it is superstitious to react so, that it was, at least in part, to renounce superstition I left the convent. I squeeze her hand, trust it is enough.

Barbara doesn't hesitate. 'Did not our Lord say, "Suffer the little children to come to me"? He will not refuse an infant entrance to heaven. Your son is there now, I'm sure of it…'

She pauses, and I think of the family portrait hanging in their Stube, and the three ghost-children Lucas included. It is a tradition I think more cruel than kind, likely the reassurance she offers Anna for herself also, and baptised or not, the loss of her own children a pain equally sharp. I cannot but admire her courage as she continues, 'There are many children in heaven, three of ours among them; always in the sunlight, always happy, and' – she takes a deep breath – 'however hard it is, I know they wouldn't choose to come back, even if they could.'

32

CHAPTER TWO
WITTENBERG, AUGUST 1525

The idea that germinated in the first weeks of the Karlstadts' visit takes root and grows in the days that follow. And by the time they are ready to leave, the plan is fully formed in my mind. To take in students is so obvious, I do not expect any opposition. There are many details to be worked out and preparations to be made; and with the house almost empty once more, I set to with a vigour and enthusiasm equalling my initial attack on the cloister. It is an antidote to the silence; no pitter-patter of children's feet as they chase each other up and down the stairs, their high piping voices echoing in the corridors, and no companionable chatter as Anna and I sort winter clothes for them. She stopping their wriggling while I pin and tuck and tack and think how fine it will be if we are so blessed.

I have never lost the convent habit of waking before dawn, nor been able to remain in bed once awake, and it stands me in good stead now. Martin appears by turns amused, rueful, and on occasion mildly exasperated, but I am becoming used to him and take no hurt from his gentle mockery. If I have learnt anything from my years in Wittenberg, it is that words, good or ill, are not always matched by deeds. Martin is proving a kind and considerate husband, and for that I thank God daily.

The Karlstadts have been safely installed in their own place for a week when Martin appears in our kitchen mid-morning. I am elbow-deep in suds, and startle, swinging round, gobs of foam flying from my fingers. My first thought is of some trouble to bring him home at this time, his ready smile as he steps back to avoid being splattered, reassuring. I scoop up a handful of suds, as if my intention is to scrub him also.

'Good timing, Doctor Luther, the water is warm.'

He looks down at himself in mock consternation. 'Frau Luther! I am a reformed character, am I not? And almost worn away with washing.'

'Reformed, certainly … in doctrine at least, but as to practicalities' – I tilt my head to the side – 'that I am less sure of.'

'Perhaps this may convince you.' He slips a hand into the pocket of his Shaube. 'If you are to persist in the endeavour, Käthe, you will have need of this.' He takes my hand, and placing a key in my palm, wraps my fingers around it.

It is warm from his touch, but inside I am warmer still. I think of the Reichenbachs, of Elsa, and how she was required to account for every pfennig; and of the Cranachs, where, despite Lucas' generosity, it is still he who controls the finances. Whatever Martin may say or think of my plans for the cloister, however often I see a hint of uncertainty in his eyes, I will be confident in this: he trusts me to hold a key to the coffer and I can plunder

34

it at will.

'Martin, I…'

He places one finger against my mouth. 'Shh. Squirrel it away quickly, lest I am tempted to change my mind. When we married I knew you to be sound in faith and virtue, and with a quickness of mind and seriousness of purpose I appreciated, even if others did not.' I know he thinks of Philipp Melanchthon, as I do, for he is not yet reconciled to our marriage and has not visited us since the Wirtschaft. He shakes his head, as if to clear it, and continues, 'In these past weeks you have proved yourself to be industrious and capable and a worthy helpmeet.' A hint of a smile. 'As Barbara assured me you would.' He clears his throat, as if embarrassed by the sentiment. 'I thank God for the day he brought us together.'

I look down and see a trail of mud-clods across the flags, fallen from his boots; and to cover my embarrassment, I say, 'You should also be glad Barbara warned me of the work I would face, else the shock might have been too much for me.'

He follows my gaze, his expression comical. 'I'm sorry, Käthe, I'll get the brush, but later, for there is more I wish to say.' There is a new, more serious note in his tone. 'It may not be possible for you always to run to me when money is needed, especially if I am called away.' He nods at the key in my hand. 'This is a safeguard, that whether I am at home or abroad, our work here will continue.'

It is the first time he has said 'our work', the first open admission he approves, at least in principle, of what I seek to do with this mausoleum in which we live. I dip my head again, lest he misinterpret the tears standing in my eyes. It is an odd thing, and can be a mite inconvenient,

35

that when I am happy or especially moved, I am like to cry, yet when something bad happens, inappropriate or not, it is laughter that bubbles up inside me.

The first students are not long in coming, and whether it is my determination to offer good value, the price I place on board and lodging modest, or the lure of the opportunity to sit at table with the good Dr Luther himself that proves irresistible, the rooms are taken as quickly as I can I make them ready. Martin is in his element, his conversation at dinner an extension of his teaching, so that it isn't long before some are spending more time scribbling away in the margins of his pamphlets than in eating.

In the privacy of our chamber I express my concern. 'It won't do, Martin.'

He turns, one stocking rolled down to his ankle. 'What won't do?'

'All this talk while the students should be eating. They are paying to be fed in stomach as well as mind. I do not wish them to return home half-starved. It would reflect ill on us both.'

'What can I do? They ask questions. I cannot refuse to answer them.'

'We must set rules.'

'We?' There is a note of surprise in his voice.

'We,' I repeat firmly, and then to sweeten the pill, 'They will, of course, be presented as *your* rules, and, as such, will be accepted.'

He straightens his shoulders, and I see I may have a fight on my hands, but it is one I am minded to win. Barbara's voice rings in my head, *He needs a wife, Katharina, and not some pretty little thing who would be all Yes, Martin, and No, Martin, and Anything you say, Martin. He needs someone who wouldn't be afraid to challenge him if she thought him wrong, nor to shrivel if he reacted badly to the censure.* It has already proved valuable advice in relation to small things, but this is the first major issue. I touch his arm. 'It is not only the students who will benefit, but you also. We teach children not to eat and talk at the same time for a good reason, and it isn't just to avoid seeing the half-chewed food in their mouths. *Your* digestion will benefit from the chance to work without competition from your tongue. And your health be improved as a result.'

'What do you suggest?'

He is halfway to capitulating, so I press on. 'Institute a time for discussion *after* supper.'

He is clearly considering, but remains silent.

Another idea pops into my head, one so appealing I think he cannot fail to approve it. 'If it is afterwards, others, who don't board here, will be able to join in. Like the discussions you used to have at the Cranachs', only on a larger scale.'

'I must have a name for it.' His enthusiasm is building and I smother my smile, for if he can be brought to thinking it his own idea, it will ensure a speedy implementation.

He stretches out on the bed, his hands linked behind his head, pronounces, 'I shall call it "Table Talk".'

37

Chapter Three
Wittenberg, September 1525

The name sticks, and as word spreads, the number that wish to join our gathering increases almost daily, and I form a new idea. It will mean more work, but the two maids I have already employed to help in the running of the household are competent and I am sure I can find another equally so. It is as well to be prepared in any case, for, although I have no experience of the matter, I suspect I may not be able for heavy work before long. Barbara, when I ask if she has a recommendation for another servant, looks at me appraisingly.

'Someone is unsatisfactory?'

'No...'

She laughs. 'I thought not. I take it is to relieve you of some of the burden, so that you will have time for other things?'

'How did you know?'

'I *have* had children, Kat, and know the signs.'

I look down at my waist, still trim. 'But there is nothing to show as yet.'

'Not bodily, no. But your eyes betray you.'

'Do you think Martin…?'

'Has also guessed?' She laughs. 'If he has, he will be the first new husband of my acquaintance to do so, and I think that unlikely.'

I am twenty-six years old and feel as ignorant as a bride of fifteen, and I am grateful I have Barbara to fill the void of the mother I lack. 'How soon should I tell him?'

'How far on are you?'

'I have missed my monthly courses only once.'

'Early days then. If all goes well, and I shall pray it does, let it be a Christmas gift. That will be soon enough. Much as it is nice, on occasion, to be treated as if you are as fragile as glass, and as precious, the restrictions soon pall, as Eva found. It is one thing to be confined to home near the end, when the effort of going out is almost too much to make in any case, quite another when you begin to feel more alive than you have ever felt before.'

'Will I?'

'Of course. For the middle months at least.'

I feel the fear, which has been pressing like a weight on my chest for the past two weeks, begin to lift, but a kernel of unease remains, and although it will further display my ignorance, I ask, 'Should I feel sick? I have a constant churning inside, as if I could vomit at any moment. Though as yet it is a feeling, nothing more. I don't feel like eating, but have forced myself, for a lack of appetite Martin would certainly notice.'

'Didn't you know to expect that, Kat? It's perfectly normal, and in the natural course of things it will pass soon enough.'

I know her well enough to realise she doesn't mean her amusement to prick, but it does, nevertheless. 'How could I, when my only experience is with cows, and they can hardly tell me how they feel.'

She puts her arm around me, squeezes. 'I'm sorry. You have adapted so well I forget sometimes how little experience of ordinary life you have had. If there is anything, anything at all you want to ask, you know you can come to me.' After a fractional pause she turns me to face her, all hint of laughter gone, and says, 'It would be remiss of me not to warn you, Kat. There are always risks. To the babe, and to the mother. Plenty of young widowers can testify to that.'

The warning is unnecessary, and I look away, willing her not to remember my own history, lest it embarrass her.

'But you are sturdy and in good health and have as good a chance of a happy outcome as any, and likely better than most.'

I nod my thanks and in an effort to change the direction of the conversation broach the other reason I have for seeking a new servant, for I wish Barbara's opinion on that too. 'There is something else I wanted to ask.'

'Ask away.'

'You know how popular the Table Talk is? And how many seek to join us?'

'I know there are inns in the town whose profits have increased as a result, though the comfort of those who stay in them must be in doubt.'

'That's just it. *We* could take in guests in addition to the students; folk who wish to come to listen and debate with Martin, for a night or a week or a month even. What do you think?'

'There is space enough. But have you considered the cost? Room is one thing, but you will need extra

40

furnishings: beds and bedding, seating, a larger table, and then there is the food and servants to prepare it all.'

'I know. I have ideas about that too.'

'Have you broached these ideas with Martin, or is it something else you are hiding from him.'

'Not hiding, exactly, just waiting for the right moment: as you once counselled. We would need to charge for their lodgings. I cannot see any other way. But Martin…'

'Will think it God's work and therefore wrong to profit from it?'

'Is that what *you* think?'

'Of course not, but that *is* the reaction you fear?'

'Yes.'

'And you need a way of convincing him it isn't profit you seek, but simply a way to make it possible without driving you into penury.' She is looking past me, to the window and the would-be garden outside. 'Perhaps Lucas…'

It is a kind offer, but one I don't allow myself to accept. 'This is something I need to do myself. But it is important to know *you* do not think me crazy, and therefore others may not either.'

Her voice is firm. 'I have never thought any idea of yours crazy, Kat, and I don't imagine I ever will. But Martin, as we both know, has his own notions, and it will likely take all your ingenuity to circumvent them. But if anyone can do it, you can.'

I am about to thank her for her confidence in me when there is a knock at the door.

One of the maids pops her head around. 'Begging your pardon, Frau Luther, you have a visitor. Will I show him up?' There is a hesitancy in her voice that cannot

41

be explained merely by the fact the visitor is a man, for Barbara's presence makes that acceptable.

'Who is it?'

She moistens her lips with her tongue. 'Herr Melanchthon, Frau Luther. I wasn't sure if you would want me to ask him to return when Doctor Luther is here.'

My heart is thudding in my chest and there is a pounding in my ears. Under the cover of the table I ball my hands into fists, but my voice is steady. 'Show him up. There is no reason for him to go away, when I expect the Herr Doctor home at any moment.' I turn to Barbara. 'If you will keep us company in the meantime?'

'Of course. I am in no hurry, and we have not seen Philipp ourselves for a week or two, nor his wife. I shall be glad to hear how they do.'

I nod a dismissal to the maid and she scurries off, her feet slip-slapping on the stairs.

Barbara, as if to avoid any comment on Melanchthon's unexpected appearance, focuses on the maid. 'That girl's shoes are ill-fitting. Aren't you worried she'll come a cropper?'

'I cannot persuade her to let me buy her new ones. It is a misplaced pride, but I admire her for it.'

'She has your independence of spirit.'

'Yes, and similarly came to Wittenberg with little to call her own. That's why I cannot force her, but I must respect her desire to save for what she needs. If there was a way of adding to her wage packet I would do it, but it would do her a disservice if the others thought her favoured.'

There is a heavier tread on the boards outside, the creak of the handle as it is turned, and I add a mental note to put

42

oil on the list of purchases that must be made. Barbara grasps my hand and whispers, 'This is but a minor test, and you are able for it.'

It is the second time in as many minutes she has expressed her confidence in me, and never more needed.

We rise and curtsy in unison. 'Herr Melanchthon.'

I am scrabbling about for something to say that will sound neither effusive nor unwelcoming but remind myself the awkwardness between us is not of my making and so determine to speak as if I am perfectly at ease. 'Please.' I indicate a seat at the table, Barbara and I sitting down opposite him. 'I expect Doctor Luther to return shortly and you are welcome to wait for him.' An imp of mischief prompts me to add, 'Frau Cranach and I have been setting the world to rights. Though you may not consider that an appropriate occupation for women.'

Under the table Barbara presses my foot, and for a fleeting moment I think of Martin and wonder what his reaction might be to my baiting, but in the past he defended my right to think for myself, and by inference the right of any woman of intelligence. Melanchthon was no more in accord with him then than he is likely to be now, but he is on my territory, and all the more reason for me to control the conversation. I summon up my broadest smile, choose to let him off that particular hook, but trap him on another.

'I have not seen your wife and children since my marriage. I trust they are all well?'

There is a pink tinge to his normally pale face,

betraying discomfort. 'Yes. All well. Katharina is kept busy of course.'

Once again Barbara presses my foot, as if to warn me not to react to what might be construed as a barb. This time I ignore it.

'A pity she isn't with you. I would have been pleased to see her.' I wave my arm around the room. 'While I have a way to go yet in making the cloister comfortable, my friends are welcome here at any time. As Doctor Luther's have always been.' I pause for a moment, tilt my chin. 'Please convey my greetings to her, and say I trust our friendship is of such standing she need not wait for a formal invitation to visit.'

'Of course.' He is floundering, seeking for excuses. 'We have had visitors ourselves of late, and workmen in the house…'

His relief is clear as we hear Martin's booming voice in the hallway.

'We have a visitor? I'd best present myself then. And bring some beer. I am as dry as a ditch in summer.'

Melanchthon rises to his feet and I hide my smile as Martin enters, and flinging off his cloak, he bows to Barbara, then turns. 'Philipp. Good to see you here. And not before time. You will stay for Table Talk?'

Those who have joined us for Table Talk have left to return home or find their own lodgings. The students have retired, the servants also, and the candle on the top of the unlit stove is almost burnt down; but still we sit, in companionable silence, watching the flickering flame. We

44

will have to move soon, or get undressed in the dark, but I have no wish to be the first to break the spell. Taken in the round it has been a good day.

Martin leans back in the chair and stretches out his legs. 'I knew Philipp would come to his senses, given time.'

I slip onto the floor at his feet, rest my head against his knees. 'A pity it could not have been before the Wirtschaft.'

'His loss, not ours.'

'Katharina's loss also, and ... mine.'

'Yes,' he concedes. He pats my hair, and I know he means the gesture as a consolation as he continues, 'But no doubt, now Philipp has made the first move, you two can renew your friendship, any awkwardness forgotten.'

It is an optimism I don't altogether share, for while Philipp may wish to heal the breach with Martin, and rightly so, I'm not convinced he will favour the kind of social contact we previously enjoyed at the Cranachs'. But he is one of Martin's oldest colleagues, and it pained me our marriage caused a rift between them, so I'm glad it is at least part way to being mended. And whatever my reservations, I say, 'I do hope so, for these past weeks I have missed her.'

'I'm surprised you've had time to miss anyone, the wonders you have worked here. If I didn't know it was the place I have lived in for more years than I care to remember, I would think it somewhere else altogether.'

I smile up at him, the compliment pleasing. It is as good a time as any to broach my latest plans for the cloister. I capture his hand. 'There is something else I thought to ask your opinion of.'

'Concerning the house? That is your territory.'

'Concerning what we do with it, which is also yours.'

'Go on then. The sooner you tell me, the sooner I can object, as no doubt I should.' The warmth in his voice belies his words.

'Your Table Talk is becoming daily more popular, not just among students and colleagues, but people from further afield also.'

'Indeed. It is a cause for satisfaction God's Word is spreading and I have some small part in it.'

There are many who do not think Martin Luther humble, and with good reason, for he voices his opinions as if they are the gospel itself. When he writes, the words pour out of him like a river in spate, and once committed to paper, he refuses to edit them. It is a streak of stubbornness, an undoubted failing that most of his closest friends regret and have often attempted to moderate, without success. But though I share their frustrations, there is another side to him that is less bullish. I have seen his private face and know that oft-times he struggles to think himself worthy of his calling. And while he has not been struck down by melancholy since our marriage, barely three months have passed, and I am not so foolish as to believe he will never suffer from it again. If my latest idea is to survive his scrutiny, it is encouragement he needs, so I say, 'You are too modest, Martin. Think of how far folk come, the privations they suffer to be here.'

'Privations?' He seems genuinely surprised at my choice of word.

'Barbara was here earlier, and talked of the quality, or rather lack of it, of some of the accommodation in the town. She confirmed my own opinion and the plan I have been considering.'

The candle gutters and I hurry on, not wishing to have to start all over again at some other time. 'How many monks lived here when the cloister was full?'

'Around forty, perhaps at times a few more.'

'We have only a dozen students. What if we were to take other visitors also?'

'If you think you can cope, no reason why not.'

To have him agree in principle is the easy bit. I take a deep breath. 'We will need an extra servant, and more provisions, and to make the remainder of the rooms habitable, buy furniture for them...'

'Ah.' He backtracks. 'A fine idea, but how are we to finance it? Our resources aren't limitless.'

This is the crux. 'We must charge board and lodging.'

'Charge? To have opportunity to discuss God's Word? It is one thing the students paying for their keep, but visitors who come only for the Table Talk? That is a different matter altogether.'

'We wouldn't be charging for the Word.' I will him to understand the difference. 'We would be charging for them to be fed and made comfortable, as they are not in other places.'

'They do not come here to be made comfortable, but rather to be challenged.'

'In thought, yes. Of course. But it is their physical needs I think of.'

'I was not altogether comfortable in the months I spent at the Wartburg, but I cannot regret it, for the German New Testament was the result.'

'But were you flea-ridden? It is hard to think clearly when being killed with the itch. Only tonight, I saw Herr

Ritter scratch at his wrists until the flesh was almost raw. It wasn't hard to see he suffers from fleas and most likely picked them up here in Wittenberg. Is that what you wish? For folk to take more than the Word away with them? What kind of a witness would that be? And fleas might be the least of what might be contracted, for as you well know there are parts of the town less than savoury, and disease never far away.'

The candle gives one final splutter before we are plunged into darkness. After a moment, in which we each readjust to the gloom, Martin says, 'This is too big an undertaking to be decided on a whim. I will think on it.'

And that is as much progress as I can expect at one sitting.

CHAPTER FOUR
WITTENBERG, OCTOBER 1525

Barbara and I are in the room I have turned into a laundry, stacking bedsheets and blankets on the shelves Andreas Karlstadt has made for me. Anna has been working all the hours for the past two weeks, cutting and hemming and pressing, and my stockpile grows daily. I do not regret giving her the work, but I do need reassurance. 'I hope I am not asking too much of her, Barbara. With the children and her pregnancy and her own house to sort?'

'You are giving them both the chance to earn something, and until Andreas has proper employment I'm sure they are grateful. Besides, she is at the "nest-building" stage of her pregnancy and likely has more energy now than she knows what to do with.'

Without realising it, I touch my own stomach.

Barbara nods at my hand. 'You are sure, now, you also are expecting?'

'Yes.' I'm dismayed to hear the reservation in my voice, for I'd rather keep the fears I have to myself.

'And the sickness?'

I make a face, relieved Barbara has jumped to the

obvious conclusion. 'Worse every day, and now I *am* vomiting, but only first thing in the morning, and so far I've managed to get to the privy and be done with it without Martin realising anything is amiss.'

My relief is short-lived as she narrows her eyes. 'There's something else troubling you, isn't there?'

'It is a foolishness I should be able to ignore.'

'Sometimes,' her voice is gentle, 'sharing such thoughts diminishes them.'

I think of the first problem I shared with Barbara, and of how she had whisked me from the Reichenbach's house and into her own before I had time to protest. How right she was then, how often she has been right since. But this... I take a deep breath. 'When I was at Nimbschen, Abbott Balthazar often preached of the Antichrist: that he would be born of the union of a monk and a nun. It was his favourite sermon, alongside his rants regarding a too lax approach to the rules of our order.'

'You don't believe that nonsense?'

'No ... not really. But it is hard not to think of it... And what if he *was* right? What if this baby...'

Her response is swift. 'If he was right, there have been thousands of Antichrists through the ages, and assuredly this child is not one of them.' She takes both my hands in hers. 'God brought you and Martin together, Kat. You know that.'

'I believe it. But believing and having confidence can be two different things.'

'You know what Martin would say to such superstition. And he'd be right.'

That thought is enough to make me laugh, and together we turn back to the pile of sheets.

She opens a new topic. 'How *did* you convince Martin about taking paying guests?'

'I talked so much and so often of the privations those of our visitors who couldn't afford to stay at The Eagle, or who found all the rooms taken, were suffering in other establishments and the risks they ran of fleas and worse. And claimed you were of the same opinion. By the end of it I had him scratching and feeling unwell himself. I cited poor Herr Ritter's problems in such detail his ears must have been burning.'

Barbara is laughing. 'And was Herr Ritter really scratching as vigorously as you described?'

'Oh there was no need for exaggeration, I promise you. Indeed, I was watching carefully in case I saw something jump, for I had no desire to catch one myself. I did think to offer him a salve, but I wasn't sure he would want attention drawn to his discomfort.'

'Better that than be killed with the itch, I'd have thought.'

'So would I, but I caught his eye at one point, and he coloured so furiously and tugged his sleeve down over his hand, so I thought it best to leave it. Those of his class are sensitive in these matters.'

'As you would know.'

I nod my head, recognising the reference to my own knightly background. 'True enough. My brother Hans was nearly boiled alive in the bath Anna insisted on when she thought he'd caught a flea from one of the hunting dogs.'

'Poor Hans. The remedy seems almost worse than the ill.' She deftly folds the last blanket and slides it onto the shelf. 'And is Herr Ritter one of those who will be your first guests?'

'Yes.' I make a face. 'And I don't mind telling you, I am a mite concerned about what other guests he might bring along with him. I can hardly insist he bathes in lye first.'

The new venture, as with the students, is an immediate success. And though it is even more work than I thought, the servants prove equal to the task. Dorothea is invaluable and quickly becomes not just my second-in-command but a friend. I would like to share the news of my pregnancy with her, but it doesn't feel right to tell anyone else in the household before Martin. Sometimes I catch a speculative look in her eyes and imagine she suspects, but she doesn't ask. And for that I value her even more.

In the early weeks there is little time for any social contact other than with our boarders at mealtimes, and missing Barbara and the hours we managed to snatch together, I begin to look forward to Table Talk on my own account.

The discussions, far from being entirely theological, are wide-ranging: on princes and parenting, lawyers and laziness and, of most interest to me, diseases and their remedies: some so bizarre it's hard to credit anyone could take them seriously. Martin's contributions are sometimes serious, at others spiced with humour, often directed against himself, and have the company roaring with appreciation, the students in particular seeming to relish the discovery that Dr Luther is not just a fiery theologian, but a wit also.

The noise of the clatter of dishes generates a discussion

on the divisions of labour in a well-run household.

Martin waves his hand in the direction of the sounds. '...when I begin to trouble myself with brewing and cooking, be sure I am about to die.'

'As might we all,' I say, 'for nothing short of a miracle could protect us from your efforts.' For a moment there is silence, the eyes of the assembled company fixed on me, those most disdainful of my presence radiating disapproval.

Martin's 'You've got the right of it, Käthe' deflects their censure, his accompanying guffaw encouragement for others to laugh also.

It is the first time any comment of mine has produced merriment in this company and, however ridiculous it seems, it feels like a milestone: in our marriage and in my journey towards acceptance among those who throng to our table. Milestone it may be, but it is not the end of the journey, as I discover soon enough. For there is humour in which I cannot share. I question Barbara, 'Why is it men consider it amusing to talk of bodily functions, and in such a forthright manner? We do not speak thus.'

'Women do not think thus. Or not in my experience at any rate.' She is staring at the goblet in her hand, running her thumb up and down the curve of the cup, her tone reflective. 'Sometimes it seems we are a different species. I see it in the children, from the moment they can walk and talk, actions, attitudes, everything different. And the older they get the greater the differences become. You had brothers, Kat. Did they think as you did? Or act as you would have done?'

'We were all different. Hans protective. Me rebellious. Klement ... just ... Klement. Taking pleasure in poking

53

fun, in annoying or frightening me, and as different from Hans as could be. And Franz only a baby. If I had seen them grow up perhaps I might have found similarities between them, as it was... And as for Johannes and Emil...'

'Who? You've not mentioned them before.'

'Stepbrothers. And the reason – or their mother was at least – why I was sent away.'

Barbara is biting her lip. 'I'm sorry, Kat, I didn't mean to stir up difficult memories. But men and women *are* different. I'm convinced of it.'

I drag my thoughts back to the problem of Table Talk and my place in it. 'Last night the discussion was particularly wide-ranging, the humour coarse and, in my opinion, more suited to the alehouse than our table. I couldn't stop myself protesting, but it was clear from the expressions of those around me that they thought my comments inappropriate, both as a woman and as a wife. Should I have kept silent?'

'In principle, no. In practice? Probably, yes.'

'Afterwards I overheard one of the students talking on the stairs, expressing sympathy for Martin in having to suffer a wife who didn't know her place. I could perhaps have ignored that except for the response, "If word of her forwardness gets out, Martin's reputation will suffer as a result". If it gets out? How can it not with Viet Dietrich having taken it upon himself to be the chronicler of all that is said.'

Barbara is thoughtful. 'And does he?'

'There are several of them. Scribbling away as if Martin's words are gospel itself, every one of them important.'

'And they aren't?'

I ignore the amusement in her voice and pursue my own thought. 'I do not imagine I will escape their commentary.'

She sobers. 'I don't imagine you will.'

My desire to know her opinion wars with a fear of her answer. Desire wins. 'Am I forward? Growing up where I did, as I did, shut away, I find it hard sometimes to know what is the right thing, and harder still to do it.'

'Forward? No. Forthright, yes, and sometimes' – she makes a moue of apology – 'a little unwise perhaps in the timing and manner in which you express your opinions.' She sucks in her bottom lip. 'If I may offer some advice?'

'Always. You know that.'

'Well then, if in public you must seek to be circumspect in what you say and do, in private you may speak your mind. And perhaps in time what you say in private will moderate what Martin says in public. For whatever anyone may think, he values your opinions … as he should.'

I am worrying at a slub in my skirt. 'Sometimes I wish it could be as it was last year, in your Stube, when the only censure I received for speaking out was from Melanchthon. And that I could ignore, for it was clear Martin paid no attention to his criticisms, so why should I?'

'Are his reactions different now?'

'No. He treats me just as he does any of the others. If he agrees with my opinion, he says so, and if not, he is his usual dismissive self. But it is clear many of those present think it a fault in him.' Not for the first time, and despite that it is more than two years since I escaped from Nimbschen, I am conscious of how little I really understand of the workings of the world outside the convent. How much I still need to learn. 'If, before our marriage, when he had no reason to give me any special consideration, he could support me without it reflecting badly on himself, why should it be thought so wrong now, when there is every reason?'

'It was easier for him to support you then, Kat, precisely because of the lack of connection. Because he couldn't in any way be held responsible for your views. Whether we like it or not, the world sees a wife as an adjunct to her husband, and he, like Adam, is to be held to account for her actions.'

'So I am Eve, even when I am in the right and Adam wrong?'

She shrugs. 'In the eyes of the world, yes.'

I open my mouth, but she gives me no chance to speak. Her tone is firm, almost stern, as if she is a lecturer and I a student who needs to be convinced. 'Do not judge your influence by the thoughts of others. You have a husband who has proved his willingness to take account of your opinions, and as you have seen, sometimes to his own detriment.'

'So what *should* I do?'

She repeats her earlier advice. 'In public give him the deference convention demands, and in private chastise him to your heart's content; neither will do him harm and both may do him good.'

'If I am always to keep silent at Table Talk there is little point in my being there at all.'

'To be there at all is a statement of the respect in which he holds you. Take it slowly, Kat, and choose your battles. In time, those who are privileged to sit at his table, whether the great and the good or lowly students, will be used to your presence and may even come to recognise and value your contributions, as those of us who know you best already do.'

It is a comforting thought, but I'm not sure how true it is, or how far it may stretch. 'To Justus Jonas and Bugenhagen, yes, and Lucas of course, but I cannot count on any supporters beyond that, though I know of many detractors, and some with the power to make significant difficulties for us.'

'Have patience, Kat. Between your chidings and the demands of Table Talk, Martin is persuaded to take at least two good meals a day and all of that is your doing. No one who has been familiar with Luther can dispute the improvement in his appearance since your marriage. His shirts are clean, his cuffs no longer trailing threads, the Shaube, gifted to him by Duke Frederick, always freshly brushed and free from stains. In health too he is improved: his skin no longer pallid, his cheeks filled out, the whites of his eyes jaundice-free. You can take pride in it, for I know it is not always easy.'

'You can say that again. I do take pride that for the most part he eats regularly and well, for he has had many years to develop the bad habit of shutting himself away when he is writing and ignoring everything and everyone else until he is done. Acceptance that our marriage has been good for Martin in physical terms is one thing, but it's a long way from considering my *opinions* valuable.'

Don't fret, Kat. Recognition in other respects *will* come.'

'I hope so. If I had a gulden for every time in the last three months I have said "It will not do, Martin", I would already be a wealthy woman.'

Barbara laughs, which was my intention. 'I doubt that. You would no sooner receive it than he would give it away again.'

'True. "Generous to a fault" doesn't even come close. But I am learning to be creative in shepherding our finances. Someone needs to be.'

'And none better.'

As the weeks progress, I wrap Barbara's confidence around me like a blanket and determine to take her advice to heart. For the most part I bide my time, confining my contributions at Table Talk to the posing of questions, and even then, only when I judge the discussion uncontroversial. Though some frown upon any comment I make, my husband does not. His willingness to allow me to be part of it, despite protests from some quarters, is a constant source of encouragement. And often, when everyone else has retired, he re-ignites the discussion, as if he recognises both that my earlier reticence is in deference to him and that I may have something of value to add, and we continue far into the night, our exchange of opinions open and honest and free-flowing.

It serves to distract me from the fear of the child blossoming inside me that, despite Barbara's reassurance, still surfaces from time to time. And though I pray for peace in this matter, I derive little comfort, for compared to the fervour of our devotions in the convent, my prayers, now when they matter most, seem feeble and weak. I choose a moment when we lie companionably close, the afterglow of intimacy drifting us towards sleep to say, 'Under the Pope we prayed so ardently and so frequently. If we seldom found answers to satisfy then, can we really expect more, now that our prayers are less rigorous?'

He sits up, once more fully awake, and I sense a perplexity, as if he wonders why I should ask a question of such seriousness at this particular moment. But his response is swift and clearly intended to be encouraging. 'Do not fear for your own weakness, Käthe, for it is on God's strength we depend. You know His promise – He will always give us more then we can ask or think.'

I hope so. I really hope so. Mindful of Barbara's caution, I resist the urge to share the news of my pregnancy, but I begin to wish for December to come and the moment when it will be safe to do so. And I try to embrace Martin's confidence as my own, making a conscious effort to quash my other twin concerns: one, he may not wish for this child as passionately as I do; and two, when he is told of it he may also be disturbed by the superstitions of the day.

The days are shorter now. Darkness stealing upon me when I have scarcely had time to enjoy the light. When I comment on it to Paul, he opens his mouth as if to contradict, then snaps it shut again as if he thinks better of what he was about to say. And I am glad, for I am too tired to argue with him. Nor do I wish to. Besides, it is not good for a child to correct a parent, I have taught them all that, though they haven't all paid the same heed. And perhaps it isn't surprising, for they are used to hearing the cut and thrust of discussion between their father and I, the tossing back and forwards of ideas. And as Martin is often outrageous in his comments, how can I expect otherwise of our children. Young Martin is the argumentative one, always ready with a response, whether appropriate or not. He is like my brother, Klement, a sobering thought, for he has always been trouble. But lately I have thought Young Martin is also a little like his father, lacking in understanding of when to speak and when not. I must encourage them both to take more care.

I shift sideways on the mattress, seeking to find a more comfortable position, but each day it seems the lumps and bumps increase, digging ever more deeply into my spine. We haven't had it very long, but perhaps we should see about getting a replacement. Margarethe is closing the shutters, and as she turns I beckon her over. 'Ask Barbara,' I say. 'She will advise you.'

'About what, Mutti?'

Who will make me a new mattress, one that will last and at a fair price. This one has not proved suitable.'

She bites her lip, faint colour tingeing her cheeks. 'It isn't

60

ours…'

'You needn't be embarrassed. She won't mind, she never does.'

'Barbara isn't here,' she says, settling beside me, her forehead knotted. She takes my hand, strokes it. 'Barbara is dead, Mutti.'

I look over her shoulder and smile. 'Nonsense. Here she is. You can ask her now.'

She hesitates. 'Mutti…'

To save her discomfort I say, 'Never mind. I'll do it.' Behind her the candle gutters. 'Can you fetch another candle? I do not wish us to be plunged into darkness when we have a guest.'

She stands up, moves towards the door, as if relieved to escape. 'Of course, Mutti.'

Barbara has a dress draped over her arm, and though I am used to her gifting me clothes from time to time, I wasn't expecting anything today. It distracts me from the problem of the mattress, and fishing for clues, I say, 'Barbara, how kind. Have we a special invitation?'

She is smiling. 'I looked this out for you this morning, for I guessed you will be needing it soon. And my need of it is well past.' She spreads the dress out on the bed and I see the extra fullness in the skirt, the raised waist.

She was right. I did need it, sooner than I'd imagined.

Chapter Five
Wittenberg, December 1525

November slips into December almost unnoticed, the days, though short, marked by crisp, clear mornings and cloudless skies, the virgin blue overhead paling to almost white on the horizon. Now that my sickness has abated, and I can safely leave Dorothea in charge of the morning chores, I take to walking into the town every day, to purchase any needed provisions. The daily exercise is as good a way as any to make use of my increased energy and dispel the restlessness that makes sitting inside impossible.

The new gown Barbara has lent me rustles as I walk and complements my heightened colour, and I bless her for her thoughtfulness. I go through our gate onto the thoroughfare, disturbing the spiders' webs hanging from it, sparkling, silver, like the finest of lace. An icing of frost cracks underfoot and I lift my face to the sun to feel the welcome warmth, and step out more confidently knowing it brings a becoming flush to my cheeks. That thought is followed immediately by a twinge of guilt that I should indulge in such vanity. And balancing it, an image of Eva, of what her reaction would be: the mischievous, gentle mockery. 'Welcome to the real world, Kat.'

I do miss her. I touch my hand to my stomach, think – it will be a fine thing if we can get through the winter with weather such as this. Brisger, whose cottage abuts the edge of the cloister grounds, straightens up and raises his hand in greeting. His sleeves are rolled up to his elbows and he is breathing heavily, clearly unused to the effort he must make as he turns over the soil in the beds cut for the growing of vegetables. I dip my head in return, remembering Martin's response when I'd confessed to a sense of guilt that Brisger left the cloister shortly after our marriage.

'No need,' he'd said. 'It may be the making of him. See how industrious he has become. An industry sadly lacking when we lived together in the cloister. I would never have guessed he would develop an interest in horticulture. But needs must, I suppose.'

'Needs must indeed,' I'd repeated, keeping my face straight. 'I have planned out a vegetable plot and likewise need the soil turned ... I bought you a spade.' I am not the only one who can poke fun.

Now, as I stroll along the Collegienstrasse, I smile at the memory of Martin's face.

'Perhaps we could hire a gardener.'

'Perhaps we could.' I pretend to consider his proposal before dismissing it. 'There is little use at this season. It will be soon enough in the spring for that. In the meantime, if the soil is turned over, the frost will break it down and it will be ready for sowing when the time is right.' Strange that what began as, at least in part, a jest, results in one of the many surprises in our marriage, for Martin takes to

63

digging with a will, as if husbandry had been a lifelong ambition.

Barbara is in the queue at the fish merchant, and with a sideways glance at the gown, says, 'Well? Have you said anything yet?'

'No. Though I think it cannot be long before he guesses, for he has already commented on my restlessness. And that I do not wish to quell, for fear of idleness overtaking me.'

'Idle? You could never be idle, Kat. You don't know the meaning of the word.' Her eyes are alight, and her mouth curves in a smile. 'If you can risk a moment or two of leisure, come back with me. I have a pattern for a shift I thought to ask your opinion of.'

When we are seated in her Stube she waves her hand towards a piece of paper lying on the desk by the window, weighed down by an ink bottle and quill. 'There is *my* list: jobs to be done, things to be sorted. Not half the length of yours. When you have ticked everything off, then we may worry about you becoming idle. And in case you are concerned, neither work nor walking will do any harm, to you or the babe, and both may do you good.'

It is a welcome answer to my unspoken fear that perhaps I might cause damage to the babe by too vigorous activity, and I smile back; she should know, for they have a goodly family to their credit.

Martin is home from the university when I return from my walk, empty-handed, aside from a telltale parcel of comfits that caught my eye and which I hastily conceal under my cloak.

'Is your brain becoming addled?' he asks. 'You were at the shops yesterday. Surely you made all the purchases you needed then? Or did you go looking for another spade, that you may keep me company in my labours?'

It is the ideal opportunity to share my news, but though Barbara's questioning has confirmed me in the knowledge the danger period is past and there is no longer any need to fear disappointment, I am suddenly shy and put it off until later. Somehow it seems more appropriate to speak of such things by candlelight, and in the intimacy of our bedchamber, rather than in broad daylight in the Stube, when a servant or a visitor could appear at any moment. A mistake, as it turns out, for he hears the news in another way and in far from pleasant circumstances.

We are invited to the wedding of Johann Lubeck. It is my first formal invitation as Martin's wife, the first time since our marriage we have opportunity to parade through the town arm in arm and in a large company, and though I am somewhat nervous, I look forward to it. But, two days before the Wirtshaft, I try on my best gown, an earlier gift from Barbara, to discover the lacings barely meet, and when I do succeed in forcing them together, I can scarcely breathe.

I call in at the Cranachs', and Barbara, taking one look at my face, says, 'Don't tell me, you're worried you cannot fit in the gown you hoped to wear to the wedding?'

'Yes and…'

'Come upstairs.'

She stands back to allow me to precede her into the room. I have been in it often in the time I lived with them, but it is the memory of the first occasion that comes back

65

to me now, as sharp as the taste of lemons on my tongue. It is the room we were taken to when we arrived from Nimbschen, and for a moment I see us all as Barbara fitted us out, her judgement as to colour and style unerring. I remember my own initial disappointment at the dress I thought drab, until she commanded me to turn around and I saw how it shimmered and changed colour in the light as I moved. Now, as then, there is a skirt laid out on the bed, in what has become my favourite olive green, and beside it a blouse with soft pleats. A black velvet jacket hangs over the back of a chair, the upturned collar finishing in twin points, the sleeves decorated with jet at the wrist.

'How did you know…?'

'I gave you that best gown, remember? It wasn't hard to guess how soon you would outgrow it.'

I lift the skirt and hold it against me, feeling how little it weighs, how soft the wool is. Barbara's head is tilted to one side, the way she holds it when she is thinking, and I wait for her verdict. She reaches forward and grasping the hem flares out the pleats that hang unstitched from the waistband.

'There is plenty of material there, and the waistband itself I can alter to allow for growth, but you'd best try it for length. And even if it touches the floor now, in a month or two it will have ridden up and require some addition at the hem.'

When I step out from behind the screen my feet and ankles visible, she makes a face.

'No time like the present I suppose. Leave it with me, Kat. I shall add a band to the hem.' She moves to the chest under the window and begins to rummage through the contents, finally emerging with a velvet cloak, the edges

66

shiny and worn. I hear the satisfaction in her voice. 'I knew this fabric would come in useful someday, even if as a cloak it is too shabby to see the light of day.' She spreads it out on the floor and runs her hand across it, the nap in the central section springing under her fingers. 'There is ample here for what we need.' She grins up at me, rocking back on her heels. 'It's as well it's a doctor you have married, else convention would debar its use.'

I have no idea what she means. 'How so?'

'Haven't you ever noticed the differences in the clothing of the wives of academics? Those whose husbands have a doctoral degree may have gowns banded with velvet or silk, those whose husbands are mere masters may not. It is an indication of the status marriage has conferred on them. And you are one of the lucky ones.'

'Lucky in more than that I hope?' Lucas is standing in the doorway. 'Good morning, Katharina, I didn't realise you were here; when I heard voices I thought to find one of the servants with Barbara.' He looks at me more closely, his eyes narrowing.

I feel the heat in my cheeks, and looking at my stockinged feet, I sit down abruptly and pull them under the hem on the skirt.

Barbara says, 'Martin doesn't know yet, so please, be careful you don't let the news slip out. It is for Kat to decide when to speak.'

He reaches down and, taking Barbara's hand, helps her to her feet, slipping his arm around her waist. 'I promise I won't say anything, but I wish you joy, both of you.'

67

There is a breeze blowing as we leave the Lutherhaus. It is a name coined by some of the students, but it seems to have stuck, and I am glad, for repeated references to 'the cloister' bring back memories that still have the power to unsettle me, despite the two years I have been away. The skirt Barbara altered for me swirls around my ankles and I have to hold it down to avoid it lifting in the wind, and I regret refusing the offer of lead weights in the hem, thinking the velvet heavy enough to do the job. But there will be dancing to follow the Wirtshaft and I shall be glad of the freer movement then, even though it will only be in the more sedate of the dances I shall participate. I am counting on Barbara and Lucas to distract Martin when the effort might be too risky for me, for, though it has been nearly a fortnight since I came home from the Cranachs' determined to speak, I have not yet found the right moment to share my news.

We are passing the Melanchthon house when the door opens, Philipp and his wife emerging.

Martin stops. 'Well met, friends.' He shakes Philipp's hand, bows to Katharina Melanchthon, then waves towards the church spires. 'Shall we walk together? It is a fine day for such an auspicious occasion.'

I step forward, pleased to have opportunity to walk with Katharina, for though Philipp has been a regular at Table Talk, my suspicion he wouldn't extend his converse to the purely social has been correct, and she and I haven't spoken since before our marriage.

'Frau Luther.' Her bow is the minimum courtesy demands, her tone cool, and I wonder if she too feels awkward. I make a conscious effort to avoid any note of censure, any sign the lack of support from the

Melanchthons has been hurtful. We have not issued a formal invitation to any of our friends, yet there are those, like the Cranachs and the Jonases, who have proved their loyalty by coming of their own accord; and by laughing off my embarrassment at the state of the Lutherhaus, they have allowed me to do the same.

'I'm sorry we have not had opportunity to entertain you since our marriage, our Stube is not yet suitable for a social occasion. And the hall is scarcely better.' Conscious of the numbers attending Table Talk, of which she will be very well aware, I qualify the statement. 'One that includes ladies, that is. Your husband and mine and the students who follow them are so caught up in the topics of discussion of the day they scarcely notice the comfort or otherwise of the furnishings. And a good job too, for they are at present basic at best.' I attempt a laugh. 'But at least they are clean, which is more, I believe, than could have been said in the latter days of the cloister.' I rattle on, aware I am speaking fast, likely betraying my nervousness, and take a deep breath, attempt to slow down. 'I hoped our paths might cross in the marketplace some day, or we might meet elsewhere, but I haven't had much leisure to socialise myself of late.' It is an attempt at excusing her by offering an excuse myself, but without effect. She remains stiff, an attitude I take to be an extension of Philipp's reserve. Hoping to break it down by a friendly gesture, I reach out to slip my arm through hers, but she steps back, pulling her arm tight into her side, and I have no alternative but to fall into step beside her, without making any further attempt to link.

It is a relief to reach the Castle Church and join the people clustered outside. Dr Luther and Melanchthon have moved closer to the church door, as befits their position in the community. Kath Jonas, as she is now called in our circle, to avoid confusion, waves, and threading her way through the crowd gives me a quick hug, before standing back to look at my gown.

'What lovely material,' she says. 'And the velvet band is the perfect complement to the jacket.' She looks across to the far side of the square where the Cranachs are standing. 'Barbara?'

'Who else? She is such a good friend to me.'

Kath turns to Katharina Melanchthon. 'Doesn't she look well?' And to me, 'Marriage suits you.'

Katharina Melanchthon looks, if anything, more distant than before. 'Frau Jonas, Frau Luther. Please excuse me. I must rejoin my husband.'

Kath makes a face at her retreating back. 'What's wrong with her? Did I say something?'

'I've no idea…' I begin, and then remember Barbara's comment on the protocols of dress. If she thinks I flaunt my status as Martin's wife by the band on my skirt there is little I can do about it and even less point in speculation. Instead, I express my disappointment. 'When we met on the way here I thought to use the opportunity to renew our acquaintance, now Philipp and Martin have patched things up. But we might as well have been walking on opposite sides of the street for all the conversation I could get out of her.'

Kath squeezes my arm. 'Well, let's not worry about it now. This is a celebration. We should think only of happy things.'

And we do. For a time. It is the first Wirtschaft I have attended since my own, and it brings back a rush of memories, which are, for the most part, pleasant. Bugenhagen gives the homily, as he did for us, though shorter, perhaps as a result of the nip in the air, and I suspect I'm not the only one glad when the band strikes up for the processional and we head towards the Lubeck house where the meal is to be served and the revelries to follow.

'At least,' Kath says, linking my arm again, 'we haven't far to walk, and once we are inside we will be warm. A packed hall will see to that.'

Justus and Martin have joined us, Martin expressing his pleasure at the turnout.

'I'm glad to see Johann Lubeck so well supported. It is a testament to the regard in which he is held, and well deserved. And the gifts that will be presented will no doubt be more than welcome.'

I am thinking of the crowds that blessed our union, and Justus' encouraging words then. 'As they were for us,' I say. 'We have much to do yet at the Lutherhaus, but without the wedding gifts, we wouldn't have been able to do anything at all.'

Kath says, 'What's next on your list?'

'Lime,' I say. 'Every room needs the walls freshened, though how many bucket-loads it will take I dread to think.'

'Cartloads, more like,' Martin says, his expression droll.

We are at the tail end of the procession, waiting our turn to enter, the newly-weds already inside the house, the musicians, who had paused by the doorway, moving aside to allow the guests to follow the happy couple in.

Kath is laughing. 'Make sure your head is well covered

or you will look an old woman before you're finished. Our neighbour's hair was as white as snow when she painted her Stube, and it took several washings to get the lime out.'

Jonas laughs with her. 'Maybe you should let Martin do it. It is one thing, and perfectly natural, for an old man like Martin here to go grey, young wife or no, but...'

There is a commotion to the left, a woman thrusting through the well-wishers to confront us, jabbing her finger at Martin's chest.

'It is a disgrace, *you* are a disgrace, an affront, to the church and to God.'

She has a face as sharp as an axe blade, her words pouring over us like vitriol. Those nearest to us step back, opening a ragged space around us with Martin and the woman facing each other at the centre, like a pair of cocks lined up for a fight. Except Martin doesn't react to her attack but remains silent, his expression carved from stone. Bugenhagen gestures frantically to the musicians to form up again, in a transparent attempt to drown her out. They make a half-hearted effort, but falter as she raises her voice to a screech and continues her abuse, the guests who have not yet entered the house turning to listen. 'You call yourself a man of God. You stand in the pulpit and presume to lecture *us*, who are good decent people, on how *we* should live. While you are a lecher, and she' – she turns her glare on me – 'is a whore.'

I step back, my face flaming, and out of the corner of my eye see a small man also pushing his way towards us. He grasps the woman's arm, pleading, 'Come now, Clara,' but she tosses him off.

'They have no right to come here, to sully this marriage

72

with their presence, when their own, so-called marriage, is a union made in hell, an abomination in the eyes of the Lord.' She jerks her head towards me. 'And the babe *she* carries will be the spawn of Satan.'

The small man is trying again. 'Clara, please, this is not...'

She half turns, her gaze raking those who surround us, her contempt clear. 'Has no one the courage to join me in denouncing this evil?'

Bugenhagen has come up on her other side and steps between her and Martin, his palms upraised.

'Frau Jessner! That is enough!'

I hear his controlled anger and bless him for it, and for its effect, for the woman's shoulders slump, her voice dying to a mutter under the power of his gaze. She is led away, Bugenhagen holding one arm, the man who had first tried to stop her holding the other; the crowd parting to let them through.

Now it is over, I am shaking, the ground threatening to move beneath me.

Kath takes a firmer grip on my arm and, disdaining the impropriety, challenges Martin. 'That was horrible. Why did you not defend, if not yourself, at least Katharina? To remain silent, is it not taking "turning the other cheek" too far?'

I sense the tension in him, as if he is a coiled spring ready to burst its bonds. But when he speaks it is with uncharacteristic restraint, matched by a formality of address that serves to emphasise how public this confrontation has become. 'You give me more credit than I am due, Frau Jonas. It was not to "turn the other cheek" I remained silent, but rather, had I allowed myself to speak, my very words might have been a disgrace and an affront to God, though our marriage is not.'

His heightened colour is another indication of how much of a struggle he had to retain control, and I cannot but be glad he managed, for I remember when he castigated the peasants under Müntzer, and in the privacy of the Cranachs' Stube or not, it was an ugly thing. I lift my head, speak clearly, that all around might hear and understand I do not place any blame on my husband for what has come to pass. 'You did well, Herr Doctor Luther, not to abuse her in return.'

Kath looks unconvinced, but before she can say anything else, Justus Jonas nods towards the Jessners' retreating backs,

'I would not be Eberhard Jessner for all the world, wealth or no, and have that shrew for a wife.'

It is a clever tactic, drawing attention away from us, and under cover of the murmurs of agreement that come from all sides, Martin says, 'Better a dry crust...'

He is looking directly at me, and I meet his gaze, the other half of the quotation: 'Where love is' a beacon of hope inside my head.

He takes my hand, and this time his words are for me alone. 'Have no fear, Katharina. Our marriage is pleasing to God, and regardless of what malicious tongues may say' – I see the question in his eyes – 'our children, should we be so blessed, will be also.'

'This wasn't how I meant for you to learn...' I begin, but he shakes his head to silence me, queries:

'Are you sure?'

'Yes.'

'Well then, let us take pleasure in it and forget what

74

has been said today.'

'I think,' Justus says to Kath, 'we should go home.' And to us, 'Will you join us, that we may raise a glass in honour of this good news.'

It is clear neither Martin nor Justus place any credence on the prophecy dogging me these three months past, and the knowledge gives me a measure of relief, but as the wedding guests begin to drift into the Lubeck's house, though a few cast us a sympathetic glance as they go, there are others whose expression is hard. Bugenhagen may have succeeded in stemming the flood of Frau Jessner's accusations, but I suspect the damage is done.

Chapter Six
Wittenberg, January–February 1526

It seems I am right, for though Clara Jessner is publicly censured and fined two Schockgroshen for reviling us, the mud sticks. And when my pregnancy becomes obvious, there are many, even in this supposedly evangelical town, that cross the street to avoid meeting me and surreptitiously cross themselves, as if they fear the evil eye. Martin is by turns amused, contemptuous and finally angry on my behalf. But when he talks of preaching against their credulity, perhaps regretting his silence when Frau Jessner first attacked us, Bugenhagen counsels otherwise.

'Leave it alone, Martin. You will but fan the flames and likely do more harm than good.' He looks at me. 'How long have you to go? Five, six months? It may seem an age, but it will pass, and when the babe is born they will see what a fine fellow he is, and that will still the tongues, you'll see.'

I derive a momentary pleasure from his assumption the child will be a boy, but the fear I will never be fully accepted remains. 'If they don't find something else to criticise.'

'You have weathered storms before, Katharina. You will weather this one. And if I may make a suggestion?' He hurries on, giving me no chance to dissent. 'Hold your head high and go about your daily business as if there is nothing to disturb you. As if you are proud of your condition, as indeed you have the right to be, and think only to look forward with anticipation to the child with which God has seen fit to bless your union. Shut your ears to the mutterings, and remember this, your friends have confidence in you. Your husband has confidence in you. You must repay us all by having confidence in yourself.'

I take a deep breath. 'God grant that I can.'

As the weeks wear on, though I try to take Bugenhagen's advice to heart, it is hard not to feel perhaps Martin has made a mistake. In marrying at all, for that has attracted widespread opposition, but most especially in marrying me. Though Melanchthon himself has come round, his frequent presence in the Lutherhaus a public recognition of his acceptance of our marriage, there are many in Wittenberg who remember what he said when he first heard of it. His 'anyone but her' a phrase oft repeated behind my back, and occasionally even to my face. When I let that slip in Martin's hearing, he regards me seriously, and for a moment I fear he shares the feeling.

His response is consequently the more encouraging. 'We will prove them all wrong, you and I.'

He pauses, and in his eyes I glimpse again the Luther who proposed to me; unsure of himself and perhaps even afraid of my reaction. The Luther who has no problem saying exactly what he thinks, and in the most dogmatic terms, about any religious or political topic or indeed a social ill; but who finds it hard to articulate his personal feelings. He takes my hand, focusing on my palm, massaging it with his thumb.

'You must know, Käthe, in the months since our marriage I have come to realise that, far from being a last resort, there is no one who could have suited me better than you.'

It is the approbation I need, then and later, when news trickles in from Ducal Saxony. Duke George has publicly denounced us, writing to the Diet of Speyer. His accusations are wild and inaccurate, claiming Martin has driven all the monks from the cloister so that we two may 'feast in carnal lust' on the provisions that once fed forty.

Martin says, clearly enjoying the pun, 'He has written to a Diet of our diet, Käthe. And in the most glowing terms. I did not know we fed so well. No wonder you grow plumper by the day. I thought it was a child you carried, not a paunch you are developing through a surfeit of rich food.'

He may find it amusing, but despite his expressed confidence in me I find it chilling, for I am a Meissener, and the name Duke George still has the power to trouble me. 'Don't joke, Martin. Do you not fear the harm he might do to your reputation? We have enough to contend with here, and Speyer is not Wittenberg; who knows how far abroad the word may spread.'

He is dismissive of my fears. 'All the world knows Duke George is no friend of mine. Those who will believe him were never my supporters, and are therefore no loss.'

He may be right in that, but I am also, for as word of

78

our marriage and my pregnancy spreads across Europe, so the critics multiply. I had not thought to be notorious but so I have become. There are many who claim my pregnancy predates the marriage, among them those whose opinions carry weight. It is a hurt I seek to keep to myself, for Martin cares little for the criticism of others, be they peasant or prince, and expects me to do the same. When word comes that the king of England claims Luther has renounced his vows and seeks to destroy the church out of his lust for a profligate nun, Martin's response is to frame a repudiation. He bursts into the kitchen waving a copy of the printed pamphlet and thrusts it into my hand, his glee plain.

'What do you think?' he says. 'Shall I address it as I did before? For was it not inspired?'

I look down at the words *'Martin Luther, minister by the grace of God; to Henry, King of England by the disgrace of God'* and suggest, 'A new title perhaps?'

His alternative is no less inflammatory: *'Against the Blasphemous Book of The King of England'* but I let it rest. And, gradually, what Martin does by shouting, I learn to do by quiet resistance, in public, moving about Wittenberg as if oblivious to the gossip that follows me. Even to Barbara and to Kath Jonas I put on a good face, and only to Eva, when I write, do I confess the fears that, as my belly swells, continue to trouble me. Her response, in which I detect an underlying sympathy, is forthright and clearly designed both to amuse and to encourage me.

If you can be brought down by whatever the gossips say, then marriage has surely changed you and not for the better. The Kat I knew would thumb her nose at such nonsense. Antichrist indeed! Pray for the child by all

79

means: for his health and strength and above all for an easy passage into this world. As for the rest, concentrate on yourself and build up your strength. You may not think you need rest now, but once the babe is born you will wish you had slept for a month beforehand to prepare yourself.

I can hear her voice in every syllable, and though it magnifies the distance between us, it is also as if she's right here, standing in front of me, and I find myself smiling as I read her final sentence.

I shall look forward to meeting the little 'monster' so soon as Basilius can bring me to visit you and you can meet mine. For all children can be 'monsters' on occasion, as you will shortly find out for yourself.

And the relief neither Martin nor Bugenhagen can bring, despite all their admonitions, Eva accomplishes at a stroke.

February comes in on a bitter east wind, which Martin, rubbing his hands together to bring colour back into them as he enters the Stube, says must have blown all the way from Muscovy. I cannot disagree with him, for when I stick my nose out, intending to go to the market, the sharpness of the air sears my nostrils and I retreat, in much the same way as a snail does when he pulls his head into his shell. Dorothea, who proves her worth a dozen times a day, bustles me back to a chair by the stove. 'You've seen sense then? Not before time. Aside from the cold, which is like to shrivel you like an apple lain too long in store, the chances of falling and breaking a limb are high, and then where would you be?'

I'm tempted to say, 'Right here and you looking after me', but I know the question is rhetorical.

'We need...' I begin.

'We need nothing that cannot wait. With the provisions we have at present we shall none of us starve, and if our diet is less varied than is usual, it is only to be expected with the weather as it is. Any complaints from any of our lodgers' – she puffs out her chest – 'I shall deal with.'

And that, I think, with amusement, would put the fear of God in all but the most difficult of our students. It's as well we do have a well-stocked storehouse, for the storm that follows piles the snow against our gable wall and fills up the street outside the gate, making it well-nigh impassable. Martin and Brisger and half a dozen of the students between them dig a channel as far as Philipp Melanchthon's house and he takes up the challenge and joins them in extending the track as far as the university.

Martin expresses his satisfaction. 'It is pleasing to see our students are sufficiently concerned about their studies to lend their hands to physical work. At least we will not miss any lectures, and a good job too, for who knows how long this weather will last.'

'Who knows indeed?' I stifle a smile as Dorothea, despite what she said to me, tackles Martin as he prepares to head for the university. 'Take the spades with you. It is very little farther to the market. And though we aren't at the point of privation yet, some flour and oil wouldn't go amiss.'

When he returns it is with a note from Eva. 'It arrived at the print house enclosed in a letter from Basilius and has been lying there for some days. Lucas intended to bring it to you, but since the weather broke it has been

81

all he could do to keep his own work on track.' There is a hesitation in his voice, and I suspect he knows, or at least guesses at, the contents and isn't altogether sure how I will take it. A suspicion confirmed when he bends his head to examine an imaginary mark on his Shaube and mumbles, 'I daresay there is little of moment in it, but it will perhaps relieve the tedium of being confined indoors.'

He leaves me alone to read it, which is an additional sign that, contrary to what he says, the news it contains is likely of significance.

I imagine Eva sitting by the window in her Stube in Torgau, watching the snowflakes swirling past, and know her thoughts must likewise have been whirling. To write or not to write. To tell me, or leave me in ignorance. I don't know which, in her place, *I* would have chosen, but both the letter and the act is done now and cannot be undone.

Jerome Baumgartner is married. Three weeks ago, to his fifteen-year-old bride.

I wish him joy of her, she writes, and I sense her disdain, imagine the tilt of her head as she continues, *though I doubt he deserves it.*

I doubt it too, but bitterness, as Barbara once said, is an uneasy bedfellow, and I have enough worries of my own without seeking to add to them. I want to wish them well … I *do* wish them well, for if in our marriage I have not experienced the intoxication a union with Jerome promised, I have found happiness of a quieter and perhaps more lasting kind. Nevertheless, there is a fluttering in my stomach I cannot quite quash, a flood of memory I find unsettling. And I wonder if, as he spoke his vows, he too felt a momentary regret; and if it is unworthy of me to hope so. I see the question in Martin's eyes when he comes to lead me through for supper and I summon up my best smile and say, 'Eva has told me of Jerome's wedding. But you already knew that.' He looks a mite shamefaced, like a child caught in a fault, and I tuck my hand through his arm, make my voice firm. 'You needn't have feared to tell me. It was all a long time ago and I'm glad he is settled.' A less noble impulse prompts me to add, 'And no doubt his parents are also.'

Martin's shoulders relax, his smile all the thanks I need for the effort I have made.

'There is one more piece of news,' I say, 'but this is mine and not Eva's.'

'Oh?' A flicker of concern crosses his face, and though I am tempted to tease, in this it would be unfair.

'I felt the babe move today. It is the first time … and timely.' It is the nearest I will come to a confession of any residual feeling for the love I have lost, and I determine once again, as I did on my wedding night, to look forward, not back.

Chapter Seven
Wittenberg, June–August 1526

I had not expected it to be easy, but I did not expect this. The first pain came as I swept the flagged floor in the kitchen, and I bent over the broom handle, my grip on it fierce.

'Breath with it,' Barbara had said, when she was preparing me for what was to come. 'Long and slow, until it fades. As it will, at first. And take note of the respite between pains, for it is only when they start to come close together you need to think of sending for the midwife.' I nodded, but perhaps she saw the apprehension in my eyes, for she added, 'You can send for me immediately, of course. I will be happy to come from the outset. You have been like a daughter to me, Kat, and it is a mother's privilege to share in this most joyous of events.'

'Joyous?' I say, when she appears in the doorway and finds me once again bent double, pain like a hot poker boring through my spine and into my stomach.

She is brisk. 'When it is over, then you'll know. For now, you must bear it as best you can and think of the blessing to follow.'

84

When I straighten she takes my arm and parades me up and down the floor, as if using the length of the room as a means of measuring time, and talks to me constantly between contractions. It is the first time I have heard Barbara chatter – inconsequential conversation that I forget instantly with each following spasm. The third contraction is stronger than the second, the fourth stronger still. I lose count after the twelfth and think only of controlling my breathing as Barbara urges. Her words roll over me and around me, a steady hum in the background, like the sound of bees at a beehive, also holding the promise of good things to come. I make no effort to reply, for my mind is focused on the cycle of sharp pain and dragging respite, and as the morning wears on I wish for it to speed up, as she has warned it will, and for it all to be over. And when the space between contractions dwindles and the pain becomes almost too much, she leads me to our chamber and sets me down on the birthing chair and gives me a rag to bite on. I think of the apothecary in the convent and the distillation of poppy seed the infirmaress brewed when one of the sisters suffered great pain, and wish she was here now. Wish she could give me the respite of sleep; that I could wake when it was done.

As if she reads my thoughts, Barbara is firm. 'I cannot give you the relief you might wish for, Kat, for I need you to be awake and strong at the finish.'

Sweat breaks out on my face, glistens like spilt oil on my neck and shoulders and trickles between my breasts. My hair is plastered to my head, my shift drenched and crumpled, and I no longer care what I look or sound like. A mare may be able to birth without squealing, but I cannot.

85

I arch my back and scream as another spasm takes me, the rag slipping from between my teeth. I am gripping tight to the uprights of the chair and wonder if the torments of hell could possibly match this pain. Barbara disappears for a moment and I hear her calling for Dorothea. And then she is back at my side, her grip on my hand strong.

'It will soon be over, Kat.' The bell of the Town Church is ringing out noon as the midwife appears. She is brusque, her voice reminding me of someone and I struggle to place it. I shut my eyes to better concentrate and it is as if Frau Seidewitz is bending over me. *She* never intended me to come to this. I begin to laugh, great choking laughs that hurt my chest. In this at least I have defeated her.

Barbara leans across and slaps my face, my laughter dying. 'I'm sorry, Kat,' she says, following up her slap by stroking my forehead, 'but whatever the cause, hysteria will not help.'

The midwife is bustling about, issuing orders, calling for tepid water and old cloths. I focus on the word, feel a spurt of anger.

'I don't want my babe swaddled in old cloths,' I say.

'And do you wish your floor bloodstained?' Her voice is dry, almost contemptuous, and, my anger submerged under the knowledge I must be both stupid and inadequate, I clamp my mouth shut.

Barbara glares at her, says, 'You're doing well, Kat...'

I feel an alteration in the pain, a solidifying, a bearing down, as if of a weight pressing on my back and in my groin, and they are on either side of me, gripping my hands and shoulders, the midwife ordering, 'Pant, Frau Luther, pant.'

86

And as we practised, Barbara is panting also, and I match my breaths to hers.

From a distance I hear the midwife. 'And push, and push, and once more … push.'

There is a grinding and a tearing and a rush of wetness between my thighs. A moment of silence, then another slap, not of me this time, and a cry as if of outrage.

The midwife is smiling broadly as she places the babe in my arms. 'Well done, Frau Luther.' She nods, satisfaction in her voice. 'Between us we have birthed a fine boy.'

I smile back at her, thinking – she doesn't sound like Frau Seidewitz after all. And maybe I am not so inadequate. And thank God it is a boy, for once is enough. I turn to Barbara. 'I pray I will never … ever have to do this again.'

She laughs. 'That's what we all say, Kat. And the feeling never lasts.'

Martin kneels by the crib, exultant. 'Look what a fine fellow he is. We shall call him Johannes.'

'For your father?'

'Yes.' A fractional pause. 'You don't mind?'

'Of course not. It will give him the pleasure he deserves. After all' – I think of Martin's father's joy in our marriage – 'this is partly his doing. And besides, my father was Hans also. So it is doubly fitting.'

'Indeed.' Martin's mind is clearly already running on. 'I have sent word to Rörer to prepare the baptismal font. This young man neither looks nor sounds sickly, but it must be done today, nonetheless, that we may all sleep quiet in our beds tonight: knowing he has received the grace of God.'

I laugh, for this may be my first child, but even I know that sleep is likely to be in short supply.

Martin reacts sharply. 'It is not a laughing matter, Käthe.'

This is not the moment for theological debate, and if I see vestiges of the old religion in Martin's theology, who am I to judge, for there are habits I find hard to break; and there was more than a moment or two during the last hours when I would dearly have loved the comfort of the rosary.

'It is not the baptism I laughed at, but the idea of sound sleep. We will not be enjoying that luxury for quite some time to come. Or I will not at any rate. Indeed, if you don't wish to be disturbed, you'd best take yourself off to a chamber at the other end of the house, for this young man likely won't know day from night for a month or two.'

As if on cue, Johannes wakes, his crying lusty and sustained, and I am back at Lippendorf, with baby Franz waking three or four times a night until he was five months old. But now isn't the moment to share that thought. In the quiet of the afternoon his cry echoes around our chamber, Martin's expression bemused.

'He's so small! And the cry so loud! Is he...'

'Normal? Yes. Perfectly so ... in every way.' I pick Johannes up, settle him to my breast, smile up at Martin. 'And he will get louder, I promise you.' I change tack, wish Eva was here, or any of the Nimbschen sisterhood. 'If the baptism is to be today, who will be the godparents?'

88

It's clear it's something Martin has considered well in advance, his mind already made up, despite his inclusion of me in his response.

'We must choose wisely, and though they will not all witness the baptism, that will not debar them from the task. Justus Jonas will stand for the university and Christian Beier for the court, Müller for Mansfeld, Lucas, of course.' He pauses, and I suspect by his narrowed eyes he has moved beyond friends and is thinking now of those whose patronage might be important. It is a strangely worldly-wise Luther, quite unlike his normal attitude, an indication of the power of fatherhood.

'I think it will be politic perhaps to invite Mayor Hohendorf's wife.'

'But we scarcely know her,' I begin. 'Or, at least, I don't.'

He rests his hand on Johannes' head. 'She has influence and her approval will go a long way to stop the wagging tongues.'

'What about Barbara?'

'Not this time, Käthe.'

'But she…'

'She will understand why she is passed over and will have the sense to know Lucas represents them both.' Although his voice is firm, I sense his need of my approval. 'Barbara is already your friend, but there are others in this town who must be encouraged in that direction, and harnessing Frau Hohendorf to your cause will be an important first step.'

Perhaps Barbara *will* understand, but I determine to make sure she knows it was no choice of mine to leave her out. She has been too good a friend to me for that.

I had not known what to expect of Martin, but imagined his initial enthusiasm for the child would fade, and I would be left, as likely most mothers are, to deal with all the day-to-day tasks of caring for this latest addition to our household. But in this I am wrong. Though he returns to his lecturing and preaching, he becomes more regular in his hours and makes it a priority to spend time with Hans, eager to dandle him on his knee and bounce him up and down and croon to him, his nonsense songs and childlike babble a side to him at odds with the austere face the outside world sees. I wish Eva was here to see how young it makes him seem. He writes with ever more vigour, as if his outpourings have a new impetus. As if he now writes not only for those whom God is leading into the light of the true Gospel, in Germany and across all of Europe, but especially for this child, our child.

He reads his latest pamphlet out loud to me as I suckle Hans, prefacing his reading with, 'God has granted us this child, Käthe, and with him comes both privilege and responsibility. To raise him in the full knowledge of the grace of God. That he may grow up a good Christian, and none may say, Martin Luther's son is reprobate.'

I can't keep the amusement out of my voice. 'He is but two months old, Martin, and can hardly be expected to learn anything yet.'

'Do you doubt the Word of God can penetrate even the simplest of souls?'

Put like that there is no point in arguing, and besides, if it means I will have more of Martin's company as I look to the child, that is a benefit I don't want to lose. He surprises me in other ways too. I write to Eva, asking when she will visit, and add, *You will be surprised at my good 'old' man. He is a doting father, willing to help with anything he can. He plays with Hans, bathes him, even changes his tailclout, and walks the floor with him when he is colicky. I cannot ask for better, and I have no doubt there are many 'young' men who would be less supportive.*

I am touched by his willingness to share his satisfaction in our marriage with more than our close circle of friends, and to say to others in public what he has said to me in private. But, as always, he is devastatingly honest, and is genuinely bewildered when I am less than impressed by the terms in which he does so.

We are sitting in the Cranachs' Stube, enjoying a rare escape from the aftermath of Table Talk, when he appeals to Lucas, 'I wrote to Herr Amsdorf that, though I did not burn for Käthe, she is so much better for me than I could ever have imagined. What is wrong with that? It is the truth. And now it seems she would have preferred me to keep my thoughts to myself.' His expression is comical. 'I don't understand it.'

Lucas is trying very hard to contain his amusement. 'Damning by faint praise, Martin? No wife wishes that. Either be fulsome or keep silent. It is by far the best way.' He winks at Barbara. 'As I have learnt.'

Barbara, pointedly refusing to rise to his comment, says, 'Perhaps you should stick to the Scriptures, Martin. Understanding *them* is more your forte.'

There are footsteps on the stairs, a slap, slap as if of ill-fitting shoes. That girl, I think. One of these days she will have an accident, but I will not be to blame, for I have told her a dozen times to go to the cobblers and get new shoes. The door opens and the maid manoeuvres herself through the gap, her arms full of logs.

'I've come to stoke the stove.'

I nod.

She smiles a gap-toothed smile. 'I thought to do it now, for the Fraulein says you may have a visitor today.'

I focus on her mouth. 'You had the tooth out? I'm glad.'

'Yes.'

'I told you, didn't I? Now if you would just listen to me about your shoes.'

She sets the logs down and bends to open the stove and rakes out the ash, ignoring my comment.

I give up on the lecture, ask, 'What visitor?'

'The Fraulein didn't say.'

'They come to see the baby.' *I cock my head and hear a faint cry, like the mewling of a kitten.* 'Listen. He's awake. And just in time.'

There is an odd expression in her eyes as she turns, as if she doesn't quite understand.

'They want to check if he has two heads,' *I explain.* 'And I swear some of them are disappointed to find he has not.' *I try to laugh, but it hurts my chest and I end up coughing instead.*

She has set down the poker and is edging towards the door, but turns and comes across to lift me up to put a beaker to my lips. 'Now, now, Frau Luther, you must take care.'

I am not a child and won't be spoken to as if I am by a chit of a girl. 'Bring me Hanschen,' I say, in my firmest voice. 'Else the visitors will have a wasted journey.'

'Hanschen?' she repeats.

Perhaps she doesn't mean to patronise. Perhaps she is a little wanting.

I wave my hand at the ceiling and prompt her gently, swallowing my irritation. 'The baby. He must be brought from the nursery if visitors are expected. There was the prophecy, you see. Martin laughed it off, but he didn't hear the whispers on the street as I passed. And though Barbara also took me to task for giving it credence, I couldn't altogether dispel my own fear, not until I saw him for myself. Healthy and whole and entirely normal. You do know he is, don't you?'

'Of course, Frau Luther.' She bobs a curtsy. 'Of course.'

I know by her repetition she doesn't mean it, but I don't blame her. There were many folk hard to convince.

Chapter Eight
Wittenberg, August–December 1526

If I thought the birth of Hans, manifestly *not* the two-headed monster our opponents had predicted, would silence all the naysayers, I am sorely disappointed. There is less open criticism among Wittenbergers: matrons, who would previously have crossed the road to avoid having to speak, now stopping to offer their congratulations as if they had never doubted for a moment the validity of our marriage, nor given any credence to the rumours and superstitions that had circulated. The tradesmen, who had served me in the past, out of a loyalty to the Cranachs perhaps, or a fear of losing the university trade, but without the courtesy of conversation or gossip, now add a little something to my order as if in apology for their previous reticence. Most pleasing of all, Katharina Melanchthon appears at our door with a gift for Hans and accepts the invitation to join me for some refreshments. We sit by the fountain Martin built for me, the sound of the water a soothing backdrop aiding our conversation. Though it is at first stilted, when Hans wakes she indicates the crib and says, 'May I?'

I nod, and she lifts him out and he grabs her finger. She takes a deep breath. 'I'm sorry, Frau Luther…'

'Please,' I say, 'we were not always so formal, and need not be now.' Before I can change my mind, I continue, 'Call me Kat. It's what Barbara and Kath Jonas do. And it will make life easier if we three that share a name can refer to each other without confusion.'

Her cheeks are scarlet and her eyes remain troubled. 'This past year, I have not been fair…'

'This past year there have been many misunderstandings, many difficulties best forgotten. And I, for one, have no wish to remember them.' Hans' head has dropped onto her shoulder and he is sucking at her gown. I reach out my arms. 'Perhaps I'd best feed him, before he ruins your dress.'

She hands him over, turns as if to go.

'Stay', I say. 'He won't take long, for he has his father's appetite.' Then, to give her an escape route if she wishes it, 'If, that is, you won't mind his lack of manners. He takes after Dr Luther in that too, as noisy when feeding as he is vigorous. Heavens knows what he'll be like when he starts to talk.'

'Unstoppable?' she says. Her hand flies to her mouth. 'I'm sorry, I didn't…'

I laugh. 'Maybe,' I say. 'But I hope not.'

The elector, Duke John is also supportive, and his generosity goes a long way to helping, not only in practical ways: with wood for the stoves and supplies of grain and venison, wine and fish; but also with an increase in the salary he provides for Martin, which is a more than welcome addition to our household income. There is rarely a night when we don't have guests who are willing to pay for the privilege of sitting at Martin Luther's table, but increasingly there are others, less fortunate, who rely on our goodwill and our hospitality without the ability to pay. In this, Martin and I are agreed, we will not turn away anyone in need, though we are less in accord as to how to provide for them. Martin's thoughts seldom stretch further than a week ahead, and though I do not agree, I cannot but admire his consistency, for no one could accuse him of saying one thing and living another. He is a walking example of the belief of which he is quick to remind me every time I raise the issue.

'Sufficient unto the day, Käthe.'

We have been married for more than a year, and with every passing month my confidence has grown and any residual reserve I may once have had about voicing my opinions, or challenging Martin's, in private at least, has gone. 'That's exactly it,' I say, 'the ground surrounding the Lutherhaus is insufficient. I cannot feed the numbers we are accommodating with the vegetables it can produce, far less have room for any stock. For that we need land.'

He is unconvinced. 'We cannot afford land, Käthe, and besides, what money we have should be used for the good of others, not to increase our status.'

'What money we have will soon be gone, if we do not husband it properly. How then will we profit others?'

He gestures towards the chest in the corner and to the wall cupboard, which holds the silverware we received as wedding gifts. 'When the coffers are empty, we have silver, and to spare, that can be sold. And besides,' he sighs, as if to suggest I do not understand what is at stake here, and reverts to his stance when we were first married, 'it is God's work we do, and He is no man's debtor. If money is required, it is His to gift.'

For a man who can be so earthy in conversation, too much so at times, and so focused on relating faith to everyday life, in matters of finance he is hopeless. Maybe I *am* less spiritually minded, but one of us needs to be practical. 'Perhaps God expects us to use the gifts He has already given,' I say. 'Common sense, for one.' I stop, for if I have learnt anything in the last year it is that a steady drip of contrary opinion is better than a deluge: less likely to attract an instant and vigorous response, and therefore the more likely to be effective. For, in life, as in his writings, once Martin Luther has made a pronouncement, he will not be moved, though the four horses of the Apocalypse were ranged against him. I make a strategic retreat. When the moment is right I will tackle him again, and next time with a fully fledged proposal. For now, I rest my hand on his arm, the pressure light, imagining the approval of all the good wives of Wittenberg as I say, 'But you're right, Martin, we are not destitute yet, nor anything like.'

He rewards me with a smile, which fades as he turns to the Shaube thrown over the back of his chair and fishes in the inner pocket. When he straightens, a pamphlet in hand, his expression is sombre and a shiver runs through me. It's clear as he turns the crumpled paper over and over it raises a difficult issue and he isn't sure if he should speak of it or not.

I would much rather know than be forced to speculate. 'What is it, Martin?'

He smooths out the pamphlet on his palm. 'Criticism

of myself I expected, and even welcomed, for it is a sign the Devil is disturbed by what I do.'

It is such a typical Martin reaction I almost laugh, but by his face I see it isn't a laughing matter.

'For you, Katharina, to be branded so… Perhaps by marrying I did you wrong.'

The tension in him, the renewed vulnerability, the use of my full name, now a rarity, troubles and warms me at the same time. I lean forward, take the paper from him. 'Whatever this is, we will face it together.' It takes every ounce of self-control I possess not to allow revulsion to show on my face as I read. I'm glad I'm already seated, for if I was not I think I might fall down. I did not expect marriage to Martin would be easy, but I had imagined any problems would be personal, between our two selves. For, if I am honest, I am as capable of a strong will as he and knew sparks might fly. When opposition came from those around us, I clung to Barbara's counsel to hold my head high and the storm would pass. And so, in Wittenberg, for the most part, it has. It is an altogether more difficult thought that I am a byword for everything unsavoury, not only in Saxony, but in the world beyond; that there are those who hate me so much they can produce such bile. I fold the pamphlet in four to give myself a moment, then, 'Who writes these things? Who prints them? No one here, surely?'

'No!' Martin's colour is rising. 'If it originated here I could challenge them directly, as it is…'

'As it is' – I stifle my own feelings, seek to calm him – 'we must ignore them.'

'Can you bear it?' he asks.

This time I do laugh, but I hear the note of hysteria in

it and pray he does not. 'What our enemies say matters less than the opinion of our friends, and we have plenty of those.' I inject confidence into my voice. 'I will bear it.'

The flood of scurrilous pamphlets and letters to us and about us continues.

I am a 'so-called wife', a 'dancing girl', a 'prostitute' who has 'led astray many nuns by my misbehaviour'.

'That last,' Barbara says, seeking to make humour of it, 'is certainly true. And something to be proud of. Even now, more than three years after your own escape, many are finding the courage to follow your example and grasp the freedom you have found. Lucas was talking only last month of another group of thirteen nuns who slipped the net.' And when I don't immediately respond, she says, 'There are many who have good cause to bless your courage. Think on them.'

She brings it close to home. 'Think of Florentina von Oberweimar, of how she looked when she first arrived in Wittenberg, of how she looks now. If there was ever an example of the good you have done, she is it.'

'I do think of her, often. And take encouragement from the thought. But I would rather not read that Martin, by marrying me, risks the fires of hell. I might have expected Rome to react, but to be the talk of half of Europe … is unexpected.' I think back to the pamphlet Martin wrote in response to the English king. 'As to why the English king weighs in against us, that I cannot even begin to imagine.'

'He relishes the approval of the Pope, and the title of *Defender of the Faith*. And sees pillorying Martin as an easy way to maintain it. You are caught in the crossfire. That is all.'

When I raise an eyebrow, for in general Barbara has scant interest in the world outside our own little corner of Saxony, she blushes. 'So Lucas says.' She grasps my arm, her voice firm. 'Forget him, Kat, forget them all.'

I wish I could take her advice, but Martin is increasingly angry, his frustration building with each new accusation. And though I appreciate his concern is for me, I find myself glad the presses from which they come are *not* within reach, for I very much fear his actions if they were. He prowls around our chamber like one of the bears in the pit at the castle in Torgau, alternately morose and explosive.

I try once more to calm him. 'They are not here, so there is nothing we can do.'

He slams the latest pamphlet down on the windowsill so hard the glass in the frame rattles. 'If they were, I would see them shut down, every copy burnt, their presses destroyed.'

I think, but don't say, for fear of releasing another torrent – we have had our surfeit of violence in these last years and should not seek to add to it.

It is clear the situation has become a more general topic of discussion when, two days later, Justus and Melanchthon arrive in the Cranachs' Stube in the late afternoon. Lucas and Martin are still at work, Barbara and I snatching a few minutes of leisure, and I suspect the timing of the visit is deliberate. It is hard not to regret the disturbance, for it is a rare treat just to sit and enjoy Barbara's company, but I chide myself for such selfishness and summon a welcoming smile, which dies when I see the paper in Melanchthon's hand. He stands, his back to the window, and faces me, his tone a match for the stern expression on his face, and I can't help wondering if, despite the thaw in our relationship, he still attaches some blame to me for the damage to Martin's reputation. But perhaps I misjudge him and it is just his manner. Maybe the students at the university think he hectors them too.

He crumples the pamphlet in his palm and tosses it into the space below the stove, where a fire is set in winter. 'These pamphlets ... they are the work of evil men, stuffed with scurrilous lies and do not improve in the telling. Martin does not fear for his own good name, or his work, but I do.'

Barbara is carefully looking anywhere but at the crumpled paper and I feel for her, knowing it is only her desire not to embarrass a guest that stops her leaping up to remove it. For a moment I think about Melanchthon in his own house, if he is untidy there, if all men are, and all wives destined to tidy up behind them. It is the first time I have consciously thought of myself as part of this new sisterhood, and a warmth spreads through me.

My train of thought is broken by Justus Jonas, who is characteristically gentle.

He gestures towards the crumpled paper. 'He fears for you, Katharina, and with reason. And as Martin's friends we feel for you also, for you would not be human if you did not find these distressing.' He glances at Melanchthon, who nods as if in corroboration. 'If you need evidence of the esteem in which those who matter hold you, Katharina, look how many guests are flocking to your door.'

'They flock to Martin, I cannot take credit…'

He cuts me off, but I can forgive him his curtness,

'Without you and what you have done with the Lutherhaus, they could not flock at all.'

I look from him to Barbara, and finally to Philipp Melanchthon, and this time my smile is genuine.

Barbara says, 'Many good things have come into your life, Kat. Focus on them.'

I think of Hans and the blessing he is. And when doubts arise in the weeks and months that follow, I swivel the ring on my finger and remind myself it is a gift from King Christian of Denmark. If one good king approves of me and of my marriage, why should I be concerned about other, less worthy, folk, whatever their station.

Chapter Nine
Wittenberg, Spring 1527

The fruit trees are in bud, and everywhere the signs are of new life, when I discover I am expecting for the second time. Hans is a lively ten-month-old, and he has found his knees and elbows, crawling so fast I have only to turn my back for a second and he is away and into mischief. Martin roars with laughter when I bemoan that he upended my mending basket and scattered wools and threads all across the newly restored Stube floor. The ill was compounded by Tolpel, our new mongrel puppy, who, clearly thinking it had been done just for him, proceeded to tangle himself and Hans and the table legs by running round and round in circles with a ball of wool between his teeth.

'It is no laughing matter,' I begin. 'I had to cut him free. And that shade of wool was hard to come by, and will be harder still to replace.'

'It has been worse,' Martin says, and I know he is referring to the offerings Hans deposited in every corner of the room when the maid, distracted by the need to remove the basin of hot water in which she had been bathing him in front of the fire, allowed him to crawl about without the

103

benefit of a tailclout. A mistake that has *not* been repeated.

I struggle to keep my face straight. 'Maybe so, but that particular episode is something I have no wish to remember.'

He comes to stand behind me, pulling me against him, my head resting under his chin. 'On the contrary, I find it highly amusing,' he says.

'I daresay,' my tone is dry, 'like many men whose taste in humour runs to the crude.'

His laughter at my unintentional pun is unrestrained. 'Well, well, Käthe, finding your humour at last?'

I ignore the comment, continue with my own thought. 'There is no need to recount the tale to everyone who might be remotely interested, and even those who are not.'

'He is an infant,' he says, 'and it was but proof of it, a tale plenty of folk have enjoyed.' He nods in the direction of the mess of wool still lying on the table and rubs his chin in my hair. 'And that will be another.' And as an afterthought, 'If the wool was to darn my socks, you need have no concern for colour on my behalf.'

'More's the pity,' I say. 'Two years ago a mismatched darn would have bought you the sympathy of half the matrons of Wittenberg. Now it would be my reputation at stake were you to appear in that state.'

'I hope you do not suffer from pride, Käthe? For that would place my reputation at stake. Think of the gossip if the wife of Martin Luther is caught in one of the seven deadly sins.'

For a moment I fear he might be serious, before the corner of his mouth lifts and I see he is teasing.

'Unfair,' I say.

'Yes.' His smile broadens. 'But if I cannot tease my

wife, who can I tease?'

I give in to the impulse to laugh with him, my eyes saying what my voice cannot, that this is a new and unexpected turn in our relationship. And welcome. I glance across at my workbasket, at the thimble winking among the wools, and for a moment am reminded of Jerome, who was also wont to tease, but dismiss the memory as no more than a needle-prick which fails to draw blood.

Barbara has come calling, and we walk together in the garden as she admires the new beds Martin has cut. When she commends his industry I agree, but when she asks, mischief in her eyes, if Hans has repeated his puppy-dog marking of territory, I sigh.

'Martin is not still spreading that story about is he?'

'I suspect so, for I heard it in the queue at the butcher's shop, and it seems it's going the rounds.'

'I wish he wouldn't.'

'He is proud of the boy,' Barbara says, 'and looks for tales to tell.'

'Well, he could surely think of something better.'

'There isn't much to note in an infant of ten months, aside from how many teeth he has and that he is on the move. You must admit, in terms of an infant's prowess, the story has the merit of being out of the ordinary.'

'It has the merit of embarrassing me now and no doubt Hans in the future. He'll likely tell it at the boy's wedding.'

There is a mischievous lilt to Barbara's voice. 'I heard he boasted of the exploit to Justus Jonas.'

'And did you hear Justus' response? I thought better of him. He sent a gift for the boy, which pleased Martin mightily and me not at all.'

'Not at all?'

'The gift is fine enough, of course, but I'd prefer he didn't encourage Martin in such talk.'

'Martin won't change, however little encouragement he gets. You know that. Remember the gift and forget the cause and' – a serious note creeps into her voice – 'be grateful for a father who loves his child and isn't afraid to show it. Many, perhaps even most husbands, have little interest in, or time for, a child. At this stage at least. We are fortunate, you and I.'

'Children.' I correct her automatically, and she leaps up to enfold me in a hug.

'When?' she says.

I know her joy for me goes far beyond that of a neighbour and friend.

'December, I think.' I shiver and wonder if it is a premonition. 'I trust it will not be a hard winter.'

'Don't go looking for trouble, Kat. We have the summer to come. Think on that, and let the winter take care of itself.'

She is worrying at a loose thread on her sleeve, and I know I have triggered thoughts of the children winter stole from her, and am sorry for it.

She bends her head to nip the thread off with her teeth, and when she looks up again, I see the effort she makes to focus on my news and not her own ills and I bless her for it.

'I wonder which it will be? Will you mind, Kat?'

'So long as it is healthy, no, but I don't know what

Martin will favour. Perhaps another boy? To carry on the family name?'

'Perhaps, but fathers oft have a soft spot for a daughter and can be apt to spoil them. Something you may need to watch.'

This time I tell Martin of my pregnancy early and see the smile spread across his face. He picks up Hans and tosses him high into the air, the boy crowing with delight. When he catches him again, he holds him at eye level and says, 'You, young man, are going to have a little brother or sister. And will have to be a good example to it.' He tosses him up again, higher this time, and Hans giggles louder.

'Careful,' I say, 'if he falls and lands on his head he may not be able to be an example to anyone.'

'Trust me, Käthe. I won't let him fall. Will I, Hanschen?' He perches him on his shoulder and hunkers down beside me.

'Will you mind,' I ask, 'whether it is a boy or a girl?'

'Not in the least. A boy can follow in my footsteps, and as for a girl, I cannot have too many ladies to look after me.' He is hesitant, and I wonder if he is being entirely truthful. 'I have some news for you. Basilius and Eva...'

'What about them?'

'I'm sorry, Käthe, but Basilius has been offered the position as physician to Duke Albrecht.'

I look away, so he will not see the tears springing to my eyes. 'Torgau was bad enough, but there at least we could visit from time to time, but Prussia!'

Martin sets Hans down on the floor and turns my

107

head, forcing me to meet his eyes. His voice is soft. 'You would not want to hold him back, Käthe. And where Basilius goes, Eva must go too. Thank God you had their friendship when you needed them most, and if it comes to it, take care to wish them well.'

I put my hand on my stomach, think – I want them now. Instead, I say, 'He deserves the recognition, and I *will* wish them well, but I cannot pretend it isn't a loss that will be hard to bear.'

He tightens his grip on my chin and speaks in the tone I have come to think of as his sermon voice, which brooks no contradiction. 'There are many losses in this life, Käthe, and most of them hard to bear, but there are also blessings. Think on them. There are plenty in this town who are already your friends and plenty more who would wish to befriend you.'

I cannot stop myself. 'And also those who would not.'

'Of course.' He waves his hand dismissively. 'I of all people know that. And do I care? No. You should be the same.'

Easier said than done, I think.

Martin is silent for a moment, pursuing his own thoughts. But when he begins again it is the same topic. 'I too am losing a good friend,' he says.

Whether deliberate or not, as a means of distracting me it is effective, and I am genuinely curious as I ask, 'Who?'

'Brisger. He is for Altenburg. I wish him well.'

It is gentle as reproofs go, and I smile for him. 'And I. Though it will seem strange to see the cottage empty.'

'We could move there.'

That makes me straighten. 'Are you serious?'

108

'It would be cheaper, and easier on you, and' – there is a ghost of a smile on his face – 'I believe the cottage roof does not leak.'

It is my turn to be dismissive. 'We cannot move out now, Martin. Think of all those who come to see you. Those who need our help. All the work we have already done. Two and a half wagonloads of lime have gone on the walls of this house, and you suggest I walk away?' There is something in his expression, a sheepishness that gives me pause. 'You have not spoken of this to anyone else?'

He shifts. 'I did just mention it to Spalatin … but only in passing. He will not think anything of it, I'm sure. Nor say anything to the duke.'

I am *not* sure. 'I hope not, for it is scarcely practical. By all means think of the cottage as an annex, to extend our bounds, the garden ground a useful addition for our table. But as an alternative to the Lutherhaus? Talk sense, Martin.'

As if to emphasise my point, one of the maids appears, a letter in hand. She bobs a curtsy.

'This has just come, Doctor Luther, and the messenger waits for a reply.'

When he looks up his expression is bleak, but his tone is businesslike. 'Tell him we shall be glad to receive the child, and will treat him as our own.'

She bobs again and disappears.

I move to look over his shoulder. 'What child?'

'My sister Kaufmann's son, Andreas.' There is a catch in his voice. 'Her husband cannot manage to look after him and hopes we can see our way to taking him in.'

I am equally brisk, to counter the emotion welling

within me, as it always does when I hear of a motherless child. Nor do I wish to threaten his control. 'Of course we can. He can join Hans in the nursery. There will be plenty of room for three.'

110

Chapter Ten
Wittenberg, June 1527

I wake as usual at four o'clock and pad down to the kitchen and out to the garden. I love this time, when I can be alone to enjoy the morning sun as it spills across the meadow and sparkles on the water of the Elbe flowing silent and slow beyond our wall. I pause beside the newly pruned fruit trees, head cocked, to listen to the dawn chorus, a glorious burst of birdsong, as if they too share my relish of this empty hour, before the hustle and bustle of the day drowns out their singing. Slipping through the gate onto the riverside meadow, I make for the water's edge and sit down to slip off my shoes and dabble my toes. A fish breaks the surface of the water and falls again with a plop, and I think it must be for joy, for there is no practical reason for it to leap so. I envy it, and imagine what it would be like to join it, gliding through the water, the sunlight sparkling on me. Martin would laugh at such fanciful notions, and no doubt think the child growing within me responsible, but on mornings like this I remember sitting by the shallows in the brook that bounded our farm at Lippendorf, while Hans and Klement jumped from the bank showering me.

The sun slips behind a cloud. I have been two years married and have not yet seen my brothers. It is not for want of an invitation, but they have not come, and despite the affectionate tone of letters I have received from Hans, I cannot help feeling a niggle of worry that they disapprove of what I have done. Martin pooh-poohed the idea when I confessed it to him, but then Martin is apt to pooh-pooh every thought not in accord with his own, so I cannot take comfort from that.

Barbara is more thoughtful when I express the same doubts to her. 'It isn't always easy to make time away from home as you well know. You haven't stirred from the town since your escape from Nimbschen, other than to look at the garden ground you thought to buy. And even that time was snatched. Their lives will be equally busy, and from what you told me, their circumstances may be straightened and they may be unable to spare either time or money. When both are in less short supply they will come.'

Now, as I stare into the water, I think on her response and allow her confidence to become mine also.

The new Castle Church clock chimes the half hour, and I dry my feet on the hem of my gown and wriggle them back into my shoes. Martin will be up soon, if he is not already, and needing his breakfast before he shuts himself in his study to write. Barbara is right. Life is full and to bursting. There are fires to light and bread to bake, the maid to send for milk, pickles to set down, fish to salt and, and, and... So many chores, but I relish them all, or at least I relish the sense of satisfaction when they are done. For as the number of our visitors grows, so does the work required to look after them, and it is often late

112

in the evening before I can sit down, knowing all the preparations are made for the day ahead. Martin chides me to take more rest, more time to myself, especially as my pregnancy has progressed, but I feel more alive than ever before, my energy almost boundless.

'Nest building,' Barbara says, when she comes to find me as I am going through the linens, laying aside those requiring repair. 'You are like a bird, Kat, diligently preparing for the birth of this little one, and it is to your credit you work so hard. But Martin is right. You cannot spend all the hours God gives working, or you may wear yourself to a shadow. Besides that your friends will think they have been deserted.' She settles herself on a bench. 'You'd best sort out the remainder of those quickly, for I have come to drag you away.'

'But I have…'

'Nothing else to do that can't be done tomorrow, and the reason I want you can't wait.'

I have my back to the door, the draught that alerts me to it opening. As I swing round, the bedding in my arms drops to the floor. I have imagined this moment so many times, but never imagined the hesitation, in either of us.

Eva is the first to break the silence, to cover the distance between us. 'Kat!' She wraps her arms around me, holding me so tight I struggle to breathe. I gasp and she loosens her hold and steps back a fraction. 'You're looking well.' She pats my stomach in an almost proprietary manner, as if she is part responsible for my marriage and hence my condition. As I suppose in a way she is, for had she

113

showed any inclination towards Martin, he would not have held back to marry me.

'Eva, oh, Eva! How good it is to see you. When did you come? Where are you staying? How long will you be here?'

'Whoa! One at a time, please, else I will answer one thing and you'll have already asked another and it'll make no sense at all.'

'Eva and Basilius are staying with us,' Barbara says. 'And so you see why I have demanded your attention.'

'I will call for some refreshment…'

'No need. Everything is already set at our house.'

'But first,' Eva says, 'I'm desperate to see what you've done here. Barbara says you've worked miracles.'

'Hardly miracles,' I allow a note of pride to creep into my voice, 'but you will notice a difference from last you were here.'

She gives an exaggerated shudder. 'I should hope so. I didn't enjoy the extra visitors who shared our beds.' She wriggles her back as if to dispel an itch. 'Indeed, talking of them almost makes me feel them now.'

'Don't worry. They were the first to go, out with the straw. Closely followed by the spiders, who held a protest march on the stairs as they went.'

We are moving through the main rooms, the refectory, the kitchen, the room we have taken as a Stube.

'And where,' she says, looking around, 'is all the staining on the walls? The mould on the ceilings?'

'Concealed under two and a half wagonloads of lime.'

'And most of it applied by Kat,' Barbara cuts in.

Eva whistles. 'So not the good Doctor Luther then?'

'No. But he does plenty else, particularly with

114

Hanschen. Which is more than many in his position would do.'

'So I heard.' A pause, a moment of seriousness. 'I am glad, Kat… You know I had my doubts of your wisdom in marrying Doctor Luther, after…' Eva stops, bites on her lip.

'You can say his name. I have long ago forgiven Jerome Baumgartner for his defection. And perhaps his parents were right to hold him back. If he had not the courage of his convictions when faced with their disapproval, I dare not think how he would have managed in standing with me against the world. My "good old man", as you once called him, is proving himself steadfast, indeed the problem is how to restrain him in his defence of me, not encourage it.'

We are back in the refectory, one of the maids preparing the table for supper, the door of the cupboard where our silverware is kept standing open. Eva looks across, a sparkle in her eye.

'Do you remember when the abbess took you to Torgau for the fair, and how I envied you the chance to escape the cloister, even if only for a day or two? How we all fed, like sparrows, on the crumbs of tales you brought back for us, of the market, the stallholders, the sounds and the smells, bringing it alive. How far removed it was from our experience. I remember the longing in your face when you spoke of the silversmith. Who would have thought it then, that we would be here now, and you would have your own silver, and plenty of it.'

'Not I, for sure.' I shut the cupboard, make a face. 'Though how long I will keep it is another matter.'

'Why wouldn't you?'

'Martin…'

'Thinks it ungodly to have such possessions?'

'On the contrary, he sees them as God's richest blessing, but one we should plunder at will when the need arises, generally to share with others who purport to be less fortunate than ourselves. I take a somewhat different view but have yet to fully convince him of my argument.'

Eva's silvery laugh fills the room. 'I almost feel sorry for him, for if what you have accomplished so far is an example of your determination, he will not be able to withstand you for long.'

'I hope not, for the poor we always have with us, and must feed and house and clothe them, somehow or other. And the price of a few goblets, however pure the silver, would not last for long.'

Eva looks at the line of trenchers set out down the length of the table. 'Hmm, I see your problem. Not exactly a quiet family meal. Nor, I imagine, what you expected when you agreed to marry him.'

'I didn't know what to expect. But now, I find a satisfaction in all of it.'

'Lucas was right then. He said I would find you the good wife of Proverbs.'

'Lucas said that?' I look at Barbara, who nods.

'He did. And I agree with him, though' – she appears reflective – 'lest you get puffed up, I have heard him comment on other, somewhat less convenient qualities.' She laughs. 'I'm sorry, Kat, You needn't look so deflated. We are none of us perfect, and a streak of stubbornness is exactly what is needed in dealing with a household such as this … and with Martin.'

Eva interrupts. 'Wives we may be, but I didn't come

116

all the way from Torgau to talk of housekeeping and how to manage a husband. You were, you are, my best friend, Kat, and we have more important things to share. Where's the child?'

'Children.' I grin again at her surprised expression. 'We have some waifs and strays staying with us, and I find I enjoy to hear the noise they make.'

As if on cue Hans appears, his chubby fingers held tight by a little girl scarcely taller than himself, though clearly older, the pair of them trailed by one of the maids, who flushes scarlet when she sees us.

'Pardon me, Frau Luther, I didn't know you had visitors.'

Eva slips her hand into the purse hanging from her waist and brings out two comfits, hunkering down and holding them out to the children. Hans doesn't hesitate, grabbing one and stuffing it into his mouth, but the little girl hangs back until I nod my approval.

'Danke,' she says, dropping an awkward curtsy, which results in her overbalancing and plumping down onto the floor, her legs outstretched like a rag doll.

Eva sits down beside her. 'What's your name, Liebchen?'

'Ana Marie.' It is no more than a whisper.

'Pretty name. I have a little girl like you. She likes comfits, too.'

I catch Barbara glance across at the sand clock and nod to the maid. 'Take the children to the kitchen for a drink. And then they may play outside for a bit before supper. I will be at Frau Cranach's and Doctor Luther will be joining me there.'

117

Eva and Basilius stay three more days in Wittenberg, and we two make the most of the time, Eva spending each afternoon at the Lutherhaus. The weather is kind and we work together in the kitchen garden, tending to the plants as we once did at Nimbschen. We chatter constantly as we work, a feast of remembrance: the hopes and fears and dreams we once had, how far we have come. I am proud of our garden, of the produce we grow there, for it isn't only the common vegetables – cabbages and carrots, beets and beans, onions and radishes – but others less usual. Eva is impressed, and I think perhaps a mite envious, as we weed around the pumpkin and melon plants, the striped fruits lying along the soil like stuffed cushions on a bench.

'Where did you get these?'

'All Martin's doing,' I say. 'He has taken an unexpected interest and often begs for folk to send or bring us unusual seeds. It is a bonus I could not have anticipated, for he didn't have the reputation of a man who favoured husbandry.'

'As I recall, the cloister garden was a disgrace when we arrived in Wittenberg, and perhaps it could hardly have been anything else with only Herr Brisger and Doctor Luther living here, besides that he had more important things to do with his time.'

I pause, remembering the pamphlets that found their way into Nimbschen. 'And if he had not, we – and hundreds of others – would still be treading the mill of works and bound by the fear of hell.' It is a sobering thought, and in an unconscious echo I say, 'Untidy as it was when we first saw it, by the time of our marriage it more closely resembled a wildwood than anything else. It took some clearing I can tell you, and to do Martin justice, he wielded a spade with vigour, as he does everything. The results as you see.'

A dimple appears in Eva's cheek. 'Maybe he isn't so old after all, and, though it pains me to admit it, maybe I was wrong to question your wisdom in marrying him.' She gestures towards the lilies and roses lining the path, their mingled scent filling the air. 'And were they Doctor Luther's idea also?'

'In a way. I spoke once of my mother's garden at Lippendorf, and a week later I came upon him planting seeds in a tray, which, when I asked what they were, all he would say was "Wait and see". I thought it likely some other exotic vegetable, so to find them a flower, planted purely for my pleasure, was entirely unexpected. As for the rose bushes, those he begged from the castle gardens, as a present for my name day.'

'Another sign I misjudged him.'

I laugh. 'We all did. All we saw of him at the start was Luther the reformer, the fiery preacher, the scourge of Rome … and our saviour. And to be truthful, I knew little more of him than you, even when I agreed to marry him. But I have since discovered Luther the man is very different from what we, any of us, imagined. And for the most part in a good way.'

The air cooling, I gather up the last of the weeds we have pulled and, tossing them into the barrow, lay the tools on top.

'Let me,' she says, grasping the barrow. 'You should take more care.'

'Bad enough,' I say, 'Martin being solicitous, without

119

you weighing in on his side. I am past the danger point and have no intention of sitting around doing nothing while I wait for this little one's arrival.'

She doesn't relinquish the barrow, but as we head towards the outhouse where the garden implements are stored, she looks back. 'All this, hard work as it must be, and with less privacy than I could handle, seems to suit *you.*'

'Yes. It seems I have a hidden talent for organisation...'

'For telling people what to do, you mean?' Her laugh rings out. 'I could have guessed that.' There is a mischievous glint in her eye. 'Does it include your husband?'

'This is my territory, and it includes everything and everyone in it, without exception... Even my enemies would say so, though they would think it an offence, as I do not.'

'A job well done,' she says, and I know she isn't only referring to the gardening.

But overhanging the memories and the laughter and our pleasure in each other's company is the understanding we are living in borrowed time, though we do not talk of it until the final day. Basilius has accepted the new position of physician to Duke Albrecht, and we both know that when they move to Prussia, we will never be together again.

'But still friends,' Eva says. 'That will never change. And we can write. That at least is something to be thankful for from our years in the convent.'

Chapter Eleven
Wittenberg, July–August 1527

The university term is ended, and with many of the students gone home we have one of those rare evenings without Table Talk. Martin arrives home just in time for supper and I hear voices in the hallway. He sweeps into the Stube and throws the door wide.

'Look what the wind has blown in? I take it there is plenty of food to go round, for I came upon these pair leaving the Town Church and prevailed upon them to join us.' For all his bluffness, I sense an uncertainty and am quick to offer reassurance.

'Friends are always welcome, and particularly so just now.'

'With Eva gone?' Kath Jonas hugs me. 'If I had not known the Axts left yesterday, I would not have been persuaded to come unannounced, but in the circumstances I thought you might welcome company.'

'You thought right. It is hard to think I might never see Eva again. She was more than just a friend, she was…'

'Your closest companion?'

'Yes. And though Nimbschen is long gone and I would not wish it to be any other way' – I hesitate, afraid I may be disappointing Martin by my admission – 'a little bit of me has gone with her.'

'Of course.' Justus nods. 'How could it not. But a little bit of her will remain with you also, and you will both be the richer for it.'

Supper over and Aunt Magdalene putting the children to bed, Kath and I are sitting in the window seat enjoying the last rays of sunshine, while Martin and Justus are talking about the proposed programme of lectures when the university recommences. Their discussion is cordial, their voices a background hum to our own conversation.

Kath is entertaining me with Sophie's latest exploit. 'I had stopped to pass the time of day with Frau Hohendorf, Jost and Sophie fidgeting behind us, when I heard Sophie announce, "I wouldn't like to have *her* nose. Mutti was right, it is as sharp as a hatchet".'

'Did Frau Hohendorf hear?'

'She couldn't not, and though she didn't say anything, the look on her face was enough. It was a salutary lesson not to speak so candidly in front of the children.'

Our laughter is cut off midstream as Martin gets to his feet, one hand pressed to his left ear. His face is white. 'I'm sorry,' he says. 'I need to lie down.'

I am at his side in an instant. 'What is it?'

'Pain in my ear, a loud ringing, as if I were beside the bell in the church tower and it chiming the hour.' He is clutching onto the edge of the table, and as he lets go and takes a step towards the door, he staggers. I grasp his arm, but Justus is at his other side.

'Let me help, Katharina.'

Martin nods. 'Thank you, Justus.'

We support him to our chamber, and together help him out of his clothes and into the bed, barely managing it before he loses consciousness. I fly to the physic cupboard and call for Aunt Magdalene, sending up a prayer of thanks for her recent move from Nimbschen to join us in the Lutherhaus. When I return he looks up at me, his eyes barely focused. I take his hand and he clutches at it.

'Hanschen,' he says, 'bring Hanschen.'

There is a tightness in my chest and I sink to the floor at his side, turn for support to Magdalene, but she's no longer there.

'Käthe.' He is moaning, repeating my name over and over, his voice barely audible.

Magdalene reappears and moving to the other side of the bed raises his head to trickle a liquid into his mouth.

'Mutti?' Hans is leaning against me, rubbing at his eyes, his bewilderment clear. Dorothea hovers in the doorway, her usual briskness replaced by uncertainty.

Martin stirs, struggles upright, stretches out his hand and places it on Hans' head. 'Hanschen. Dear boy ... look to your mother and do as she bids. Your father commends you to her, and to God. They will look after you.' And to me, 'Käthe, I did not mean to leave you so soon...' His head falls to the side.

'No! No!' I turn and pull Hans close, burying his head against my chest.

Justus grasps my shoulders and I allow myself to be raised to my feet.

Magdalene straightens. 'He hasn't gone, Kat. I have given him something for the pain. That is all.'

I want to believe her, and as Justus draws me away I

look back and am relieved to see the rise and fall of his chest.

'See,' she says. 'Take Hanschen back to bed. I will stay with Martin.'

I am in the brewhouse with Dorothea, overseeing the mashing of the barley malt. Brewing is one of the chores that brings me most satisfaction, for the beer that results is considered one of the finest home brews in Wittenberg and represents a substantial saving for our household accounts. Martin has been up and about again for several weeks now, but the fear of losing him hasn't left me, for although he hasn't had another recurrence of the pain that so prostrated him, he still suffers dizzy spells from time to time, striking without warning. Hearing the creak of the gate, I say, 'I don't know if I could have borne it.'

Dorothea wipes her hand on a rag. 'You have one child and another on the way. Of course you would have borne it. But thank the good Lord Herr Doctor Luther has been spared and you do not have to.'

'I know. I do, but...'

'You cannot add an hour to his life by worrying, so there is little point in causing yourself distress. Sufficient unto the day?'

Her echo of Martin is unintentionally prophetic, for his dizzy spells pale into insignificance against a greater threat. Plague has come to Wittenberg.

When word of the first cases in the town reaches us, Aunt Magdalene nods her head, as if it is an answer to a question troubling her. 'There will be much work here, many families in need of support. Perhaps it is for this God called me from Nimbschen.'

It may be so, but my concerns are closer to home, for Martin, for Hans, for the unborn babe and the other children in our care.

The university flees to Jena, the Lutherhaus echoing with the lack of the students who lodged with us. And as the town is caught in the grip of disease, the duke sends word we should follow, not just for Martin to continue his lecturing, but for our own safety.

Martin is adamant in his refusal. 'Our place is here, to help as we are able, and not only ourselves. It is the responsibility of every pastor, deacon, doctor, nurse and city official to remain.'

Deep inside I know he is right, though my heart quails. When Hanschen falls ill, I am consumed with anxiety, but I do not wish to share it, for fear speaking the worst will make it so.

Aunt Magdalene, coming upon me as I am kneeling at his side, wiping at his face and neck with a cloth wrung out in cold water to reduce his temperature, is quick to offer reassurance. 'Take heart, Kat. He is a sturdy child, and this but a childhood fever, not the plague.'

I look up, my fear translated into almost hostility, for it isn't her child tossing and turning, shivering and sweating in equal measure. 'Children die of fevers every day. Why should we be spared such pain?'

'Why indeed.' She pauses, as if in recognition of my right to question, continues, 'But we can give him good care and the right medicines, and by the grace of God we will recover him.'

Martin shares her opinion, and I find myself alternately

resenting and craving their strength of faith, which I struggle to match. His fever lasts for twelve days, Aunt Magdalene, Dorothea and I taking turns to sit with him. When he finally opens his eyes, and whispers, 'Mutti, I thirsty', instead of rushing to get him a drink, I remain rooted to the floor by his pallet, my shoulders shaking, the tears I couldn't shed while he was in danger, flowing freely.

Aunt Magdalene bustles forward and moves me aside. He sips from the beaker she holds to his mouth, then smiles and murmurs, 'Danke, Lena,' before his eyelids flicker as he drifts into an easy sleep.

Torgau: October 1552

Margarethe is hovering at Paul's shoulder as he questions me about my pain. I smile encouragingly at them. 'I am much better today,' I say. 'I think I could sit awhile.'

'Are you sure?' he says, his expression dubious. 'It is only three weeks since the accident and the bone will scarcely have begun to knit.'

I am well aware of the risks and slide my hand over my pelvis feeling the misalignment. I know it will never be as it was before, that once I am up and about again I will be misshapen and walk with a limp, but take comfort the deformity at least will be hidden under my skirts. That much Paul has conceded when I insisted on discussing my care, but still they try to hold me back. 'You know I cannot lie here forever, for there is danger also in failing to move. A little extra valerian,' I say, 'that's all I need, and help to get into the chair.'

'I have sent to the pharmacist, for we appear to have used up all we had.'

Paul is looking at Margarethe instead of me, and I suspicion he is not telling the truth.

'You were never a good liar, Paul,' I say. Not like Young Martin. He could swear on his own grave he was innocent of a misdemeanour I'd seen him commit.'

They both flush, Paul looking down at the floor, Margarethe studying her hands, and I take pity on them. 'I know you have the best of intentions, but I must get up soon, for there are folk more ill than me to look after. Ask Basilius. He knows.'

'There are no…' Paul begins.

He is interrupted by Margarethe. 'At least wait until the doctor comes.'

'Jerome Schurf?' I say. 'He's already here. '

She is chewing her finger. 'Doctor Schurf is in Wittenberg, Mutti.'

'Where else would he be, other than with us when there is such need? But it is good of Hanna to come too. And put herself in such danger, now that we are a plague hospital.'

CHAPTER TWELVE
WITTENBERG, SEPTEMBER–NOVEMBER 1527

The Lutherhaus is full to bursting, the rooms vacated by the students taken up by plague victims the main task of nursing them shared between myself and Aunt Magdalene who, following Hanschen's lead, we all begin to call Muhme Lena. Dorothea shoulders the burden of the rest of the household tasks, aided by the maids; all of us working with a will, dropping into bed, night after night, exhausted. And as soon as we lose someone, there is someone else to take their place, the number of those falling to the disease increasing throughout September and October so that we are fast running out of linens. With every death, all clothing and bedsheets must be taken beyond the Elster Gate and burnt to avoid the transfer of infection, the stench of burning wool an ever-present reminder of the dangers we all face.

Though the university has gone, a remnant of students remain, Martin continuing to provide lectures for them alongside the preparation of sermons and his writing. And as if that isn't enough, he takes on the harvesting of the produce in the garden with an enthusiasm which surprises us all, including himself.

He comes into the Stube and throws himself down on the settle. 'I understand now,' he says, 'the attraction husbandry has for Andreas Karlstadt, for it is easy to see God in the bountiful provision He has given, and, as I kneel in the mud pulling cabbages, to thank Him for it.'

Clods of earth trail across the polished floorboards, but I scarcely notice, for we have different priorities now. The babe moves within me, pressing against my ribs and, with a glance at Martin, I stretch upwards, to relieve the discomfort in my chest and stifle the desire to laugh at the irony of my situation. In my first pregnancy I found Martin's concern at times suffocating and longed to be free of restrictions. Now, with dragging tiredness a constant companion, a little concern would be welcome.

'We are indeed fortunate that with the help the duke provides we have food, and to spare, for all here. But when we are fully into winter it may be a different story.'

I can see he isn't listening and I sense he has something else of import to say, anxiety once again gnawing at my stomach.

There is a renewed weariness in his voice. 'Deacon Rörer's wife has been taken. God rest her soul.'

My anxiety hardens into a knot. 'Has anyone else succumbed?' I slip onto the floor at his knee, thinking of the Bugenhagens, who lodged in the pastor's accommodation adjacent to the Rörers. 'What of Walpurga?'

'Both she and Johannes are fine, but they have asked to come here.'

'Out of the skillet and into the fire surely? They will not be safe from infection here.'

'They do not ask to escape danger, but rather that

130

they might be of assistance.' He places his hand on my stomach. 'I have not counselled care, Käthe, for the task facing us is great, but I do not forget your state. You and Muhme Lena and Dorothea do well, but I know help will not go amiss. And although Walpurga is also expecting, she assures me she has energy aplenty and would wish to use it for good.'

'I cannot deny we would appreciate another pair of hands, but I don't wish to put her in danger or threaten her pregnancy.'

'The whole of Wittenberg is in danger, and it is only by God's grace we are still standing. If they wish to help, it is their decision to make. Our place to be grateful for it.'

And grateful we are, and for the Schurfs who also move in to help in the nursing of the most seriously ill. It is a sobering thought that it has taken a crisis such as this to break down Jerome Schurf's resistance to our marriage.

'Not before time,' Martin says, the gruffness in his voice concealing the gratitude he feels.

In the town the death toll increases daily, the plague doctors, in their beaked masks and black cloaks, scouring the streets and alleyways, searching out the ill and marking their doors with a cross.

Dorothea, who treks in an out of town collecting supplies of milk and flour, is grim. 'If this continues, Wittenberg will be a ghost town, for many have fled, and those who remain, if they do not die of the plague, will likely die of cold or hunger, for lack of anyone to look to them.'

Muhme Lena is tearing cloth into strips and placing them in buckets of cold water. She looks up with a sigh but doesn't pause. 'We are only so many and must do what we can without fretting over what we cannot.'

It is an uncharacteristic fatalism that chills me, and as the weeks wear on, one which threatens to infect us all.

'Is it a scourge from God?' I ask her as, night by night, the rumble of carts carrying the corpses outside the city for mass burial is a continual hum stealing sleep.

Her brow puckers. 'I think it more likely a natural consequence of something people have done or not done, Kat, and if we only knew the cause we could perhaps halt the disease.'

Dorothea's bleak assessment ringing in my head, I determine to see what is happening in the town for myself. It is indeed a melancholy sight, for in every street there are shuttered houses, wooden spars nailed across the doors, traces of the chalk marks still visible. The marketplace, once bustling, is silent, the stalls that remain open almost devoid of customers. I regret I did not bring my purse, for if I had I would have bought something from every one. On the Mittelstrasse I look up at the roofline and see, interspersed among the forest of smokeless chimneys, occasional thin wisps of smoke struggling upwards to reach the sky and think how it must be to live among such dereliction. Retracing my steps, I halt outside the Melanchthon's house, an impulse I regret so soon as the maid opens the door a fraction, only to shut it again with a muttered, 'Wait.'

'Kat?' Katharina Melanchthon appears and I see with surprise she also is heavy with child and the birth likely imminent. 'I'm sorry you were shut out, the maid…'

'No. It's I who should be sorry. Why shouldn't she fear? I should have thought before I called, for no doubt it is common knowledge the Lutherhaus has become an infirmary for plague victims.'

She steps back to allow me to enter, but I shake my head.

'I'll not come in. I hadn't realised…'

She glances down at her stomach and then at mine. 'I cannot deny it frightens me, for it's hardly the best time to bring a babe into this world. And with Philipp at Jena…' She shrugs. 'Perhaps it is as well one of us is safe. There will be enough orphans, and to spare, when this is over.' She hesitates, then, 'If you will not come in, I will walk with you. Some air may do me good.'

I doubt it, for it cannot be called fresh, but I welcome her suggestion nonetheless.

By tacit agreement we take the path down to the riverside meadow, where the clearest air is to be found. Katharina bends awkwardly to pick a stem of wild garlic, breathing in deeply. 'There was something you wanted to ask?'

I pause, follow her example. 'Yes, but it doesn't matter, not now.'

She looks down at her stomach again. 'Why should this make a difference? Ask me anyway.'

When I finish, she remains silent for a moment and I don't blame her. 'Of course, I cannot expect you will be able to do anything now.'

'Why not? I may not be able to walk fast, but I am not bed-bound yet. How can it be right to refuse while daily you and Hanna and Walpurga pour yourselves out to help those in need. Visiting women who are not ill, but nevertheless need help and advice, that they may not succumb, is hardly the same risk. I should be, am, honoured to be asked. Besides, we are all in the same boat.' She makes a sound halfway between a laugh and a sob. 'If you cannot leave Hanna to carry the burden by herself, neither can I. If this babe is anything like the last he won't be quick in coming, and it will occupy me while I wait, and besides, I am better placed to hear of those in the town who most need help.' She tucks her arm through mine. 'I shall walk you home, but' – a flicker of a smile – 'you'll forgive me if I don't come in.'

In mid-November there is a brief respite, the number of deaths decreasing, our hopes rising that the grip the disease has on the town is on the wane. Serious as the issue still is, Martin seeks to make a jest of it.

'We have lost five pigs. May Christ our comfort allow the plague to be content with this tribute and cease.'

It is humour I find inappropriate, allied to a fear God will too, and when Hanna Schurf is struck down, I am sure of it. My unspoken desire to challenge Martin, to lay the blame at his door, is a weight on my chest, turning the relief I once felt for the help Hanna has been in the Lutherhaus to guilt that we brought her into danger. Paradoxically, as we all pray for her, Jerome Schurf becomes increasingly supportive, of Martin and myself, and as I experience the truth of the saying that adversity deepens friendship, so the weight begins to lift. To be dispelled altogether by the rejoicing when, against all the odds, she recovers, with only scarring to indicate where the pustules have been. She reappears in the Stube, leaning on Jerome's arm, her skin parchment-sallow, her cheekbones prominent, eyes dark-rimmed. Her first question is for the pregnant and needy women in the town she had visited before she fell ill.

She names them one by one. 'Have you seen them?

How have they fared?'

'We visit them all, at least until...' I tail off, for it is hard to name those who have been taken.

She reaches out her hand, her once plump fingers slender, the veins blue-black under her skin. 'Even if we only saved one life, Kat, it would still be worth it. I shall be glad to resume my visits.'

Jerome is gentle, but also firm. 'When your strength increases, my dear.'

Late in in November, Dorothea returns from town with the news of the arrival of the latest Melanchthon. 'A boy, and baptised George,' she says.

'They are both well?'

'Frau Melanchthon is a mite tired, as is to be expected, but' – her expression is troubled – 'the boy seems a puny thing, though perhaps that will change.'

The nearer it comes to our own time, the more insistent everyone else is that Walpurga and I restrict ourselves to helping Dorothea, two of the maids replacing us in tending to the sick. And to be truthful I am glad, for when I think of Hanna I am struck by how fortunate we have been thus far; and I have no wish to take any further risk than those we run simply by being here.

Chapter Thirteen
Wittenberg, December 1527

December sweeps in in a flurry of snow and hail, driven by biting winds from the east. The stoves are stoked up, despite our dwindling supplies of wood, and I fear they won't last out the winter. Martin sends to the duke and receives in return a promise of logs, to be delivered so soon as the track from the woods on the other side of the Elbe is passable.

Muhme Lena comes in as Martin is reading out the reply.

Her eyes are troubled. 'We may pray it is soon or it may be more than heat we will be lacking.'

I think of the winter in Nimbschen when the road through the valley was blocked, the convent cut off for weeks. How the fratress' brow was constantly puckered as she eeked out what supplies we had: watering the soups, serving ever-thinner slivers of cheese, reducing the portions of salt cod. Likely what is in Muhme Lena's mind also.

Dorothea is brisk. 'No sense in looking for trouble where there may be none. We are warm and well fed at present and can ride out a week or two without shortage. Let that be sufficient for us.'

'Indeed, Dorothea.' Martin smiles his approval. 'God is no man's debtor. He has not let us down before. He will not now.'

Whether it is the babe inside of me making a dent in my confidence, or my own lack of faith, I envy his certainty, but when I voice my doubts to Walpurga, she laughs.

'You needn't trouble yourself, Kat, for who can expect to match up to Doctor Luther's faith? Not I, for sure.' Then, more soberly, 'And in my experience pregnancy does something to a woman.'

'Addles her brain, you mean?'

She laughs again. 'That's one way of putting it. Though I would not think to admit it to my husband, nor recommend you do either. Still, we will be ourselves again soon. And in the meantime may concentrate our prayers on a safe delivery for both of us.'

I do pray, every day, for the memory of my first labour, though it dimmed with time as Barbara had said it would, has now resurfaced, sharp and clear, as if it were but yesterday. I miss Barbara, for I cannot share my fear with Martin, and Muhme Lena, though no doubt she would be sympathetic, does not have any experience to draw on. Contrary to all our hopes, the plague rages, unabated, despite the wintry weather, the snow piled in drifts against the cloister wall, and it seems whatever the root cause of the disease, it isn't destroyed by cold. The Bugenhagens have now moved into a chamber at the other end of the

137

Lutherhaus, as far removed from the plague victims as it is possible to be, and Dorothea, backed up by Martin, insists I follow suit. Used as we are to a north-facing Stube, it is nevertheless odd to wake in a room where the morning light is dim, and I find myself less inclined to get up.

Muhme Lena's eyes crinkle with amusement when I confess to the laziness. 'Nothing whatever to do with being close to your time?'

'I don't remember feeling thus with Hans.'

'That was summertime and with sunlight to wake you. Everyone feels more energetic in fine weather. And though I know you weren't short of work to occupy you then, we are all stretched to the limit now, and with your added burden it's little wonder you should be tired.'

'I just wish...'

'For it to be all over? It will be soon.'

I don't want to hurt her feelings by saying it is Barbara I wish for, that I miss her sorely, so I content myself with, 'I know.' I stretch upwards to relieve the pressure under my ribs and move to the window to look out. It is no longer snowing and the wind has dropped, leaving an eerie silence. I sigh. 'I miss the hustle and bustle of the street too, for with the inclemency of the weather few are venturing out, and those that do are not coming here.'

'And who could blame them, for we are more like a plague colony than a house.'

'I know that too,' I say, 'but it doesn't make it any easier.'

I am in the kitchen, kneading dough, the rhythmic movement soothing, when I hear a knocking at the front door.

Dorothea looks up, surprised, and I feel a sudden

138

surge of hope. Quickly followed by the knowledge that if Barbara *were* to arrive at our door, I should be forced to refuse her entrance, for it would not be well done to put her at risk.

'I'll go,' Dorothea says, drying her hands and straightening her apron.

I listen to the soft shuffle of her slippers as she hurries along the flagged corridor, and the screech of the bolts as she pulls them back, straining to make out the murmur of voices.

'More poor souls needing help,' she says when she returns. 'I have set the maids to see to accommodation for them.'

For the first time since the beginning of the outbreak her voice reveals a weariness at odds with her usual disposition. She sets her mouth in a firm line and resumes the shredding of cabbages and chopping of vegetables, attacking a turnip as if it was solely responsible for our current plight. The knife slips, slicing into her finger, blood beading along a cut an inch long, and she subsides onto the bench, sucking on it, while I scrabble in a basket for a clean strip of rag to staunch the flow. When I turn around she is crying, a loss of control that sends a shiver through me. She is still clutching the knife and I kneel by her side and gently release her grip, before pulling her other hand from her mouth and binding the cut.

In the privacy of our chamber I settle beside Martin. Ever since my conversation with Muhme Lena, and her confidence that the plague isn't God's doing, I have worried away at the thought it is lack of prayer, of fervency, of faith, that is the root cause. For whatever may be the case for others, for sure I cannot match the intensity of my convent prayers. I am almost afraid to ask his opinion, for fear he will despise me for my uncertainty, but I need to hear it, nonetheless. If he has confidence, perhaps it will restore mine also. I focus on a snag in his stocking, mentally adding it to the mending piling up in the basket, say, 'How long can this go on? So many people are dying. Have we not prayed enough?' And then, with a deep breath, aware it might be blasphemy I speak, 'Or is God not listening?'

He rests his hand on my head, stroking my hair as if I were our mongrel puppy, Tolpel, and I don't know whether to laugh, or cry, or pull my head away. I will him to say something comforting, to hear the Martin Luther whose confidence in God is unshakeable.

'God always listens, Käthe. And He *will* answer.'

I relax a fraction, but he hasn't finished.

'We are none of us immune from doubts, but in our weakness lies His strength.'

It isn't enough for me. 'What if we do not get the answer we want?'

'Then we must bow to His will.' He cups my chin in his hands, tilting my face to meet his gaze. There is anguish in his eyes, but his voice is firm. 'However hard that may be.'

The pains come with the dawn, the panic that has been building over the last weeks replaced by a fatalistic calm

140

allowing me to slide from the bed and pad up and down the chamber, breathing into each contraction, deep and slow, as Barbara taught me. Her voice is in my head, instructing and encouraging, and it enables me to work through the first hour without the need to wake anyone.

When Martin stirs I am bent over the end of the bed, gripping the frame, my knuckles white. He is out of bed and by my side.

'Should I fetch Muhme Lena or Dorothea?'

I concentrate on riding out the spasm, and when it subsides, I relax my hold of the wood and straighten. 'Let them sleep. It will likely be hours yet and I know what to expect, what to do.'

'Can I...? Is there anything...?'

He is floundering, out of his depth, and I remember Barbara's comment that if men had to give birth, there would be less people in the world.

'Get dressed. Walk with me. When the next pain comes I will be glad of your hand to grip.' I smile in encouragement and add, only partly in jest, 'Though you may end up with the scars to prove your participation.'

We establish a rhythm, walk, pause with each pain, Martin supporting me as I breathe through it, walk again. I remember Barbara's chatter, wish Martin could similarly distract me, but I can see it is as much as he can do to be here, and with each pain the tension in his shoulders increases. The contractions are becoming longer and more painful. When I bite on my lip and draw blood, he blurts out, 'I'm sorry, Käthe, I had no idea... I didn't mean for you to suffer so... Is it always...?'

He is interrupted by a knock on the door.

Dorothea's face registers surprise. 'Doctor Luther!

141

This is no place for a husband.' And to me, 'Why did you not call? You know I would have come the instant you needed me.'

'I know. But I wanted to let you sleep. And Doctor Luther has coped admirably.' I shut my eyes against the next wave of pain, imagine a change in it. When I have ridden it out, I relinquish Martin's hand and, running my thumb across the marks where my nails have dug into his palm, say, 'I think perhaps it *is* time for Dorothea to take over.'

His expression is a mixture of hesitation and relief, but she grasps him by the arm and propels him to the door. 'Fetch Muhme Lena and a maid. The best thing you can do now is to keep Hanschen and the other children occupied, and out of earshot. And shut the door.' She takes my arm in his place. 'You think it will be soon? Do you wish the chair?'

'I thought so, but perhaps I was wrong. The last pain…'

'No matter.' We parade the length of the room again. 'It was an opportunity to get the good doctor out of the way. This is women's work. No doubt he was fine enough for the start, but when the real work comes, it is something no husband should see … or hear.'

The labour continues well into the afternoon, and though the progression is steady, the light is fading before we are done, Muhme Lena hurrying to put Martin out of his misery. I stare down at the scrunched-up face, at the cap of dark hair and the tiny hand gripping tight to my index finger, and listen to her steady breathing and thank God.

'Has Doctor Luther chosen a name for her?'

'No,' I say. 'I have. I will call her Elizabeth.'

'Will you now?'

He is framed in the doorway, and when I look up and smile, he smiles back, and I wonder if it is a better sense of what we women go through causes him to capitulate.

'Elizabeth it is then, though who in the world will we say she is called for?'

'Herself.'

His shout of laughter seems as much a relief of tension as amusement, and he leans over and touches the babe's head, as if in blessing. He looks towards the window, at the encroaching darkness. 'I must call for Jonas...'

'It is too late today, Martin, and no fear this little one won't last the night. Tomorrow will be time enough for the baptism.' Muhme Lena ushers him from the room. 'Straightforward as this birth was, Katharina needs rest.'

Elizabeth is three weeks old, Walpurga standing by the cradle, swinging it back and forwards, her expression wistful. Elizabeth stirs, hiccups, settles again, and Walpurga turns towards me with a smile, which becomes a grimace as she presses her hand to her stomach with a sharp intake of breath.

'It's coming, isn't it?'

She grabs hold of the arm of a chair, gasps out, 'Yes, thank God.'

'We'd best get you to your chamber.'

Her labour is fast and the midwife is once more adamant in her refusal to come to the Lutherhaus, but this time it is Muhme Lena who takes charge. Of all of us it is I who has experience in the matter and should

143

therefore be best placed to help Walpurga, but, whether it is because I am still at Elizabeth's beck and call and can be needed at any moment, or to spare me the memory of my own recent confinement, I am dispatched to boil water and organise clean linen and help with the preparation of supper. Whatever the reason, it is ineffective, for as I stir soup and cut bread and lay the table in the refectory, I can think of nothing else.

I slip to the door seeking a clearer air than can be found in the kitchen, but step out into a hailstorm and last only a few moments before scurrying back inside, my cheeks stinging.

Dorothea looks up and grunts. 'If it's fresh air you're needing, you could feed the chickens, for I don't expect Muhme Lena will be doing it tonight.' She nods towards the cloak hanging on the back of the pantry door. 'But I suggest you wrap up first, for we don't want you catching your death of cold.'

'Death by battering, more like', I say, 'for it's coming down hailstones the size of pebbles.'

'Best wait awhile then. I daresay it won't last forever.' And then, as if she knows what I'm thinking, 'I never set great store by omens. If a babe is healthy, the worst storm in the world won't alter that. But content yourself, we'll likely have a long wait yet.' And then, with an expression of disbelief, she drops a spoon with a clatter and cocks her head. 'Well I never, the babe safely delivered so soon, and a lusty one, to go by the cry.'

We fly upstairs to find Walpurga propped up on cushions on the bed, the babe in her arms swaddled so tight I'm surprised it can breathe, never mind cry. Muhme Lena, perhaps guessing at my thoughts, is defensive.

144

'It is security the little mite needs just now, see how contentedly he lies.'

'That was quick,' I say.

'Quick maybe, but not easy,' Muhme Lena is bustling about, removing the bloodstained cloths, mopping at the stains on the floor.

Walpurga looks up from her study of the infant, her face chalk-white, eyes luminous, and I wonder just how much blood she has lost and if she will be able to recover it fully. I dispel the thought, for it comes uncomfortably close to home, raising the question – am I also diminished? – does every birth diminish a woman?

'I could have wished for an easier labour,' she says, 'but thank the good Lord there is nothing amiss.' Her smile is for me. 'I have a son, and mayhap a husband for your daughter.'

Chapter Fourteen
Wittenberg, January–February 1528

With the turn of the year comes relief, from the weather and the plague. There is no way to describe why or how, but one day there are twenty deaths, a few days later only ten, then five, then two, and finally a few stragglers, and though the plague doctors still insist on their burial outside the town, and the burning of all the clothes and bedding, there is a general feeling we are at last waking from the nightmare of the past months.

The final burials take place, not at night, as the others have done, but at dusk, a small crowd following the cart out to the burial ground and standing at a distance to raise a ragged cheer as the bodies are laid to rest.

'It was somewhat inappropriate,' Martin says, when he tells me of it, 'but we none of us had the heart to reprove them. For which of us is not glad to see the back of the plague? Pray God it is a long time before we suffer thus again.'

'Or ever,' I say.

He lifts one shoulder in a semi-shrug. 'That, Käthe, is perhaps *too* optimistic.'

Maybe it is, but it doesn't stop me hoping. And when a service of thanksgiving and petition, led by Johannes Bugenhagen, is held in the Town Church, I look around me and see many lips moving in silent prayer and suspect they feel as I do. The ravages of the plague are seen everywhere, inside the town and out: in the empty houses, half-filled pews, shuttered shops and undug gardens. But as if by common consent, the talk among the townsfolk is all of mundane problems: a faulty lock on a pantry door, a chimney that smokes despite thorough sweeping, a ham over-salted, seed that has suffered from the frost and will need to be replaced. I wonder how long it will be before we are able to gossip of happier things.

Gradually, as the days lengthen, the university returns, and with it comes a sense of normality, as we all begin to look forward instead of back. But far from lifting Martin's spirits, now that he does not have the plague to concern him, he begins to sink into a depression. It isn't just the dizzy spells that trouble him, though they continue, but a deeper malaise I find hard to understand and even harder to know what I should do. I share my concern with Justus. 'If it was the decimation the plague wrought, I could understand, or even the problems with his own health, but when I challenge him, though he mentions his frailty, it is only in passing, his primary concern the colleagues who are no longer here in Wittenberg. How they are spread far abroad and he longs for them all to be together again. But he sent them out, that the freedom of the gospel might be shared. Why would he wish them back again?'

Justus is sympathetic, but can offer little comfort. 'This depression of his, it is not logical, nor easy to explain. I have seen it before, though not perhaps as severe as now.

147

He does not fight it as we think he should, perhaps because to him it is his cross to bear. An affliction as troublesome as any physical ill.'

'What can I do?'

'I'm not sure there is much you can do, bar making sure he eats and sleeps, so that while he is struggling in mind, his body remains strong.'

I cannot keep the anguish from my voice. 'I cannot just sit back and wait.'

He sighs. 'I will speak to him, Katharina, but I cannot promise he will listen.'

Inwardly I scream – make him listen! Outwardly I hold myself in check, take a deep breath, say, 'Thank you.'

When Justus appears in our Stube, Martin barely stirs.

'How are you, Martin?'

He shrugs, exhibiting a listlessness that frightens me more than ever his explosions did. 'How should I feel, when all my friends are gone? When daily I fear I do not have the strength to finish the work God has given me to do?'

Justus is gentle, but I sense resolve. He sits down opposite Martin. 'As you once said, the Kingdom of God must be proclaimed in other towns, not just in Wittenberg. You know it is for that Amsdorf is in Magdeburg, Spalatin in Altenburg, Linck in Nuremberg, besides the countless others who have left here with your blessing. Will you withdraw it? Summon them back?'

I interject, 'How can you say you have no friends here, Martin? There are many who love you: Melanchthon, Bugenhagen, Justus here who cares enough to come to seek to jolt you out of your depression.' I pause, take a deep breath, risk, 'Your wife and children.'

That draws a response, but not the one I wished.

'Ah yes. You have been a true wife, Käthe, but perhaps I did you wrong in marrying you. If I leave you a widow, with the burden of children to care for, what good will I have done?'

I feel a spurt of anger. 'Our children are not a burden, but a blessing. The Martin Luther I married wrote and preached and taught thus. This is the Devil speaking. Will you let him extinguish your fire?'

Justus gives a shake of his head so infinitesimal I'm not sure if I've imagined it. 'We none of us know the day or the hour when God may call us home, Martin. But that does not mean we refuse to live to the full the life we are given. You left the cloister to embrace the opportunities God gives, not to shirk them. And there are opportunities aplenty here. And all the more, because many of our friends are occupied with God's work elsewhere.'

Whether it is my reference to the Devil or Justus' challenge, Martin thrusts back his chair and leaves the room without a backwards glance, the door banging on its hinges and bouncing against the wall.

I look at the handle-shaped dent in the plaster, anger draining out of me, leaving a sense of hopelessness in its wake. 'I'm sorry, I should never have asked you to…'

'Don't be. Any reaction is better than none. He may have stormed off now, but once stirred, you may find tomorrow the anfechtung has left him.'

'Should I…?'

'Go after him? It's not my place to say, Katharina, but if you want my opinion…'

'Yes, yes, I do. I may be his wife, but you have known him for much longer than me and this is my first

149

experience of the anfechtung, as you call it.' I am rubbing with my thumb at a roughness on a fingernail, staring at it intently, not entirely comfortable with unburdening myself in this way, but unable or unwilling to stop myself. 'It frightens me.'

He is sombre. 'It frightens us all, Katharina, to find even Martin Luther has feet of clay.'

He bows his head, his hands clenched as if in prayer. Then, aware of my scrutiny, looks up. 'But perhaps it is good for us to see that no one, however strong their calling, is immune from Satan's attacks, and only the power of God can help us to withstand them.' He looks past me, towards the picture of the Virgin and child hanging opposite the stove. 'As for what you should do? My suggestion is to leave him to his demons tonight and pray, believing God will rescue him. As I will also.'

Our prayers are answered. The next morning Martin wakes with the dawn. As the light slips into our chamber, filling up the room and chasing away all shadow, I see the lines are smoothed out in his face, the anguished expression of the previous days replaced by a quiet calm.

He pads across the floor to where I am sitting at the desk, already poring over accounts, and lifting my plait, he traces a weaving line down the hair from where it comes together at the nape, to the tip. I feel rather than hear his sigh, and recognise it as a sign of a weariness of body but no longer one of mind.

'I'm sorry, Käthe,' he begins, but I swivel round and, reaching up, place my hand against his mouth, afraid if he

150

says too much I will cry.

'If you are yourself again, that is enough for me.' I look him full in the face. 'I will not say these past weeks have been easy, but we must not dwell on them, rather thank God for your release.' I hesitate, unsure of the wisdom of what is in my heart to say, but, remembering the hurt expression on Hans' face, blurt out before I can change my mind, 'I don't seek or need an apology for myself, but Hans deserves one. He is too young to understand anything other than that he sought his father's company and was sent away.' There is a moment's silence, a flush creeping upwards from Martin's neck, and I wonder if I have overstepped the mark.

'You're wrong, Käthe.' He lifts my hand and turns it over, staring at it as if to memorise the pattern of lines etched into my palm. 'You both deserve an apology, along with everyone else who has suffered alongside me. And you shall have it. With my thanks: for your forbearance and your honesty. Both qualities I prize.' He imprisons my hand in his, with the first glimmer of a smile. 'I am well aware of how much courage it took to speak as you did, both yesterday and today, and I am grateful for it.'

Andreas Karlstadt, in common with all the labourers and craftsmen in the town, has more work than he can handle, as houses are repaired, walls freshly limed, timbers treated. I walk along the Collegienstrasse, the air ringing with the sounds of chisel on stone, of hammering and sawing, of the clanking of buckets and creaking of ladders, of whistling and shouting, laughter and oaths. I

151

feel my spirits soar, despite the lime dust and soot which stings my nostrils and catches at the back of my throat. But when I call to see Anna, I find her subdued.

'I am glad of the income, of course,' she says, 'and thankful we are all still here, though I cannot but feel guilty we rejoice when others do not.'

'You have had your share of pain in the past. It is not wrong to be grateful this time you were spared.' I become brisk. 'Bugenhagen would remind us we must rejoice with those that do rejoice and weep with those that weep. We were never promised a lack of weeping, but I for one am happy to be able to rejoice with you.' That brings a tremulous smile. 'And am come to invite you to supper, before the Schurfs and Bugenhagens return to their own place. We will be full up with students and visitors soon enough, all eager for Table Talk to recommence, so must take the chance while we can.'

She looks doubtful and, ignoring her expression, I press on.

'I won't take no for an answer. We are all due some pleasure, and the Cranachs and Melanchthons and Justus and Kath Jonas are already contracted to come, so *you* mustn't disappoint us.'

'Andreas has not found it easy to be sociable…'

'Justus has promised to tackle Andreas, and mild as he appears, he isn't used to being refused. Indeed, he had reason to speak sternly to Martin just three days ago, and with good effect. If he can jolt Martin out of a depression, I do not think Andreas will be able to withstand him.' She remains silent, and guessing at the reason for her uncertainty, I offer, 'This is no time to remember recent ills, but rather to reinforce old friendships. Barbara, in

152

particular, is looking forward to spending an evening with you free of shadows.'

'It is not a recent ill that concerns me, but rather a longstanding one, which has come again to the fore.'

There is only one issue that could so unsettle her. 'The Anabaptists? Has Andreas…?'

'He has not re-baptised anyone, but I fear it may only be a matter of time. If someone should request it, I do not think he would refuse…'

I finish her sentence for her 'And that, Doctor Luther could not countenance?'

Her lip is caught between her teeth, and I think back to the autumn, when word trickled in of the persecution of the Anabaptists; the horrifying stories of those burned at the stake or drowned, heretics in the eyes of both Catholic and evangelical alike.

'I am right, am I not?' she says.

'There are two things you should know. Martin argues for infant baptism, yes, but he recognises his argument is based on tradition, not theology, and, in private at least, he has expressed admiration for the bravery of those Anabaptists who have been martyred. But he fears disunity, and it would indeed be a problem should your husband speak openly in their favour. He has not done so yet, nor has Martin said anything of the kind, so there is no reason why you cannot accept this invitation.'

'We have no one to look to the children…'

I demolish her last remnants of resistance. 'You are all invited, for the children too have missed the company of friends. And the Lutherhaus has been scoured to an inch of its life, so they can chase about to their heart's content, without fear of infection, or indeed of censure. Besides,

153

there are babies to admire all round, and it will be good for us to concentrate on the lives just begun, rather than those that have passed.'

The candles are burnt almost down, the stove beginning to cool, when Lucas Cranach gets to his feet. The buzz of conversation dies away as he clears his throat.

Barbara whispers in my ear, 'I trust this will not be the beer talking.'

I smother a chuckle. 'If it is, I think for once he can be forgiven.'

On my other side Kath Jonas turns a laugh into a cough. 'If it is, at least it is good Einbeck beer. We may hope the speech matches it.'

Walpurga Bugenhagen puts a finger to her mouth. 'Shh, it's not often Lucas takes the stage.'

'Thankfully,' Barbara says.

Justus looks across at we six clustered by the hearth, shakes his head in mock disapproval. 'Damen, please. Give him a chance.'

Lucas raises his tankard. 'The evening is almost gone, but I thought I should get in before Martin, for my speech, beer fuelled or not' – this with a bow towards Barbara – 'will be short.'

We all laugh, but he waves us into silence.

'My courage may stem from the Einbeck, but my sentiments do not. We are in a new year, and how better to go forward than in friendship and fellowship and thankfulness to God. Despite the ill that befell our town, we all have benefitted from His protection in the year that has gone and will, we trust, experience blessings in the year to come.'

He sits down amid a chorus of 'Amen', as heartfelt as if we were in church and his speech a prayer. There is a moment of silence, broken by a squeal as the door flies open, Jost Jonas tumbling through, Hans on his tail. They skid to a halt, panting, Hans' thumb straying into his mouth, as if he's unsure among so many adults. There is the sound of running footsteps, the other children piling in behind them, the room alive with laughter and cries of 'I won.' 'Found you.' 'You pushed.' 'It's not fair. I wanted to be first.'

Barbara gathers in her two youngest. 'Well now, perhaps it's time these children were in bed.'

There is a chorus of protest, but Kath Jonas and Katharina Melanchthon follow her lead, Hanna Schurf moving quickly to shut the door lest any of the children escape.

Hanschen's mouth wobbles and I pull him close.

Over his head Barbara says, 'We'd best get away before laughter turns to tears. It has been a good night and we don't want to spoil it.'

CHAPTER FIFTEEN
WITTENBERG, APRIL–JUNE 1528

In like a lion, they say, and out like a lamb. And so it proves, March sliding into a balmy April, day after day filled with sunshine, with only a light breeze to ruffle my skirt as I stroll to the market square. I carry Elizabeth in the sling I have fashioned from a length of linen, in defiance of the convention that it should only be those who cannot afford to do otherwise who demean themselves by doing the work of a servant. She stares up, unblinking, and I tell myself perhaps she is looking at the clouds trailing across the sky like strands of white wool. I tell myself her stillness, her lethargy, is something she'll likely grow out of once she is old enough to be on the move. That perhaps she is simply by nature a quiet child. That to compare her to Hans is a foolishness and I should not fret so. But I cannot bear to be parted from her, for there is a kernel of worry deep inside I cannot quash, however much I overlay it with other more ordinary concerns. I cannot avoid thinking of Walpurga's son, Johannes, born just weeks after Elizabeth, already taken from us, the after-effects of the plague perhaps responsible and my child likewise in danger.

Hans is clutching the string attached to Tolpel's collar, now ahead of me, now lagging behind each time the dog stops to nose at a doorway. He crows with delight when Tolpel lifts his leg against a barrel, as if it is an achievement to be proud of, and my reprimand is choked in my throat, for I have just begun training Hans and congratulate him every time he asks for the pot.

Wittenberg is truly alive again, the square bustling, cries of stallholders rising above the rattle of wheels on the cobbles. The creaking of axles, the lowing of oxen and the whinnying of horses is a comforting cacophony of sound, signalling, as Lucas had predicted, a past put behind us and a brighter future ahead. It takes me twice as long as I intended to make my purchases, for at every step it seems there is another woman who stops me to peer at Elizabeth and pat Hans on the head and wish me well. For me it is the final piece in the puzzle, a sign our world, my world, is finally righted; and it goes some way to relieve my fears for Elizabeth.

Despite the time I have already been abroad, I cross the square to call in on Barbara, as was my previous custom. 'I finally feel our marriage is accepted,' I tell her, pleasure in my voice.

'A pity it took the plague to give you the place that should rightfully have been yours all along.'

Through the open windows I hear a burst of birdsong, so in accord with my own feelings, I cannot but smile. 'It hardly matters now. Not when the sun is shining and the beds in our garden are alive with fresh growth, buds forming between the leaves on the fruit trees. We will have a fine show of blossom and a goodly crop to follow.'

157

We are walking in the garden in the cool of the evening, stopping now and then to turn over a leaf or test the strength of a stem. There is no sign of disease, nor infestation, and I smile to myself as twin thoughts flit through my mind – it is a little Eden, and hard to believe three years ago it was a wilderness, what plants there were valiantly struggling against the weeds threatening to choke them.

We stop at the fence bounding our territory, separating it from the riverside meadowland beyond. As if he can read my thoughts, Martin looks across the garden towards the rear of the house.

'You have done wonders, Käthe.' He sweeps his arm in a wide semicircle, taking in the vegetable beds and the herb garden, and the miniature orchard, finishing at the pen where the chickens peck and cluck. 'We are well provisioned, and all your doing.'

I tuck my arm through his. 'I have a good labourer … though he took some managing at the first, I admit.'

'He has learnt well then?'

'Quite well. Though there may be room for improvement yet.' It is the first time I have indulged in teasing Martin, another milestone in our marriage. I imagine the reaction of some of the most prim of our neighbours, were they to hear us, the thought making me smile.

'What are you thinking?' he asks.

'Nothing. Just counting my blessings and hoping for good things to come.'

'It is easy to feel blessed surrounded by all this.' He

turns me to face him.

'When we married I esteemed you, and through the encouragement of Barbara Cranach, who was best placed to know, having lived with you many months, thought you like to be a good wife, if a mite forthright at times.'

I laugh, remembering his proposal: the epitome of practicality, without a shred of romance. 'As I recall, you thought we'd do very well together.'

'As I recall, I did. An understatement of the highest magnitude, as I now know. Though I did not expect to have to altogether relinquish the lordship of my demesne.' He turns me back to face towards the house, and this time his sweeping gesture encompasses not just the garden and the Lutherhaus, but the outbuildings also: the brewhouse and stables and piggery. 'How does it feel, Käthe, to be lord of all you survey?'

I don't know how to answer, and I lean back against him, hoping my closeness will convey more than words ever could.

His hands are on my shoulders, his chin resting on my hair, and there is ease in the silence between us. And that, too, a milestone.

I hear from Eva. They have passed another milestone in their marriage too, but a less happy one. They have lost a child. But unlike many, it is not an infant who has not yet had time to make a mark on the world. I think of their little girl, skipping between us as we headed for the stall selling comfits, her curls tossing, her impish grin so like the Eva I remembered from our own childhood. Barbara would say it is the common lot to lose a child and must be borne as best we might. That we must take comfort in those left to us, and spare a thought for the poor unfortunates who have none. I know she is right, but it doesn't halt my tears as I re-read Eva's letter. *I am bereft, yet cannot show it, for fear Basilius will not understand my sorrow, or if he does, it will but increase his own. And the worst of it, Kat, is though she has been gone but one month, already her face is fading. If I had only asked Lucas to paint her likeness, I could have kept her with me forever.*

I hurry to the nursery and hang over the edge of the cradle, looking down at Elizabeth, sleeping sound, one arm thrown back above her head, her fingers loosely curled, the other bunched under her chin. And determine to take Eva's unspoken advice.

'I will pay Lucas, of course,' I say to Barbara.

'I doubt if he'll take it. Though perhaps if you could persuade him it might be best … not because we want the money,' she adds hurriedly, 'but because I know how busy he is and a favour would likely be pushed to the back of the queue.'

'And rightly so,' I say. 'Will you ask him for me?'

'I can do, only I fear if *I* ask, it may be months you wait, not weeks.'

And so it turns out. I count the months as they pass, April blending into May, May into June, but once the request has been made through Barbara, I do not feel I can ask, especially as what holds him up is a commission for the Town Church.

'It is easily his biggest project yet,' Barbara says, by way of an apology, as we walk together by the riverside, Hans and Jost Jonas taking turns to throw a stick for

160

Tolpel, who never seems to lose interest in chasing after it and bringing it back, only for it to be thrown again.

I nod towards them. 'It tires them out. And makes Tolpel less likely to tear around the house leaving devastation in his wake.'

'A pity children didn't have the single-mindedness of a puppy. I used to despair of making them concentrate on their lessons for more than five minutes at a time.'

'There are other problems with puppies,' I say, 'especially excitable ones.'

'I believe some children think they're puppies.'

'Don't remind me. That is one memory I'd prefer to forget.'

As we walk back towards the house, Barbara halts at the entry leading to the workshop. 'Would you like to see how the painting is progressing?'

It is something I haven't consciously thought about since leaving their house to marry Martin, but now the offer is made I realise I've missed seeing Lucas' paintings come to life. 'Is it very big?'

'Big enough I suspect it will be a struggle to get it out the door once it's finished.'

'Lucas will not make that mistake, surely?'

'No, and I daresay it will look smaller when it's mounted in the church, but in the workshop, well ... wait and see.'

It is huge, and though only partly sketched out, the complexity of the design is already clear. We stand back, so as not to disturb the work. There are two apprentices filling in some of the outlines Lucas has drawn, while Lucas himself is delicately colouring a face. He turns, and wiping his hands on a rag he comes to stand beside us.

161

'I always loved looking at your work, but this is something else. The vibrancy of the colours, the lifelike expressions on the faces…'

He nods. 'Thank you, Katharina.' His focus slides back to the picture, his head tilted to one side, a faraway look in his eyes.

Recognising that however polite Lucas is attempting to be, we are a distraction he'd prefer to be without, I say, 'I'd best be going home. Before those children get too restless outside and make some mischief.'

'Come anytime,' Lucas says. 'You're always welcome.' He lifts his brush and turns back to his work, and I sense we will be forgotten before we are through the door.

'Are they all Wittenberg folk?' I ask Barbara, as she accompanies me to the corner.

'Most are. And some less capable of standing still for an hour than others. Your Elizabeth will be an easier subject, provided he can take her likeness while she is asleep.'

'Asleep or awake she is…' I don't know how to describe it, settle for 'not lively.' She casts me a sharp glance. 'And it worries you?'

'Hans was crawling by now. She shows no inclination to move at all.'

'Children are different, Kat. Are there other worries? Does she cry much?'

'No. Sometimes I wish she did.'

'Laugh, then?'

'Not that either. She smiles, and plays with her fingers, so I know she sees them, but sometimes…' I have never said this to anyone and I'm not sure if I should now, but I go on anyway. 'Sometimes I think there is a blankness

162

in her eyes, as if, though here in body, her spirit is … missing.'

Barbara is catching at her top lip, a habit she has when deep in thought.

'Barbara?'

'She is eating well enough? Sleeping?'

'Yes. And yes.'

'Well then, try not to fret just now. In a month or two, if she doesn't begin to progress, it will be soon enough to worry. For the moment, enjoy that she is content, for there may be nothing to worry about.'

I walk home, Hans and Jost darting back and forwards at my side, Tolpel weaving in and out of our feet and, nuisance as he can be, I know I would hate to be without him, for he has wormed his way into our affections and is as much part of the family as the children are. When I reach the entrance to the Lutherhaus, I look up at the sun and moon, both hanging motionless, like giant lanterns in the clear sky – tomorrow will be warm again, perhaps even hotter than today. Maybe Barbara is right and there is nothing to fear. But as I turn in through the gateway, I glance back and see in the distance a cloud the size of a man's hand and, despite the heat, I shiver.

The cloud is not for me, but for the Bugenhagens, and my heart is breaking with them. The infant Johannes, who Walpurga had jokingly proposed as a husband for Elizabeth, lives barely four months and he is but six weeks in the grave, the ground barely settled, when their other son, Michael, also becomes ill. Though it does not at first appear to be more than a minor childhood ailment, it develops into a fever and in the middle hours of the third night he is taken. We stand by the graveside for a second time, Walpurga ramrod stiff, holding their daughters, Sara and Martha, tight against her side. Bugenhagen's head is bent, as if he fears to disclose the anguish in his eyes. At the last moment, as Martin pronounces the final commendation of Michael's soul to God, Walpurga crumples like a rag doll, Bugenhagen reaching out but failing to stop her fall, the girls falling with her. Barbara is on her knees, holding a vial to Walpurga's nose, and as she stirs, Lucas and Bugenhagen lift her between them and half support, half carry her towards the cart that brought the body.

'Here. Lean against this.' Bugenhagen is guiding her backwards to the edge of the cart, but she recoils.

'I cannot!'

'Please.' His voice breaks. 'We have lost enough already, I need you to be strong, for the girls' sake. It is only a cart.'

Torgau: October 1552

It is mid-afternoon, Frau Karsdorfer sprawled in a chair by the stove, snoring. Margarethe asked her to sit with me in case I need anything, but it's as well I haven't for she was asleep almost as soon as the door shut. I wish I could sleep so easily and so sound. Her mouth is lying open and there is a trickle of saliva at the corner, and if I could only reach across I would wipe it away. The church bell tolls the quarter hour and she startles, her snoring interrupted by a snort, before she settles again into her rhythm. The sound reminds me of Tölpel, lying on the rag rug by the kitchen stove, his snores equally loud. I smile when I think of him, his limbs stretched out, his nose twitching as if he is dreaming of a particularly tasty bone. I hope she wakes before Margarethe comes back, for she has the impatience of youth and doesn't understand that old people are wont to sleep in the afternoon.

As if in response, Frau Karsdorfer stirs, wiping at her mouth with her sleeve and then rubbing it against her apron. I look away, for it is unkind to be critical and perhaps she does not have a handkerchief. She bustles across to the bed, her eyes with that only just wakened look, and leans over me. 'Do you need anything, Frau Luther? You have only to ask.'

I shake my head. 'Only your company.'

She settles again on the chair.

I nod towards the door. It is ajar, the smell of cherries floating up from the kitchen. 'Is someone making a cherry pie? Martin will be pleased, for it is one of his favourites.'

165

'Your son, Frau Luther? Are you expecting him?'

'Margarethe hasn't said. No. I mean dear Doctor Luther.' She draws in a breath, but doesn't answer and I rattle on. 'It was a good day when I convinced him to plant cherries against the south-facing wall, and they are doing so well.'

There is a note of relief in her voice. 'Did you have a good harvest this year?'

'Yes, though I am glad Martin was too busy to help, for the temptation to eat as many as he put in the basket might have been too great for him.' I smile for her. 'I hope he is back in time to enjoy the pie straight from the oven, for he likes his pies hot.'

'Back from where, Frau Luther?'

'From the Town Church, of course. Don't you know he's preaching there while Bugenhagen is away?'

CHAPTER SIXTEEN
WITTENBERG, AUGUST 1528

It is the time of the cherry harvest, our crop, like that of most of our neighbours, exceptional. As if, after all we suffered last year, nature is offering a compensation. Martin, who has taken over the preaching in the Town Church in the absence of Bugenhagen, sent to assist in the official adoption of the Reformed Church in Hamburg, expresses his disappointment that he has little time to assist.

'I fear, Käthe, you must find another labourer, and I must rest content to share in the spoils.'

'A chance for all the crop to find its way into the storehouse then, rather than half be eaten en route.'

He affects an injured tone. 'At the apple harvest last summer you didn't find me surrounded by dozens of telltale cores.'

'Dozens, no. Though I did notice one or two had unexpectedly found their way onto the midden. And I do not suspect Hans, for eating several apples at once would likely have brought on a stomach ache.' I laugh at his expression. 'Which leaves either me or you, and it certainly wasn't me.'

'Sometimes, Käthe, I think your accounting skills rather too accurate for comfort. What is an apple or two among friends?'

'I must concede we had plenty and to spare. But cherries are altogether more tempting. And the risks of employing you all the greater.'

His change of subject is abrupt. 'Have you pinned down Lucas yet, to paint the likeness of Elizabeth?'

'How did you know…?'

'There are few secrets in this town, Käthe, and even fewer between our two houses. I had it from Muhme Lena, who heard it from Dorothea, who heard it from the Cranachs' cook, and so it goes on.'

'It was something Eva said, but if you object…'

'Not at all. I'm just surprised that with your powers of persuasion it isn't already hanging on our wall.'

'Barbara agreed to ask him on my behalf, and I don't like to pressure her.'

'I daresay he'll get round to it, once his latest commission is finished. I shall look forward to it, for she takes after her mother … fortunately for her.' There is a flash of the self-deprecating humour I think one of his best characteristics. 'A girl with my looks might find it hard to snare a husband.'

'Snare? Martin.'

'Attract, catch, snare…' His grin is almost boyish. 'Most men would say what's the difference?'

I laugh with him, thinking of Eva. 'Many women would too.'

I am melting a film of wax to seal the last jars of cherries, humming Martin's latest hymn as I work. He sang it to me last evening, strumming his own accompaniment, and the tune has been running around in my head ever since. The moments when he shares his compositions with me before anyone else can hear them are one of the great pleasures of our marriage. Music has been important to me all my life, and I thank God for a husband who loves it too, and who is talented in that respect. Through the open window I can hear Hans' running footsteps in the garden, and by the joyous barking accompanying them, I know he is chasing Tolpel. We are one of the few households in the town to keep a dog purely as a pet, and though Dorothea isn't yet altogether in favour of the notion, he certainly keeps Hans entertained.

As I trickle the wax into the final jar, I look at the shelves laden with rows of preserves already set down and cannot avoid a sense of satisfaction that we are indeed well provisioned for the year to come. There is no sign of a recurrence of the plague and, the weather holding, folk go about their business with smiles on their faces, the atmosphere throughout the town a happy one. Week by week, as Martin preaches, the Town Church is full to bursting. The singing, if it isn't always as tuneful as it once was at Brehna, is enthusiastic and heartfelt, and that, Martin says, when I comment, is worth more than the odd flat note. Though we are barely into August, he is already looking forward to the Thanksgiving service to follow the harvest, and planning whom among the poor should receive the bounty.

I am pouring the remainder of the wax into a dish when

I hear the church bell chime and realise it is well past Elizabeth's feeding time. It is one of the minor sadnesses that I found myself lacking in milk for her and had to resort to goat's milk. Hardly surprising, I suppose, for as Dorothea said, we were all run ragged looking after the plague victims, and with barely enough energy to keep ourselves going, never mind two. It has been a blessing in a way, releasing me for other jobs, and I suspect for Muhme Lena a secret joy, for it is she who has taken a major hand in the feeding, her patience endless, especially at the first, as hour by hour she trickled warmed milk into Elizabeth's mouth from a spoon. I haven't said anything to anyone yet, but I suspect I may be expecting once more, and this time, I hope it will be different.

Tolpel yelps and I hurry outside, afraid Hans may have grabbed hold of his tail as he sometimes does. I hunker down beside them, pet the dog, and am about to scold Hans, when I hear the first scream. Dorothea, who has been picking peas, hears it too, and we run to the house and up to the nursery. I don't need to see Muhme Lena sitting on the floor, rocking backwards and forwards, the motionless bundle cradled in her arms, nor to hear her keening, to know what is wrong. She looks up as we enter, her eyes dry, but with a hardness in them I've never seen before. Wordlessly, she holds out her arms and I subside onto the floor beside her and take Elizabeth. The blanket falls open and I see her limbs are relaxed, her face strangely peaceful, but though her eyes are open, there is no light in them.

We are still sitting on the floor when Martin rushes in. I have wrapped the blanket around Elizabeth again and am holding her against my chest.

170

'She is so very cold,' I say. 'So very, very cold.'

He kneels down beside me and makes to take her from my arms, but I tighten my hold.

'She's gone, Käthe,' he says, his touch on my shoulder gentle.

'I know. I think I always knew it would come to this.' I look up, pleading for understanding. 'But I'm not ready to give her up yet.'

There is a catch in his voice, tears standing in his eyes. 'God will look after her now.'

'Please, just for a little while. We had her for such a short time. God will have her forever.'

Beside me, Muhme Lena chokes and, struggling to her feet, rushes from the room.

'Go after her, Martin,' I say. 'Comfort *her*. For her loss is also great. And when you are done…' – I feel tears threatening but hold them in, for I do not want to rain on her face – '…when you are done, come back. I will be ready then to let her go.'

I don't know how long I sat, rocking her to sleep. I was aware of no conscious thoughts nor feelings: not anger, not despair; and when Martin comes to lift her from me, I continue to rock, still feeling her weight in my arms.

He returns with a candle and hunkers down beside me again. 'Käthe.'

I see with surprise the light has gone, and as he raises me to my feet I come without protest. For what else is there to do.

The funeral service is short and simple: a hymn, a committal prayer, the scattering of blossom and the lowering of the tiny coffin into the grave, the final tossing of earth. Afterwards, when our friends have melted away, we two stand and stare down at all that remains of the child who hovered briefly on the edge of our lives, but flew away before we could truly know her. Martin places his arm around my waist and as he pulls me against him I feel him start to tremble. I have never seen Martin cry, and it terrifies and comforts me in equal measure.

We are in a flurry of preparation, for at last Martin's father is coming to visit, along with his brother Jacob and wife and his brother-in-law, George Kaufmann. It will be Herr Kaufmann's first opportunity to see his son since he sent him to the Lutherhaus, and I hope it will be a happy reunion. I think back to Brehna and how I might have felt had my father visited, and though I think I would have been pleased to see him, I think I would have been angry also at his abandonment of me. In the event it is a happy time, despite that Margarete Luder is unable to be with us, and for the first time I have the opportunity to see the affection Martin has for his wider family and they for him. His father, who had been so good to me at the time of our wedding, is delighted with his grandson and namesake. He has brought Hanschen a whistle, and though he is not quite three years old, they spend hours in the riverside meadow while he teaches him how to use it to attract songbirds to the traps set for them. At supper, when I look at the plate stationed in front of Martin, for, of all dishes, songbirds are his favourite, I think back with nostalgia to our wedding feast, warmed by the thought our marriage was not a mistake.

Martin, as if he reads my mind, leans towards me. 'Whatever storms have come our way, we have weathered them and will do so again.'

I would rather we had no more storms to weather, for my latest pregnancy is well advanced, but I look forward with both hope and trepidation, mingled with a sense of guilt. Some days I want the babe to be a girl, to replace the hole Elizabeth has left; at other times I think if it is I will not be able to love her as I ought. I don't share my thoughts with anyone, for all those closest to me have had their own losses to bear and I don't wish to add to their pain.

Martin has been released from carrying out any further visitations, and though I am glad to have him at home, I am concerned for him also, for his health remains precarious. The lingering illness of February has left him weakened in body, but strengthened in a determination not to waste any time. He shuts himself away for days at a time, his writings pouring out ever faster, so that I think we must kill an extra goose or two just to keep up with his demand for quills. He is working on two catechisms at once, and delivers sermons on them three times a week: on Sunday afternoons, when servants and young people attend church, and on Monday and Tuesday mornings for everyone else. The numbers of students, which had dwindled when both Martin and Melanchthon were away, have increased again, a welcome relief to counter a worrying shortfall in our income.

Of the catechisms, the sections on the Ten Commandments, the Apostles' Creed, the Lord's

174

Prayer and the Lord's Supper are uncontroversial, even the section on baptism raising few ripples to disturb Wittenberg's pond, but as always, when peace among the reformers threatens, another issue arises to divide them. This time it is an argument between Agricola and Melanchthon regarding repentance; Agricola maintaining an emphasis on forgiveness will remind people of their sin and encourage repentance, while Melanchthon is convinced emphasising it will discourage a genuine desire to change. I cannot help but be amused to find Martin taking the middle ground. When I relay the arguments to Barbara, she almost chokes.

'Martin the Moderate? This is a departure.'

'One to be welcomed, if it would only last, which I doubt.'

She laughs. 'I doubt you would recognise him if he truly became "Martin the Meek", or indeed enjoy the new man.'

'Perhaps not, though I would like to have the opportunity to try. And I would prefer that some of the judgements he is called to make might not be so public, nor expressed with such vehemence.'

'You cannot blame him for calling out Elector Joachim, surely? The treatment of his wife, his infidelities, the hypocrisy of the threats to execute her for daring to take both bread and wine at the sacrament, beggars belief.'

'I know, and I don't blame Martin, but there is a spiteful tone to some of his pronouncements and that is a new development ... and troubling. Fire and passion I understand, vitriol even, as when he railed against the violence of the Peasants' Revolt, but spite? That is something different.'

175

She takes what seems a long time to answer, and when she does I sense she is choosing her words carefully. 'Martin has extraordinary gifts, but he is an ordinary man, with the failings and frailties we all share. And when someone is suffering physically, it isn't unusual if they become peevish. It has been a difficult two years for us all, at home and abroad, and perhaps for Martin more than most. Besides that' – here she hesitates again – 'when someone is pregnant their sensitivities are often magnified, their tolerance level reduced. Do not judge him too harshly just now. Think on all the good things, and forget the bad.'

It is sound advice, but hard to follow, for it seems the nearer I come to my confinement, the more the external pressures increase. The Turks besiege Vienna, and though it seems far from us, it is the reformers who are blamed for their advance. In April, word filters back from the Diet of Speyer that the decision to allow Lutheran reforms has been rescinded. I expect an explosion from Martin, but he is surprisingly dismissive, both words and tone moderate; for him at least.

'Let them do their worst. What do we care of decisions made in human courts? God has opened a door that no man can shut.'

That is all very well, but when Duke John orders the building of fortifications around Wittenberg, once again the air is full of swirling dust and rings with the sound of chisel on stone. This time, although the stonemasons are happy enough, with the extra work and guaranteed pay, the implication the town may be in danger of invasion is a shadow hanging over us all; while I fear our latest babe will be born in a time of trouble, as Elizabeth was, and perhaps with similar consequences.

It is a girl, the birth straightforward, and, to honour Muhme Lena, is baptised Magdalena. From the first Martin dotes on her, and I come on him sometimes hanging over the edge of the cradle, his fat forefinger clutched tight in her fist, a smile playing around his mouth. Unlike Elizabeth, she is responsive from the start, smiling early, and crowing with delight when Martin lifts her and tosses her into the air, as he used to do Hans. I am so pleased with her liveliness I forget to worry she might be dropped. Muhme Lena too is delighted with her, and takes upon herself the role of nursemaid, and I suspect if it weren't for feeding her, I mightn't be needed at all. The Bugenhagens have been away almost a year, and I miss Walpurga and wonder if she too has a new addition to their family to fill the shoes of the children they have lost, or if Sara is destined to be their one 'ewe lamb'.

As May moves into June, Martin, who once relished writing letters to all and sundry, struggles under the burden of correspondence. Barbara, who has called while he is out at the university, mentions Lucas' concern at Martin's grumbles about the pressure he is under.

'It's most unlike him to complain about work.'

I cast a quick glance at the new clock, sent as a gift from Nuremberg, see that he is not expected for a while, and say, 'Come and see his study.'

She looks surprised at the suggestion, but that is nothing to her expression when I open the door and usher her in. She takes a step back and subsides onto the only

177

available seat with a whistle. Every other surface, the table and chairs, desk, stools and windowsills are piled high with letters, boxes stacked on the floor, correspondence spilling out of them too.

'No wonder he's overwhelmed. Where are they all from?'

'All over,' I say. 'Even from as far as England, though the foreign ones no longer get the priority they once did.'

'I'm not surprised! They aren't all just letters, surely?'

'I wish they were. Some are, of course, but most are not. There are disputes folk want him to settle, petitions for help, enquiries and requests for advice: on points of doctrine and practice.'

'The price of fame.'

'Yes. And one I think he would gladly relinquish, was there anyone to relieve him.'

'Oh' – her face clears – 'I almost forgot. There may be soon, for Duke John has ordered the Bugenhagens back to Wittenberg.'

'That is good news. When are they expected?'

'Word is it'll be no more than a week or two.' She waves her hand at the piles of documents. 'With luck, Bugenhagen will chew his way through these in no time.'

'Martin will be so pleased. As will I. It will be good to see Walpurga again, for I have missed her.'

'I've missed her too, for you cannot have too many friends. I imagine it has been hard for her too, to be away so long.' Barbara settles back onto a window seat and looks out towards the street. There is the rumble of wheels on the cobbles. 'I hear you have three more nuns seeking sanctuary.'

'Yes, from Freiberg. They escaped with their parents'

178

help but couldn't return home, for Duke George is reputed to be furious.'

'When is he ever not?'

'Indeed, Barbara.' Martin appears and, throwing his Shaube over the back of a chair, sits down, stretching out his legs towards the stove. It is an unconscious gesture that never fails to make me smile, especially when, as now, it is unlit.

'Have you heard about the Bugenhagens?' I say, by way of welcome.

'You know?' He sounds disappointed. 'I thought to be the first with the gossip, but I might have expected Frau Cranach would beat me to it, for her house is the centre of Wittenberg in every sense of the word.'

'And why not? But perhaps you have an idea of the timing of their return? That morsel of gossip hasn't yet reached me.'

He produces a letter with an air of triumph. 'This,' he says, 'is direct from the horse's mouth. They are on their way home and will be here in less than a fortnight. And I don't mind telling you, I shall be counting the days.'

'What will you do with all your extra free time, when you can relinquish much of the preaching at the Town Church?' I say. 'Clear the backlog of correspondence?' I mean it as a jest and expect some witty response in return, but instead he rubs at one eye as if there is a speck in it, and I know he has something less palatable to say. There is a hint of apology in his gaze.

'I thought to help Justus Jonas with the visitations, now I am fully myself again.'

179

He doesn't get his wish, but I don't get mine either, for as he hoped to go on visitation, I hoped he would remain at home. Instead, he receives an invitation to a colloquy with Zwingli at Marburg.

'Waste of time,' he says, when Justus, who is also summoned, comes to discuss it. 'I know his position and he mine. There is no room for compromise.'

'There is much common ground, Martin. Could you not agree to disagree on what little is in dispute?'

I'm waiting for the explosion and am not disappointed,

'The Lord's Supper? Little? Zwingli's views are blasphemous. How can we agree to disagree on that?'

Justus refuses to be intimidated. 'Count Philip wishes to support reform. Should we not be willing to help?'

'Count Philip wants a Protestant military alliance to safeguard his own territories, and he sees theological agreement as the way to achieve it.' Martin slams his fist down on the table. 'I am a theologian, not a political pawn.'

I sense Justus' frustration. 'We are caught between the emperor on one side and Suleyman on the other. Our reforms are already threatened by the Old Church, but if we are overrun by the Turks? What price theology then? It will not be details of doctrine that are at risk, but Christianity itself.'

'I do not hold with military resistance against our emperor.'

'Pope, emperor, there is no difference. Resist one you resist the other. Bow to one, you bow to the other. Is that what you want? To wipe out the hard-fought reforms of the last twelve years?'

Martin switches the argument to the practical, producing what he clearly thinks will win it. 'You know I am forbidden to travel outside Saxony. Do you wish me to flout that edict?'

Justus is dismissive. 'It is Hesse, and on our doorstep. There will be little danger in it. The duke…'

Listening to Justus I can see someone should go, the truth in his argument plain; but I hope, for myself and the children's sake, it isn't Martin. I interrupt. 'Is it wise for you to go where there is *any* danger?'

I know it is the wrong thing to say so soon as it is out of my mouth, Martin's volte-face confirming it.

'It is not danger I fear, Käthe, only of a misuse of the time I have been given. If Justus thinks I should attend and the duke gives permission, I shall go.' His head is up, his stance combative. 'And perhaps, with God's grace, I shall be able in person to do what I have failed in print, and convince Zwingli of his error.'

Justus glances at my face and, likely as consolation, says, 'We will be a large party, Katharina, and joined by others en route, therefore no danger in it at all.'

'When must you leave?'

Martin counts on his fingers. 'The colloquy is the first week in October, so you will have to suffer me at home for nigh on three months yet.'

⊗⊗⊗

'I blame myself.' I say to Barbara, when I meet her in the square. 'Why could I not have stayed silent? Perhaps then he would have worked himself up into a refusal that couldn't be retracted.'

181

For a moment I think her silence is an acceptance that I was, at least in part, at fault, until she says, 'How are your melons doing?' and I realise she is speaking for the benefit of the two women within earshot, the widening of her eyes a signal for me to respond in kind.

'Well, so far, though we could do with some rain, so that they wouldn't require constant watering.'

The women's chatter fades into the background and Barbara casts a glance over her shoulder, then takes my arm and propels me out of the main thoroughfare. 'Marriage is a lifetime of learning how to handle your husband, trust me on that. And even then you may not judge it right every time. Besides, he would likely have come round to the idea with or without your intervention, for he is a principal in this and has never yet voluntarily avoided a confrontation, especially one he hopes to win.'

'And if there is stalemate?'

'Then we are no worse off than before. But one thing is certain, the threat from the Turks is real, and who can blame Count Philip for seeking to protect his lands. A strong alliance may protect us also.'

'But why must religion be involved? If the Turks are such a threat, surely religious differences could be set aside for the greater good of all.'

Unexpectedly she laughs. 'Sometimes I forget how little time you have spent in the world, Kat. Some things are so tightly entwined that to divorce them is impossible, religion and politics a prime example. Among princes and potentates at least.' She shifts her basket onto her other arm. 'I'd best get back, and you should too. You have melons to water.'

They are the least of my concerns, for July and August

prove hot and breathless, the water level in the well dropping, and I fear it may run dry. I share my concern with Dorothea. 'If we become solely dependent on what we can draw from the Elbe, we will be in competition with every other dwelling and brewhouse along the riverside, and we may all be the losers.'

'Besides the consequences for the fish stocks.'

That was something I hadn't thought of, another worry to add to the many burdens we already carried. The new fortifications are almost finished, and though intended to give confidence that Wittenberg could withstand attack, to me they are a sign of the threat Suleyman poses. Rumour and counter-rumour filter through: he has reached Vienna; he has been repulsed; he has a hundred thousand men and ten thousand horse; his troops have been decimated by an outbreak of cholera. He is a great leader and a saviour of his people. He is a monster, who favours the raping of women and killing of babies and orders men be ripped open from throat to groin, their bodies left for carrion to feed on. When I overhear women whispering of Suleyman's savagery I cannot help thinking of the aftermath of the Peasants' Rebellion and the atrocities carried out by our own men on the orders of Duke John. And when the subject of the Turks' barbarity comes up at Table Talk I find myself saying, 'Are we not all barbarians at heart? All capable of the most terrible acts?'

There is a bristling all around me, a palpable sense of outrage that I should equate good Christians with infidels, and a renewed resentment I should be allowed to speak at all.

Martin cuts through the mutterings, and though he does not directly endorse what I have said, the implication

183

is clear. 'We are all born in sin and shapen in iniquity, and it is only by God's grace we conquer our baser instincts.'

Later, when we are retiring for the night, he asks, 'What were you thinking of at Table Talk, Käthe? It wasn't just a general comment, was it?'

'That it is only four years since our soldiers butchered their own countrymen and left widows and orphans to starve. And though I deplored those actions, I am not guiltless. Not in heart, even if in deed. Are we not taught that if we hate, it is as bad as murder, if we covet, as stealing. That petty jealousies and tittle-tattle are also a sin, and that he who is guilty in one point is guilty in all. If we, who have God's grace, cannot keep the Commandments, how can we expect anything of a pagan horde who do not?' My voice breaks. 'That if they come, our children will not be safe. That Elizabeth will have the best of it.'

I bless him that he doesn't offer me platitudes, nor quote the many other Scriptures that should give comfort. They are already flooding my mind, but at this moment it isn't eternity that concerns me, but my family here and now. Instead, he says, 'I love the children too, Käthe, and you.'

If I doubted his affection, the last weeks before the delegation to the colloquy departs are all the proof I need. Magdalena is a demanding baby, but, as long as she is well fed and given attention, a happy one. Martin spoils her, as Barbara warned me he might, lifting her on the slightest pretext and carrying her around nested against his shoulder. When I am tempted to protest I think of

Elizabeth's simple headstone in the new cemetery outside the town and haven't the heart to say anything. For, as I say to Katharina Melanchthon, 'We are fortunate she is here, and healthy, why not let Martin enjoy her.' Hanschen, who I worried might be jealous of a new sister, follows his father's lead, and when Martin is at the university he sees to it I am not allowed to ignore her crying for any cause.

'Cutting a rod for your own back,' Dorothea says with a shake of her head, but Martin laughs her off.

'When I am gone to Marburg, you may introduce whatever regimen you please. For the time being I intend to give as much time to my daughter as I can, and I defy you to prove it a mistake.'

She sniffs, and later when I come upon her in the kitchen kneading bread, she looks up and, accompanying each word with a thump, says, 'When he has gone to Marburg it is we who will suffer the consequences of his spoiling.'

I touch her shoulder. 'I know, but when you have lost a child, the one you have is the more precious. Besides, she will be too big to dandle soon enough and the issue won't arise.'

CHAPTER EIGHTEEN
WITTENBERG, SEPTEMBER–OCTOBER 1529

September comes all too soon, and though I don't allow Martin to see it, large party or not, I fear for the journey he and the others are about to take.

Barbara calls after supper and finds me back in the brewhouse, scrubbing out a vat. As always, she seems to know what I'm thinking without being told. 'Working to take your mind off Marburg?'

I look down at the scrubbing brush in my hand. 'It needed done, but yes, it didn't need to be tonight. It's just … the closer we get to their departure, the more nervous I become.'

She puts on her most encouraging voice. 'It's not as if Martin will be travelling alone. Aside from the half-dozen from here, others are joining them along the route, and word is for the last leg of the journey in Hesse they will have a military escort.'

'And that is supposed to make me feel better? To be accompanied by soldiers implies there is a risk.'

'Not necessarily. It is often ceremonial, a recognition of status, of importance. Have you ever seen the duke travel without an escort? Even here, where he is most safe.'

'I know. And I know also for most of the route Martin will be on familiar ground, and may even enjoy the journey and the opportunity to see old friends. If Eva was still in Torgau I could almost wish I was going myself.'

'A good job she isn't then, or you might stow away in a baggage cart.'

I laugh, but it doesn't deflect me from my primary thought. 'I can't help worrying, however foolish.'

'Five weeks,' she says, 'and he will be back. Before you've had time to miss him.' She hesitates. 'Has he talked of the issues to be discussed?'

'Only the Lord's Supper. Though Justus has implied more. But Martin is so strong in his convictions regarding it, if that is the only thing to be discussed, it would be enough.'

'That explains it then.'

'What?'

'I met Anna Karlstadt yesterday. If you are nervous, she is ten times worse.'

'But why? Andreas isn't going.'

'Apparently he has become convinced by Zwingli's arguments and bound to be in conflict with Martin all over again. She fears they may have to leave Wittenberg, unless some accommodation between Martin and Zwingli is reached.'

'Poor Anna. I wonder if she regrets her marriage?'

'If she does, she won't say so, for her loyalty to Andreas is unquestioned.'

'As you once told me every wife's should be.'

Barbara looks at me sharply, as if she finds something

187

in my tone worrying. 'You don't have any regrets?'

'No, or none that matter anyway. And if sometimes I wish I could shake him, I imagine most wives feel the same on occasion, though they may not always be prepared to admit to it.'

She nods her agreement. 'I certainly have, though I wouldn't say so in front of Lucas, or indeed most of our acquaintance…' She pauses and cocks her head. There is a commotion in the hallway, Martin calling for refreshment, other voices murmuring in the background. 'Time to go, this is a dangerous conversation for mixed company, and I would hate to let anything slip out.' She gives me a quick hug. 'Five weeks, remember, and it will all be past, and pray God no harm, and maybe some good done.'

They assemble at the Elster Gate on the 15th September, the morning cool and clear, and though Martin is still grumbling about the likely waste of time, I sense his suppressed excitement. Melanchthon and Justus Jonas and Caspar Cruciger are in good time, and we stand, the men in one cluster, wives in another, waiting for Georg Rörer, the last member of the party. The older children are there too, at their and their fathers' insistence, and I cannot help wondering if under it all they think there is a possibility of disaster, and they may not all return safely. Lippus Melanchthon, Jost Jonas and Hans, who have become almost inseparable, are chasing each other around in a game of their own devising.

To distract myself I focus on them. 'At least it doesn't involve tying Tolpel in a blanket and putting him into the barrow, as they did yesterday. Dorothea heard the yelping, and when she went to investigate it was to find him nearly strangled in the rope and frantic to escape.'

'At least it wasn't Magdalena,' Kath Jonas says.

'True, though if it had been it would have been more than a slap on the legs Hans would have got.'

'And the others,' Kath says. 'I'm sure they were all equally culpable.'

There are rapid footsteps behind us as Rörer appears, his breathing noisy.

'There you are, Georg. What's keeping you?' Philipp Melanchthon heads for the first cart. 'We should make the best of it while the weather is fine, for who knows how long it will last?'

Katharina Melanchthon grins and drops her voice so only we can hear. 'Ever the optimist. I shall miss him of course, but not his tendency to think the worst of everything.'

– Including my marriage, I think, but don't say. Thank God he has come round.

The farewells are brief and circumspect, as befits the public nature of them, the men piling into the first cart. As the cavalcade moves off, the carts creaking and swaying, I repeat Barbara's words over and over in my head in a silent litany, 'Five weeks, only five weeks.'

I find it hard to think of returning to work as if this were a normal day, and I suspicion the others do too, for, as if by common consent, we stroll back to the Lutherhaus and, releasing the children into the garden, settle in the Stube, Muhme Lena joining us.

'Do you know the route they intend to take?' Elizabeth Cruciger asks.

'Didn't Caspar...' Katharina begins, but sensing Elizabeth's embarrassment I cut in.

'I think Martin planned it all, and as far as I'm aware it includes Torgau, Erfurt and Jena, for I saw him write letters to make arrangements for accommodation. Beyond that I can't be sure, though I think they intend to pass through Weimar and Grimma on the way to Altenburg. Others are to join them there.'

'Wasn't there talk of a military escort?' That is Katharina again.

'Yes. When they reach the border of Hesse.' I repeat Barbara's words, as much to convince myself as the others. 'Clearly a mark of respect, for why would they need protection in Count Philip's own territory when it is at his invitation they come?'

'No reason at all.' Kath Jonas, ever practical, ever sensible, changes the subject. 'I hope those boys aren't trampling all over your vegetables, Kat.'

'Not many left to trample; with the weather we've had, we've harvested most ahead of time. The cherries are well past, and the boys are too small as yet to reach the apples and plums.'

Elizabeth sighs. 'We had no blossom on the plums at all this year, and last year they were loaded.'

'We were the opposite,' I say.

'According to Elsa Reichenbach...' Katharina tails off, flushes.

'I never had a problem with Elsa,' I say. 'Indeed, I wish I could renew our friendship, for I cannot forget her kindness to me when I first came, but somehow...'

'Philipp Reichenbach is not noted as the easiest man in the world, nor the most humble.'

It is the nearest I have heard Elizabeth come to outright criticism of anyone, and I love her for it. 'Yes, well … anyway, what did Elsa say?'

'That plums fruit best once every two years, the plant resting in between.'

'A bit like people then.' Kath Jonas' retort is instant, her immediate embarrassment equally so.

Katharina looks scandalised, then her lips twitch and we are all laughing, the dangers our menfolk may face forgotten.

A messenger comes from Marburg.

We arrived safely, escorted by forty horsemen, the cavalcade winding around the town, the track spiralling upwards towards the castle perched on the hill. Zwingli required safe passage, and while we sweated in the wagons, his party had the pleasure of a boat trip on the Rhine. We are to have our first meeting tomorrow evening, though I have little expectation of a good result. But don't fret, Käthe, for I have promised Justus and the others of our delegation I will speak in a reasonable manner. As I always do, of course…

I imagine the little twist at the side of his mouth as he writes, for he has many faults, but self-deception isn't one of them.

Count Philip is delighted we are all here, for the news is the Turks are camped outside Vienna and outnumber their troops three to one. Barring a miracle, it seems the city must fall. And then, as if he wished to distract me from the sombre tone, *You would like Marburg. Philip*

191

is a popular ruler and the inhabitants for the most part seem cheerful. They whistle as they go about their daily business, though how they have the breath to do it I don't know, when with every step they must go either up or down. I am exhausted even thinking of it.

I can't help but smile, for he does carry a little more weight nowadays than is good for him. His conclusion is typically Martin.

Tell that little scamp, Hanschen, to behave for his moder and toss Magdalena in the air for me. It seems strange to think that when you read this we will be finished with the business and already preparing to return home. I do not need to exhort you to rise early and take care of our domain, for I know you can do no other, Your loving husband, Martin Luther.

When I read the letter to the other wives, I omit the last sentence, for I want to keep something for myself.

Elizabeth focuses on the news of Vienna, a pucker of worry on her brow. 'The Turks are really coming then?'

Kath's hand is behind her back, the fingers crossed, but she looks straight at Elizabeth, her tone matter of fact. 'It is a far cry from Vienna to here, and winter is coming. Who knows how long the siege may last, or if they will be successful.'

'But there are so many of them.'

I back Kath up. 'Many mouths to feed and so very far from home. We should wait for real news before we torment ourselves with fears of the worst.'

When real news comes it is the best we could have hoped

for on two counts.

'I shall never complain about mud again,' Dorothea says when she returns from the market to relay the news the Turks have been defeated, not by the Viennese troops, nor the strength of the fortifications, but by the weather. I smother a smile as she leans her elbows on the table and prepares to share every detail. Even making allowance for a degree of exaggeration, it appears to have been a defeat of Biblical proportions.

'Can you believe it? The Turks were forced to abandon all their heavy artillery in the Hungarian mud before they even reached Vienna, and after repeated failed assaults, simply packed up their sodden camp and melted away into the rain. If we ever doubted God is on our side, this is the proof of it.'

Kath Jonas, optimistic when the outlook was bleak, is cautious now there is room for optimism. 'Suleyman may have his tail between his legs, but I don't think he will run far. When the conditions are more favourable he will return, and we may pray God we are prepared.'

'We will be.'

'Justus!' Kath swings round and leaps to her feet. 'We weren't expecting…'

'Count Philip closed the colloquy early, so here we are. Returned safe and sound.'

'It was a failure then?'

'On the contrary, like the defeat of the Turks, it was a success and will likely pave the way for further co-operation among the states, in military terms at least. Which was Philip's primary concern. And I see' – he grins – 'yours also. I had not thought to come back to a wife so well versed in world affairs.'

'Don't tease, Justus. When we first heard the Turks had reached Vienna, we feared for Saxony, for ourselves...'

His expression becomes serious. 'There is still room for concern, as you so rightly said, but the omens are better now than when we left, and we may thank God for that.'

Martin is hovering behind him, strangely silent, and with trepidation I bring the conversation back to the colloquy. 'What happened at Marburg? And why was it stopped?'

'Because of an outbreak of the English sweating sickness, to which,' Justus adds hastily, 'none of us succumbed. Nor any of the other delegates, but Philip felt it politic to leave the city and so gave us all leave to do likewise.'

'But the result of the discussions?'

'Fifteen articles, with full agreement on fourteen of them. A success in anyone's book.'

He sounds confident, but I'm not convinced. Martin still says nothing, and it is so unlike him I know whatever the problem with the fifteenth article, the blame lies at his door. I have to ask.

'And the remaining article?'

Justus shifts from one foot to the other, looks at Martin, then away again.

Kath steps forward, takes Justus' arm, and as so often when she senses tension, seeks to dissipate it. 'We should go home. Tomorrow will be soon enough for the detail. Tonight there are children who deserve to know of their father's safe return.' And with a glance at Caspar and Melanchthon, 'And your wives also.'

Muhme Lena looks as if she may be about to comment,

but I catch her eye.

'Tomorrow then,' I say. 'You will all be welcome for supper.'

There is an eruption of sound on the stairwell, a medley of children's voices, Hans outraged, Jost protesting.

'Time to go, indeed,' Justus says. 'Before these boys come to blows.'

He is smiling, but I sense an undercurrent in his words and wonder if he and Martin also came close to a fight.

Supper is a subdued affair, even the children quiet, as if they too sense all is not well. Martin stirs himself to talk of Marburg, of the Hessian cavalry, of the castle, the turrets rising through the morning mist as if in a fairy tale, and the fat burgesses puffing their way up the hill with supplies. I can see his heart isn't in it and I know the children do too.

When Muhme Lena gathers them up and shepherds them away, I think of the long night ahead and decide I must tackle him now, for a silence heavy with unspoken thoughts is worse than anger. Outside there is the steady drip, drip from the cracked waterspout, indicating the drizzle of earlier has likely strengthened into rain, but there is no wind and it isn't cold. I move to the window and rub a gap in the moisture on the glass to look out. 'Will you walk with me in the garden?'

'In the rain?'

'Why not? We will not die of damp and it cannot be any more bleak outside than in.'

He has the grace to look ashamed. 'Best I suppose you

hear it from me,' he says, 'and without the possibility of other ears to flap.'

The path squelches underfoot, and when I have to catch hold of his arm to avoid sliding into the mulberry patch, I think of Dorothea's pronouncement and stifle a laugh, though I suspect there is nothing funny about what he has to confess. We reach the bench by the plum trees and I take one look at the puddles of water lying on it and choose to continue walking. He keeps hold of my arm, and though it would be tempting to imagine it a chivalrous gesture, I think it more likely he wants to avoid any chance of me walking away.

'Well? This fifteenth article? I take it, it refers to the Lord's Supper?'

'He would not change his view.'

'But you expected that, and still went. The other fourteen articles you do agree on, are they not sufficient for some accommodation between you?'

'His position is blasphemous, and I told him so.'

The tension building in me is matched in him, a kettle gathering a head of steam and his grip on my arm tightens; but I don't dare say he is hurting me, for I need to hear it all.

'He swore he desired my friendship, that there was no one else he looked forward to meeting more than me, that he wished my pardon for his sharp remarks.'

'And your reply?'

'That we cannot have the same spirit. That his resistance of Christ's words is false and malicious. That I commended him to the judgement of God, for I could do no other.'

I shut my eyes, think – Martin, Martin, Martin, seek

for words, but he isn't finished, his vehemence matched by a devastating scorn.

'He shed tears! As if by a show of weakness he might move me to relent.'

I wrench my arm away and fail to keep the bitterness out of my voice. 'The great Martin Luther doesn't know the meaning of relent.'

'Käthe?'

I turn and stride towards the house, leaving him standing, the rain peppering his hair and shoulders and splashing mud onto his Shaube.

CHAPTER NINETEEN
WITTENBERG, FEBRUARY–OCTOBER 1530

Jacob Luder writes from Mansfeld. Martin turns the letter over and over in his hand, his face white. 'My father is gravely ill.'

'Should we go to them? Or can your parents be brought here? I could care for him … for both of them.'

He is already scribbling a reply as he calls for a maid. 'Is the messenger still here?'

'No, sir. He left the letter and went. I don't know where.'

'No matter. Can you call my nephew?'

She bobs a curtsy and disappears.

He continues to write, his lip caught between his teeth. 'I cannot leave my lecturing and you also are needed here. If they can come that is by far the best solution.' He nods to himself. 'Cyriac should go. No one better, for he can travel fast and it is his grandfather after all.'

I read the letter over his shoulder. It is a note of consolation, a confirmation of faith, and for a moment I think back to my father, dying long before Martin's reforms, the thought troubling. 'What of those who died in the old faith, who did not have a chance to understand the truth of God's grace?'

Martin reaches up and covers my hand which bites into his shoulder. 'We look on the outside, Käthe, God on the heart. And does not Romans teach us that everyone since the beginning of time who recognised God as Creator and claimed His promises will meet Him in heaven. Cling to that. As for my father, we will see him here if he is spared, but if he is to be taken, we must pray his journey to the next life is easy and short.'

When Cyriac returns with the news that the old man is too ill to travel, Martin gathers the children around them and says, 'Grandfather Luder is on his way to heaven and when the time comes he will be there before he can blink.'

'Will he be singing?' asks one of the orphans who live with us.

'Singing his heart out.'

Hans looks up into Martin's face. 'One of your hymns, Father?'

There is a lump in my throat. 'One very like,' I say.

The Emperor Charles is back in Germany, fresh from his coronation by the Pope.

'Will it make a difference to us?' I ask Bugenhagen.

'There will be a diet for sure, to emphasise his new status, but whether it will serve to draw factions together or drive them apart is another matter.'

He is right. Word comes from Torgau: a diet has been set for April, to take place in Augsburg, and a delegation from Wittenberg will accompany the duke. Melanchthon is keen to go, for he still harbours hopes of some kind of reconciliation between the Catholics and the reformers, but Martin is typically dismissive.

'Catholics, Turks, Jews, enemies all. I have no truck with any of them.'

Justus shakes his head. 'Just as well it isn't safe for you to go, then.'

My sigh is one of relief, for the memory of his last absence is still fresh, the rift it caused between us and the effort it took on both sides to heal, something I'd rather not repeat. When Justus has gone, Martin comes to stand beside me at the open window, the breeze stirring the wisps of hair on his forehead. His tone is tentative, as if he expects opposition.

'I am not to go to Augsburg, Käthe, but I am summoned to accompany them part of the way.'

'Must you go?'

'Only as far as Coburg. I will be safe from confrontation there. If I die of anything, it will likely be boredom.'

And judging from his first letters it seems he is right, for the content is nothing more than a description of the fortress and the folk in it.

There are thirty men working here, and twelve of them watchmen. Hanschen would no doubt like to see the men guarding the towers for they have bugles to sound in the event of danger, but I don't expect to be woken in the middle of the night by them, for I believe I am as safe here as at home. I tell you this only because I must write something and there is nothing else to write about. Except it is a sad place without friends and I hope I shall be able to return to you soon.

I imagine him pacing about the fortress like one of the

bears in the castle pit in Torgau, frustrated by inactivity and perhaps growling at everyone around him. Bugenhagen, however, snorts when I say so.

'Martin will not be content to do nothing. He may not be at Augsburg but I suspect he will be involved nonetheless.'

'How can he be?'

'There will be letters going back and forth, for Melanchthon will not present a confession without seeking Martin's opinion, and Martin will not be slow to give it.'

Word comes from Justus and I sense the undercurrent of concern in what he writes. *Martin has sent a letter to the clergy at Augsburg, if something covering almost forty topics may be termed merely a letter, pointing out all the errors of the 'pretended' church as he calls it, and showing how the Lutheran reforms are necessary to address them. We may all thank God he is not here to speak to the assembly in person and that the emperor has not yet arrived, so that the letters may be forgotten by the time he does.*

I think back to Martin, a year past, standing in our Stube, legs apart, arms folded, declaring, 'For this I was born: to fight against devils, hack away thorns and thistles, drain the swamps. I am the coarse woodsman who must blaze a trail. Master Philipp comes neatly and quietly behind me, cultivates and plants, sows and waters, according to the gifts God has given *him*.'

'Melanchthon will be more circumspect?'

'Oh, indeed. But whether it will be enough to satisfy the emperor, who can tell.'

'How long will they be away? Martin talks of coming

201

home soon.'

'I suspect he will be sore disappointed. A diet is measured in months, not weeks, and nothing will even be started without the emperor's presence.'

Martin's frustrations are not confined to the Diet. His latest pamphlets, entrusted to Schirlenz for printing, have not yet appeared, and when I, for want of other news, let slip about the delay, he is caustic. *They are making dried fruit of them. If I wanted them stored I would have kept them with me. Insist they send them back, Käthe, and put them instead to Herr Rau. He I trust will do better.*

Barbara is thoughtful when I show her the letter. 'Perhaps it is not such a bad thing. If he worries about minor issues such as this, he will have less time to think about the Diet.'

'Less time to meddle in it you mean?'

'Yes and that cannot be anything but good.' She hands the letter back. 'Besides, to involve you in this way is a sign, to you *and* others, of how much he trusts and depends on you.'

'Or another reason to criticise me. As yet again I overstep the mark.'

My concerns about the pamphlet pale into insignificance when word comes in May: Martin is ill again, with spells of dizziness and blinding headaches so severe he cannot even read, far less write. Fear gnaws at me while we wait for further news.

Bugenhagen, as usual, tries to be encouraging. 'He will be well looked after, Katharina, for the duke has ordered his personal physician to send medicine, and it will be the best money can buy.'

'But he cannot know what Martin needs without

seeing him. If he were here…'

'If he were here he would ask for your prayers, not your anxieties, which accomplish nothing. This is an old ill and his symptoms well known. Trust me, we will hear he is recovered soon. In the meantime, is there anything you can send to improve his spirits?'

I think of the charcoal drawing of Magdalena one of Lucas' apprentices has done for me. Although darker than I would have liked, at least it is her likeness, so that should anything happen, her face will not fade beyond memory as Elizabeth's has done. As I parcel it up I remember the new glasses that were delivered for Martin shortly after the delegation had left. He hasn't found any to satisfy him up to now, but I add them to the parcel anyway. And when Muhme Lena appears as I'm packing them in sheep's wool to ensure their safe arrival, she nods.

'Good idea, perhaps they will help, if he can be brought to wear them. It is hardly surprising he suffers from eye strain, with all the poring over books and parchments he does, and little wonder he has headaches as a result.'

I suspect the headaches cannot be explained away so easily, but I let it pass.

We receive two letters in quick succession. Reading the first one, my initial tension drains away. It is Martin back to his old self.

I am well recovered and grateful to have the picture of Magdalena to remind me of my little bud. Though whether it is the glasses you sent, which I don't mind telling you are the worst I have ever had, or the quality of the drawing, it isn't as clear as I'd wish. If the latter, it is to be hoped the apprentice who drew it – I imagine it wasn't Lucas – will speedily improve or he may cost Lucas work. You need no longer worry I suffer from boredom, for I am overrun with visitors who disturb my work and are all too often free with their opinions and advice. To which, as you know, I am always open… I laugh aloud at that, for giving advice to Martin is not to be undertaken by the faint-hearted, requiring patience and a certain manipulative skill based on a close knowledge of his psyche, unlikely to be found in a casual visitor. He continues, *Argula Grumbach has told me how best to wean the little bud, though why she thinks I need such knowledge I've no idea. I pass it onto you and pray you take no offence, for busybody as many think her, she has a good heart, and, when all is said and done it was she who bullied me into taking a wife, for which you and I both must be grateful.*

I read that last bit aloud to Barbara, and she laughs with me. 'Must you indeed? If you thought you might ever turn Martin into a romantic swain, Kat, a comment like that would finally convince you otherwise.'

The face of Jerome Baumgartner flashes across my brain and is as quickly gone again. 'I learnt long ago that romance is an over-prized commodity, and I am not sorry for it now. Martin has other qualities, and for most of them I am grateful.'

I am alone in the garden when Dorothea brings the second letter, a knot of concern on her forehead. She hands it over and waits for me to open it, another sign of her unease.

'It's from Coburg,' she says, 'and the messenger came in haste, so…'

I read it quickly, relief flooding through me, accompanied by a pang of guilt. 'It is Martin's father.'

'Gone?'

'Yes. And I cannot help but feel…'

'Glad it isn't Doctor Luther?'

'Yes.' I crumple the letter in my hand. 'But I should not think it. Hans Luder welcomed me into his family when others would not. I should mourn him as my own father.'

'No doubt you will, and would have done already if the good doctor had been standing beside you when you received this news. It was only natural to fear for him and therefore natural to feel relief before anything else.'

Belatedly I ask, 'Who brought the letter?'

'Viet Dietrich… I left him standing by the front door.' Her hand is at her mouth. 'That was not well done.'

I smile at her obvious embarrassment. 'I daresay he won't hold it against you. But you'd better go to him, offer him refreshment, a bed for the night. And perhaps he will have more to tell us.'

'Frau Luther.' In the Stube Dietrich bows first to me, then to Muhme Lena. 'Frau von Bora.

'Fraulein.' Her correction is automatic, borne of much practice.

He bows again. 'My apologies, Fraulein.' He looks back at me and I see the travel stains on his clothing, the sweat marks under his armpits, the dust on his boots.

'Supper will not be long delayed, but in the meantime, will you take something to drink?'

'Thank you, a beer, if I may.'

'I'll go.' Muhme Lena bustles away. I indicate a seat, impatient to question him more fully.

'How has Doctor Luther taken the news?'

'I won't deny it hit him hard. He read the letter, then took his psalter and retreated into his room. We could hear him weeping and he didn't reappear that night. The following day his eyes were still red, the skin around them swollen, and he admitted his head ached. But when he spoke of his sadness, he spoke also of his comfort in knowing his father lived long enough to see the light of the gospel. How long he will mourn inwardly I don't know, but by the time I left he was picking up the pieces of his writing and busying himself again.'

We get evidence of that two weeks later, when a letter arrives addressed to Hanschen. I read it to him, and help him to follow the words with his finger. It is both a fanciful tale and an exhortation to good behaviour, the combination so typical of Martin it brings him close to me as I read.

To my dearest son, Hanschen ... I know a beautiful garden with many children ... ponies with bridles of gold and silver saddles ... learn and pray and tell Lippus and Jost to do likewise that you may come into the garden together.

'Read it again, Mutti,' Hanschen says, when I stop. 'Read it again.'

Over the next few days we read it so many times, to Hanschen and to Lippus and Jost when they appear to play, I know it almost off by heart. I sit with Kath Jonas on the bench at the end of the garden while the boys gallop up and down the paths on the imaginary ponies Martin conjured up for them in his letter.

'I had no idea he could be so lyrical,' Kath says, 'though perhaps I should have guessed, when I think of his hymns. He is a far cry from the Luther of his polemics when he addresses children. A side to him few people see.'

The boys skid to a stop in front of us and Hanschen asks for the umpteenth time, 'Are the ponies' saddles

206

really silver?'

'So your father writes.'

Kath stands up, puts her arm around Jost. 'I should gallop these boys home, before their ponies are worn out with riding.' She overrides the chorus of protest. 'It will be suppertime soon and your mother will be looking for you, Lippus.' Above our heads the sky is flushed with colour, the wisps of cloud rose-tipped. 'There will be plenty of time tomorrow to resume your game.'

Hanschen tugs on my arm. 'May we?'

'If you are all the good children your father has written of, then yes. Of course.'

Kath hears from Justus. She comes to me to share the news, her voice bubbling with excitement. 'The emperor has arrived at Augsburg at last. And with him an entourage of one thousand soldiers, as well as falconers and two hundred hunting dogs. I wish I could have been there to see it.'

'I'm glad it isn't me has the feeding of them!'

'Justus says he brought his own cooks and apothecaries and more – it is the whole court on the move.'

'What else does he say?'

'There has already been controversy, over the Corpus Christi feast and public preaching, but a compromise has been reached. I don't imagine it pleases anyone, for neither the Catholic clerics nor the Lutherans can preach publicly, but at least it allows the diet to proceed. Melanchthon's confession has been presented to Charles and they await the Catholic response. He is hopeful of a reasoned

207

outcome, for Melanchthon's tone was moderate.'

'Does he have any idea when it will end?'

'If he has he doesn't say so.'

'It's been four months already. I had no idea it might be so long.'

'None of us had, but what can we do but wait?'

July slips into August and August to September and the harvest is gathered in and still no word of the diet being completed. Each time Justus writes home, Kath comes to share his news, but it doesn't make good reading. The compromise he hoped for doesn't materialise, instead the emperor finds in favour of the Catholic position.

His final letter is brief and to the point. *He has given us, along with all the reform parties, seven months to return to Rome.*

'What will this mean?' I ask Bugenhagen, but he shakes his head.

'When the duke returns, maybe then we will know.'

It is a sombre party that rides into Wittenberg in mid-October, Duke John at its head. Their faces are drawn and travel-weary, no one inclined to go anywhere other than to their own homes. There are new lines etched into Martin's forehead and I can tell by the way he slumps into the chair his weariness is more than physical. When I ask of his health, he brushes away the question as if it is an inconvenient fly buzzing around his head.

'There are more serious problems to be faced than whether I am troubled by headaches.'

'But are you?' I press.

He sighs. 'Headaches, dizziness, weakness and congestion. All of those and more. But what are they compared to war.'

208

I sink down on the floor at his feet, winded. 'War?' There is a pounding in my ears, a feeling my head might burst. 'Will it really come to that?'

His voice is devoid of emotion and the lack removes any doubt of exaggeration. 'I see no other outcome.'

Torgau: October 1552

Paul and Margarethe are standing by the open casement. I watch them through half-closed eyes and wonder what they are whispering to each other... They never used to be so secretive. But lately, when I ask something, I see the covert glances that fly between them. She leans out, her shoulders turned sideways to fit through the gap, her neck bent down as if she peers at something on the street below.

Paul says, 'Can you see anything?'

'Not yet. Are you sure they'll come this way?'

'What other way is there? They will make straight for the castle, I'm sure.'

'Who?' I say, but they don't seem to hear. I try again, louder this time, but with no effect. I reach out for the stick that lies against the bedframe, that I use to thump on the floor when I want something and there isn't anyone here. It slips from my grip and falls, but the clatter is clearly enough to catch their attention for they both turn, Margarethe catching her head on the window frame as she pulls herself in. She is dancing from foot to foot, rubbing at her forehead.

Paul is laughing as he comes towards the bed. 'What is it, Mutti? Do you want a drink?' He reaches one hand behind my shoulders to lift me up and with the other holds a beaker of water to my lips. I purse my mouth, shake my head.

'I want to know what's happening,' I say.

'They say Count Philip is coming to the castle. To see Maurice. There is to be a reconciliation.'

There is a suppressed excitement in Margarethe's voice, a

210

light in her eyes. She is interrupted by a commotion outside the window, the steady clip-clop, clip-clop of hooves, the clinking of bridles, as if a procession passes by. 'There they are.' She ducks her head out again, craning to look along the street.

'It's not Maurice,' I say. 'It's Duke John he comes to see. They don't need to be reconciled. For they are already friends.' I sigh. 'But your father is right.'

Paul sets aside the water. 'Right about what, Mutti?'

'That war is coming.'

'The war is over, Mutti.'

'You're wrong,' I say. 'It's only beginning.'

CHAPTER TWENTY
WITTENBERG, OCTOBER 1530–APRIL 1531

Philip of Hesse is to travel to Torgau to seal an alliance with our duke against the emperor. All the talk in the town is of the possibility of war, of what it may mean: for Saxony, for Wittenberg, for the reformation, and most of all for Martin and the other leaders who have also been ordered to attend.

When I go to the market I am aware of people hurrying, their 'Guten Morgen's no more than a mutter. They avoid my eyes, but I catch their sidelong glances and wish I could say something to reassure them, for I know their awkwardness no longer signifies disapproval of me as it once did, but rather a sympathy they are afraid to voice.

When he returns from Torgau, Martin is uncharacteristically silent about the proceedings, and once more I fear he isn't altogether comfortable with his own contribution to them. I consider challenging him, but he continues to suffer from recurring weakness and headaches lasting sometimes for days, so I leave him be. It is clear he chastises himself sufficiently, without me adding my weight to his unease. In typical Martin fashion he does not stop working, however he feels. There is an irony in the topic he is preparing for the students, for it is the Song of Songs, and I wonder how he can lecture on love when all around is hate.

In contrast, autumn is kind, the days dry, the winds light, and as a consequence the leaves turn without dropping. I know it will not be long before the branches are bare and winter takes a hold, but in the meantime it is a daily pleasure to glory in the medley of colour in the trees on the far side of the Elbe. And though it be trivial in comparison, I cannot help but feel a sadness war may rob us of that joy too.

Justus Jonas calls one afternoon at the end of November, when Muhme Lena and I are alone in the Stube, a pile of sheets to be turned heaped on the floor. I scoop them up and set them aside, with a murmur of apology.

'It is I who should apologise, for coming unannounced and disturbing your labours.'

'Not at all,' I say, and taking a deep breath, I ask him what I have not dared to ask Martin since the evening he returned from Torgau, 'What of this League? Is it growing? Or will it crumble away without loss of life?'

He is silent for a moment, as if considering how best to respond. 'Martin has said nothing?'

'Nothing. And I have not questioned him. The memory of the horrors of the last conflict is still fresh in my mind, and when I think of Martin's part in it ... of what may come again ... I am afraid.'

Another silence, then a settling of his shoulders as if a decision has been made. 'We are all of us afraid and none wishing for war, but it may be inevitable. There is to be a meeting in December at Schmalkald and a League formed

213

of those states and cities that cannot accept the emperor's edict.'

'And Martin, will he be part of it?'

'The signatories will be secular authorities. But Martin's approval has been sought. I sense a hesitation. 'He has made a distinction between what princes may do and what is appropriate for individual Christians, whose duty is to submit to worldly authorities.'

'Is that not...'

'A sophistry? Yes. But perhaps a necessary one in the circumstances.'

'But if the authorities are themselves at war, who do we submit to? Our duke or the emperor?'

'Exactly so.'

A part of me is disappointed Martin has allowed himself to be squeezed into a position of compromise, presenting the situation in shades of grey, when the Martin I first met was as black and white as the painting of the timber-framed walls of our chamber. His opinions then, clear and unequivocal. A small voice inside of me adds – and dangerous.

In the momentary pause, I hear Magdalena cry, and as Muhme Lena leaps up to go to her, waving me back into my seat, I feel a hard knot tightening in my stomach. Guilt I could even think such a thing colours my cheeks, but I have to ask. 'Is it a selfish thing to bring children into such a world?'

His answer is unexpected. Not the usual 'Children are a blessing from the Lord', but an altogether more sombre thought.

'It is our duty, for if we do not, who know how to bring children up to fear God and live aright, others, less enlightened, will; and the world be full of Godless and evil men.' He answers the question I haven't asked: why Martin and Melanchthon should be dragged into the discussions.

'The quarrel with the emperor, while it is territory and authority at stake, is nevertheless rooted in religion, and any alliance formed against him will be likewise based. For the Protestant states there remains the single issue of the Lord's Supper to divide us, and in Count Philip's view it must be resolved for any alliance to be strong.'

Whether it is resolved or not remains unclear, but I have other, more personal concerns, for Martin's dizzy spells have become increasingly troublesome, and early in December he reluctantly stops his lectures. He continues to preach, but that too is halted when he is forced to leave the pulpit in the middle of a sermon. It is the first time since our marriage I have given much thought to the age disparity between us and that I may be widowed young. Something of what is going through my mind must have shown on my face when I bring him a potion to relieve the pain, for he reaches out to grasp my wrist.

'Sit with me a moment, please.'

I perch on the edge of the bed, looking at the lines etched into his forehead, trying to remember if they were there when we first met, and if they were, if they are much deeper now.

He takes hold of my hand. 'You are concerned for me, Käthe, and that is a comfort. But I want you to remember I was an old man when we married, and with indifferent health. And under the constant threat of death. You took a risk then; it is no greater now. We must both live one day at a time and be content.'

If I thought his ill health would mean he would take things a little more easily, I am sorely disappointed, for he determines if he cannot speak he must concentrate on writing. His first thought is to finish the revision of the psalter, laid aside since returning from Coburg.

'Why can he not rest?' I say to Barbara, when she calls in to enquire of his health.

'He has never been able to rest, unless illness lays him flat on his back, and you don't want that.'

'These dizzy spells...'

'Are worrying, I know, but perhaps stopping preaching and lecturing will be enough to allow him to recover his strength. Writing will exercise his mind and keep it occupied, which may not be altogether a bad thing. Left with nothing to do, he would be a smouldering ember the lightest breeze might ignite.'

The breeze comes all too soon, when, at the beginning of January, word trickles back from Schmalkald of the formation of 'a Christian association for defence and protection against violent assault'. I have no idea what Martin's reaction will be and am relieved when he is enthusiastic, but without exhibiting undue agitation.

He looks at me over the top of his latest spectacles. 'A petition has been sent to the emperor asking he soften the terms of the Augsburg Edict.'

'Is it likely to have effect?'

'With sixteen cities and states willing to sign a charter, he would be a fool to ignore it.' His shoulders are relaxed. 'Perhaps it won't come to war after all, for with three and a half months left before the edict is due to come into effect there is time for negotiation.'

By mid-January his health is improving and I fear he may rush back into his university work, but he has made a different, more momentous decision.

'The psalter,' he says, 'is a worthy task, but the people have need of a translation of the whole Old Testament, for if they have only access to the New, they cannot understand the whole purposes of God.'

I steel myself to be firm with him. 'You cannot think to do it on your own?'

His guffaw is welcome as an indication my fear is groundless; and doubly so, for laughter has been in short supply of late. 'No, Käthe, I may have managed to translate the New Testament while in the Wartburg, but this is not the Wartburg, and I have no intention of becoming a hermit. Besides, the Old Testament is three times the length, and a different matter altogether. No. This will be a team effort.' His grin is almost boyish, his tone laced with mock concern. 'But I'm afraid you must be prepared to set more places at our table, for it is here we will come together to discuss the work.'

'Rather here than anywhere else,' I say, mindful of the children and how little time they have had with their father over the past months. 'I shall feed them all with pleasure, but will keep you to your promise not to be a hermit, for your family has need of you also.'

He is true to his word, continuing to work at his normal pace, but making time for the children, and for me. Table Talk is once more a feature of our routine, but afterwards when we are left in peace, we toast our feet at the stove and resume our late-night discussions. Sometimes Martin shares the debates the translation team are having.

'It isn't always the words that pose a problem, but how to understand the culture from which they come *and* translate them into ours in a way that makes the true sense of them clear. For that we need both Hebrew scholars and Jewish theologians, however unpalatable that is to some.'

'And to you?'

'How better to understand the world of the Old Testament than through the eyes of those who still live by its tenets, however much I might wish it to be different.'

It is a side to Martin only those closest to him see, a reasoning and reasonableness largely at odds with the tone of the pamphlets that still leap from his pen in between his translation work.

People need certainty, not equivocation, Käthe,' he says, when I comment on the disparity. 'Not everyone can be trusted to think for themselves; some need to be told what to think.'

As Easter and the date when all Lutherans are supposed to return to Rome approaches, the tension, which had dissipated in the autumn, increases again. All the talk is of what the emperor will do to those towns that disobey him, what sanctions he may impose. Watching the children and feeling a new stirring in my womb, I am less worried about the impact on commerce, or on the churches, than on what might happen to our family, and if we are at more risk than others. Hanschen is almost five and as mischievous as ever, Lippus Melanchthon and Jost Jonas his constant companions. And boisterous as they are, I am glad they spend more time at the Lutherhaus, where I can keep a watchful eye, than they do in their own homes. Magdalena toddles along behind them, a miniature shadow attempting to copy their every move. Martin, who can be harder on Hanschen than I would like, is ever indulgent to Magdalena, and I sometimes fear he will ruin them both. When I say so, he responds with a laugh.

'Come, come, Käthe. Will you have me damned if I do and damned if I don't?' He slides an arm around my waist, as if by so doing he will alter my opinions. 'If I am prone to extremes, which on occasions I admit, it is a blessing I have a wife who will moderate me.'

'Blessing indeed.'

We swing round to see Justus and Kath Jonas standing in the doorway, and I note the suppressed excitement in Justus' face and the letter crushed in his hand.

'Albert Mainz...' he begins.

Martin's face darkens. 'What has the old goat done now? I might have known he would cause problems.'

'Quite the contrary.' Justus thrusts the letter at Martin. 'See for yourself. He has asked the emperor to consider negotiations with the alliance.'

My mind is jumping ahead. 'Is there a renewed threat from the Turks?'

'They are rumoured to have thirty thousand troops in Hungary, and Vienna once more at risk. But money to fend them off isn't the only reason Charles may consider a compromise.'

'What then?'

'To buy votes. For his brother, Ferdinand, who has ambitions to become king of Germany.'

'Would that be a good thing? For Germany? For us?'

219

'Better than the emperor's wrath. Better than war.'

Kath draws me away to the window, and we lean on the ledge side by side, the sound of the children's laughter floating upwards from the garden. 'Thank God,' she says. 'Thank God they will no longer be at risk.'

The Easter service in the Town Church is joyous, a celebration of the Resurrection, but also a festival of liberation from the spectre that has hung over us all since Augsburg. Matrons of the town who previously had little to do with each other because of some minor offence clasp hands and offer the compliments of the season, as if they have always been the best of friends. When one who has always treated me ill heads towards us, her voice raised and her hand outstretched, I turn to Kath, as if I haven't heard or seen her. Kath's reprimand is gentle, her voice no more than a whisper, but her grip on my arm is firm as she turns me round.

'Today is for celebration, Kat. Do not spoil it by a remembrance of past sins, nor scorn new friendships.'

Martin, when he joins us fresh from the pulpit, is equally buoyant. I slip my arm through his and, indicating the crowds milling in the square, compliment him on the turnout and on his sermon. There is a sardonic twist to his mouth.

'I am not so foolish as to think it all a response to my preaching. Balaam's donkey could probably have kept their attention today. But it is a cause for thanksgiving just the same.'

Chapter Twenty-One
Wittenberg, April–July 1531

Light is peeping around the shutters when I wake, the silence in the Lutherhaus absolute. I look at the mound that is Martin lying beside me, at the tousled hair curling over his ears, and the line around his neck dividing the weathered skin from the pale, and decide today is a good day for serious conversation.

His breathing is deep, but I cannot wait and so shake his shoulder. 'Martin.'

He startles and sits upright, and it is clear, however relaxed he may appear, there are underlying fears troubling him. 'What is it, Käthe?'

'Only that I have news and wish to share it, before it becomes obvious to all.'

He is fully awake now, leaning back against the bedhead and smiling. 'And when is this child of peace to be born?'

'You knew?'

'Guessed.' He reaches over to tug gently on the plait lying across my shift. 'But I had no wish to spoil your pleasure in telling me. Or mine in hearing.'

'It will be November, or thereabouts, and we may hope for a gentle winter to welcome the babe in.' I pause, rest my hand on my belly.

There is a 'What-are-you-going-to-ask and will-I-like-it' look in his eyes, but I have made up my mind. It is as good a time as any to approach once more the question that has burdened me almost from the beginning of our marriage. I go for an oblique approach. 'There will *be* peace? You are certain of that?'

'As certain as we can be of anything. The League is powerful, the emperor needing their support, for the Turks are a continuing threat in Hungary.'

'But not to us?'

'No. Not to us, or not directly at least.'

'You *are* pleased about the child?'

'Of course.' A shadow flits across his face. 'Though I wish my father was still here to see it.'

I want him in a happy mood, not a sad one, so say, 'I think Magdalena will be pleased, for she will likely imagine it a doll to play with.'

His eyes light at the mention of her name. 'Judging by how she cradles the kitten, I think she will be a fine little mother.'

I pull myself further up in the bed, leaning back against the bedhead beside him, our shoulders touching. 'Herr Heffner in Zahnaerstrasse is wishing to sell his property. I thought it might be a useful addition to our holdings.' I hesitate, unsure of whether to give him a chance to respond, but when he remains silent, plough on. 'There is a small house, though he wishes to be allowed to remain in it for his lifetime.' To skim over that small difficulty, I add, 'No doubt the price will reflect that. Besides, we have

222

no need of the house, and the garden and field come with benefits not always easy to find hereabouts, especially within the town boundaries.'

I can tell from his expression he's prepared to hear me out, so I am over the first hurdle.

'Benefits?'

'There is a barn and a ready water supply.'

'A well?'

'Better. The Faul brook runs through it, and the word is the fish are plentiful and varied, trout and pike, perch and carp. How good it would be to have a ready supply of our own, without recourse to the fish merchant. And the land will be ideal for stock.'

He has not said no, so perhaps we will not have the fight we had over our garden outside the Elster Gate. It was a good buy and I haven't regretted it, though I have regretted the pleadings and tears I used to get my way. This time I hope we will come to a suitable conclusion through reasoned discussion, rather than the appeasement of a distressed wife.

There is the patter of feet on the corridor outside, the door pushed open, Magdalena poking her head through. Martin swings his legs over the edge of the bed and stands up just in time to catch her as she throws herself at him. He lifts her up and spins her round and she bounces in his arms and giggles, and when he sets her down on the floor she tugs at his hands. 'Again, again.'

'Later,' he says, turning her and propelling her to the door. 'When we are all dressed and in our right mind. Now … off you go.' And to me, 'We will talk more of this later.'

223

I stroll along Zahnaerstrasse to see Herr Heffner's property for myself, so that when next I raise the subject I will have all the details at my fingertips.

Afterwards I call with Barbara.

She is kneeling on the floor with Anna standing on a chair in front of her, while she pins up the hem of her dress. Nodding me to a seat, she finishes the task before removing the handful of pins from between her lips.

'I've just been along to see Herr Heffner's property, as much as I can see from the road, that is.'

Surprise registers on her face, and I wonder what she knows that I don't. 'I heard it was for sale, though I wouldn't have expected you to be interested.'

'Why not? You know I have long wanted more land, and Martin seems more amenable now than he once was. It looks good.'

'It would need to.'

'What do you mean?'

'Do you know the price?'

No. How much is it?'

'Nine hundred gulden ... if the rumours be true.'

I let out a long breath. 'That would take all we have and more.'

She nods, and in an obvious attempt at encouragement, says, 'There'll be others I'm sure. And maybe more affordable.'

She is probably right, but over the next few weeks, every time I go out I find myself taking a detour past Herr Heffner's and pausing to look across the field towards the barn and the fence beyond marking the boundary. And each time I look, it becomes more desirable. I talk to

Martin again, and this time the discussion is serious and wide-ranging, and it is clear he too has taken the trouble to investigate the possibility.

'You know,' he says, 'we would have to borrow against it?'

'Much?'

'A modest amount, I admit, but borrow nonetheless.'

This time I won't plead, for I know how hard it is for Martin to think in business terms, and he does not like risk, though in this I think it a small one. I focus on practicalities: the limitations of the space in our own gardens, of what we might save if we can increase our stock, the convenience of releasing stalls at the Lutherhaus if the horses can be stabled elsewhere. Finally I tackle the issue of money, focus not on the base price but on the proportion we don't currently have. 'If it isn't a lot we need, we could soon pay it back.'

He is silent for a moment, then, 'Perhaps you should have married a farmer, Käthe, not a cleric. I care nothing for land.'

'It's not the land itself, but what we can do with it.'

'Is it?'

'Of course. We have so many mouths to feed.' I mean what I say, but afterwards, when I am in the brewhouse drawing off a flagon of beer, I think of the farm at Lippendorf and wonder if Martin is right; if it is my background and upbringing that drives me in this regard. If land and the ownership of it is my security. It is an uncomfortable thought and so I don't bring the subject up again, but to my surprise the Heffner property is bought. When Martin comes to me with the deed of purchase and drops it into my lap, I determine I will shoulder the responsibility for the working of it, and make it pay.

As the days begin to lengthen and the babe within me quickens, we settle into a new routine, Martin resuming his lectures, me with increased responsibilities inside and outside the Lutherhaus, and we thrive on it. In the evenings, when Table Talk is done, and the participants departed, I finish my own chores and we spend a companionable hour together before bed. It is a time we both prize, building, as it does, the sense we are equal partners in the business venture our home has become. It is a noisy household, between the student boarders, whose exuberance often outstrips their sense of decorum, and the children, whose running footsteps and high voices echo along the corridors. Besides Hanschen and Magdalena, we have a succession of waifs and strays, some related to us, some not, to look after, but I find it easy to love most of them at least; and in caring for them it seems Muhme Lena too has found her true vocation. There are some visitors who complain it is impossible to find sufficient peace to think, but while I sympathise, I am *not* prepared to straightjacket the children; the thought of it raising memories I would rather forget: of the strictures of the cloister and, sharper still, of my five-year-old self suffering under the sternness of Frau Seidewitz.

We are never short of people requesting to be part of Table Talk, but when we begin to have so many crammed into the room not all can be seated, I protest. Martin doesn't wish to exclude anyone, but I insist.

'It is for safety sake if nothing else. You do not want

someone to faint, or worse, for lack of air.'

'But how can we refuse?'

I think it obvious. 'We can have a waiting list, and when there is space, others can join us.'

'You are a braver woman than me,' Barbara says, when the latest criticism of me goes the rounds of the town. 'You know the gossip is all of the "petticoat rule" in the Lutherhaus? And it is not helped by Martin jokingly calling you "My Lord Käthe" in the wrong quarters.'

I shrug off her concern. 'They could say worse, but what matters is I have brought Martin round to my way of doing things. Which you must admit is sensible.'

'Undoubtedly, but I wish you could achieve it without detriment to your own reputation.'

'There are some folk I will never please, whatever I do, and it is little use in fretting over them. Our friends know better, and that is enough for me.'

There is a moment of silence in which I recognise her unspoken conclusion: 'It may need to be', before she turns the conversation. 'I hear folk are writing Martin's words down, and there is talk of printing the discussions, that they may be shared with the world outside of Wittenberg.'

I nod. 'There are several self-appointed chroniclers who scribble away furiously in the background. I just hope they are accurate in their reporting. I am not privy to what they write, and when *I* offer an opinion I wonder if it is recorded … or quietly ignored.' I grimace. 'Perhaps it's better not to know.' I can tell from her smile, she agrees.

In May, when the thorn is in blossom, our quiet equilibrium

is disturbed once more, for we receive word Martin's mother is gravely ill. He dashes off a letter to her and fully intends to travel to Mansfeld in person, but his letter is no sooner sent than another arrives telling us she has died. My only memory of her is of the days surrounding our Wirtschaft, but I warmed to her then and so mourn her sincerely now. I take it upon myself to tell the children, to spare Martin the task, for it is clear he feels the loss keenly. When Kath Jonas comes to offer condolences, it is Martin she asks of.

'It is the natural order of things to bury a parent...' The memory of Elizabeth hovers between us, neither, I think, willing to speak it out. 'His main regret is he didn't manage to visit before she died. And that I share, for I remember how hard it was to hear of my father's death when I had not been able to say goodbye.' I hesitate, unsure if what is in my mind makes sense. 'It was harder to believe he was gone when I didn't see it for myself, and I wonder if it is the same for Martin.'

Kath is brisk. 'Talk to him of her. In the past tense. It will help.'

'She was proud of you,' I say, coming to stand beside him as he stares out of the window looking towards the Elbe and the wooded land beyond. 'And she understood your responsibilities here, and wouldn't have wished you to lay them aside for her sake. Think of her as you last saw her, rejoicing at our wedding; as she likely thought of you with pride in her last hours.'

'I know. And I do.' His words are a sigh, and the

thought comes to me that perhaps to lose his second parent emphasises his own age, his mortality. That he is wrestling with the understanding he is now of the generation next to go. A suspicion confirmed when he says, 'I wish for your sake, Käthe, I was not so old, and like to leave you a young widow.'

'People die at every age, young and old, and we none of us can predict which way it will go. Only God knows. You have always taught we must rejoice in every day God gives us. Now you must live as you teach.'

He doesn't have long to fret, for problems small and large are brought to him in increasing numbers for his judgement. Some are easily sorted: when Magdalena Staupitz visits to request his intervention, so that she doesn't lose her house, he is quick to offer reassurance. 'This is an unintended consequence of the repossession of convent property. I will petition Duke John. Your house is safe.'

I draw her away to the Stube, and settle her on a window seat. 'It is so good to see you, also an unintended consequence, but in this case a lovely one. We are all so scattered, and to have a chance to be together again, even if only for a day or two, is an unexpected pleasure.'

'Unexpected, perhaps, but not surprising. We were a family at Nimbschen, and those of us who escaped together close knit as a result.' She leans towards me. 'Now that my house is safe, perhaps you will be able to visit me. It is not so very far.'

I scarcely need to ask, for she exudes an air of contentment, despite the problem that brought her to our door, but I do anyway, wanting to hear it from her own lips. 'The school goes well? You are happy in it?'

'Yes, and yes. It was a good day for us all when I wrote to Doctor Luther. But I must admit, I did not expect...'

'To see me married to him?'

She nods. 'I wouldn't have thought it the inclination of either of you.'

'It wasn't. Or not at first. But I have no regrets, nor, I think, does he.' I mean it as encouragement, that she may return home without any concern on my behalf, but as soon as the words are out of my mouth I realise, perhaps for the first time, how true they are, warmth spreading through me.

'I can see that.' She gives me a quick hug. 'We were not encouraged to be demonstrative in the cloister, quite the reverse, and I find it hard sometimes to overcome the training, but I am very happy for you both.'

Other issues require Martin to be stern and cause him real grief; like the case of the Wittenberg bailiff caught consorting with prostitutes.

He paces up and down our chamber, and though it is to me he is speaking, it is as if he needs to justify his decision to himself. 'I cannot do else than deny him the sacrament, for his sin is flagrant. I am not harsh for harshness sake, but rather to bring him to repentance; but I see no sign of remorse and so fear him damned.'

I try to offer reassurance. 'You have given him every opportunity to mend his ways.'

'But is my preaching so ineffective he cannot see how far he has strayed? Am I failing to lead others likewise?'

I think of the Jews, also seemingly intractable, and

of his anger alternately directed at them and at himself that they have not flocked to convert. Fearing this new disappointment may likewise lead to one of his intermittent bouts of depression, I lead him to a seat and kneel beside him, grasping both his hands in mine. I will him to listen to me. 'It is not your preaching at fault, it is the hardness of his heart.'

His eyes are shut, as if he prays.

'You can only show people the narrow way. It is their responsibility to enter the gate, and did not even our Lord weep over those who would not?' I risk a stern tone. 'A servant is not greater than his master.'

He pulls one hand free, and for a moment I think I may have gone too far, but he places it over mine, his expression wry, and in a partial echo of an earlier reprimand says, 'As even the great Martin Luther needs to be reminded from time to time.'

231

CHAPTER TWENTY-TWO
WITTENBERG, JULY 1531–FEBRUARY 1532

The six months that follow are a period of calm, a time when we are all able to enjoy the small pleasures of our life, the rumbles of war with the Turks receding. As the summer takes hold, Martin, his health good, and as a consequence his natural ebullience returned, begins his lectures on the Galatians Epistle. It isn't hard to see it is a book that suits both his theology and his temperament. He bounces back and forwards between the university and the Lutherhaus, those of us who aren't privileged to hear the lectures in person treated to an enthusiastic reprise of them over breakfast, lunch and supper. I have to look away at times, for I have never liked the thought of anyone seeing or hearing my own chewing, and my stomach churns at the sight of food revolving in Martin's mouth. At least the sound is masked by his voice:

'Galatians is all about freedom ... from rules, from rituals... All those who disagree: Papists, Anabaptists, Zwinglians, Muslims, Jews' – he sweeps his arm around the room as if it is full of them – 'contradict that simple message...'

It is the Martin I first heard, confident in his own opinions, equally dismissive of all those who do not share them, whether Christian or otherwise, displaying the fearless arrogance that endears him to his supporters and so antagonises his enemies. I admire his certainty but cannot help hoping the commentary that is to be the result of his labours may be more measured in tone.

Hans, as he insists we call him now that he has a tutor of his own, mutters into his porridge, repeating some of the choicest phrases. His mimicry of Martin is so perfect I almost choke trying to contain my laughter, and attempt to stare him into silence. He tilts his head at me, his grin impudent, and for a moment I see my brother Klement, but stifle the thought. He is only a child.

Nothing can take away from the satisfaction I find in supervising our increasingly large household and all our enterprises, within and without. The garden, once a wilderness, is bursting with good things, the seeds Martin begged from far and wide producing a crop, ten, twenty, a hundredfold. The Heffner land too, has proved profitable, the grass lush, the cattle and pigs we keep there fattening nicely, and I am confident we can over-winter sufficient of them to ensure fresh meat to enliven our diet in the darkest months. The Faul brook lives up to its promise, providing a constant supply of fish, the smokehouse racks always full.

In the town the streets dry up, dust rather than mud settling on the hem of my dress when I head into the market square.

'A lot easier to deal with,' Dorothea says as we brush our skirts. 'Let's hope the weather holds.'

And hold it does, the sun continuing to shine until

233

harvest, the fields outside the town glowing golden, tall stalks of ripening barley waving in the light breeze. It is a good summer too for songbirds, and Hans is assigned the task of checking the net trap daily. Martin is delighted with every catch and compliments him as if it were all the boy's own doing. I am more reticent, for I cannot forget the momentary resemblance to Klement. I think of his flash of cruelty as he exulted in chasing field mice among the stubble, toying with them as a cat would, and pray my son will not follow in his uncle's footsteps.

In November, after my easiest pregnancy yet, aside from the heartburn that latterly plagued me, I am delivered of a second son. Barbara is my first visitor and comes with a gift Eva sent in advance, along with a note of congratulations. She writes in her usual irrepressible style, and though it makes me laugh, it brings a lump to my throat also, that she is so far from us.

I see you are determined to people Wittenberg with little Luthers. I wish I could be there to see it, for I cannot imagine the good doctor as an infant.

'How did she know it would be a boy?'

Barbara laughs. 'She didn't. She wrote two notes, with instructions to me to deliver the appropriate one.' She looks down into the cradle, where Young Martin lies on his stomach, bottom up, knees tucked under his tummy, his head poking from the blanket swaddling him. 'I knew it,' she says, indicating his cap of coarse dark hair, 'that's what caused such discomfort for you.' She strokes his head, the hair springing back from her hand. 'And Eva is right. If he doesn't lose it, he will be Martin all over again.'

'His nose is already,' I say, 'and the double chin.'

234

'No need for Lucas to paint his likeness then…' She trails off, the shadow of Elizabeth hanging between us, a passing cloud briefly blocking the sun.

I turn the conversation into a jest. 'If he favours Martin, there will certainly be no need, for pictures of him can be picked up from a dozen market stalls for a few pfennigs apiece. Though why anyone would want Martin gracing their wall is beyond me. Less trouble than the real thing, of course.'

'Is it indeed?' Martin appears unannounced and comes to stand beside us. He places his finger against the curled fist, and he is rewarded when the babe opens his hand and fastens it around the finger.

I smile at him. 'I didn't know you were there.'

'Clearly,' he says, 'or you might have spoken of me more kindly.'

'Possibly,' I say, 'then again, maybe not, for' – I look across at Barbara, laughter in my voice – 'is not falsehood a sin?'

November and December fly past, Young Martin growing apace. 'As interested in his food as his father,' I say, when Kath Jonas and Katharina Melanchthon come to see the latest arrival. 'So it's little wonder he is stretching, faster even than Hans did.'

'He is sturdy, I'll give you that.' Kath lifts him up, delighted when he opens his eyes and rewards her with a sleepy smile.

Magdalena pushes between us. 'My turn, my turn.'

'Shall I?' Kath glances at me for approval.

235

'If you want to nurse him, Lenchen, you must sit down. I've told you that before.'

She plumps down onto her bottom, holds out her arms, Kath hunkering beside her to hand Young Martin over.

'She likes him then?'

'For a moment or two at a time. Much as she likes the new kittens in the barn: something small and warm to nurse. Until he becomes too wriggly, or cries. Then it is definitely *my* turn.'

Katharina Melanchthon is by the table, her mind clearly on more serious matters. 'Philipp says Doctor Luther's lectures on Galatians are his greatest work yet. Well prepared, well structured, well rehearsed and comprehensive.'

'All that and more,' I say, unable to keep the dry note from my voice. 'I can vouch for it.'

Kath Jonas' mouth twitches, but Katharina, seeming not to be aware of any undercurrent, indicates the pamphlet lying on the table. 'Is this it in print already?'

'Yes. They are in great demand. Sometimes I wish…'

Both of them look at me.

'Nothing.' I hunker down on the other side of Magdalena, and as if on cue, Young Martin begins to grizzle. 'I'll take him, sweetheart. He's hungry.'

She thrusts him at me, and scrambling to her feet, heads for the door. 'I'm hungry too.'

Katharina is still holding the pamphlet, turning it over in her hand. 'Philipp says this may run to thousands.'

'Yes. So does Lucas Cranach.'

'Who will take the profit?'

The question is so close to my own I don't want to answer for fear I reveal my thoughts. Kath rescues me.

'The printers, I imagine, who bear the costs of the venture and any risk.'

'There can be no risk, surely.' Katharina is worrying at the issue like Arlo with a bone. 'Anything Doctor Luther writes sells well.'

I am more abrupt than I intend. 'There must be something of more interest to talk about than Martin's writings, important as they are.'

Once again Kath comes to the rescue. 'They say Duke John is ill, his flesh wasting away. Johann Frederick will sign the Peace of Nuremberg on his behalf.'

'As long as someone signs, does it matter who?'

'I don't suppose so, but it is hard to think Duke John may soon be gone, and it doesn't sound the most pleasant of ways to die.'

I agree with her, but though I don't say so, I cannot help thinking there is an element of justice in this, for all the suffering he caused following the Peasants' War.

◯◯✖◯◯

January comes in with a flurry of snowstorms, the winds driving along the Collegienstrasse and piling snow in drifts in every opening. Marooned in the Lutherhaus, I am concerned for the animals we have at the Heffner property, until Johann, the swineherd, comes to tell me he will sleep in the barn there, to better see to the stock.

'You have enough blankets? And a brazier?'

'The barn is windproof and watertight, and well heated by the animals. There is no fear of me freezing while I sleep.'

I imagine him breaking the ice on the drinking troughs

and struggling through the snow to draw water from the brook to refill them, his fingers blue even in his woollen gloves. 'And in the daytime?'

He shrugs. 'I work outside and am well used to cold.'

'We are fortunate to have you,' I say, 'and must see you are well provisioned.'

In February, in a temporary thaw, word comes from Torgau. Martin holds the opened letter in his hand and I cannot tell from his expression whether the news is good or bad. As if he reads my mind he says, 'Which do you wish to hear first? The good or the bad?'

'The bad. It will not improve with the waiting, though the good might.'

He doesn't bother with any preliminaries, though I imagine Chancellor Brück's letter is generous in that regard, for he isn't noted for brevity. Instead, Martin moves straight to the important paragraphs.

It is with sadness I have to report the wasting of flesh Elector John suffers has resulted in the amputation of a toe. And though the physicians hope it may halt the disease, I suspect the duke is less confident...

'Poor man,' I say, picturing in my mind my last sight of him, sitting upright in his carriage as he entered Wittenberg flanked by outriders: the carriage, horses, and men all alike clad in the black and yellow of the house of Wettin, Hans jumping up and down beside me as we stood in the crowd in the market square to watch him pass, acknowledging the cheers with a regal dip of his head. 'He was so vigorous. It must be hard to be unable to move unaided.'

Martin is looking beyond me towards the window and the world outside, and it's clear his thoughts are

238

also anchored in the past. 'He was a good man, for all his warlike tendencies. And even now he thinks of others in what might be his final days.' There is an odd note in his voice, as if he doesn't approve the duke's actions, however altruistic they might be.

'What has he done?'

He turns the letter over, skips down to the bottom of the page, chews on his lip, his tone out of kilter with his words. 'This is the good news.'

I imagine Brück at his desk in Schloss Hartenfels perhaps blowing on his fingers to warm them and lessen their stiffness, pausing to dip the quill in the ink, as he writes,

You may not wish for this, but the duke has instructed me to draw up a deed of gift of the Lutherhaus. It is to be an outright bequest, free of any taxes...

'Ours' – I cannot keep the joy from my voice or the smile from my face – 'entirely ours.'

Martin is not smiling. 'Generous as the duke is, he may be placing a millstone around our necks. The maintenance is already an expense we can ill afford, and if anything major were to go wrong...'

My mind is already on things that could be done, improvements that could be made, if we can only find the money. 'Ours,' I repeat. 'I never dared to wish for this.'

'I wish...' Martin begins, corrects himself. 'It might have been better had we taken him up on his previous offer to gift us a smaller property in the town. One that would have suited our, *my*, advancing years.'

'No. No!' My enthusiasm is growing with every moment. 'There is so much we can do with this. It is security, for the future, for the children. A kindness we must gratefully accept.'

'A kindness we have no choice *but* to accept.' He settles his shoulders. 'And perhaps it is as well it pleases you, for the management of it all will rest on your shoulders. I have neither the time, nor the inclination.'

– Nor the competence, I think, but don't say. I am barely listening to him, for I have become used to his lack of drive for anything but his writing. As perhaps it should be. And if I am to be allowed to follow my inclination, what I secretly think of as *my* calling, I will be content. I would like to read the letter for myself, for I can't quite believe our good fortune, but when Martin shows no sign of handing it over, I content myself with asking, 'What else does he say?'

'Only that he trusts whether he lives or dies it will enable us to continue the good work of the Lutherhaus, and wishes us joy in it.'

There is a warm feeling in the pit of my stomach, and on impulse I reach up and place my hand against Martin's cheek, willing him to share it. 'That will not be so hard, surely?'

The tension in his face slackens. 'I daresay not…'

I appreciate the effort he is making, as he jokes, 'If My Lord Käthe is in charge.'

CHAPTER TWENTY-THREE
WITTENBERG, JUNE–AUGUST 1532

The excitement I feel when we first receive the news of the gift of the Lutherhaus increases as spring drifts into summer, my plans for the building developing also: the initial thoughts of renovation and repair metamorphosing into ideas for extension. Along with the building has come permission for a licence, not just to brew beer for our domestic consumption, but to sell it also.

Muhme Lena finds me standing in the doorway of the enlarged brewhouse, watching as the new vats are installed. There is a gentle mockery in her voice. 'Standing idle, Kat?'

I turn with a smile and lean back against the warm stone. 'You know brewing was my favourite occupation at Nimbschen, but I had no thought then of the value and significance that training would come to have.'

She is silent for a moment, her expression serious. 'No more had I, Kat. When you first came to us, you were so full of life I burned with anger against your father for sending you, and even questioned God for allowing you to be shut away so. I watched you grow up, and though you caused us no grief, it was no surprise when you chose to leave. Indeed, I rejoiced in it, though of course I could not say so openly. Living with you here, seeing the confidence you have in all you do, I understand now.'

'And the abbess?'

'If she were here, she would feel as I do, proud of what you have become.'

Her affirmation encourages me to enlarge my plans further. I tackle Martin after supper. 'There is one major lack in this building.'

He narrows his eyes, waits for me to continue.

'The cellar is in need of major reconstruction, for we have insufficient cold storage.' I hold my breath, waiting for refusal, but it doesn't come, only the query,

'Is it really necessary?'

Encouraged, I am emphatic. 'Yes.'

'Well then, have drawings prepared and we can discuss it further.'

We spend many evenings poring over the plans, until, eventually, it is decided.

When the building work commences I take pleasure in listening to the whistling of the masons and the ring of chisel on stone, and the smell of cut timber pervading the house. Martin complains his head is sore and that it is hard to think straight with all the hammering and banging, but it is with a smile, which belies his words. The children dart about, ever inquisitive, and get under the workmen's feet, but when I seek to be stern with them, the men smile and tell me to let them be. Hans' interest, I suspect, is driven by a desire to escape his lessons, and I cannot but have some sympathy for him, for sometimes I think Martin pushes him too hard.

June is a gentle month, the weather perfect. We take to inspecting the works in the evenings when the men have gone home, my excitement mounting as the cellar project nears completion. We are standing in the centre, waiting for our eyes to accustom to the dim light. In my head the shelves are already well stocked, groaning under the weight of cheeses and jars of pickles and preserved fruits. I see smoked hams hanging from the hooks embedded in the vaulted ceiling, and barrels of salt fish lining the rear wall, and, in the corner furthest from the door, a tower of slatted racks to hold the apples already forming on the trees.

I turn to Martin, my eyes shining, and as if he can follow my thoughts, say, 'Carefully stored they may last to Yule and beyond before the skins begin to toughen and the flesh to dry out.'

'What may last, Käthe?'

'The apples, of course.'

He smiles down at me. 'Oh, of course. How foolish of me not to read your mind.'

I am just about to respond to his teasing, when I notice a spiral of dust sifting from the roof, followed by a shift in the curve of the vault. At first I think it a trick of the light, but there is a low rumble, as if of a cart on the cobbles, and then more dust, the noise increasing. We have scarcely time to jump backwards to the entrance before we see the crack opening in the ceiling, stones beginning to fall. It is only a few minutes, but it seems like hours we stand at the edge of the path, watching and listening until the sound has stopped and the dust billowing through the open doorway settles. I scarcely dare look at the wall above for fear I will see it begin to crumble also, nor at Martin, lest

243

I see blame in his eyes.

In the silence that follows he draws me to the bench below the kitchen window, and as I sit down I begin to shake. He pulls me to him. 'We are safe, Käthe. That is all that matters. We are safe.'

The collapse is only partial, but it is a shock nonetheless. The cost of repairing the damage equally concerning.

'Two hundred gulden?' Barbara is as horrified as I am.

'We have no choice. Without suitable underpinning the whole building may come down.'

'Where will you find the money?'

'No idea, at least none I want to contemplate. There is Herr Heffner's land, but though selling that would solve our short-term need, it would feel like a backwards step.'

'And Martin? What does he think?'

'I don't exactly know, but it's clear he is worried as to how and where we will find the money. As I am.' I square my shoulders, dare her to contradict me. 'It must be found somehow, but I will not sell land. I will pawn all the silver, jewellery, the gold cups, anything but land.'

She pats my shoulder, nods. 'If anyone can, you will do it, Kat.'

We beg and borrow and pawn and sell, and though it embarrasses Martin, I am delighted and relieved when the elector grants us an extra one hundred gulden a year towards the maintenance of the building.

As a precaution while it is shored up, we do not use the rooms above, and for as long as the work continues the children are forbidden to go anywhere near it. I don't wish to frighten them, but Martin insists the only way to ensure their obedience is to tell the older ones, and in that group he includes Hans, how close we came to death.

As summer wears on, it is another death that concerns not only us, but all of Saxony. Elector John lingers much longer than anyone expects, and it seems his is not to be an easy end, the decline steady but slow. In August he calls for Martin and for Melanchthon and they are at his bedside at Schweinitz when he suffers a final stroke. They accompany his body as it is rushed to Wittenberg.

'Lack of balsam for the embalming,' Melanchthon says, a note of reproof in his voice. 'Despite that there has been plenty of time to prepare.'

Martin's thoughts are focused elsewhere, as he relays their last discussion, clearly moved by the elector's distress. 'He asked me whether it is possible for soldiers to be saved?'

'Which was another way of asking if it were possible for him?'

'Yes.'

'No wonder,' I say, 'for if I, who had no part in it, cannot forget his actions in the aftermath of the Peasants' War, it's hardly surprising it preyed on his conscience.' When Martin remains silent I press, 'How did you answer him?'

'As I would answer any sinner. That if there is repentance, God's grace is sufficient.'

He speaks with his usual confidence, but something in his stance suggests an element of diffidence that makes me uneasy. I am tempted to ask, 'Do you believe there is no sin that cannot be forgiven?' But lacking the courage, or perhaps fearing the answer, I ask instead, 'And did that

245

suffice?'

'He died depending on the Cross of Christ... Thank God...'

This time I don't break the silence, but wait for him to continue, his hesitation indicating it is something else which troubles him.

'I am to speak no eulogy at his funeral, but I fear how the people will react.'

'If they will take it as criticism of him?'

'If they will see it as a lack of respect, for the office as well as the man.'

I am conscious of the implied irony that Elector John, a known reformer, called 'John the Steadfast', will be laid to rest in the classical manner of a Latin funeral; while Frederick, who made no such claim, was given an evangelical one, Martin's sermon full of praise. I ask, 'What are Duke Johann Frederick's wishes in the matter, surely as his father's heir it is he should decide?'

'He will not be here in time for the funeral.'

Martin must have seen my surprise, for he adds, 'We are ordered to proceed, and hold a second memorial next week.'

Summer it may be and hot, but privately I question if it would not be more appropriate to wait for our new elector, but I don't share my thoughts with anyone, not even Barbara.

The funeral service is short, the procession accompanying Elector John's body to the Castle Church long, indicating the regard in which he is held. A wooden cross is carried aloft, the clergy, faculty and students lining up behind. From the moment the cortège crosses the river the church bell begins to toll, sombre and sonorous, echoing throughout the town, a metronome counting out the elector's last hour. Horsemen flank the bier, peeling off to the side as they reach the entrance to the church, to form a guard of honour through which the remainder of the mourners pass, heads bowed. The choirboys chant in German, Martin preaches a sermon harking back to the Augsburg confession, and at the interment Melanchthon gives the traditional Latin oration. Standing to the rear, beside Barbara, I think about Duke Johann Frederick, our new elector, about his youth and inexperience, and wonder what will happen to the League now. What will happen to us, to me, to the new life already quickening inside me.

Torgau, November 1552

It is raining, battering the window and sliding down the glass with a hiccup as it crosses the crack. There is a steady drip, drip, drip, and I think of the broken overhang that I always meant to have fixed. 'It should have been done,' I tell the girl when she comes to shut the shutters and light the candle. 'But somehow, even though other, more important, jobs were, this one slipped through the net.'

She nods, as if indulging me, and busies herself with straightening the covers. 'Do you need anything more tonight, Mutti?'

I want to ask why she is calling me Mutti, but I don't wish to upset her, for she has been good to me. And her face is familiar – perhaps she is one of the orphans we have taken in. I wave my arm around the room. 'Will you help me? There are so many things to sort. And so little time. I meant everything to be ready.'

She pats my arm. 'There's nothing that won't wait until tomorrow, Mu…'

'Tomorrow…' I say, 'There is something special about tomorrow, but I can't remember what it is. I shut my eyes, concentrate. 'Tomorrow is my birthday.'

'It's only Novem…' she begins.

'January isn't the month I would have chosen but that we cannot choose.'

Her top lip is caught in her teeth, as if she is stopping herself from speaking.

'When is your birthday?' I ask.

Her voice is cracking, her eyes moist. 'Don't you remember?'

'Should I? Have you told me before?'

She makes a choking sound. 'It's December.'

I smile at her. 'Just before mine then.'

She doesn't answer, instead picks up a comb. 'Would you like me to comb your hair?'

'That's kind,' I say. 'Margarethe used to comb my hair. Do you know Margarethe?' I reach up and touch a strand of her hair. It is the same copper colour and has the same unruly wave in it. 'She looks a little like you.'

She moves to the side and undoes my plait. I can't see her face, but sense her agitation in the movement of her fingers. Thinking she is concerned for me, I seek to reassure her.

'Oh, don't worry, there is always a fear,' I say, 'and to birth a babe is hard, harder than you can imagine, but it is always worth it in the end.'

CHAPTER TWENTY-FOUR
WITTENBERG, JANUARY 1533

It is not how I thought to spend the eve of my thirty-fourth birthday, sweating and straining as I ride wave after wave of pain, until with a final savage thrust I usher the latest Luther into the world. He is born one hour after midnight, and although throughout the labour I would have been glad for it to end, I cannot but feel a special joy we will forever share the day of our birth. He is the best gift I could wish for: a sturdy child, whole and healthy, with a pair of lungs to rival a bellowing calf. In the morning when Magdalena is brought to see him, she counts his fingers and toes and pronounces herself satisfied, and states he will be welcome in the nursery. Dorothea, who has brought me a posset, looks as if she is about to reprimand her, but I pull Magdalena close. 'I'm glad of it, poppet. I'm sure he will thrive in your care.'

He is baptised Paul, after the apostle, the service held in the Castle Church, Prince John Ernest, our new elector's young half-brother, standing as one of his godparents, an honour that pleases Martin and me both, and one I hope will serve to counterbalance the weight of responsibility his name confers.

I look down at him as he lies content in the cradle, the only sound his even breathing and an intermittent schlup, schlup, as he sucks on his thumb. It is hard to believe in less than eight years I have given birth five times. For a brief moment I think of Elizabeth, but lock that sadness away and concentrate instead on the good fortune of four live children to my credit. Though I would not have admitted to it, I had hoped for another girl, to dilute Martin's spoiling of Magdalena, but now he is here I wouldn't have anything other. Paul stirs and stretches, his arms upthrust, and I think of Hans, his matriculation at the university already set for the autumn, though he will be but seven years old. I cannot but hope this child will not be so pressed.

Elector Johann Frederick surprises us all. Although his father and grandfather had protected Martin and his fellow reformers, they had largely depended on ignoring demands for censure, rather than outright refusal of them. Johann Frederick has no such scruples, declaring openly it is not only Martin's right to advise all evangelicals on their form of worship and mode of life, but also his duty. Endorsement and challenge both, though I would not admit it to Martin, make me fear for him.

He works harder than ever, but it is not always labour of his choosing. No longer simply the single-minded, fiery reformer I married, but now a man of many parts. Preacher and teacher, roles he relishes, but also counsellor, administrator, pastor, and judge of all manner of issues, important and mundane. He does not keep count, but when Melanchthon, who has a penchant for records and figures and lists, announces Martin has written briefs for more than six hundred marital disputes alone, his response is a flash of his old wit.

'Only six hundred? I thought it more like six thousand. Indeed, I have begun to fear there will be no marriages left in Saxony that do *not* require my judgement.' A hint of a grin. 'Excepting those present, of course.'

'It is no laughing matter,' Melanchthon begins, his expression typically lugubrious.

I have to look away to hide my amusement, and I can see by the corner of Martin's mouth he is also struggling not to smile.

'I take these matters as seriously as you, Philipp, but if we did not laugh sometimes, we might cry. And indeed' – his expression sobers – 'maybe we should, for there are those among our followers whose acceptance of grace is more an excuse to avoid the rules of Rome than any true faith.'

To turn the conversation, I ask, 'You did not bring Katharina with you tonight? I trust she is keeping well, and her pregnancy progressing as you would wish?'

Melanchthon turns to me with a smile, and I think how much has changed between us from the early days, when his disapproval of me was obvious to all.

'She's tired.' The lines on his forehead are more visible than usual. 'I suppose it is only to be expected, though...'

'She has a house to manage, and two other children to run after; of course she will be more tired than in her earlier pregnancies. And if what we see of Hans and Jost Jonas and Lippus' behaviour while they are playing here is anything to go by, no doubt they will take some running after at your house also.' For a moment he looks somewhat taken aback, and I wonder if he thinks my comment an implied criticism of his son, so I add, 'I enjoy to see the liveliness in our children, but I must admit, in the last months before Paul's birth, I had a hard job to keep up with them.'

'Better boisterous than sullen,' Martin says, nodding at Melanchthon. 'It is a fine thing our children share the friendship of their parents.'

Melanchthon turns back to me, sucking on his lip. 'I will be glad when her time comes, and I know she will be too … for she misses the company of her friends just now.' The rising inflection of his voice turns his statement into a question.

'Paul is nearly a month old, and the weather kind for February. If it holds I could visit her?'

'She will be glad to see you, I'm sure.'

There is a new warmth in his voice, a sense of relief that makes me wonder if there is perhaps more amiss with Katharina than he wishes to admit, so I resolve to go as soon as I can.

Martin rises and adds a log to the stove, poking at the embers noisily, a sure sign he is bored with this conversation, and before he can introduce something contentious, I ask, 'How is the translation work coming along?'

Both of them answer at once, Melanchthon saying 'Slowly', Martin 'Well.'

'Slowly and well?'

Again they speak simultaneously, Melanchthon saying 'Perhaps better than we could expect', and Martin 'Not as

253

fast as we'd planned.'

Laughing, I say, 'If this is an example of how your discussions go, it's a wonder you have made any progress at all.'

They have the good grace to laugh with me, and this time it is Martin who manages to get in first. 'We will be finished it this year, I am confident of that, and it will be a good translation, one the ordinary people will be able to read for themselves.'

Melanchthon nods his agreement, but adds a note of reservation. 'If we do not have to spend all our time on settling other, less important, matters.'

'The work is enough to keep us all busy, that's for sure.' Martin sets aside the poker.

Another thought strikes me. 'Will ordinary people be able to afford it?'

Chapter Twenty-Five
Wittenberg, March–September 1534

The translation of the Old Testament isn't finished as quickly as Martin hoped. The work is fragmented by periods of inactivity when he is called away to deal with matters in other places, and without him the impetus is lost. And even when he is at home, there is other work: lectures to prepare, sermons to write, hymns and catechisms and pamphlets concerning all manner of evils. The volume is enough to keep a host of printers busy and could provide us with a steady income, if Martin would but accept payment. His determination not to profit from them is a frustration I have not yet found sufficient confidence to tackle. 'Is money a bone of contention in other marriages?' I ask Barbara.

'Oh yes. There are plenty of wives of my acquaintance who find it so, but in general it is tight-fisted husbands they complain of, not the over-generous.'

'No one could accuse Martin of that.' My smile fades. 'Am I wrong to worry about such things? Or to strive to increase our income?'

'If you did not, you would both be in penury, and the

work you do here impossible. Think of Table Talk, of the visitors who flock to sit at Martin's feet. Think of the waifs and strays you are always ready to welcome under your roof. Without you, they would have no means of support.'

'How can I not welcome them, when every request reminds me of my own good fortune, of the generosity extended to me when I needed it most?'

Barbara's face is pink, as if embarrassed at my oblique reference to my time in her house. 'You are the perfect counterpoint to Martin's other-worldliness, and I am only sorry that others, more critical, cannot see how needed you are.'

Events in the world outside Wittenberg, good and bad, also conspire to slow the translation work. I suspect Melanchthon still harbours hope, even at this late stage, that a compromise between the Catholic Church and the reformers can be reached, but Martin does not.

'Too little, too late,' he says, and I am inclined to agree, for the twin memories of the tall walls at Nimbschen and the theology that likewise imprisoned me, though dimming, still have the power to send a shiver up my spine.

It is not Catholicism, however, that produces ripples of fear throughout town, but word that radical Anabaptists have taken Münster. When Martin brings the news I sink onto the bench, clasping my hands together to stop their trembling, my fingertips white. I can manage no more than a whisper. 'Will this be the Peasants' War all over again?'

'We may pray not,' Martin says. His voice rises, his scorn clear. 'The leader, Matthijs, predicts the world will end at Easter and invites all true believers to join him in his "New Jerusalem".'

'Surely few will answer such a call?'

'There are always those who can be swayed by false teachers. And though I hope the numbers will be small, I fear otherwise.'

His fears are realised, one thousand 'believers' flocking to Münster to be re-baptised. Neither the Lutheran nor the Catholic parties can afford to ignore the threat this poses, and Protestant Philip of Hesse and Catholic Bishop Franz come together to besiege the city. It was not the compromise Melanchthon wanted, but a compromise nonetheless. Matthijs' reaction to the siege is violent, expelling two thousand souls who refuse re-baptism, forcing them to flee the city with little more than they can carry. I cannot help thinking of the Karlstadts, and Andreas' Anabaptist leanings, and pray, for Anna and his children's sake, he is not sucked into the conflict.

The world does not end at Easter. I sense an unexpressed relief in the faces of the worshippers as they spill from the Town Church on Easter morning and an added joy in the affirmation greeting 'Christ has Risen' reverberating around the square.

Barbara halts beside me, echoing my thought. 'However much we profess to look forward to the Second Coming of our Lord, there is a part in each of us that clings to this life.'

Justus Jonas and Martin are weaving through the crowd towards us.

'What will happen at Münster now?' I say, as Martin

takes my arm.

'Who knows?'

'Will the siege be lifted?'

'Only if the Anabaptists surrender control, and I cannot see that while Matthijs is in charge.'

Justus is equally grim. 'Even if anything should happen to him, there are others ready to step into his shoes. This will not end anytime soon.'

Word comes that Matthijs has been killed in a skirmish outside the walls of Münster, and I cannot help feeling a leap of joy, hope building that the worst may be over. I am wrong and Justus is right, for a new and more controversial leader takes Matthijs' place. John of Leiden, as he is known, styles himself the new King David, and advocates polygamy, his views spreading like wildfire across Saxony.

'It is the topic of gossip on everyone's lips, causing outrage and protests from even the most timid of women,' I say, as we prepare for bed.

Martin pauses as he unrolls his stockings. 'The day may come when a man may take two wives.'

'Indeed,' I say, fixing him with a glare. 'Well I would not stand for it. I'd sooner return to the nunnery.'

He touches my shoulder as if in apology. 'Käthe, I did but jest.'

Later I say to Barbara, 'There are some things that should not be a cause for amusement.'

She is more sanguine. 'Granted, but you should know by now men have different ideas about many things. What they find amusing, we find offensive. If no offence is meant, none should be taken. It is by far the best way in any marriage.'

258

'Sometimes I wonder if I am suited to be a wife, for I cannot hold my peace if I think something wrong.'

'I've told you before, Kat, you are suited to be *his* wife, none better, for without someone to challenge him and rein in his excesses, who knows what might happen.'

Despite Leiden's views, or perhaps because of them, his following among men increases, and it isn't long before he sends out missionaries, as if he were Christ himself. Though I do not condone his ideas, and pray they will be defeated, I am saddened when word comes that eight of his followers have been executed.

'Why must there always be violence? Do they not remember how many have already died in the name of religion?' I ask Martin.

He takes a moment to reply. 'It is precisely because they do remember, that we see deeds such as this. Fear breeds violence.'

'Can you not preach peace?'

'In the face of such heresy? No. I cannot. Whatever the consequences.'

The summer stretches out with little to break the cycle of long fine days under clear skies, at odds with the news continuing to trickle in from Münster, besiegers and besieged both settling in for a long struggle. The talk in the marketplace is all of the justice of Count Philip's cause, the need to destroy the scourge that is Leiden and his followers, the Old Testament admonitions to allow none to live. And though it does not touch us, I cannot look at our own children without thinking of the innocents of Münster, imprisoned within the town by the actions of their parents. And justice or not, my heart aches for them.

And for Martin, when in July he is called away again. I write to Eva

I had not realised the hole in my heart when he is not here, until I received his latest letter. He signed it, 'Your true love, Martin Luther'. Who would have thought, when we first arrived, he would come to think of me like that? Or I him? When we married a part of me envied you the love you had found with Basilius, the love I never expected to find again. But find it I have, in my 'good old man!' I hope he will be home soon.

When he returns, it is to throw himself into the task of translation with renewed vigour, and to push the others also. 'We are so nearly there, Käthe, so nearly there.'

I am pleased for him, and for myself, for there is a promise of a good harvest with plenty of grain to see us through the winter to come. Barbara calls in after a trip to the market, and as we walk in the garden I point out the beans, which are threatening to take over a section of garden, but comment on the additional work required to ensure they have enough water to swell the pods.

She is unable to keep the amusement out of her voice. 'Farmers! Never satisfied. Wanting rain when there is none, and no doubt a return to dry weather at the first hint of drizzle.'

'Guilty as charged,' I say, drawing her to the bench. I look out at the neat rows of vegetables, the cabbages beginning to heart and swell, the tops of the turnips pushing through the soil as if demanding to be gathered. On the fruit trees the apples and pears hang heavy, almost ready to drop. A cloud passes across the sun, and in the sudden coolness I wave my hand over the garden. 'Is it not hard to see all this produce and not think of those who may already be starving?'

'We cannot change the world, Kat, only look to our own little corner and be grateful for what *we* have been given.'

It is good advice, but not always easy to follow. As summer drifts towards autumn, I look to the house, and to giving it a final scouring to prepare it for winter.

'Nest building again,' Barbara says, when she finds me knee deep in children's clothes. 'But don't overdo it.'

Good advice, but equally hard to follow. Closets are tidied, floors are scrubbed, sheets are mended, preserves and pickles are set in ordered lines on the pantry shelves, hams and salt fish are stored in the newly refurbished cellar. I am polishing silver when I hear Martin's booming voice on the stair. Our collection is spread out on the table in front of me, the contours of the candlesticks catching the last of the September light as it spills through the leaded windows. I always leave the chalice, a wedding gift from the university, until last, taking especial pleasure in its curves, and finding amusement in the distorted face smiling back at me as I buff it to a shine. I start to put it all away in the wall cupboard where it belongs, for what is a delight to me is somewhat of a trial to Martin, but he bursts into the room before I have finished. There is a bounce in his step and his glance at the silver is cursory, as he waves a sheaf of papers at me. I know immediately what he's going to say and pre-empt him with a smile. 'The Old Testament is finished then?'

He places the papers on the table and sets a candlestick on top, to stop them being stirred by the draught from the open window, then takes both my hands in his. 'Finished, Käthe,' he echoes. There is satisfaction in his voice. 'The whole Bible in German. It is well done.'

I dip my head to hide my smile. Modesty is not his strong point, but in this he has a right to be proud, for the effort he and others have made.

He is looking over my shoulder towards the window, his face tilted upwards as if to sniff the smell of newly scythed grass, which drifts in from the meadow by the Elbe. He pulls me close and turns me round, my back against his chest. Sliding his arms around my waist, he rests his chin on my head. 'There will be three harvests this year,' he says. 'By God's goodness we will be triply blessed. With food for our bodies, nourishment for our souls, and' – he pats my stomach twice and I feel the babe stir within me, as if it recognises his touch – 'joy for our spirits also.' He spins me round again to face him, his face alight. 'The husbandman you have made of me rejoices in the first, the cleric in me in the second, and the father in the third.'

I cannot think of a suitable reply, but I understand what he means.

He captures my hand again, his enthusiasm bubbling over afresh. 'I will set you a challenge, Käthe. I will give you fifty gulden if you can read the whole Bible by Easter.'

I cannot refuse him, however daunting I find the idea. 'Accepted,' I say.

There is a moment of companionable silence before the frame of the casement rattles, and we turn together to see Magdalena in the doorway, her face streaked with tears, one hand hidden underneath her apron. She hurls herself at us, and Martin swings her up into his arms.

Her voice is muffled against his chest, her words barely distinguishable through her sobs, only one name clear. I stroke her hair, striving for a neutral tone, for it may not be the boy's fault, and ask, 'What has Martin done now, poppet?'

She lifts her head, her wails beginning afresh, and withdrawing her hand, she opens it to reveal her rag doll, the head lolled to the side, stuffing escaping from the neck. An old image of Klement in our nursery flashes into my head, my doll similarly violated. Our son, Hans, is not Klement, but it appears Young Martin may be. I uncurl her fingers and cradle the doll in my hand. 'It will mend, poppet. I will make it right.'

Chapter Twenty-Six
Wittenberg, May–August 1535

There are some things that cannot be made right. I am at Herr Heffner's field, assisting with the pupping of the sows, when the word comes. Margarethe, our third daughter, born in December, when Wittenberg was in the grip of winter, cut off from the rest of the world, is with me, lying in a basket, well wrapped up despite the spring sunshine, her rhythmic breathing a comfort. She is an easy child, and appears to thrive. Nevertheless, I do not like to leave her.

Dorothea, as usual, had tutted when I gathered her up. 'We are capable of seeing to the babe without your constant oversight. Especially as anyone can see to her needs.'

I don't need reminding that once again I have insufficient milk and so have had to resort to feeding her goat's milk. It is a failure I find hard to accept, hidden from all but my closest friends.

'It isn't that I think...'

'We know.' Muhme Lena has shaken her head at Dorothea. 'It is no shame to struggle with feeding a babe.

264

And only natural you should want to compensate by keeping her close in these first months. Once she is on her feet, then you will be able to be confident about leaving her in our care.'

The lad who proffers the note sways from foot to foot as I open it, but when I look up he is staring at the ground, as if afraid to meet my eyes.

'Thank you. Tell Doctor Cruciger I will be with him just as soon as I have rid myself of the smell of pigs.'

He lopes away, and despite the sad news, I find myself smiling at the disproportionate length of his legs, as if he were a cricket, not a youth.

Johann, who is kneeling on the ground helping a piglet to a teat, rocks back on his heels as I approach.

'It is Frau Cruciger. She…' I feel tears welling. 'I must go. To be taken so young, it is…' Conscious of my status as Martin Luther's wife, I stop myself from saying it isn't fair. 'Those poor, poor children.'

He stretches out his hand as if in comfort, and as quickly pulls it back again, colouring. 'I will manage here,' he offers.

'I know, and thank you.'

Muhme Lena meets me at the door and takes Margarethe. Her eyes are also luminous, and there are streaks on her cheeks as if she has newly wiped away tears. 'You will be going to the Crucigers'' – she wrinkles her nose – 'but not without a change of clothes I hope.'

Caspar Cruciger is sitting in their Stube, his shoulders slumped, the children clustered around him, red-eyed. He looks up as I enter, but doesn't rise.

'I'm so, so sorry.' I want to put my arms around him but am constrained by the impropriety of such an action and

265

instead place them around the youngest of the children. As I draw them to me, the littlest turns her face into my skirts and begins to sob.

Caspar stirs. 'Your dress...'

But I shake my head. 'Will take no harm. We all loved her, and will feel her loss sorely.'

He subsides back onto the chair. 'She was so young, so full of life, her music and her hymns so full of joy, and now...'

'Now she is singing in heaven,' I say. He looks up, his gaze accusing, and ashamed of the platitude, I tighten my grip on the children and allow my own tears to fall.

At home, Martin gathers our children together. 'God has chosen to take Aunt Elizabeth to join the heavenly choir,' he says. 'You must be very kind to her children. But though she is lost to us, her music remains, and every time we sing one of her hymns we will remember her.'

I know what he is trying to do, and commend him for it, but later, as we lie side by side in the bed, I stare at the ceiling as if to memorise the pattern of small cracks that mar the plaster. 'It could have been me,' I say. 'And our children motherless.'

He takes my hand, 'His ways are not our ways, Käthe. You know that.'

'I know it here.' I stab at my head. 'But I don't feel it. Not here.' I press my fist against my chest. 'Not here.'

Some things cannot be made right. And it seems this year has more than its fair share of ill. In June we hear Münster is retaken and John Leiden and two of his followers sentenced to death.

'An eye for an eye,' Martin reminds me, when I shiver.

'What of "love your enemies" and "do good to those who despitefully use you"?'

He is uncharacteristically patient. 'There is a difference, Käthe, in what an individual must do and what the civil law demands. Leiden's rebellion was against the powers and authorities of the land, as well as against God, and he has suffered the consequences of his actions as a result. To do less than execute him risks the danger of anarchy. And likely many more dead.'

That, I can accept the justice of, for he has been responsible for so much suffering. But when a messenger arrives and favours us with the details of the deaths, I have to turn my face away to hide my revolt at the relish in his voice.

'Maimed with hot tongs,' he says, indicating by a crude gesture what part of their bodies he is referring to. 'Horribly painful, and no more than they deserved. Their remains are suspended in cages on the tower of St Lambert's Church and are there yet unless' – he leers and winks – 'the crows have finished them off.'

There is a firm set to Martin's mouth as he ushers the messenger out, and when he returns he slumps down on the bench, his silence speaking volumes.

'That was not well done,' I say.

'It is not our place to judge. Who knows what any of us would do when relieved from such a circumstance?'

'Vengeance is mine, says the Lord.' I hear the hard note in my voice, but have no wish to soften it. 'We may hope it isn't us he takes vengeance on.'

'We may pray,' Martin corrects me, 'indeed we must,

lest worse befall us.'

Prayers or not, the worst does come, for in August the plague returns to Wittenberg. I think of Elizabeth, born in the last outbreak, and living only a few months thereafter, and thank God I am not pregnant this time. But as we prepare once more to provide what help and comfort we can to those affected, I fear for us all.

Muhme Lena is brisk. 'We can but take care, and seek to avoid infection and trust God for the rest.'

It is Martin who makes the error that so nearly brings us to grief. Day after day as he visits the sick and the dying, he is meticulous about removing his outer clothes and washing by the well in the garden before entering the house. So I don't think to question when he rushes into the Stube. Margarethe is sitting on the rug, propped all around by cushions, and he sweeps her up, jigging her and putting his finger to her mouth when she chuckles.

'Hush, Margarethe, I have news for your mother.'

His eyes are alight as I ask, 'What is it? Is the plague diminishing at last?'

He stills, his face draining of colour, and he sets Margarethe down.

I hear the panic in his voice as he rushes to the door and calls for Dorothea to bring water and soap.

'What is it?' I say again, frightened.

He looks down at Margarethe. 'I omitted to wash my hands. I was so keen to give you the good news. What if I…?'

Dorothea is there, a basin in one hand, a small bowl in the other, concern in her eyes too. The water is steaming, the smell of lye strong. Martin pushes his sleeves up and plunges his arms into the basin up to his elbows, scrubbing vigorously. I am rubbing at Margarethe's mouth with a moistened rag, but she screws up her face and presses her lips together and turns her head away. I turn it back and imprison it with one hand and, when she opens her mouth to wail, slip a rag-wrapped finger inside and run it round the soft flesh. She protests even more, but I rinse and re-rinse the rag in the bowl and rub and rub until Dorothea gently takes her from me and hugs her close, shushing her.

'You have done all you can. Pray God no ill will come to her.'

For a week we all watch her closely, looking for any sign of fever, my prayers as repetitive as if I still used the rosary, my words a constant pleading refrain that God may spare her, and us. I do not know if I will be able to forgive Martin if she should die, and it is a shadow hovering between us, holding us apart. Each time he looks at me, I see the haunted expression in his eyes and know he tortures himself, but I cannot offer him any comfort, nor look to him to ease my pain.

It is Muhme Lena who first dares to suggest the child will be all right. 'I think our prayers are answered. She should have shown signs of fever by now if she had been infected.'

It is the release we all need, permission to smile again, to think of other things.

Martin comes to me, cups my face in his hands. 'I am sorry, Käthe, to have caused you such distress. I will not be so foolish again.'

I take a deep breath and reach up to touch his hand, my voice cracking as I attempt, 'I trust this hand is washed?' It is a poor jest, but he recognises it as such, his answering smile tentative.

'I am forgiven?'

I should say, 'there is nothing to forgive', but I have not reached that point yet, and make do with a nod and a squeeze of his hand. It seems sufficient for him, for his shoulders relax. It is much later when I remember the cause of his carelessness and ask, 'What was the news you were bringing?'

'It is old news, now, and for that I am also sorry. Your brother, Hans, has returned from Prussia and is working…'

'Here? In Wittenberg?'

'Ah, no. He is managing the cloister of Saint George in Leipzig. And once this crisis is past, there will be no reason why he may not come to visit.'

I sit down abruptly, my legs like jelly, memories washing over me like a flood. Hans leading me to the pasture to show me the newborn foal. Hans helping me to spell out the catechism. Hans showing me where to find the choicest brambles, the whitest mushrooms. Hans picking me up when I fell, dusting the dirt from my skirts. And, most of all, Hans protecting me from Klement's cruel teasing. I look up.

'That is the best of news. I hope he will not be long in coming.' But afterwards I worry away at the thought he will have changed, as I have, and perhaps both of us, beyond recognition. I share my fears with Barbara. 'Thirty years … it is such a long time. We may no longer have anything to say to one another. What if the affection we once shared is gone?'

As usual, it is her common sense that sets my mind at rest. 'If it was, he would not have taken the trouble to send word of his new appointment. It's likely if the plague

270

was not here he would already have come. But it would be a foolish person indeed who would visit Wittenberg just now.'

'Pray God it is over soon.'

'Amen to that.'

we and those we could help ... have spared her. It would
be a foolish person indeed who would visit Wittenberg
just now.'

'Perhaps it is over soon.'

'As God wills.'

Chapter Twenty-Seven
Wittenberg, November 1535

Summer slips into autumn, the cooler temperatures
bringing relief from the intense heat of August and from
the plague. We have lost no one in the Lutherhaus and
for that we are all grateful, but as one trouble diminishes,
another takes its place. Münster may be back in the
hands of the proper authorities and Leiden dead, but the
Anabaptists are not defeated. A flurry of pamphlets are
written in an attempt to counter the heresy, and Martin is
asked to write prefaces to many of them.

'I know his name will lend credence to them, but is
it really necessary?' I ask Justus, when he calls with an
invitation to supper from Kath.

He looks uncomfortable, and I suspect he is fobbing
me off when he says, 'They seek Martin's endorsement
and Cranach's printing, for they are both good publicity
and will ensure a wide circulation.'

When Martin comes in, I pass on the invitation and, as
he makes himself ready, question him also. He pauses in
buttoning up his shirt, as if he is unsure whether or not to
answer, then sighs.

272

'I am writing the prefaces, Käthe, because this heresy threatens me directly.'

I was not expecting this. 'How?'

'Many of the Anabaptists once followed my reforms. There are those who claim I am therefore responsible for the extremes to which they have taken them.'

'That is unfair!'

'Unfair, maybe, but it is the case nonetheless.'

'What have you said in reply?'

'As Jesus was not the Devil because Judas was a traitor, neither is Martin Luther the Devil because early sympathisers are now heretics.'

It is the first time in almost a year I have heard him speak in the pithy style of the Luther of our early acquaintance, and it seems to take years off him. I find it unsettling that though I have spent ten years trying to moderate his outbursts, in some ways I have missed the firebrand Luther I married.

We are sitting after supper, Martin and Justus having disappeared into Justus' study, when I say so.

Kath laughs. 'You cannot have it both ways, Kat.' There is a teasing note in her voice. 'Of course, it may just be he is mellowing with age and he may be a veritable pussycat before long.'

That conjures up an image so ridiculous we both dissolve into laughter. We are still laughing when Martin and Justus look across as they reappear.

What's so funny?' Martin says.

'Nothing,' we say, simultaneously, and it starts us off again.

'Perhaps if we go out and come in again, we will be met with more sobriety?'

'Perhaps,' I say, still choking. 'Or perhaps not.'

Whether it is his outspoken and robust defence, or the content of the pamphlets themselves, I don't know, but the circulation is widespread, though their effect on the general populace is harder to gauge. There is one consequence, however, and it shows me a facet of Martin's character I would never have dreamt of. It is November, the air with a bite to it nipping my face as I head to the market square. For several years now I have been able to walk about in Wittenberg without constantly feeling the pressure of eyes boring into my back and the sense I am the subject of gossip and criticism; of conversations nipped off as I pass. There are still those who will never forget my origins, those who feel the stigma of the renunciation of my vows as something that should dog me to my dying day. But they are a minority, and I have learnt not to be concerned by them. Today is different. Once again I am aware of sidelong glances, of whispers behind hands, and my first thought is – what has Martin done now?

But when I return to the Lutherhaus, far from any sign of trouble there is an air of excitement. Even Dorothea, usually so phlegmatic, is flustered, preparations for the meal forgotten as she stands over the simmering copper, prodding away. It is not the normal washing day, or time, and I pause in the doorway. 'What...?' Magdalena skips around me, her plaits flying, singing a made-up song to herself, which makes little sense to me. I catch hold of her. 'What about Vati and a barber?'

She hops from foot to foot and tugs at my hand. 'Come

and see!'

We meet Hans on the stairs.

'What *is* going on?' I say again.

He rolls his eyes and makes a throat-cutting motion and shudders. Magdalena tugs at me again. 'You'll miss it, if you don't come quickly. Vati is…' She claps her hand over her mouth. 'You'll see.'

Martin is sitting in our chamber, a towel pinned around his shoulders. His hair is damp, one side the usual: tousled and unruly, as if it hasn't been combed for a month, though I know it has. The barber is working on the other side, snipping away, hair falling onto the floor around him. He looks up as we enter, acknowledging me with a nod.

'Frau Luther. You will scarce know your husband when I have finished with him.'

That much is obvious, but it's the reason for it that concerns me.

Martin turns his head and is rewarded by a sharp, 'Sit still, if you do not want to lose an ear.'

He pulls a comic face and winks at me. 'How will you like your new neat husband?' he says.

'No idea,' I say, 'until I know why.'

'For shame,' he says, and I hear the underlying laughter in his voice. 'You have spent years brushing and tugging and straightening me. Mending my stockings, chastising me for every little tear. Polishing my boots to within an inch of their life. And now, when I am tidying myself up, you aren't sure if you'll like it?' He half turns his head again and yelps as the barber nicks his ear.

'I told you to sit still.'

There are few people who can address Martin in this fashion, and I find myself taking to the man. I affect my

275

most disinterested voice. 'If you will not tell me what the occasion is, I shall go away again and leave you to Herr…'

'Deller.' The barber nods again.

'Herr Deller's tender mercies.'

'You haven't heard then?' Martin risks turning his head.

'Of course not, or I wouldn't need to ask.'

'Wittenberg has a visitor. An important one.'

'Oh?'

'The papal envoy, Vergerio. And here to see me.'

A worm of fear crawls in my stomach. 'What does he want?'

'I won't know until I meet him.'

There is a time for teasing and it assuredly isn't now. For a moment I forget the barber's presence, but I manage to collect myself. 'Mar … Herr Doctor, please.'

'I believe he wants to entice me to Mantua, to attend a council there.' His tone is casual, as if it were an invitation to supper.

I draw in my breath sharply. 'You will not go?'

'To meet him? Yes. To Mantua? No. Or not unless they drag me there.'

The worm stirring in my stomach uncoils, becomes a snake, its head raised to strike. 'You don't think there's any fear of that?'

'Until I meet him, who knows? But request or order, I have no desire to attend and will do all in my power to resist.' He waves his arm at the barber, and at the chair, draped in his best robe, with his medallion of office as the Dean of the Faculty of Theology slung on top. 'Bugenhagen suggested it would not go amiss to take a little bit of trouble with my appearance. I hope he's right, else all this effort will have been for nothing.'

I focus on the practical to suppress my unease. 'When is the meeting to be?'

'In the forenoon. At the castle. We are invited for breakfast. Which will be just as well as I am like to starve tonight with all the prinking and preening that is required.'

I cannot help feeling glad I will not be expected to host the envoy, for he will undoubtedly know my history and as such is bound to disapprove. 'So that is why Dorothea is washing your linens instead of preparing the evening meal? I knew it had to be something of note to throw her from her usual routine. Oh...'

'What?'

'In town. Folk were staring and whispering as they did in the early days, and I feared...'

'What?' he says again.

'That *you* had done something for which I deserved sympathy.'

He chuckles. 'That isn't sufficiently out of the ordinary to be cause for gossip surely?'

The barber has finished and is removing the towel. He bows to me, and as he looks up I see the amusement in his eyes, and I pray he isn't one for idle chatter. 'Frau Luther. Herr Doctor Luther.'

Martin runs his hand round the neck of his shirt as if to dislodge any stray hairs and then scoops up Magdalena. 'What do you think of your Vati, Liebchen? Will I do?'

She tips her head back as if to consider, rubbing her hand along his jawline. 'Better,' she says. 'Not scratchy.'

I smile. 'What other preparations must be made?'

'Only a bath, that I may smell of roses, as likely he will.'

Bugenhagen brings a carriage, and though Martin doesn't smell of roses, he *would* pass for a courtier with his neat hair and clean-shaven face, his white shirt, with the carefully ironed pleats and the gold medallion glinting at his chest. I brush his best robe while he burnishes his boots himself, Magdalena hunkering beside us, pulling faces and trying to see her reflection in them.

She is wide-eyed, and Hans chokes back a snigger as Martin gives a mocking theatrical bow and steps into the carriage, yet, even as I frown at Hans, inwardly I cannot blame him. This new, polished Martin is so unlike himself as to be almost a stranger. And though I cannot deny he has spruced up well, I find myself, however illogical, regretting the transformation.

They return in high spirits. Bugenhagen stops in front of me and, sweeping his hat from his head, bows almost to the ground. A parody, I imagine, of the papal envoy.

'You should have seen it, Katharina. Vergerio was clearly expecting an uncouth, renegade priest, likely with visible horns. When Martin stepped from the carriage, he couldn't conceal his surprise. He was impressed with the appearance of our Doctor Luther and will no doubt take a good report back, in that regard at least.' He flicks his finger against Martin's medallion. 'I suspect he wouldn't have been averse to getting his hands on this to put around his own neck.'

'While I can't wait to get it off mine,' Martin says.

Tempting as it is to enjoy their exuberance, I ask, 'What of the reason for the meeting?'

Martin is dismissive. 'Ah, a failure in the envoy's terms, I believe. Though' – he makes a face, signifying irritation – 'I am not permitted to disclose what I said, but suffice it, he is no nearer to persuading Germans to accept a council in Italy.' A pause. 'The Englishman, Barnes, was also invited. I found him a disagreeable man.'

– Perhaps clothes do affect feelings and how one reacts, as Elsa Reichenbach once said, for this is a Martin surprisingly moderate in his criticism.

'Who is Barnes? And why is he here?'

'He is but a forerunner. To prepare the ground. A delegation is to follow, for the English king seeks to join the Schmalkald League … for his own ends of course.'

I skirt around what King Henry once said of me, for I have no wish to raise those memories, concentrate instead on theology. 'But didn't he write virulently against you and your reforms?'

'Indeed.'

It is clear Martin is also remembering Henry's vitriol regarding our marriage, but unlike me he tackles it head on.

'What he falsely accused me of, he is now guilty of himself. His supposed espousal of the Reformation, some two years since, was but a means to divorce his lawful wife and wed his whore.'

I flush, and belatedly it seems he notices my discomfort. 'I'm sorry, Käthe, I didn't think.'

Bugenhagen rescues me from the need to reply, by making a jest of it. 'You, speaking without thought, Martin? I suspect Katharina is well used to that.'

'Yes. Well, at any rate, when the delegation arrives no doubt we will have to suffer endless disputes and debates, for I am not at all sure Henry's theology matches his desire to break from the Catholic Church.'

Relieved the conversation has moved onto safer ground, but puzzled nonetheless, I ask, 'Why here? Why not at Schmalkald itself? Surely the League and those who join it are forming a political alliance?'

'Politics and religion cannot be untangled. The evidence is all around us. We are tasked with sorting out the religious differences, that the political alliance may follow. Not a task I relish.' Martin sighs. 'I have had my fill of wrangling.'

A new Martin, indeed, I think … or an aging one, for he has never before shied away from argument. It is an uncomfortable thought, and one I seek to bury.

The English delegation have been here since December, the cost of entertaining them a drain on the elector. It seems an English bishop, whether leaning towards reformed doctrine or not, still expects to be looked after like a king, his entourage likewise. We do not offer any hospitality at the Lutherhaus, for we are still in debt ourselves to the tune of nearly four hundred and fifty gulden despite all my efforts to economise, though the image of Magdalena positioning herself in front of Bishop Foxe and pronouncing on his appearance is an amusing one.

Martin, who argues for restraint when I wish to invest in more land, is ever ready to give to anyone who asks. Although the individual gifts are small, taken together they are a significant drain on our resources. But when I remonstrate with him, his answer is, 'God put fingers on our hands for money to slide through, so He can give us more.'

I wish I had his confidence. The talks themselves, delayed until January to allow Melanchthon to be recalled from Jena, where the university has once more taken refuge, are in full swing, but according to Martin they are producing nothing but hot air. Night after night he returns home discouraged and grumpy. He chides the children when there is no need, glares at anyone who gets in his way, regardless of intention, and his conversation at the meal table is little more than a series of grunts. At Table Talk too, he is his most acerbic, and though I think it unlikely, I hope those who take notes of all that is said may edit them carefully.

At first I think his mood is simply a reaction to the lengthy and apparently fruitless discussions, and determine to tackle him about his demeanour, but before I have opportunity I see other, more worrying signs. The wedding of the elector's son, which should have been a happy interlude to relieve the tedium of the talks, is a fiasco, Martin suffering a dizzy spell and unable to complete the ceremony. We return home in the elector's carriage and I help him to our chamber, despite his protests that there is no need to fuss.

'It is an old enemy. A day or two in bed and it will be defeated. You'll see. By next week I shall have no more excuse to absent myself from the interminable wranglings of Foxe and his archdeacon … More's the pity.'

Fully recovered or not, he returns to what he has dubbed the talking shop and the discussions begin again. But by the beginning of March, when they have been going at it hammer and tongs for two months, and it finally seems some progress is being made, Martin is suffering again and this time it is more serious. For more than a month he can scarcely rise from his bed, reserving all his energies for struggling up to use the chamber pot, set behind a screen in the corner.

The talks he once thought tedious, he now misses, and asks Melanchthon to report daily on any progress.

'Is there any progress?' I ask, when, one evening, Melanchthon arrives to find Martin already asleep.

'Surprisingly there is. We hope to have a set of Latin statements on which we are all agreed before the delegation departs.'

'They are definitely leaving?'

'Oh, yes. Leaving Wittenberg at least, though not Saxony. They will attend a meeting of the League, now that there is sufficient common ground.'

'When will they be gone?'

'A week or two, three at the most.'

I look across at Martin lying with his head extended back and his mouth hanging slack, his snoring fit to wake the dead. 'It would have been a fine thing if he could have been there to see a resolution, but if it is to be so soon, I think it unlikely.'

'I have to agree.' Melanchthon reaches out his hand and touches my shoulder. The gesture is so unlike him that, though he clearly meant it as a comfort, the effect is quite the opposite, a chill sweeping through me.

'You think he might die?' I don't intend it to be an accusation, but so it sounds.

'I think,' he says, studying his hands, 'you should be prepared.'

Martin doesn't die, but it is a close-run thing. Day after day, week after week, as he drifts in and out of sleep, I sit at his bed and pray he will not be taken from me, that the children will not be left fatherless. Eva's words 'an *old* good man' run through my mind, a constant and frightening refrain. Dorothea and Muhme Lena take their turn, and between us he is never left alone, for I could not forgive myself if he should slip away with no one to note his passing.

The cherry trees are in blossom, the petals blowing about in the wind swirling around the Lutherhaus garden, when I hear him say my name. I have not cried since he became ill, but now I am undone by the weakness in his voice.

I slip to my knees beside the bed and, grasping his hand, rest my head on the coverlet, to hide the tears trickling down my cheeks. 'I'm here.'

His recovery, once begun, is swift, though I am convinced a weakness remains and am *not* happy when he insists on travelling the thirty-three miles to Eilenburg to preside at Caspar Cruciger's second marriage.

'It is no distance,' he says, 'and I'm not thinking of riding, which, though tiring, would likely be more comfortable than the shaking I shall suffer sitting in the cart. He is my good friend and I am honoured to be asked.'

When I don't reply, he lifts my chin and forces me to look at him. His tone is gentle, but his sentiment firm, the words so close an echo of my own thought, there is nothing I can say.

'You are thinking of Elizabeth Cruciger, and understandably, for she was your good friend. But she is not rendered any more dead by Caspar's remarriage than she was the day we buried her, and those children need a mother.'

He is right about Elizabeth, but I am right about his

lack of stamina, the journey to Eilenburg setting him back, rendering him too weak to travel to Eisenach to a planned meeting with Bucer to discuss the Lord's Supper. He sends a message asking for a week's delay.

However tempting, I refrain from saying 'I told you so' and instead make a suggestion. 'Bucer has travelled from Strasbourg. What difference will a few extra miles make? Invite him here instead. It may not be neutral territory, but you have the excuse of your illness to justify it.'

I sense a reluctant admiration as he says, 'You would have made a good strategist, Käthe, a pity you are a woman.'

'A pity?' I say, smiling in return.

'Well, in that respect at least. In all others I am glad of it, though I hesitate to be maudlin.'

'I should hope so.' Dorothea is in the doorway, briskness oozing from every pore. 'Melanchthon and Bugenhagen are here, and to judge by their expressions, with important issues to discuss.'

Bugenhagen takes the lead. 'You are not strong yet, Martin. Perhaps we need more than a week's delay for this meeting…'

'Käthe suggests we hold it here. In Wittenberg.'

There is a moment's silence, broken by Melanchthon. He dips his head to me. 'Good idea. Jonas and Cruciger are likely already on their way to Eisenach, but I daresay they can be redirected en route.'

The discussions last a week and are more cordial than could have been anticipated, matched by the concord signed at the end. Martin bursts into the Stube, his face beaming, flourishing a scroll and accompanied by Justus Jonas. He unrolls it and reads aloud, 'Dear brethren in the

285

Lord…'

When he finishes, Justus says, 'There is to be a joint communion service before our brothers depart. A visible sign of unity that has been too long in coming.'

I want to ask 'Will it last?' but don't want to dent their pleasure.

Supper is a merry meal, the children taking advantage of Martin's renewed good humour to ignore Muhme Lena's attempts to get them to go to bed.

'Let them stay,' I say. 'This is an evening for celebration. Why should they not share in it?'

In the weeks that follow we have other causes for celebration, and an air of goodwill pervades the Lutherhaus. Having refused to go to the papal council, Elector Johann Frederick plans one of his own and asks Martin to draw up a list of topics for discussion. Martin is happy to be writing again and disappears into his study for hours on end, and when he emerges it is with a smile for everyone and a willingness to play with the children, which had been sorely missed during his periods of illness. It isn't just lists he compiles, but at odd hours I hear the strains of his lute and know he takes a break to write hymns. It isn't hard to encourage him to play and sing to us in the evenings after supper. Hans is already a fine singer, his treble strong and true, and listening to him I remember my own time at Brehna, and the ambition I had then to be a choir mistress. With Martin's tenor and my own soprano and the children clustered round my knee, even Young Martin able to hold a tune, I think we are set fair to have our own choir.

Whether it is as a reward for Martin's work on the council, or a result of the elector's generous spirit, Martin is given a fixed salary of three hundred gulden. I am delighted when the word comes, though I hope it won't mean any reduction in the other gifts that flow from the elector's hand, for substantial as three hundred is, it does not match our expenses and we need every supplement we can get.

When Johann Agricola is offered a professorship at the university, I hatch another plan. The whole family has come to stay for a few weeks until they find suitable accommodation within the town. I broach the matter with Else Agricola first. 'Why not stay here? There is plenty of space and the children will enjoy having company.' I see doubt in her face, and guessing at the cause, add, 'You would be doing us a favour, for you would be able to contribute to the household in a way many cannot.'

'If you're sure?'

'Of course. It will be like old times, only better, for this time you will not be here because you are ill and require care, but rather to enjoy fellowship and each other's company. And it will be fine for Martin to have another professor under our roof, for sometimes, between Dorothea and Muhme Lena and me, I think he suffers from a sense of "petticoat rule".'

She laughs. 'I don't see Herr Doctor Luther suffering any kind of rule but his own.'

'Prepare to be surprised. For Martin the husband is a very different character from Herr Doctor Luther the preacher and teacher.'

She is surprised, and sometimes, when I catch her eye, we share a private moment of amusement. For a time, all is harmony, Martin and Johann bringing home debates from the university to carry them on at our table, but in the friendliest of terms, while Else and I take pleasure in our renewed friendship, deepening it daily. It is the calm before the storm, the weather kind, summer slipping almost imperceptibly towards autumn. The harvest is plentiful, the shelves in the storerooms groaning under the weight of cheeses and pickles and preserves. Bunches of herbs hang above the table in the kitchen and barrels of salt fish stand in the basement. Martin, straying into it one day when I am netting a ham to join the others already hanging from the hooks embedded in the ceiling, looks up, and though he smiles as he speaks, he betrays an element of concern.

'You will not overload the ceiling, I trust. We don't wish to risk another collapse.'

I tuck a stray strand of hair behind my ear and laugh. 'No fear of that. The lesson is learnt and this stonework is well made.'

The building and renovation works continue, taking advantage of the good weather, and once again I take pleasure in examining their progress of an evening, with Else accompanying me when Martin is otherwise engaged. Our new roof is nearly finished, the rows of neatly stacked slates almost gone, the heap of lime reduced to little more than the height of a dunghill.

'It will be good,' I say to Else, 'to be able to have the children playing in the garden without fearing they will reappear as snowmen, or worse.'

'I imagine it will be good to think your work here is finally at an end.'

'As to that' – I grimace – 'I suspect there will always be work, just not so extensive or a drain on our finances.'

'You don't regret it?'

'No! It has been ... is one of my pleasures to see this building brought back to life. But I fear sometimes I think more of the architecture than the people who live inside it.'

'It is a fine work you do, Kat, and without a building in a good state, none of that could happen.'

Aside from the improvements within the Lutherhaus, there is a new building under construction at the rear. Originally intended as a guest wing, I have new plans for it, but I don't intend to share them with anyone until it is ready. In a household as full as ours, where everyone knows each other's business, it is a pleasure to have a secret.

September comes upon us almost unnoticed, only a sharpness in the early morning air and the sparkle of dew on the grass in the Elbe meadow to indicate the changing season, and when the days begin to cool, I draw a sigh of relief that this year we have escaped the plague. Focused on all the blessings surrounding us, I fail to recognise the cloud, the size of a man's hand, on our horizon.

It is Magdalena who first draws our attention to the fact that Muhme Lena is ailing, and I cannot but feel guilty it took a child to notice what should have been obvious to me. I am in the brewhouse, drawing off the thin beer we reserve for the children, humming as I work, when Magdalena appears at my side, her mouth pulled down, her hands balled into fists. I try to unfurl them, but she resists. 'What is it, Lenchen?'

'Muhme Lena. She won't play chase with me.'

289

'Perhaps she's busy, poppet.'

'She isn't. She's lying down ... and the shutters are closed ... and when I went in she told me to go away ... and to shut the door to keep out the light. And...'

There is a chill in the pit of my stomach, and even as I wipe my hands and summon the boy, who has been mashing malt, to finish my task, I am thinking – what will we do without her? 'Go to Dorothea and tell her I sent you to get a comfit, for you are a good girl. Perhaps she may have a job for you only a clever child can do.'

When I enter the chamber Muhme Lena is lying on her back, her eyes shut, her breathing irregular. 'Please God,' I pray, 'let her not die. Not yet.' I'm not sure if she is sleeping and so step carefully to avoid the creaking floorboard stretching from the door to the bed, but she hears me anyway and opens her eyes.

'Katharina.' She sighs out my name, as if it takes every ounce of strength she has, and I think back over the last weeks and berate myself I saw no sign she ailed. I want to say 'We will take care of you and you will be well again in no time', but looking at the shadows under her eyes and the hollows in her cheeks I know it isn't true, and so don't know what to say. I lean over her and she reaches out to touch my face, to wipe away the tear trembling at the corner of my eye.

'Don't cry for me, Kat. I have had a good life, and these last ten years, living with you, have been the best of all.'

'How could I not see you were unwell?'

'I didn't want you to. This has been such a good summer, I didn't wish to blight it. And my prayer has been I would see autumn and the trees turning colour before I

290

go.'

'How long…?'

'Since Easter, when I felt the first discomfort. I knew something was wrong.'

I shift, about to protest, to ask why she didn't seek help, but she strokes my cheek.

'And before you say anything, I *did* consult the doctor, but I swore him to secrecy when he confirmed what I think I already knew. That there was nothing to be done.'

I am crying in earnest now, and she takes both my hands in hers, but her grip is weak. 'Don't let my last memory of you, Kat, be of your tears. I would far prefer it to be your smile that sends me to my final sleep.' She swallows, gathers her breath again. 'It was Lenchen told you, wasn't it? I did not mean to speak harshly to her. Sometimes the pain…' A spasm crosses her face. 'Will you help me, Kat? To die well? To show the children there is nothing to fear in this last journey. That I am going to God, and his arms are open to welcome me.'

'What must I do?' I whisper.

'There will be times when I cannot bear the pain. Keep the children away at those times, and bring them to me only when I can smile.' She pauses. 'The doctor has promised powders to give a measure of relief, and rest assured, Kat, I will take all he gives, but I will need your strength too, for I do not think I am brave enough to face this any other way.'

'Don't say that. You have been brave for months since, and are still.'

'And for that, I have your husband to thank, for it is God's grace has brought me thus far. And God's grace, I pray, will take me home.'

291

She gets her wish, staying with us until the leaves have turned. We move her bed so she can look out across the Elbe to see the autumn colours: the golds and bronzes and rich deep reds, the leaves twisting and turning as they drift down. And when the branches are bare, she says, 'Bring them all in. It is time for my goodbye.'

We are gathered around her bed, Martin by my side, Hans standing poker-straight, his mouth clenched, Magdalena holding my hand so tight it hurts, and Young Martin and Paul clinging to my skirts. Dorothea, her mouth working, is holding Margarethe in her arms.

At the last, Muhme Lena looks up, past us all, her face alight, and reaches up with both arms as if to greet someone, before her hands drop.

Magdalena is tugging at my hand, her voice puzzled. 'Who did she want to hug, Mutti?'

Martin answers for me. 'It was our Lord, Lenchen, welcoming her home.'

I lean over to close her eyelids and fold her hands across her chest. Martin drops to his knees and we all follow suit, his prayer one of thanksgiving for a life well spent. His words echo in the silence, and I bow my head as if to share them, but inside I am crying out, 'How will I manage without her?'

Muhme Lena's is not the only death. And the next, though it happens far away and to someone we have never met, touches Martin deeply. I had heard of William Tyndale of course, for when word came he was in Hamburg and working on a Bible translation based directly on the original Hebrew and Greek texts, Martin was jubilant.

'The word is spreading, God be praised. And we may take pride Tyndale has gained sanctuary in our country.'

I am confused. 'But his is not the first English Bible, surely?'

'That honour belongs to Wycliffe, who was burnt at the stake for his pains, and the penalty still applies to anyone found in possession of a copy. Not that there are many to be found, for without the printing press, it was easy to suppress them. This time it will be a very different story.'

News of his progress trickles back from time to time, and always to Martin's satisfaction. Tyndale's New Testament is finished. He has begun work on the Old.

Martin's optimism increases when we hear the English king has chosen to use a pamphlet of Tyndale's to justify his break with the Catholic Church. 'Not,' he says, 'that I have much truck with Henry, but if it allows Tyndale back to England, it may be for the greater good.'

The next news is less good. Tyndale is imprisoned in Vilvoorde in Belgium and like to be tried for heresy.

I wonder what he was doing there, but don't ask, for the injustice so incenses Martin, I fear mention of it might lead to an apoplexy. Word reaches us in the middle of October. Tyndale is released, not to resume his place in this world, but into the next.

Dorothea ushers the messenger into the Stube. Martin strides up and down the chamber, his face increasingly flushed, the questions he fires at the man staccato. His responses to the answers equally explosive.

'Who is this Henry Phillips? Tyndale's *friend*?' He halts, thrusts his face into the messenger's, as if he holds him responsible. 'God in heaven, who needs enemies? There is no justice if this Phillips does not rot in the hottest fires in hell.'

The messenger takes a step back.

Forgetting convention, and my normal mode of address in front of all but our closest friends, I reach out. 'Martin…'

He half turns, his gaze unfocused, as if he doesn't recognise me, and pushing away my arm he turns back and grasps hold of the messenger by the shirt. There is both anguish and uncertainty in his voice. 'Did Tyndale die well?'

'Martin!' I say again.

The messenger puts his hand to his throat, tries to loosen Martin's hold, to give himself room to breathe. He stutters out, 'His d-dying p-prayer was for the E-English

294

k-king, that his e-eyes would be op-opened to the t-truth of the G-Gospel, and his p-people might be a-allowed to have God's w-word for th-themselves.'

Martin releases him, stumbles backwards and collapses onto a chair. The colour is fading from his face, his breathing slowing. 'How was he killed?'

'S-Strangled and b-burnt.' The messenger takes another step back, as if he fears to be grasped again. 'Th-They s-say he was d-dead before the f-fire t-took.'

Martin studies his feet, as if he imagines flames licking around them, an infinite sadness in his voice. 'One blessing then.'

I take advantage of the momentary silence and lead the messenger towards the door, motioning to Dorothea to follow. 'You must be tired and hungry. Dorothea will take you to the kitchens and make sure you are well cared for.' And though I don't mean it, I force myself to add, 'Thank you, for bringing us word.'

Martin retreats into his study again, rising earlier and working late, as if Tyndale's death is driving him to greater efforts on the Schmalkald Articles he prepares for the elector. He burns candle after candle down to a stump, and I fear he will do more damage to his sight in the process. When I remonstrate, he reacts angrily.

'I must work, for there is a time coming when no man can work.'

'Maybe we *are* in the last days.' I strive to sound reasonable. 'But if we are, then as Justus Jonas says, we must carry on, living a good life, not grinding ourselves

295

down.' I rest my hand on his arm, risk, 'What use will you be if you work yourself into the grave?'

His laugh is harsh. 'What use will I be if I take my ease? It is little enough I can do. But what I can, I must.'

Barbara, when I meet her in the market square, is sympathetic, but counsels, 'Give him time. This death has hit him hard.'

'Why should this one be more difficult than any other? We didn't know the man.' I answer my own question with another. 'Because it was for translating the Bible Tyndale is martyred?'

Barbara's answer startles me. 'Perhaps because Martin is not.'

'I don't understand.'

'He is alive and Tyndale dead. And that, in Martin's book, may prove a lack of worthiness on his part.'

The square around me begins to tip and tilt, her voice coming from far away. Her hand is grasping my elbow and holding me upright, and after a few moments the world rights itself.

Barbara's grip loosens, but she doesn't let go. 'Steady. I didn't intend to make you faint.' She glances at my stomach.

'No,' I say, 'I'm not pregnant... How can he even think he's not worthy? If Martin Luther is not, who is?'

'You know that, Kat. I know it. But despite Martin's bombast, you of all people must know his greatest fear, ridiculous as it may seem to us, is that he will not be found worthy. How many times have we heard him say God honours those who have honoured Him most, and martyrdom the clearest sign of his approval.'

'I have always thought that a foolishness. And besides,

Tyndale's work was unfinished. How does…?'

The answer comes from behind me. 'In our eyes, yes. But in God's? Who are we to determine the worth of any man's work?'

I swing round to see Bugenhagen at my shoulder, the sudden movement causing me to stagger again, Barbara renewing her grip on my arm.

He is apologetic. 'I didn't mean to startle you.' He nods to Barbara, as if seeking her approval, turns back to me. 'If you're heading home, Katharina, I will walk with you.'

I give Barbara a quick hug, and turn towards the Collegienstrasse, taking his proffered arm. As we walk, I ask, 'How can we know if a man's work is finished? Or if he pushes himself too hard and for too long?'

'Martin?'

'Yes.'

'I suspect he will always push himself beyond what God requires of him. Our job is to seek to moderate him.' His face crinkles into a smile. 'In all things.'

It isn't enough. Not Bugenhagen's initial exhortations, nor Melanchthon's gloomy predictions of the effect of such diligent effort on Martin's health, nor my pleading. In the middle of December gales buffet the Lutherhaus, the roof timbers creaking, so that I fear it will lift altogether, destroying all our good work. And as if we do not have enough to concern us, Martin is struck down with chest pains so severe he cannot write. I send for Bugenhagen, confident he will support me in making Martin rest.

Instead, he refuses to meet my eye. 'Time is short, Katharina, the articles must be ready for the end of the month. We will get Martin a scribe. It will be less taxing for him.' He rests his hand on the pile of papers already on the table, as if to give weight to his argument, and attempts to make a jest. 'You know words avalanche from him when he has a specific task in hand. If we force him to keep them in, his head may burst.'

It draws a smile, as I suspect he hoped it would, but it doesn't deflect me from seeking to extract a promise from Martin. 'When this is done, you will take some rest?'

'Of course,' he says.

He doesn't convince me, but I fix my sights on calling in the promise when the time is right.

'Depend upon it, I *will* insist,' I say.

When I tell Barbara what I have said she raises her eyebrows, the action more eloquent than words could ever be.

◯◯◇◇◇◯◯

The articles are finished and Lucas Cranach has printed off copies to be circulated among all the proposed signatories. Martin is up and about, but far from strong.

'Remember what you said, Martin. Now is the time for rest.'

He looks at me in astonishment. 'You must have known, Käthe, that we are all to go to Torgau, for the articles to be signed in the presence of the elector' – and with a slight hesitation and a shamefaced glance – 'en route for Schmalkald.'

'You have written the articles. Is that not enough? You

are surely not thinking of going yourself?' I wave towards the stove. 'Look at you. Sit any closer and you'll be inside it. Be sensible, Martin. You are not well enough.'

He shifts his chair back. 'I must go.' And then, as if he has some small recollection of the promise he made, 'But not for a week or so yet. Ample time for me to regain my strength. And when we reach Torgau, there will be time for rest there also.'

'But why are you needed?'

'That I may defend my position. Explain more fully to any that have not the learning or capacity to understand for themselves. Being born a prince does not guarantee intellectual ability … indeed' – he grimaces – 'often quite the reverse.'

He shuts his eyes, as effective a way of closing the conversation as any. For if I am trying to convince him to take some rest, I can hardly disturb him when he apparently follows my suggestion.

I write to Eva. She is far enough away that what I say will not come back to bite me.

I might as well spit as try to get Martin to slow down and think of himself. Of his health. Of me and the children. If he were not so well made, I fear he would wear himself to a shadow.

I pause the pen, amused despite myself at the picture I paint, then stoke up my indignation again and continue.

I am supposed to be able to handle him. Or so Barbara says. And sometimes I can. But not always. And not in this. There is not one of his closest friends who seeks to dissuade him. I wish someone would take him to task. If Argula Grumbach was here she would not hesitate to speak out.

299

I pause again, acknowledging the irony, for when she sent advice to me on the weaning of Magdalena, I was not disposed to accept it.

I fear for him, Eva. But he laughs at my fears and is determined to go ... If nothing else I wish I could accompany him, for at least then I could be confident he would not have to sleep in a damp (or worse) bed, nor be fed rancid food. In a real war I could take my chances as a camp follower, but in this war of words I am debarred.

When the letter is dispatched, I suffer a qualm of conscience, aware of more than a hint of disloyalty in what I have written, but what's done is done. And whatever the distance between us, Eva is still the person who understands me most and will judge me least.

If I expected Martin to truly spend the last days before their departure resting, I am disappointed, for it seems there is to be a last minute addition to the articles. I am interested, despite myself, and surprised Martin is prepared to countenance it. I cannot resist questioning him. 'Allow the Pope precedence over other bishops? Surely that goes against everything you stand for?'

He is unusually tentative, and even as I listen to him I am thinking – this isn't Martin speaking.

'This Pope is not the venal fiend of the past. His doctrine is wrong, but his heart may yet be touched. And the precedence is conditional. He must first recognise the gospel. I once said the Pope, any Pope, is but the bishop of Rome, and I stand by that. But just as there is seniority in practice, if not in name, between pastors, so, if we allow bishops at all, as it seems we must, it may be so with them also.' His tone becomes confidential. 'To be truthful, Käthe, I do not think it likely we *will* have to

300

bow to him, but it gives the appearance of a desire to be conciliatory, *and* keeps dear brother Philipp happy.'

'Oh, of course,' I say, 'I might have guessed *you* would not be the strategist.'

That brings a grin to his face, and for the first time since he became ill, we are at ease with each other again.

'I wish…' I begin,

'That you could accompany us? I know. And if it were possible I would wish it too. For it will be a spectacle. And one I think you would enjoy.' A teasing note creeps into his voice. 'And as a *von* Bora, more fitted to the company than I.'

It is a rare reference to my background, an acknowledgement that, whatever folk may say or think, I was not some nobody elevated by my marriage, but entitled to a status in my own right. And though pride is a sin, I take some pleasure in it.

He continues, 'If it goes on for a long time, it will be a burden on the folk of Schmalkald. Our elector is likely grateful Count Philip has chosen to host the League. For to feed and accommodate perhaps six hundred visitors at once will be no mean task. Though it's likely the nobility will bring their own cooks, and it's only we poor theologians that will have to rely on the town.' He grins again. 'I give you my word I shall take every invitation that comes my way to dine with princes, and if I have not the leisure to write, when we return I will make time to bore you with every detail.'

'That,' I say, 'is a promise I will hold you to.'

It is with a lighter heart I see medicines are packed, and a sheet from the Lutherhaus.

'Really?' Barbara says.

I have an answer ready and one that makes both of us laugh. 'He may have been used to a flea-ridden mattress once, but those days are long gone.'

Torgau: November 1552

When I open my eyes it is dark, and I listen to hear if there is any movement downstairs, for if it is silent, I will know it is still the middle of the night. I have never lost the habit of waking early, winter or summer, and lately have struggled to sleep more than an hour or two at a time. There is a scuttling sound in the corner: I must remember to ask Paul to set a trap, for I have a fear of a mouse running across the bed when I am asleep, or perhaps burrowing under the covers and biting my toe. I do not like mice in the house, for they are dirty creatures. Martin never minded, but then, he is a man and had lived so many years in the company of men and with more lax standards of cleanliness than I demanded. I smile now at the memory of his face when I first tackled him about the state of the Black Cloister, how he seemed genuinely surprised that I should protest so. He soon learnt.

A pity he didn't capitulate so readily on every issue. We had so many discussions, and I take pride I won more than I lost, but not where his calling was concerned. In that, he wouldn't be shifted. He used to say, 'In the house I bow to Käthe, in everything else I bow to the Holy Spirit.'

'High praise,' Barbara said, 'if a mite ill-advised.'

She was right, for it brought me much condemnation. The door is ajar, and in the grey half-light I see him standing, his back to the stove, his face turned towards me. 'There have been times,' I say aloud, 'when I wish you could be more flexible, Martin, more willing to listen to reason.'

'Am I not always willing to listen?' There is an almost

303

childlike surprise in his voice.

'Ask Barbara,' I say. 'Or Lucas. Or Melanchthon, even. When your mind is made up, there is no shaking you.'

'Would you wish me to be other than I am?'

'Sometimes,' I say, 'if I'm honest, especially when I think your own inclination matches the elector's requests. To go to Schmalkald for example, even though you were not fit.'

CHAPTER THIRTY
WITTENBERG, JANUARY 1537

They are in good spirits as they gather at the entrance to the Lutherhaus ready to depart, the mood of camaraderie and relish in the trip ahead obvious in all. Despite that it is the middle of winter, it is perfect weather for travelling, with a cloudless sky and only the lightest of breezes stirring the branches in the trees separating our garden from the one next door. There is no more than a nip in the air, though there have been moments in the last week when I wished for snow to sweep in from the east and carpet the streets in drifts ten feet deep, so that no one could get as far as the market square, far less a day's travel. Now the time has come, I am glad the ride to Torgau will be as swift and straightforward as it could possibly be, for whatever Martin claims, he is not fit, and I cannot help but fear the journeying may be too much for him.

Yesterday I said as much to Barbara as I stood in line waiting to buy new buckles for his shoes and was rewarded by overhearing two matrons standing behind us, clearly listening in.

'What did she expect, marrying a man so much older

than herself?'

'What else could she do, after Baumgartner threw her over? I daresay no one younger would have her.'

Barbara had mouthed, 'Ignore them.' And when we halted outside her house, before I made for home, she said, 'There will always be folk ready to criticise and to remember your past; and not to your advantage. But you must not allow them to upset you. You are worth ten of them.'

'I knew when I married him he thought nothing of himself or his own comfort, and indeed admired his selflessness. I learnt to relish the small victories of ensuring he has good food and clean clothes and a house and bed vermin-free.'

She laughed. 'And that was no mean feat.'

'Most of all, I learnt to be proud he proved himself willing to discuss spiritual matters with me, albeit in the privacy of our chamber. But his recurring ill health is a worry, a constant niggle I find impossible to ignore. And increasingly, Eva's phrase "He is a good *old* man" comes back to haunt me.'

'Young or old, all any of us can do, Kat, is live for the day.'

Now as we wait, her last words are ringing in my ear, but they don't bring me the comfort I imagine she intended.

Dorothea and I stand by the gateway, along with Katharina Melanchthon, Kath Jonas and Else Agricola, surrounded by an assortment of children who, having absorbed the air of excitement, are fidgeting, unable to stay still.

'Is it far to Torgau?' Magdalena tugs at my arm. 'Will

Vati be there for dinner time?'

'Not too far, poppet. Not in time for dinner, but certainly supper.'

She gives a little hop and a skip, and accidentally bumps into one of Martin's great-nieces and they both fall over. The little one opens her mouth to wail, and I pick her up and dust her down and hug her to me, Magdalena patting her hair and saying, 'Sorry, sorry.' She pulls a face, as contorted as the gargoyles in the Town Church, and successfully diverts the wail into a giggle.

Else nods at me over Magdalena's head. 'She is kind at heart, that one, and will be a credit to you one day.'

Even as I smile back, a sense of loss sweeps over me. Else reaches out to touch my hand.

'You miss Lena?'

'Sometimes the littlest things remind me of what we have lost.'

All along both sides of the street townsfolk have gathered to see the delegation leave, the chatter ebbing and flowing in waves like an outgoing tide. I look along the Collegienstrasse, searching for a sign of the Cranachs, their absence worrying.

Else touches my arm again. 'Something must have delayed Lucas and Barbara, but they *will* come.'

'I know… it's just…'

'They will be in time. They always are.'

She's right about that too, for punctuality is one of Lucas' watchwords. He is used to meeting deadlines, for printing and for his art commissions. He would be out of business otherwise. As if she has conjured them up, I see them hurrying around a group of matrons who have spilled onto the centre of the street. Lucas is striding out,

307

Barbara half running by his side, taking two steps to his one, their children ahead of them. As they push their way through to us, Barbara says, 'There was no fear of us missing this, but there was a spill of ink that needed to be sorted before Lucas could leave the apprentice to work on his own.' She makes a face. 'He is not the sharpest quill in the pot, but Lucas wants to give him a chance. It is to be hoped the philanthropy doesn't cost us dear.'

There is one of those momentary silences that happens in any crowd, a single conversation adrift within it.

'All of them away at once. It is not well done.'

'They are at the elector's command. What else can they do?'

'Well, I for one don't hold out much hope of a sermon worth listening to until their return.'

An answering laugh. 'Since when are you a judge of a good sermon? You sleep through them all.' A third voice. 'Aye and snore betimes too.'

On one side of me Kath Jonas' shoulders start to shake, while Barbara turns a snort into a cough. Only Else seems to share my unease as I look around, seeking, but failing, to find the source.

'It is a sobering thought that eight of our theologians are gone at once. If anything should befall them it would be a serious, perhaps irreparable loss.'

Kath, perhaps because she has no wish to dispel the almost holiday atmosphere, is firm. 'There will be little to fear in a group of that size. And no one in the territory they must cross to get to Schmalkald to wish them ill.'

There is a rattle on the cobbles, and the cart they've been waiting for pulls up. Mindful of the onlookers, we are all circumspect in our farewells, and I wish I had taken

308

time in private to wrap my arms around Martin and hold him tight, for, at this last moment, the fear I might never see him again sears a path through my brain.

Word comes from Torgau. The humorous tone of his letter encouraging.

We have had a light snowfall, sufficient only to dust the castle in a coating of sugar, so you have no need to fear we will be stuck here for the winter. We leave at the end of the month, and in the meantime, as I promised, plenty of time to rest. It will take only a week to get to Schmalkald. You may pray the inns along the way will be clean and comfortable, but if we must share with other, less welcome guests, I shall be the envy of everyone, with your sheet to protect me. In the meantime, the hospitality here is good and we feast like kings, so I shall be back to my ample self in no time. The bears in the pit under the bridge are at their most entertaining as they scuffle about in the snow. Which is just as well, for we have not been offered any other diversion.

I imagine him pausing, a flicker of amusement on his face.

You need not concern yourself that I will be worn out dancing with court ladies, for such fripperies seem far from the elector's mind. As for our purpose in coming here: the articles are signed and I am ready to defend them with my life.

That last phrase is struck through, though I can still read it, and under it he has written, *But I should not jest, for there will be no need for that – we will be among friends.*

We wives are gathered in the Stube, to encourage each other with news.

Kath Jonas is standing by the window. 'Of course they will be.'

'Not all of them.' Katharina Melanchthon is twisting a strand of hair escaped from her cap. 'I imagine the observers sent by the emperor and the Pope have interests other than ours at heart.'

Kath remains confident, Else and Walpurga nodding their agreement. 'They will be greatly outnumbered, and that they are there at all surely suggests a desire for compromise?'

'Perhaps,' Katharina says, but I notice the tremor of her hand and wonder what it is she knows but has chosen not to share.

I don't have long to wait to find out, for several letters come from Schmalkald in quick succession. The first is typical of Martin: a pithy account of his accommodation.

...large, unheated, and on the second floor ... my strength will increase daily with all the exercise I'm getting ... if I do not freeze to death in the night...

Of his host.

...a financial officer to the House of Hesse ... who could perhaps give me some advice on how to make one hundred gulden stretch to two ... which would no doubt please you...

And finally, of the acoustics of the church.

...they prevailed upon me to preach on Sunday forenoon, and I was, of course, happy to oblige. Until I heard myself. The building is so ill designed the assembled company were not treated to 'Martin Luther the lion', as

*they had expected, but rather 'Luther the shrew'. I shall
not preach there again.*

There is a small postscript, which I determine to take
at face value, for to do anything else would only increase
my worries.

*I have passed a small stone and bloody urine, but you
need not fear, for it came away without pain and indeed I
am the more comfortable for it now.*

The second letter is from Philipp Melanchthon.
Katharina brings it round and there is little unexpected
in it. Much drier than Martin's, it is a factual report of
the deliberations thus far. The League has had its first
meeting, perhaps fittingly in the courthouse, and has
reached a speedy decision: it will not send a delegation to
the Pope's council in Mantua. As she reads aloud, I sense
once again she holds something back, and though in these
last years we have found a level of friendship, I am not so
comfortable with her as to question her directly.

The third letter is again from Martin, and this time
as I read it, I imagine him pacing up and down, his face
flushed, his voice raised, his words intemperate.

*...Antagonism from our enemies I expected, but we
have a serpent in our midst... Melanchthon has taken it
upon himself to persuade Count Philip my articles are too
contentious, too polemical to be discussed in full session!
I do not know why I should have been brought here to be
set aside in this way. If they are not to be endorsed by the
League, I have wasted my time.*

'And risked his health in the process,' I say to Else and
Walpurga when I pass the letter over to them. 'No wonder
Katharina Melanchthon was uncomfortable. She must
have known before they left this was what her husband

311

intended. To sit here and say nothing…'

'Do not blame her, Kat. It would have been a disloyalty to Philipp to do anything else. And must have been hard for her.'

'Perhaps she would have been better to stay away.'

'And cut herself off from our friendship?' Walpurga's glance is shrewd. 'I know things have not always been easy between you, and the reason for it. But you of all people should understand what it is to suffer for your husband's actions. Do not condemn her to loneliness for the same cause.' She looks over the letter again. 'It is odd that Philipp should do such a thing, when they were apparently all agreed when they signed the articles at Torgau.'

'It is a stab in the back I suspect Martin will find hard to forgive. And for once I am in sympathy with him.' I take a deep breath. 'And I fear it may make him ill again.'

It is a fear quickly realised, Martin's next letter arriving the following day, and although he makes light of the situation, I quail at the news. He talks of sharp pains in his kidney and bladder and of passing another stone.

…uncomfortable as it has been, the biggest inconvenience is that, to my great regret, I have last evening had to turn down an invitation to dine with one of the nobles. A heavy blow, as the reputation of his cook is gossiped throughout the town, and his pastries, and in particular his songbird pie, are reputed to be legendary. Think of me, supping on a mash of bread and goat's milk, while that serpent, Melanchthon, and the others feast on fine wines and succulent meat and pastries that melt on the tongue. There is no need to fear for me, Käthe, for this will pass…

That brings a smile, for the pun is likely intentional.

...but you may weep for the lost opportunity and pray I will be able for dining out again soon. Else all the good work I did in eating my fill at Torgau may be undone and I fade to a shadow.

Else turns to me. 'If he can jest, then he is likely no worse than he claims. A plainer diet may be all that is needed to put him to rights again.'

'I hope so. I really hope so.'

CHAPTER THIRTY-ONE
WITTENBERG, FEBRUARY–MARCH 1537

It is Paul who comes running into the brewery and skids to a halt beside the largest of the vats. 'Mutti! Mutti! Dottie says come quick. You have a visitor. With a message from our elector.'

I feel my legs give way beneath me and lean against the vat. If Johann Frederick is writing to me, it is most definitely *not* good news.

Paul is dragging on my arm, the excitement in his face fading, a wobble in his voice. 'Mutti?'

I straighten and summon a smile. 'I'm coming.'

A stable boy is leading a handsome bay across the courtyard, and it shies as we come close, sidestepping, its nostrils flaring. Paul leans into me. Inside, I think – a mettlesome beast and needing some handling – this is no ordinary messenger. To Paul I say, 'It means no harm. Horses are like us, sometimes nervous of people it doesn't know.' We give it a wide berth, and as we dip through the door, I look back to see it rear up, the boy struggling to regain control, and am glad we are safely past. I push Paul ahead of me, blocking his view, for it would not be helpful to encourage a fear of horses in him. My greeting for Dorothea is intentionally loud to deaden the clatter of hooves behind us.

The messenger is waiting in the Stube, his back to the stove, and he sweeps off his hat as I enter, his bow extravagant. His clothing is well cut, his cloak hanging open from a silver brooch on his shoulder, exposing a doublet embroidered in the blue and yellow of the House of Wettin. Clearly a young buck from the court, and likely as proud as his horse.

'Frau Luther.' He proffers a letter and I slip my finger under the seal, the wax lifting. It is brief and to the point, and I hold myself very stiff, not wishing for Paul to see me crumple.

It is with sadness I must tell you your husband is gravely ill. I suggest you come to Schmalkald with all speed.

I fold it up and mark the creases, to give time to compose myself.

He is regarding me with what looks like compassion in his eyes, and I think he must know the contents, confirmed as he says, 'The elector has sent orders for a carriage to be provided for you. The ostler at the castle has assured me it will be ready at first light.'

It is more than I could have expected, but serves to add to my chill. 'Thank you,' I say. 'If you would care for some refreshment while I write a reply?'

The messenger is no sooner away than another one appears, this time with a letter from Bugenhagen. He

315

is dishevelled from the ride, and it's clear he has made the best time possible and refrained from taking time to improve his appearance before calling on us, and I am doubly grateful. Though the tone of Bugenhagen's letter is also grave and gives more detail of Martin's condition, through it all I detect a desire to minimise the danger.

...You will have heard by now that Martin has been taken ill. It is his old enemy: trouble with his bladder, but accompanied this time with nausea, pain, and diarrhoea. Unsurprisingly, he is very weak and wishes to come home. The elector has provided a carriage and a wagon to accompany it, and rest assured the journey will be as comfortable as it can be. The wagon is equipped with medicines and a copper pan to hold heated bricks, so he will be kept warm, despite the season. He would already be on his way, except that Philipp M. is insisting the phase of the moon is unfavourable for travel.

I imagine Bugenhagen stabbing with the quill as he writes:

I would wish he did not have such an obsession with astrology, for it has proved inconvenient in the past and certainly is now. Apparently...

I can almost hear his exasperation, and I share it.

...in a week or ten days the stars will be better aligned and the journey accomplished more easily as a result.

Else is helping me pack. I throw back the lid of the box that will accompany me, banging it against the wall and leaving a dent in the plaster. 'I knew it was worse than Martin said.'

'He will be having the best of medical attention. The elector will see to that. And perhaps better than could be got here. If his return is delayed, you will likely be able to

316

travel back with him, which will be a bonus.'

'If he doesn't die in the meantime.'

'Don't even think it, Kat.' And then, as if to distract me, 'You know the route he will take?'

'Yes. And I shall replicate it in reverse, and trust I shall meet him on the way.'

We toil up the hill in Altenburg and make our way to Spalatin's house. He meets me at the door, and to my surprise he greets me with a smile.

'Good news, Frau Luther. I have had word from Gotha. Your husband is much improved.'

I grasp the door frame and he puts his hand under my elbow to lend me support as he leads me inside.

'Please,' I say, 'tell me everything you have heard.'

'Of course, but first, you must be tired. Once you have had a chance to rest…'

'I don't want to rest…' I break off, aware I sound churlish. 'I'm fine, believe me. I shall rest better once I know how Martin is.'

Frau Spalatin bustles up. 'Of course you want the news first. Men do not understand these things.' Taking my arm she brings me into their Stube. 'But it is possible to do both at once.' There is a table set in the window with fresh bread and cheese and thick slices of ham. I start to say, 'I'm not hungry,' but she is sitting me down and pouring me a glass of wine. 'You eat and my husband will talk.' A telltale dimple appears in her cheek. 'He's good at that.'

To my surprise, once I begin, I find I *am* hungry and do more justice to the spread than I could have imagined.

317

Spalatin settles back in the chair beside me.

I prompt him. 'You said the news is good?'

'And so it is. I left Martin at Weimar and travelled ahead to give my wife word of his coming, so that she could make appropriate preparations.' He slides his tongue around his lips.

'What are you not telling me?'

'When he first arrived at Gotha things did not look good. In fact' – he looks over at his wife as if seeking her opinion of what to say, her fractional nod enough for him to continue – 'he wrote his will and made his confession to Bugenhagen.'

Despite myself I laugh, the sound torn from me, harsh and abrasive as sandpaper. 'Confession? When he has spent half a lifetime telling others there is no need to confess to any other than Christ himself.'

Frau Spalatin touches my hand, her voice gentle. 'I do not think he meant it to negate his teachings, only sometimes it helps to speak out what is in your heart.'

'I'm sorry, I didn't mean…'

'There is nothing to be sorry about. You have had a shock. But as my husband has said, the last word that came was much more encouraging.'

Spalatin breaks in, 'He is likely on his way now and should arrive in a day or two, and then you may travel home together.'

Frau Spalatin pats my hand again. 'And in the meantime, we can renew our friendship. There will be much to talk about.'

I think of the children at home, and how bereft I could have been. 'Indeed, and most of it good.'

But when Martin arrives, though I try to hide it, I am

shocked afresh at his appearance. His face is drawn, the cheeks hollowed and the whites of his eyes are tinged with yellow. The stubble on his chin is standing out dark against the pallor of his skin and he needs support to walk from the carriage to the house.

Else, as if she knows what I'm thinking, says, 'You know you are both welcome to stay until Martin is fit for another journey.'

I smile my gratitude. 'I think perhaps we shouldn't rush it.'

I reckon without Martin. He is keen to make for home as quickly as possible, and it is a bone of contention between us that threatens to overshadow my relief at seeing him.

'You came so very close to not coming home at all. What harm will another week or two do?'

'If I cannot be at Schmalkald, I should be in Wittenberg, where at least I am listened to.'

It's not hard to see what has riled him and still does. 'No doubt Melanchthon thought what he did in holding back the articles was for the best.'

'No doubt he thought to fulfil his own pacifist agenda.'

'Is there anything wrong with pacifism?'

'In this case, yes.' Colour is beginning to suffuse his face. 'It was a treachery I did not think him capable of.' He presses hard on the arms of the chair as if to lever himself to his feet, and seeing the effort it takes, I seek to mollify him.

'Perhaps you are well out of it then.'

He glares at me, as if I also am treacherous, but then subsides back onto the seat, breathing heavily.

'I am only thinking of your health. It is not good for

319

you to get so worked up.'

When he has recovered his breath he looks up at me. 'I know, Käthe, I know. And whatever I may say in the heat of the moment, you must believe I have never had cause to question *your* loyalty.'

We arrive back in Wittenberg halfway through March, a watery sunshine greeting us as we cross the Elbe. Looking along the meadow that lies between the housing and the river I note the grass is dotted with celandine, the buttercup yellow petals shining as if polished. I want it to be a pleasant homecoming and so fix on them. 'How good of God, to cheer us with flowers, especially those that serve no other purpose than to bring a little light into our lives.'

Martin is looking along the river, and following his gaze I see a trout leap, the flash of colour a perfect arc before it drops into the water again with a splash.

'See,' I say, 'the fish are leaping for joy at your homecoming.'

His voice is gruff, but he can't altogether hide his smile. 'The fish leap because it is in their nature.'

I draw the carriage curtain on Martin's side as we come under the archway, for I want to get him safely back to the Lutherhaus and into his own bed as speedily as possible. And though some children stop and stare as we pass, we slip into the town almost unnoticed. A quite different return from the manner of his leaving, but I am glad of it.

As we are helping him down, the children erupt into the courtyard, Hans in the lead, Magdalena next, then

Paul and Young Martin, with little Margarete trailing behind. Lippus Melanchthon and Jost Jonas are also with them, but hang back. I fend our children off. 'Steady. Your father is not well...'

He leans back against the carriage, the axles creaking, and opens his arms. 'Don't forbid them, Käthe, I have dreamt of this moment almost every night since I left. Children are a blessing. If we have not yet a quiverful, we are near to it, and every one precious to me.'

Later, as he stretches out on the bed and I tuck the sheet around him, I see the fatigue in his eyes and chide him gently. 'You should not have agreed to play for them, tonight of all nights.'

'It would not have been well done to refuse. For who knows when I might get the opportunity again.'

'Tomorrow,' I suggest, 'when you would have been more rested?'

'We cannot count on tomorrow, Käthe, any more than we can count the stars in the sky. If these past weeks have taught me anything, it is that. You know I thought I was like to die at Gotha?'

'Yes. Spalatin told me.'

'Did he also tell you I made a will?'

'Yes.'

'Did he say what was in it?'

'No. Only that it was made.'

'Well I must tell you then.' He pulls himself further up in the bed. 'I did not make provision for you and the children...'

I am ready to protest, not so much on my own behalf as on theirs.

'Hear me out, Käthe. There were more important

issues to cover and I didn't know how much time I had in which to state my wishes. You I commended to God, in the certain belief He would look after you.' He pauses. 'You do believe that, Käthe, don't you?'

I think of our children, of the cost of maintaining the Lutherhaus, of the fact that as it stands I have no rights to any of it, and want to say, 'I believe God expects us to look after our own if we have the means to do so', but I don't want to cast a shadow on this first night we will have together and so keep silent. He is stroking my hair and I kick off my slippers and stretch out beside him on top of the covers, my head burrowed into the crook of his arm.

Chapter Thirty-Two
Wittenberg, April–August 1537

We have been home a month when the others return, with fanfare and ceremony, the elector's carriage flanked by outriders, displaying his colours, the horses high-stepping and frisky. Philipp Melanchthon loses no time in coming to the Lutherhaus, and though Martin's face darkens when he is announced, he nods for him to be brought up. I stand close, my hand on Martin's arm, so that if need be I can intervene. It is Bugenhagen, however, who comes in first, and I think it a clever ploy on Philipp's behalf to use him as a shield.

He moves straight to Martin and gripping his shoulders leans back to look at him. 'Well, well. It is good to see you so hearty, Martin. The last time I saw you…' He peters out, glances at me.

'She knows,' Martin says. 'I could not keep it from her, even had I wanted to.'

'Only a blind man or an idiot would have failed to see how ill he had been.' I look at Melanchthon, cannot resist adding, 'Physically and mentally.'

He has the grace to colour, and steps towards us, his

323

hands spread, as if in apology, but Bugenhagen pre-empts him.

'This is not a time for looking back, but for moving forward. We have enemies aplenty to contend with, without driving wedges between ourselves.'

'Philipp should have thought of that at Schmalkald,' Martin begins, but once again Bugenhagen cuts in.

'You did your job, and Philipp his, and the end result is suitable to all. We should none of us allow one disagreement to sour the many years of fellowship we have shared, nor damage the work still to do.' And in a transparent effort to direct the conversation elsewhere, 'What do you think of the elector's concern regarding the principle of parishes choosing their own pastors, and the fears he expresses regarding the quality of the men so chosen.'

'I applaud his desire for the faculty to examine and ordain all candidates, and I must admit' – Martin pats my hand – 'and no doubt Käthe here would concur, there have been failures in the past.'

'Glatz, for one,' I say, willing to resurrect an old ill in order to bury a new one.

My intervention earns me a smile from Bugenhagen and a swift response. 'And your perception in recognising his flaws was fortunate' – he nods to Martin – 'for both of you.'

As spring slips into summer, the garden once more thrusting with new life, it is as if Martin too is reborn, daily growing stronger and able to resume both preaching and writing. The house is filled with music, as he compiles a new hymnbook. We hear him in the late afternoons, when his more serious work is done, experimenting with tunes, altering a phrase here, inserting an ornament there, but he refuses all requests to play them for us until he is done.

'This one is special,' he says, 'and will be worth the wait.'

He tackles with gusto the task the elector has given him to prepare viva exams for the doctoral candidates. When he finally finishes, he flourishes a sheaf of papers at me. 'These will sort the sheep from the goats.'

'What are they?'

'Theses, of course. On key points of doctrine. The candidates for ministry must defend them successfully if they are to be ordained.' He plucks one at random from the pile and hands it to me. 'This is on faith and good works, and I look forward to hearing well-argued disputations.'

The writing on the page is as densely packed as Martin's usually is, as if economy of paper is high on his priority list. I cannot resist a smile, for I'm not convinced Martin knows the meaning of economy in any other sphere.

He squints at me. 'What?'

I tease, 'If the candidates eyesight is strong and if they have been well taught.'

He ignores my first comment, refuses to be deflated by the second. 'If they fail, it is because there is nothing between their ears but sawdust. If they have paid attention in my lectures, they will all pass with flying colours.'

And so it turns out, the first ordination taking place at midsummer, the celebrations continuing well into the evening, taking advantage of the extra hours of daylight. Martin strolls home with Philipp Melanchthon in tow, and they come into the garden arm in arm. I am sitting under the pear trees enjoying the last of the sunshine, and when I see them I think perhaps the worst of our ills are behind us.

⬡⬡⬡⬡

It is mid-July, the crops well on, when Martin resumes the lectures on Genesis he had abandoned eight months ago. It is another sign of good things to come, though I find myself struggling to concentrate when he shares his insights on the patriarchs with me, verse by verse, and I cannot help wondering if some of his students find it equally slow going.

Else and I are in the pantry, washing down the shelves. The bell of the Town Church rings the hour and I imagine Martin gathering his notes and removing his glasses, satisfied with the end of another day.

As if she shares my thoughts, she says, 'It's good to see Martin so well and enjoying his teaching again.'

'Yes, though at the rate he is going, we'll all be in our graves before he is done.' I scarcely realise what I've said until I see her stiffen. She stares at me, water dripping from the cloth in her hand.

'It's all right,' I say. 'Three months ago to say such a thing would have torn my heart out. But he is so much better in every way … it is good I can make light of it now.'

We settle into the rhythm of the season, with scarce a moment to call our own, the time for idle chatter little more than a dim winter memory, and fall into bed at night, each of us in our own way tired, but satisfied, with the

326

accomplishments of the day. The children are growing up fast. Hans reaches almost to my shoulder and thinks himself a young man, with an air of arrogance that I fear he has learnt at the university, for there are many scions of good families there, and most of them with a high appreciation of their own merits. Young Martin, though not yet six, is a conundrum, sunny one moment and cross the next, exhibiting an occasional flash of cruelty towards an animal that is once again uncomfortably reminiscent of Klement. When I say so to Else, she dismisses my fears.

'He is very young, Kat. Time enough to worry when he is Hans' age and should know better.'

Paul is a delight, full of mischief but with the smile of an angel, and whatever he has been up to it is almost impossible to be cross with him. Margarethe is his shadow, trailing him everywhere, and he is unendingly patient with her, and for that alone I could forgive him anything. Dorothea huffs and puffs when I laugh at his mischief, but when his smile doesn't falter, however much she berates him for a misdemeanour, she too has to send him away before her own resolve cracks.

'That child,' she says, dropping a kettle with a clatter when a frog leaps from it as she's just about to fill it, 'will be the death of us one day, and the worst of it is we will be laughing as we meet our end.'

Magdalena has lost both her youthful plumpness and her earlier prickliness. Her character has become a match for her voice, which, though she is only eight is of such sweetness I am reminded of Brehna, and in my head I give her my old nickname: 'Linnet'. She hums and sings constantly, even when her head is bent over her lessons, and I often catch Martin watching her. I suspect she has a special place in both our hearts, though we neither of us openly acknowledge it. When I confess to Barbara, she is matter of fact.

'That's hardly surprising, coming when she did, after the loss of Elizabeth. What matters is not what feelings you may harbour inside, but that the others are not aware of any preference.'

'Perhaps,' I say to Martin one day, when we overhear her voice floating upwards from the garden, a soaring counterpoint to the birdsong all around her, 'she may be a choir mistress one day, but in a church, not a cloister.'

He looks down at the top of her head, at the auburn curls tumbling from her cap onto her collar, glinting in the sunlight. 'I have something for her,' he says, 'which I thought to keep for her next birthday, but perhaps now is as good a time as any.' He disappears to his study, and I stand at the foot of the stairs watching him take them two at a time, a feeling of wellbeing and thankfulness for his renewed good health sweeping through me. When he returns, it is with a small book, perfectly bound, and even without opening it I know what it is going to contain.

'All those evenings,' I say, 'all the tunes you experimented with, they were for her.'

He nods. 'You know I have long thought children deserve hymns of their own, with words they can understand and tunes suited to the pitch of their voices. I found it easier to compose with just one child, one voice in mind, and so have dedicated this to her.'

I trace the first tune with my finger, the notes ringing clear in my head. 'Written for one, perhaps, but sung by many I'm sure.'

CHAPTER THIRTY-THREE
WITTENBERG, SEPTEMBER 1537–FEBRUARY
1538

I should have known our peace couldn't last. The new guest wing is almost finished, and I take care Else Agricola helps in the choosing of paint for the walls and the ceiling decoration, for it is my hope that once Johann has a fixed tenure in the university, it can become their permanent home. I have grown used to her company, and if she doesn't altogether compensate for the loss of Muhme Lena, or of Elizabeth Cruciger, she comes close. She is an integral part in our Wittenberg sisterhood, and I look forward to the quiet of winter when, with less work to occupy us, we are able to indulge in more social activities.

But with the first wind of autumn blowing along the valley of the Elbe, causing the leaves on the trees to shrivel and drop, and the heat to bleed out of the sun, a matching chill settles on the Lutherhaus.

The cause is an old argument resurrected. However, this time it isn't confined to an academic disputation, but touches us all.

I am sitting on the floor of the Stube, attempting to

sort a jumble of coloured thread. The mess is courtesy of Paul and Margarethe, who clearly found pleasure in spilling them from my workbasket, and who were, when I came upon them, stirring them around as if they were the contents of a rather colourful stewpot. Arlo, the stray who adopted us and consoled the children when Tolpel died was sitting in the midst of it all scratching vigorously at a skein of yellow draped over one ear. He leapt up as I appeared, his tail wagging, and proceeded to spin round, shaking his head as if to shake off his burden, but succeeding instead in entangling his claws in half a dozen separate colours.

Paul looked around as I entered and waved a wooden spoon at me. 'Would you like some soup, Mutti? It's vegetable.'

Margarethe waved her spoon also, repeating after him, 'Vegable.'

The proper thing would have been to be stern, but they will be too old for such games soon enough. I hunker down and accept the imaginary bowl and spoon and pretend to eat, licking my lips. When I finish I untangle Arlo and send them all off to return the wooden spoons to Dorothea, making a mental note to tell her to check the next time they ask to borrow something what exactly they are wanting to do with it.

I'm humming as I work, the tune of one of the hymns from Magdalena's hymnary dancing in my head, when Martin flings open the door and, stamping in, throws himself down on the settle.

His face is flushed, never a good sign, his forehead knotted. 'This is a fine way to repay our friendship and our hospitality. It is Andreas Karlstadt all over again.'

I think of the last dispute, with Philipp Melanchthon, and wonder what on earth he has done now, and whether direct questioning or an attempt at distraction is likely to be the best option. 'Has Philipp...?' I begin.

Martin looks at me as if I have two heads. 'Melanchthon? In this at least we are in perfect agreement. Thank God.'

'Who then?'

'Johann Agricola. Having slept in our beds and eaten our food and sought our support for his professorship, he is now openly in contention against us.'

I think of Else and my plans for them, of the guest wing, of how much she has come to mean to me, and try, 'Johann has long been your friend as well as a colleague. You encouraged his return.'

'An error of judgement I now deeply regret.' He snaps his mouth shut.

'Can you not discuss whatever it is amicably? Find some common ground?'

I make a pretence of continuing to sort the threads. He stands up, his breathing heavy, but I keep my head down, and after a moment I feel a draught as the door swings open, the floor beneath me shaking as it bangs shut again. Once I'm sure he's gone, I abandon the mess and, fetching my cloak from the kitchen, hurry to Barbara's. I burst in on her and allow my fears and frustrations to spill out. 'There is some problem between Martin and Johann Agricola, and he is so angry I very much fear he will throw them out.'

She is calm, considered. 'Do you know what the dispute's about?'

'No idea. He was so incensed I thought it best not to question him.'

'Likely a sensible move.'

Below us in the square a dispute has arisen between two stallholders, their voices rising in claim and counter-claim. As suddenly as it had begun, it stops, in a flurry of backslapping and laughter. Barbara jerks her head towards the window. 'In a day or two this may blow over also and you won't need to ask. You know how Martin is. A person is either for him or against him. There is no middle ground.'

'That's what I'm afraid of. The Agricolas have lived with us in amity for months, and I hoped…'

'There have been fallings out before and all mended in the end.'

'Or not,' I say.

It's clear we are sharing the same thought, but Barbara seeks to dismiss it. 'Agricola is no Thomas Müntzer. Whatever this dispute is, I cannot see *him* leading riot and disorder.'

I cannot help but laugh at the thought of the mild-mannered Johann at the head of a mob.

She glances at me and, as if quick to capitalise on my release of tension, continues, 'Don't fret. We'll get to the bottom of this and likely with no real harm done.'

If only it was that simple. It is a week before I learn the root cause of it all. Else is as much in the dark as I, and as eager to know what ails our menfolk. At mealtimes they sit as far away from each other as possible, and any attempt to draw them into conversation is met with stony silence on both sides. They no longer sit with us in the Stube after

332

supper, a loss which Else and I both feel but are equally powerless to do anything about. Martin's continued anger is not entirely a surprise, but Johann's equal coldness seems out of character, and the longer it goes on the more serious I assume the doctrinal issue must be.

It is Philipp Melanchthon who brings it out into the open, in a heated discussion between the three of them in Martin's study, the voices echoing down the stairwell. I have just finished putting Margarethe to bed and pause at the foot of the stairs when I hear Melanchthon's raised voice.

'We ignore the law at our peril.'

Agricola is surprisingly firm. 'To preach adherence to the Ten Commandments implies good works are needed for salvation. Do you wish to add to what Christ has done?'

'We wish to ensure Christians do not continue in sin. Disregard the Ten Commandments and we have no standard against which to measure our actions.'

Martin weighs in, his words reasonable, his tone explosive. 'Christ came not to destroy the law, but to fulfil it.'

They trade quotations, their voices growing ever more strident, until the door above me opens, Johann Agricola framed in the light spilling onto the corridor. I shrink back into a window alcove as Melanchthon has the last word, calling down after Agricola's retreating figure. 'This should be disputed in a proper forum.' I imagine his disdain. 'If you have the courage of your convictions, formulate your theses and we will announce a disputation that more than we three can attend.'

At first I hope that moving the debate to the university will improve the atmosphere at home, but I am wrong.

It seems the dispute cannot be settled to anyone's satisfaction, the debates continuing through the winter and into the New Year without any sign of a resolution, Martin becoming increasingly critical and unkind. He lifts a glass at Table Talk and marks it with three lines. 'The first,' he says 'represents the Ten Commandments, the second, the Creed, and the third the Lord's Prayer.' When it is filled he tosses it back, and once refilled he holds it out to Johann, the use of the nickname adding to the cruelty of what is to come. 'Drink, Master Eisleben?'

I cannot watch, for Johann never does more than sip at a drink and will not be able to match Martin. His face is flushed with embarrassment, even before he takes the glass, and though he makes a valiant effort, he manages only to drink down to the first line. He sets the glass down, recognising defeat.

Martin is triumphant. 'I knew it. Master Eisleben can put away the Ten Commandments but must leave the Creed and the Lord's Prayer in peace.'

'How can he speak so?' I ask Barbara, when I recount the public taunting.

'Johann was his favourite student,' she says. 'This feels like a betrayal. And as the saying goes, "a wound from a friend cuts deeper than that of an enemy". And is the harder to bear.'

It's no surprise when Else comes to tell me they are leaving the Lutherhaus and taking lodgings elsewhere in the town. We cling together for a moment, without words, and I know we share the same thought, the same hope, that this schism, unlike many others that have gone before, may yet be mended.

I cannot avoid Martin, however much I am out of sympathy with him, but for a time I avoid Else, embarrassed by his outpourings.

It is Barbara who brings us together again, tricking us both into a meeting at her house. When I enter, Else is already there, and she starts up, patches of colour flaring on her neck. 'Kat, I had no…'

Barbara stands between us, a hand outstretched to both. 'Neither of you are at fault in this, nor should you suffer for it.'

Do I move first? Or does she? I've no idea, only that we are drawn together in an embrace that is as fierce as it is welcome. It is not, however, strong enough to heal the breach that has opened up between Martin and Johann. And as the dispute rumbles on it becomes the focus of gossip in the town and, perhaps naturally, the weight of sympathy is with Martin and Melanchthon, for Johann is perceived as a cuckoo in the nest, a student who thinks himself greater than his master. When he appeals to the elector to consider his case, Johann Frederick forbids him to leave Wittenberg until the issue is settled. I feel for Else, for I have been where she is now. Matrons stare and whisper and make unkind comments as she waits in line at the fishmonger, or cross the street to avoid speaking to her, as if she too is a Samaritan.

The end, when it comes, is unexpected but understandable. One day they are here, the next, gone, it seems no one knows where, and though I dare not say so to Martin, I wish them well.

335

CHAPTER THIRTY-FOUR
WITTENBERG, APRIL–AUGUST 1538

It is a difficult spring, inside and outside the house. I miss Else, and fear for her also, as the months roll on and we have no word of the Agricolas or how they fare. It is indeed the Karlstadts all over again, though not how Martin meant it. We circle around each other, equally unable to articulate the unease that lies between us in our bed at night and which casts a shadow over our days.

'Is it always thus?' I ask Barbara. 'That however strong love grows, it can be shrivelled by a single disagreement, as fragile as if it is blossom destroyed by an inopportune frost.'

She regards me gravely. 'You may not want to hear this, Kat, but whatever the rights and wrongs of the matter, your duty, to love and honour your husband, remains. There are difficult times in every marriage, but if you can hold to your vows, perhaps you may both weather this storm.'

'I will not pretend it was well done.'

That draws a smile. 'You don't have to. It's obvious to all, for you aren't the best at hiding your feelings. But have it out with him, Kat, and clear the air. You have been outspoken enough in the past and it has done no harm, to you or Martin. But once you have said your piece, let it go. Though Martin and Johann's relationship may never be repaired, there are other things to focus on. Your children, for one. You shared in the making of them, and they deserve two parents who are not at loggerheads. Think on that.' She hesitates. 'And consider also your position in this town. You fought hard for your standing. Do not throw it away now. There are still those who would love to see your marriage fail. Prove them wrong. Prove you can rise above this.'

It is late May, four weeks after Barbara's homily. In my head I accept what she says, but each time I have determined to tackle Martin, moments when I think he is ready to meet me halfway, something or someone conspires to stop me. I am hurrying along the Collegienstrasse from the market square, in the hope of beating the storm which dark clouds are threatening, my basket bouncing against my hip. The wind is against me and increasing, the coolness of the air causing me to shiver. It is only mid-afternoon but is almost as dark as if it were dusk, and as I look up I feel the first large dollops of rain on my face and regret coming out without a cloak.

'Käthe!' Martin is beside me, wrestling himself out of his coat and draping it over my head.

I put up one hand to hold it in place as he says, 'We'd better hurry, if we don't want to be washed away entirely.'

His arm is around my shoulder, and for a fraction of a

337

second I stiffen, then lean into him, and lifting my skirts high above my ankle begin to run. We collapse into the doorway of the Lutherhaus. Martin is totally soaked, his hair plastered to his head, as smooth as an otter's, water dropping from his nose and eyebrows and running down the side of his neck. Although my hem is wet from splashing through the puddles that filled every pothole, the rest of me has fared better, courtesy of his gallantry, and I find myself smiling up at him as we lean against the door to catch our breath. He reaches for the door handle, but I capture his hand.

'Wait, please.' We stand under the overhang as the rain slants down, a curtain cutting us off from the outside world. 'You know I think you are wrong in your treatment of Johann Agricola.'

He stirs, opens his mouth, but I place my finger against his lips.

'I think you are wrong, and my opinion will not change,' I repeat, 'but I am wrong too, to allow it to sour what we have, and for that I am sorry.'

He stirs again and again I halt him. 'If we cannot agree to differ, then we are both the losers, and I don't want that.'

'Nor I.' He slides his coat off my head onto my shoulders and runs his thumb across my cheek, wiping away the raindrops. 'I think, Frau Luther, we must go in, else we may catch our death, and I don't think either one of us wants that either.'

Later, in the Stube as I towel his hair dry, turning it back to the unruly curls I have come to love, he looks up, and I understand the wealth of feeling underlying his words,

'We should be grateful this day for the rain. It will provide a thousand gulden worth of corn and wheat and barley and wine to fill our bellies and gladden our hearts, and has cleared the air besides.'

It is indeed a good year for crops, with no need to fear for any shortages of basic foodstuffs, and with Johann Rischmann proving himself a capable manager of the Heffner land, I have the time to focus on our kitchen garden and to experiment further with new plants. The herbs we grow for everyday use, peppermint and marjoram and sage, flourish, and I find I need to restrict their spread, else I will have no room for anything else. Caraway, in particular, is so rampant seed cake becomes almost as much a staple in our diet as bread. When I set the latest offering on the table, Margarethe makes a face, earning a reprimand from Dorothea.

'Count yourself lucky you *have* cake, miss. There are many who don't.'

She pouts. 'Don't like pips.'

Young Martin is quick to take advantage, lifting an extra slice. 'I'll eat your bit.'

Paul tries to grab it off him. 'Not fair! *I* wanted that.'

Young Martin raises it above his head, scattering crumbs and seeds in every direction. 'I asked first.'

'Put it down,' I say. 'Neither of you asked, and those who snatch, don't get.' I take the plate, hand it to the maid hovering behind me. 'Take it back to the pantry. When their manners are improved it may reappear.'

That pleases no one, but I don't wish our table to

become a battleground, the memories from my own childhood still clear in my mind.

The rapprochement between Martin and me, begun in the rain, holds, and I think perhaps this will be a good year in more ways than one. And when he comes upon me as I am preparing the soil for the crocus corms Barbara has given me, I welcome him with a smile. He tosses one between his hands. 'All this trouble for a few stigmas of saffron?'

'These few stigmas…' I begin.

His tone is teasing. 'I know, small they may be, but they would buy and sell a pig or two.'

I ignore the exaggeration. 'It isn't hard to grow and *is* the most expensive of spices.'

'Remind me to come and watch you harvesting it.' He yawns and mimes picking the stigmas out of the centre of the flower, then mocks consternation as one is dropped.

'You may jest now,' I say, 'but you won't be laughing when I ask you to do the harvesting. That will test your dexterity and patience.' I pop the last corm in the hole I've just made and smile up at him again. He reaches down to take my hand and helps me to my feet.

'I've come to take you to the Cranachs, for we are bid there for supper, but I see I shall have to wait while you scrub half the vegetable garden from your fingers.'

'You will have to wait a bit longer than that. I want to water the fig seedlings; they aren't doing so well, and I fear it may be a lack of moisture. The mulberries also. Barbara won't mind.'

'My stomach might.'

'You are hardly in danger of dying of starvation.' I poke his belly. 'As this proves.'

340

We walk towards the back of the garden where the sun is still slanting onto the soil, and halt at my nursery bed.

'Should they fruit this year?' Martin says.

'I am not so impatient, whatever you may be. They are only two years old and it will be at least another before we can expect any return from them. And even then not guaranteed.' Unintentionally my tone becomes more serious. 'But I don't want to lose them at this stage or it will be all to do again.'

He gives my shoulder a squeeze. 'You won't. I shall promise to water them every day while the weather holds.'

That, I shall hold you to.'

He is as good as his word, which is just as well, for it seems that we survive one crisis only to face another. This time it is illness that troubles us, Young Martin and Paul both succumbing to a high fever. Dr Schurf assures me it is not the plague, but nevertheless as I nurse them I cannot quell my fear, for children die of many ailments and fever the most common among them. When two of the maids also fall ill, with similar symptoms, my time is taken up with looking after all four of them, the garden ignored.

'I could not bear it if we were to lose the boys,' I say to Barbara when she comes to offer assistance.

'And Martin?'

'I don't know. When Elizabeth died, he was sad, but perhaps more for me than for himself, for he had scarcely time to get to know her. This is different.'

'What has Schurf said?'

'That with good nursing and prayer they will likely all pull through, but he can't or won't make any promises.'

For a moment a shadow crosses her face, and I know she is thinking of the three lost children in her family

341

portrait. I blurt out, 'How did *you* bear it, Barbara?'

There is telltale moistness in her eyes, but her voice is firm. 'By concentrating on the children I had left, not the ones gone beyond my reach. But I was never offered hope they would survive, quite the reverse. In this case you have every reason to trust Schurf's judgement, and you must focus on that.'

Chapter Thirty-Five
Wittenberg, April 1539

The boys don't die, and daily I give thanks to God for sparing them. It is a joy shared by our whole household, even five-year-old Margarethe, who, though she does not fully understand, hops and skips alongside Magdalena and me as we head for the market. There is an added air of excitement, clusters of people gossiping at every stall. I feel it deep inside me even before I hear the cause, but when I do, it is as if a weight I didn't know I carried had finally been lifted from my shoulders. Duke George is dead. As we turn for home and take Margarethe's hands, I count, 'One, two, three, whee,' and we swing her off the ground. It is the nearest I can get in public to skipping myself.

'Again,' she says, 'again.'

Inside our gate, Lippus Melanchthon is being chased by his little sister and Margarethe tears herself free to follow them.

Magdalena pauses at the house entrance, her eyes troubled. 'Why are you happy to hear someone has died, Mutti?'

I look at my older daughter, nine years old and full of fun, yet sensitive beyond her years. 'Duke George was an enemy of the Reformation and of your father. It is hard not to be glad he is gone. Especially as' – I hesitate, for I have never before confessed a weakness to any of my children – 'as a child I was in awe of him, but when I left the convent it was in fear, for I was his subject and breaking his laws. The fear has never completely left me, until now.'

She looks up at me, her gaze direct, her question equally so. 'What of the new duke? Will you fear him also?'

'They say he is of the reform party, and we may hope the rumours are true.'

They *are* true, for the next word that comes, via a jubilant Bugenhagen, is that Duke Henry walked out of his father's funeral mass in favour of attending an evangelical service. Martin is equally pleased, and despite my lingering sense of impropriety, I find myself wanting to skip everywhere rather than walk.

'Perhaps,' I say to Dorothea, 'we can at last enjoy peace.'

She pauses in her stirring of a pan of soup, lifts one shoulder. 'Perhaps. But I won't be holding my breath.'

She is right and I am wrong. Ducal Saxony is declared Lutheran and Justus Jonas and Spalatin are directed to carry out visitations to stop Catholic practices, but it is not so simple. There are many priests who refuse to convert, and requests for Lutheran pastors to replace them flood

Wittenberg.

Melanchthon is, as always, pessimistic. 'We don't have enough for our own area, never mind some to spare, and if pulpits are left empty, worse errors may arise to replace those that have been lost.'

'But if there is a will for reform,' I say.

He shoots a glance at me. 'Among whom?' Duke Henry may have seen the light, but his bishops have not, though they look for a compromise.'

'No doubt in order to keep their living.' Martin is caustic. 'We have gone far beyond compromise. It is the truth we must stand for.'

There is a chill in my stomach, as if I have swallowed ice. 'Must it affect us? Here?'

'It already has.' He thrusts his hand into his jacket.

Melanchthon casts him a warning glance. 'Is that really suitable for a wife to read?'

Martin dismisses his concern. 'We have been here before, only this time we are not alone.'

I take the pamphlet from his hand. The attack on our married life and that of the Jonases and Spalatins is vicious and couched in language so strong my face flames as I read. I sit down abruptly, afraid my legs will give way. 'Have the others seen this?'

Martin shakes his head. 'Not as yet, but it cannot be long before half the world has seen it, and half of them will likely believe it.'

'How could anyone believe such obscenities?'

'People will believe what they want to believe, however cruel. If we are evil, they must be righteous.'

I turn the pamphlet over and look at the name on the front. 'Lemnius? The man you criticised for his earlier

345

writings and who fled Wittenberg?'

'Yes. He has been subverted by Cardinal Albert, or by the position flattering him might bring.'

My hand is shaking as I hand the pamphlet back. I scarcely dare ask. 'Will you reply?'

'Not to him. He is beneath contempt. It is Albert who is the principal in this.'

After Melanchthon has gone I say, 'Philipp seems particularly uneasy.'

There is a moment's silence, Martin carefully folding the pamphlet and replacing it in his jacket. 'There is a rumour his son-in-law conspired with Lemnius to have this printed.'

'Surely not!'

'I'm afraid so. And I think it true. I have counselled Philipp to issue a declaration of his own innocence, but likely some mud will stick.'

'That's why he didn't want me to see it. Did he think...?'

'This has hit him hard, Käthe. He doesn't know what to think and fears everyone's reaction, even that of his closest friends. He worried that I...'

'Well then' – I tilt my chin – 'we must show the world we do not hold him in any way responsible.'

'That,' says Martin, 'is exactly what I expected of you.'

Martin wastes no time in preparing his response. *Against the Bishop of Magdeburg, Cardinal Albert*, is typically strident, and though on occasions in the past I wished for him to be more moderate in his tone, in this I support him

346

fully. To have our friends and colleagues also maligned, and in such a manner, is unbearable, especially when they suffer for their connection to us. Martin's pamphlet is printed and distributed widely, the ripples it causes lapping well beyond Saxony into all the surrounding states.

He expresses his satisfaction. 'It is talked of everywhere. And high time Cardinal Albert is recognised for the wily old fox he is. The lip service he pays to the idea of reform is no thicker than the skin on a custard and as easily swept aside.' He is silent for a moment, then, 'And how right I was to refuse his wedding gift. That we might not be thought to be bought.'

I stiffen, smother the guilt I thought long since assuaged. At the first, in the days and weeks following our marriage, I had intended to confess my acceptance of the cardinal's gift, but somehow had never found the right moment, and as time had passed it had seemed unimportant and forgotten. I catch my lip. It was all too long ago, and impossible to bring into the open now. But if Martin were to start talking of it in the wrong circles... I shut my eyes and send up a prayer he won't hear of it from another source, for I do not want to lose his trust.

He is at home when the offer comes, more's the pity, for had he been away I might have been able to accept it. We have been married fourteen years and when he goes into the study we have set aside on the top floor of the Lutherhaus that he may work in peace, the words continue to fly from his quill in as great a volume as they ever did, even when he was single and without the responsibilities that family brings. There is a constant demand for his pamphlets, new and old, the printers scarce able to keep up with the requests for copies.

We have been lured to the Cranachs on the pretext of supper and are somewhat surprised to see other of the local printers there also. Lucas stands, an unfolded paper in his hand, the others ranged alongside him as if a phalanx preparing for battle. Barbara comes to stand beside me, as if she suspects I may need her support.

I break the silence that follows Lucas' announcement. 'Four hundred gulden a year! For the right to publish your works?' I reach for the arm of the chair, plump down onto the seat, turn to Martin. 'You surely cannot think of refusing?'

'On the contrary. I cannot think of accepting. This is God's work I do.'

'And lecturing is not God's work? You receive a salary for that.'

'That is for the university. A very different thing.'

'Very different indeed.' I choose my words carefully. 'The money half as much again, and but a fair reflection of the time you spend on it.'

His use of my full name lends weight to his response. 'Do not try to twist what I say, Katharina, it does not become you. I have never received so much as a pfennig for any of my writing, nor ever wished to.'

Lucas breaks in. 'Why should you not profit from your work, Martin, as we all do? We are here to make this offer, and in agreement that if we are granted the rights, your business alone will be sufficient to sustain us all. It will be to our mutual benefit and to the benefit of those we employ, guaranteeing them work for years to come. For even if you never wrote another syllable, what is already written would be enough. Did not Jesus himself say *A labourer is worthy of his hire*.'

348

'It is not labour. It is a gift. Of the Holy Spirit, and given for the benefit of the flock, here and elsewhere. Not for my own gain.' Martin has begun to pace, a telltale sign I choose to ignore.

'Not labour? How can you say such a thing, when there are times you shut yourself in that study and almost starve before you are done?'

Again he uses my full name. 'For shame, Katharina. Would you wish me to refuse God's prompting?'

'I would wish you to accept some recompense for what you do. If not for yourself, for...' – I was going to say 'family', but change my mind and try – 'those who depend on us for support.'

He pauses in his pacing and I think I detect a softening, and indeed his next words are more conciliatory.

'We have never yet had to turn anyone away for lack of funds.'

'No,' I concede, 'but not without selling some of our silverware.'

His tone hardens again. 'Of which we have an overabundance and can well stand the loss.'

Lucas tries again. 'Much as I appreciate the additional income, Martin, why should I and the others, who merely disseminate your teachings, take all the profit, while you, who write them, get nothing?'

'It is your business, Lucas, and as you say, a labourer is worthy of his hire. I hire you and others to do the job I cannot, and it is perfectly right you are paid.' There is a note of triumph in his voice, as of an argument well won.

'But surely...'

'Surely nothing.' He has stopped in a patch of sunlight, his hair turned to copper, his jaw out-thrust, the fire back

349

in his eyes. 'This is my last word. Do not make me act against my conscience, else it will be the Devil who profits, to the disadvantage of all.'

He looks towards Barbara and me, and though his tone is more measured, his back is ramrod stiff. 'We four have long been friends, and good friends too. I am sure we none of us would wish to jeopardise that.'

Barbara grips my hand, as if sending a message to me to bide my time. I respond with an answering squeeze, for though this money is an offer too good to refuse, in my heart I have accepted, however bitterly, it is also an argument I am not likely to win.

Torgau: November 1552

That girl is here again, the one who looks so like Margarethe. She is kind to me, and gentle, and even calls me Mutti sometimes, which I imagine is to make me feel less alone, but it isn't the same as if it was my own daughter. I miss her. I miss all three of them, Margarethe, Magdalena, my little songbird, and even the babe, Elizabeth, who scarcely had a chance at life. I am careful not to say that, though, for it clearly upsets her, and she does her best.

My hip is improving, and when they slide me up the bed and place pillows behind my head to make it easier for me to eat, I no longer gasp with pain, and indeed I wish they would leave me sitting upright, even to sleep, for if I am lying down I suffer other pains. They are like daggers piercing my chest, and when I cough it is as if my lungs are being torn apart.

There is a blast of cold air as the door opens, a maid appearing with a ewer. It is so full that water splashes onto the floor, and as she crosses to the bed steam is rising, the scent of honey strong. Between them they raise me up and set the ewer on my lap, draping a cloth over my head. I am afraid it will wobble and the water spill and burn me but, as if she can read my mind, the girl holds it steady. I bend as far as I can and breathe in, thankful for the temporary relief.

'Where is Paul?' I ask, when the ewer is removed. 'Is he with Anna?' I can forgive him for not being here as much as he once was if he is with his betrothed, for that is as it should be. 'She is a good girl and I hope they will be married soon. It will be a fine thing to have a wedding to cheer us all.'

The girl smiles at me, and once again I am struck by the resemblance. 'You will come, won't you? I think you will like each other, you and Margarethe.' I pause, wipe my hand across my eyes. 'I always expected my children to marry in Wittenberg, but perhaps it is fitting to for the first marriage to be here, where I had my first taste of freedom.'

The maid is looking from me to the girl, her expression doubtful, and I wonder if there is some kind of problem. 'The Town Church will be adequate,' I say. 'We will have no need to trouble the Duke.'

'Of course not.' The girl smiles again and pats my arm. 'I will be pleased to see Paul married.'

'I never thought to be a mother,' I say, 'far less to have borne six children.'

Somewhere a clock is striking, and I remember our castle clock, counting down the old year, my hope dissolving with each strike.

Chapter Thirty-Six
Wittenberg, January–March 1540

There is another argument I fear I am destined to lose as soon as I feel the first sharp pain. We are standing outside the Castle Church in silence while we wait for the recently installed clock to strike midnight, marking the turn of the year. I am thinking of Hans, imagining his face bright with excitement as he waits among the bell-ringers in the towers of the Town Church. It is his first time and a special honour, and I wonder if his hands are trembling as he clutches his rope, ready to ring out the celebration. Magdalena is on one side of me, Kath Jonas on the other, Barbara and Lucas and Walpurga Bugenhagen a little to my right, the assortment of younger children, who had been darting in and out playing some game of their own devising, now standing in a tight cluster, facing the heavy oak door, gazing up at the hands of the clock face, caught up in the anticipation. Martin and Justus will be lined up inside along with their fellow theologians, ready to step out as the doors are flung wide, their 'Peace be with you' a murmur that will ripple out through the assembled crowd, accompanied by a clasping of hands and a swelling of

353

goodwill, and of hope for the year to come.

The hope I have been nursing within me dissolves, and I turn to Kath, gripping her arm to enable me to stay upright. She casts a swift glance at my face, then reaches out to tap Dorothea on the arm, nodding first towards me and then to their house. Dorothea nods back and we push our way through the crowd, murmuring apologies as we go, Kath's arm around my waist.

I sink onto the bench inside their front door and bend double to regain my breath as the pain diminishes.

'I didn't know...' she begins.

'No one did. I didn't want to say.' I am picking at a rough edge on one of my nails. 'I couldn't help feeling maybe I was too old for this, and now...'

She speaks with more confidence than I suspect she feels. 'Many people suffer phantom pains, and they come to nothing.'

'Nothing is exactly what I fear this will come to. And Martin will be so disappointed.'

'Let's concentrate on getting you home to bed. Rest may be all that's needed.'

'There is too much...'

'There is nothing someone else can't do. I know you don't know the meaning of the word "rest", but you may have to learn.'

'I'm not sure I can walk all the way.'

She snorts. 'I'm sure you can't! Our wagon is out the back, and if I cannot find the boy in the melee, I shall drive you myself.'

As Kath predicted, the pains subside, and for ten days I go about trying to stifle my concerns. I am careful, walking up the stairs rather than running, refraining from carrying anything heavy, and fending off Margarethe when she demands to be swung or lifted. So careful even Martin notices, and I feel a pang of worry at the smile spreading across his face.

'When?' he says, touching my cheek.

'Five months yet…'

'And you haven't said anything? Is there a problem?'

'I'm older now.'

'But you feel fine?'

'Now I do, but at the New Year, I thought perhaps I was going to lose it.'

'Well you haven't, and by God's good grace, you won't.'

He is so positive I cannot bear to dampen his enthusiasm. 'Will you mind whether it's a boy or a girl?'

'Why should I?' He is grinning. 'Both will be useful to me in my declining years.'

When my waters break the following night, followed by sharp pains, not spread out as they had been before, but this time wave upon wave, without any respite, it is a double blow. Dr Schurf gives me a distillation of poppy seed to ease me and I slip down into darkness. When I wake I know it's all over and I find myself crying, for Martin, for myself and for the babe we have lost.

Barbara is sitting in a chair by the window, and as I turn my head she comes over and kneels by the side of the bed.

355

'Oh, Kat.'

There is something about her tone that frightens me. 'I knew it wasn't right, even from the start, and yesterday, when the waters broke...' A tear slips out of the corner of my eye and I wipe at it with the back of my hand. 'I accepted there was nothing anyone could do.'

Her tongue is caught between her lips, and with a sigh she reaches out and takes my hand, rubbing her thumb round and round my palm. 'It wasn't yesterday, Kat.'

'What do you mean?'

'You've been very ill, and...'

I try to pull myself up in the bed and find I don't have the strength, wipe at another tear. 'What day is it?' I say.

'Wednesday.' She hesitates again, but I scarcely notice.

'Three days?' I can hardly believe it.

No,' she says, taking a tighter grip of my hand, 'almost three weeks.'

When Martin comes he tiptoes into the bedchamber in stocking soles and approaches the bed without any of his customary swagger. His face seems thinner than usual and there are extra lines in his forehead.

'Have you been ill also?' I ask, trying to reach out to him, but I find even the effort of lifting my hand from the coverlet is too much.

He is on his knees beside me, the suspicion of tears in his eyes. 'Not I, Käthe, it is you who have been ill, but by the grace of God you are still here, for I do not know what I would have done without you.' He glances across at Schurf, as if asking permission before continuing. 'We thought you were like to die, and indeed had prepared the children...' – he breaks off – 'the children, they should be fetched.'

They cluster at the end of the bed, wide-eyed and silent, staring at me propped up against a mountain of pillows. Even Margarethe, who would normally throw herself at me, hangs back.

'Please,' I say, 'let me hug them.'

'One at a time then.' Martin forms them into a queue, and in turn they come forward. Hans leans over me, his arm's-length embrace revealing his awkwardness. Young Martin follows suit, bending to kiss my cheek. Paul kneels beside the bed and lays his head on my chest, and as I stroke his hair it springs under my fingers as Martin's does. Magdalena perches on the edge of the bed, careful not to lean on me, and takes my face in both her hands and kisses my forehead. When it is Margarethe's turn she stands at my side, one thumb firmly stuck in her mouth, and reaches for my hand, her touch feather-light as if she fears I will break.

'Go on,' Martin says, 'give Mutti a kiss.' But she shakes her head, and takes a step back, kissing her own hand and blowing the kiss towards me.

'It's all right,' I say. 'I won't break.'

'Are you going to die now?'

Martin gathers her up in his arms, his 'No' a little more strident than mine.

He stops, but I continue. 'I'm going to get better. That's why I was wanting to see you all.'

She tucks her head under Martin's chin, her thumb sliding back into her mouth, the sound of her sucking magnified in the silence. In other circumstances Dorothea would be pulling it out and threatening it will shrivel to uselessness if she doesn't watch out, but today none of us have the heart to chide her.

It is March before I can get out of bed, and even then I move around the room holding onto furniture as a babe does when learning to walk. 'I'm sorry,' I say to Martin as he settles me in a chair in the Stube for the first time, tucking a blanket around my knees to keep out any draughts that might slip under the door. 'I had not thought to be useless for so long.'

'All that matters is that you are on the mend.'

'But I still feel so weak.'

'According to Dr Schurf, the weakness in your limbs is from lying so long, and not from any more sinister cause. Every day you will be stronger.' He stretches out in the chair beside me. 'In the meantime, until you are able for going to the market yourself, you will have to content yourself with second-hand news ... when I remember to pass it on, of course.'

There is a suppressed excitement in his voice, but I don't want to give him the satisfaction of showing myself too eager, so I affect disinterest, looking towards the window, where clouds are beginning to build. 'Is the weather to turn?'

'I believe so, but that's not...'

'What you want to tell me? Go on then.'

'Your brother Hans is coming to visit.'

For a moment I am silent, and his smile fades. 'I thought you would be pleased...'

'Oh I am, I am. You just took me by surprise. I have waited so long for this, and now' – I wave at the rug around my legs – 'I would rather he saw me fit and healthy than

358

an invalid.'

'He will. I promise you.'

'You can't know that.'

'I'm sorry, Käthe. Maybe I shouldn't have told you so soon. He won't be here for six weeks yet. Plenty of time to regain your strength.'

Chapter Thirty-Seven
Wittenberg, April–December 1540

It is the incentive I need. But when I talk of pushing myself to walk a little, Martin tries to convince me it is too soon, and when that doesn't work, to suggest I confine myself to the vegetable garden until I am fully recovered. Something about his tone and the expression I surprise on his face strengthens my resolve, and I take the opportunity when he is at the university to announce my intention of going out to Dorothea.

'Shouldn't you wait for Doctor Luther?'

'I have been confined long enough. I will not increase my stamina by walking between the vegetable beds.'

She wipes flour off her hands and pulls off her apron. 'I'll come with you then.'

I look at the mess on the table she is prepared to leave. 'What is it you're all hiding from me?' I say.

'It was to be a surprise.'

'What?' I demand again.

She makes one last attempt to stall me. 'And all Doctor Luther's idea.'

I refuse to be put off. 'Whatever it is, I shall see it

now.'

As we come to the doorway she places her hand on the latch. 'Shut your eyes.' We step out, and I sense someone moving aside and the scrape of timber on the ground. She turns me round, commanding, 'Open them!'

I don't know what to say.

A man is resting a ladder against the wall at the side of the doorway, his hands covered in masonry dust. He gestures towards the newly carved portal, to the twin stone seats that flank the door and the elegant sweep of the arch above and there is pride in his voice. 'Frau Luther! I am not entirely finished, but I trust it meets with your expectations?'

'It's … beautiful. How long…'

He scratches his head, considers. 'Nigh on two months.'

I look at Dorothea. 'Since I first…'

She nods. 'Doctor Luther commissioned it as soon as it was clear you were going to recover. It was to be his gift to you.'

'That's why he didn't want me to go out?'

'He wanted it to be finished, and it so nearly is.'

The thought of Martin planning this, of the children managing to keep the secret, is almost my undoing, but I don't intend to cry in front of a tradesman. 'I think I am tired. Perhaps I should leave a longer walk until another day.' I turn back to the stonemason. 'I'm sorry to have disturbed you. I shall look forward to seeing it complete.'

Inside, I collapse onto a chair in the kitchen. 'Don't tell Doctor Luther I've seen it. He deserves to show me himself.'

I make a good show of surprise when Martin leads me to the door. But I don't need to make a pretence of delight. And this time I'm not ashamed to cry. 'There is none more beautiful in Wittenberg.' I reach up to lay my hand against his cheek. 'Thank you.'

My first outing, leaning on Martin's arm, is to the market square and the Cranach's house. Barbara throws her arms around me, enveloping me in a hug, then looks at me appraisingly.

'Hmm, I think you'd better come with me.' She leads me upstairs and indicates for me to sit on the bed while she rummages in the chest at its foot. She emerges with a donkey-brown skirt in fine wool and another in a soft blue, along with an embroidered blouse. 'Take these just now. You can return them when your own fit you well again. If you'll pardon me saying so, at the moment you might as well be a clothes rail, that dress hanging on you with less shape than a sack. You hardly want Hans to see you like that.'

I look down at my blouse, as loose as if it is two sizes too big, and make a face. 'How can I not pardon you, when, along with the problem, you provide the remedy?'

'That,' she says, 'is what friends are for.' She holds the blue up against me, tilts her head, delves into the chest again, and when she straightens, she has a short brocade jacket in her hand.

'But it is one of your best...' I begin.

'Shh. It will only be for a while, and if it is longer, well then, it will be a chance for me to have something made in the latest style to do in its stead.'

The rest of the year passes in a blur, good news and bad following on from each other in quick succession. As Martin predicted, I am much better by the time Hans arrives, though still, to my irritation, easily tired and in my borrowed clothes. I am in the kitchen when I hear the jingle of harness and the thump of feet on the cobbles, and a voice enquiring if the master and mistress are at home. Though it is a rich tenor, it has a note of familiarity that has me tearing off my apron and rushing to the door. There is a moment of hesitation before Hans steps forward, crushing me against his chest. He is tall and broad-shouldered and altogether bigger than I remember our father, my head barely reaching to his chin.

He relaxes his grip. 'This life clearly suits you, Kat, though Anna would have said you are a mite thin for comfort.'

I am half laughing, half crying. 'I've been ill, but am much recovered now, and all the better for seeing you. It has been…'

'Too long. I know. I'm sorry, Kat. At the beginning it was … difficult, and then when I became able to choose for myself, I had so many responsibilities and the distance so far. But now I am much nearer there shouldn't be anything to stop us meeting.'

There is so much I want to ask I don't know where to start. In the Stube I draw him towards the settle. 'Sit down, we have so much to talk about, so many years to cover.'

'Let's not go too far back, Kat, there's little point in raking over old wrongs. Let's start from where we are now. The size of your establishment is known all across Saxony and beyond; as you are. What's it like being in charge of such an enormous enterprise? And being the wife of such a prominent person? Rumour has it you hold your own. Not that it surprises me.'

'Martin might surprise you too. He isn't always the single-minded theologian folk make of him. Within the family' – I break off – 'well, you'll see for yourself. I won't deny he isn't always the easiest of men; whose husband is?' I smile to show I speak, partially at least, in jest, and reinforce it by, 'But I have no regrets. How could I, when I have been given all this. When I have the privilege of entertaining princes and duchesses and when half the world it seems wants to sit at our table.'

He is reflective. 'Who'd have thought, when you were running around Lippendorf, with Anna at her wit's end trying to teach you to be ladylike, you would rise to this?"

'Not our step-mother, that's for sure. She had very different plans for me. I wish she could see me now, for I find running this household very much to my taste. Did she know of my marriage?'

'I don't know, Kat; when Father died, she went away. I think the idea of being under *my* guardianship did not appeal.'

'I cannot imagine it would suit her to be under anyone's guardianship... What happened to Johannes ... to Emil?'

'Johannes left as soon as he could, but Emil went with his mother, for there was little for him in Lippendorf. To be truthful, there was little for any of us, for it seems she didn't bring the money Father thought she would. I suspect you could buy and sell us all, Kat, and perhaps there is justice in that.' I get the impression he is about to say something more, but he changes his mind.

I contemplate probing, but before I can say anything, there is an eruption of sound above our heads. 'You promised.' 'I did not!' 'Yes you did.' 'I'm telling.'

'I can generally get to twenty,' I say, 'before whatever the problem is lands at my door.'

I am barely at fifteen before the room is full of children, all speaking at once.

I hold up my hands. 'Whoa. Is that the way to greet a visitor?' Ten pairs of eyes fix on Hans.

'Who…?'

'Are they? Not all ours, don't worry.' I divide them up, corralling them into clusters. 'These are Martin's nephews and nieces, who also bide with us, and these' – I draw Paul and Margarethe forward, pride in my voice – 'are our own two youngest. Greet your uncle Hans,' I say with a smile.

Margarethe cocks her head to one side. 'Do you live far away?'

'Not very far.'

'Why haven't we seen you before then?' Her gaze is piercing, direct.

'Because I haven't lived at Leipzig for long. Before that I *was* far away.'

'Oh. Didn't you have a horse?'

'Margarethe. It is not polite to question so.'

Hans' mouth is twitching, as if he struggles not to laugh. He reaches out and tugs a curl escaped from her cap. 'I have a horse, but not a very good one.' He looks over her head at me and winks, and I know he is remembering, as I am, how I used to question him and how in response he tweaked *my* hair.

365

'Like mother, like daughter, I see.'

I am much better still by the time Hans leaves, the years that separated us melting away as I show him round our holdings, pride oozing from me. I take him to the Heffner land and then to the fields we have outside the town boundaries, and afterwards we walk in the cool of the evening in the garden, as he examines some of our more exotic produce, and we talk of Father and Anna and of my convent years.

When I first mention them he flushes, as if he feels somehow responsible for my incarceration. 'It wasn't all bad,' I say. 'There was a sisterhood, a sense of belonging, of safety; and I might very well have remained enclosed happily enough, for it was what I expected at the time I took my vows. Until everything changed.'

'Martin?'

'Yes.'

How did you hear of his teachings? They would be forbidden, surely.' There is genuine curiosity in his voice.

'They were smuggled in, over a period of years, and gradually took hold of a dozen of us. We became even closer as a result, and some of them' – I look down, for I don't want him to see the moisture in my eyes, – 'remain my best friends to this day, though far from me. Strange how things turn out... Nimbschen is a Lutheran convent now, our aunt still the abbess there.'

'Have you ever seen her, since you left?'

'No. I am as guilty as you in not travelling far from home, for there is always much to do here. And to be

366

truthful, I'm not sure how I would feel entering through that door again, Lutheran or not.'

Klement we talk of only once, for at the mention of his name Hans stiffens and won't be drawn, other than to tell me he struggles to settle to anything constructive. 'Least said, Kat, least said…'

Once or twice when we are sitting at dinner, the company spread the length of the table, the level of conversation rising and falling according to the food set before us, I see Hans looking at me and I wonder what he is thinking. It is when I am talking of Nimbschen and how I wanted to assist in the piggery, but it had been considered improper, that he makes a suggestion.

Martin cannot resist teasing when I tell him of Hans' offer to sell the land at Zulsdorf to me. 'Would it make you so happy to be "My Lady of the Pigsty"?'

'It is von Bora land, how could I not want it?'

'How indeed?' He becomes serious. 'It is a day's drive. I trust it will not be too much for you.'

'You said yourself, every day I grow stronger. And you know I thrive on being busy. And I'm sure I will be able to drive a wagon as well as any man.'

That makes him smile. 'I'm sure you will! All right then. You may tell Hans we will accept his offer…'

I beam at him. But he holds up a hand.

'Provided I do not find myself as good as a widower for the sake of a few pigs.'

At the height of summer he is called away to sort out a dispute. As always he is a good correspondent, his letters both regular and lively. It seems Eisenach too suffers from the extreme weather.

…all around is heat and drought, it is unbearable day

367

and night...

I imagine him mopping at his neck, sweat staining the linen around his throat, and trust whoever is seeing to his clothes will make a competent job of it.

...they say forest fires rage across Thuringia ... and no doubt will give excuse when winter comes to increase the price of firewood...

In his final letter, he sends word that in his absence I must help Bugenhagen in the choosing of a pastor for the court of the Count of Schwarzenburg. I hug the letter to my breast, the warmth in his words spreading through me like a flame.

You are prudent, Käthe and in this I trust your judgement, even more than my own.

Dorothea humphs when I show her the letter, but it is not in disapproval. 'At least he has the sense to acknowledge it.'

I wrap the knowledge of his confidence around me like a blanket and long for him to return home, so that I can share our decision in this matter and hear his 'Well done'.

But when he does return there is little time for any conversation, and part of me wishes he had stayed away, for he is vulnerable to infection and more than forty of those living in the Lutherhaus are ill. Though I am fully recovered and can oversee the nursing of them, it is a trying time. Hanna Schurf is a godsend, and we three, Dorothea, Hanna and I, take turns in preparing the special diets, herbs, massages and compresses Dr Schurf prescribes.

Barbara insists on helping by sitting with those who seem most at risk. She brushes aside my objections. 'Don't fret, Kat. I have dealt with many fevers and come to no ill.

Lucas often says I have the constitution of a horse. And while it might not be the most flattering of comparisons, I have to admit the justice of it.'

The night vigils are the most difficult, the times when fears multiply, and when I find myself constantly checking on our own children, bending close to hear their regular breathing. The guilt I feel when another child succumbs and ours do not is an additional burden. Once again Martin surprises me, both by his recognition of my unspoken feelings and his sympathy for them.

'It is only natural to be glad when your own flesh and blood are spared, even if it is at the cost of others. In heaven we will be perfect, Käthe. God does not expect it of us here, and neither should we.'

He is not there to comfort me when the next blow falls, and I miss him sorely. Melanchthon, who had been ordered by our elector to attend a meeting of theologians at Hagenau, is taken ill en route, and Martin and Caspar Cruciger are ordered to Weimar to see how he is.

The news here is as sudden as it is unexpected, and the cruellest part, that it comes when we are beginning to think the worst is over, with all but three of those ill in the Lutherhaus showing signs of recovery. At first I think nothing of it when Barbara doesn't appear, for we are well able now to cope by ourselves. I do find it strange she doesn't send word, but presume something that should have been dealt with weeks ago, had she not been helping us, is taking her attention. I leave Hanna attending to our last patients and slip out into the garden to assess the state of the vegetable beds and how much they may have suffered from my inattention. My mind is already running ahead to the following season, to crop rotation, to new plants to attempt, when I hear Dorothea cry out in the kitchen.

'No. Oh No!'

Anna Cranach is by the sink, Dorothea collapsed against the range, her sleeve touching the hotplate. Neither of them seem aware of the smell of singeing wool, and I dart forward and pull her arm away. She looks up, surprised.

'What's happened?'

Anna flinches as if I've hurt her.

'Barbara?'

She nods.

'Fever?'

'She's dead.'

'She can't be! Two days ago...'

'Two days ago she came home complaining of a headache. Today she is dead.' Anna's voice cracks.

I reach out to her and she turns and pounds her fists against my chest.

'If she hadn't come here...'

I pull her close and she drops her head onto my shoulder and we cry together, my tears wetting her hair, hers soaking into my blouse.

There is a hissing and a bubbling behind us. I turn my head in time to see the stockpot boiling over, a river of liquid streaming across the stove and pouring onto the floor, Dorothea leaping up to grab the handle and pull it off the heat. I hear her sharp intake of breath as she swings round to plunge her hand into the bucket of water.

'Count to fifty,' I say automatically. 'With luck it won't blister.' But later, as I smooth salve onto the stripes of seared skin, I wish it had been me: with an external pain to override the void I feel inside.

I have barely begun to accept Barbara's death, when other ill news comes. Justus Jonas is called to minister at Halle.

'Will he go?' I ask Kath, an empty feeling swelling in my stomach.

'We all will, and very soon.' She sighs, squares her shoulders. 'It is to be for a two-month trial, but I cannot see it coming to an end. These things never do. I have tried to tell myself it is not so far away, that we can visit, but it never seems to work like that, does it?'

I think of Eva, of the promise we would be best friends forever, and of the one and only time *she* managed to come back. How, perhaps inevitably, though my affection for her has never wavered, I have come to depend on others, Kath among them, for day-to-day companionship. And all the more since Barbara was taken. I think of the rest of the Nimbschen sisterhood, long since lost to me, and shake my head. 'No. It doesn't.'

I am determined not to disgrace myself by crying as we line up outside the Elster Gate to wish them 'Godspeed'. And I manage it, though it is a close-run thing, and had Justus not cut our goodbyes short, I don't think I would have been able to contain my tears. Afterwards, I shut myself in the privacy of our chamber and cry as if my heart will break.

Dorothea comes to get me, brisk and deliberately hearty, despite the huskiness in her own voice. 'Supper is ready.'

As I lift my head she says, 'And it isn't only you who is losing a friend. Your children need you, for they too are hurting.'

I throw cold water over my face and pinch my cheeks to bring some colour back, and drawing in deep breaths, rejoin the family clustered around the hearth.

Zulsdorf is my salvation. I can indeed drive a wagon, and derive pleasure from the surprise I see on the faces of other drivers as I wait for my turn to pass through the archway out of the town. Dorothea is understanding of my need to spend more and more time there, and we employ two more maids to cover my work at the Lutherhaus, and Martin's joking moniker 'My Lady of the Pigsty' becomes a reality. I write to Hans and tell him of the litters the sows have produced, of how I love to watch them suckle as we once watched the foal in our paddock at Lippendorf, and that in a year or two I expect it to be profitable once more. His reply is brief, but encouraging, and I smile to think how things have turned around; it is he who is now overseer of a Protestant convent, while I am a farmer. And both of us content.

It is not long before my contentment is challenged again, Zulsdorf the focus of an increasingly rare argument, but as heated as any I can remember.

It begins with a letter from Martin, informing me the Turks are once again on the move and have reached Budapest, and counselling me to sell the Zulsdorf estate and remain in Wittenberg. It is counsel I choose to ignore, trusting that by the time he returns the situation will have changed, or at least his reaction to it may be moderated. 'How can he ask it?' I say to Walpurga, who since Barbara's death has increasingly become my closest companion. 'He should know how important it is to me.'

She is typically positive. 'You should rather take it as a sign of how important *you* are to him. He thinks only of your safety… What will you do?'

'Wait. It is not an order, merely a suggestion.'

Her eyebrows shoot up. 'From Martin? A suggestion?'

'Yes, well. It isn't phrased as an order, therefore I shall not take it as such.'

But when he arrives home it is Lucas who unintentionally gives him an opening. He has taken to spending more time with us in the Lutherhaus, likely to avoid the emptiness in his own, the twin losses of his firstborn, Hans, and now of Barbara visible in the new lines in his face.

'You have heard the news from Budapest? I had not thought to find the Turks so close to our borders once more.'

Martin swirls the wine around in his glass, as if he is a taster. 'I know of the siege. Is there more?'

'The city has fallen. And they say there has been little mercy shown.'

Martin straightens. 'Then you *must* sell Zulsdorf, Käthe, Right away. I cannot countenance you so close to potential danger.'

If he had said 'I don't *want* you to be in danger', if our acquisition of it had not been so recent, if I had not been so recently ill and like to die, if Barbara had still been here to moderate me, if it had not been so much part of my own heritage, I might not have reacted as strongly as I do. As it is, I flare up. 'I *must* sell? Do I have no say in this? I have worked hard these last months to build that farm back to what it should be, and I *will not* lose it all now, for the sake of a danger that may never come.'

He is on his feet, puffed up, his face as red as the radishes I was pulling this morning. 'You forget yourself, Katharina. And your obligations. To me and to our children.'

I am also on my feet, facing up to him, anger boiling inside me. 'It is for you and our children I work myself to the bone. If it were not for me we would have been in penury long ago, and as for danger, it would have mattered little whether the Turks were on our doorstep, for with them or without them we would have starved to death.'

Dorothea is beside me, a warning hand on my arm. 'Kat...'

I shake her off, my voice as jagged as splinters of ice on the Zulsdorf pond, my glare for Martin. 'We should continue this debate in private, for the biggest danger here is we will both say something we will come to regret.'

In the event the argument is shelved, for a letter arrives which puts our quarrel in the shade. Elector Johann Frederick has been publicly pilloried: called a fat, malicious, lying drunkard, and accused of apostasy and heresy. Although they are the rantings of a duke I have never heard of, Martin is incensed. He shuts himself in his study, and when he re-emerges two hours later he is holding a paper covered in line after line of dense writing, studded with full stops and exclamation marks that cut almost through.

'How dare a reprobate, with a mistress and ten illegitimate children to his name, accuse our elector? He is a hypocrite and a coward, his own sins carefully concealed while he calls out others. Well he will not succeed.' He thrusts the paper at me. 'See that Lucas prints this, today, and by the thousand.'

I have had two days to reflect on our own argument, and though I still have no wish to sell Zulsdorf, I know my part in it was not well done. As I reach out to take the paper I say, 'Martin…'

He keeps hold of one edge of it so that we are standing close. 'No need. We have both said more than enough on that other matter, and much of it already to regret.'

We do not talk of it again, events overtaking the argument. The Turks make no further inroads into Saxony, and with the fear of them receding, Zulsdorf is kept, much to my satisfaction. And, I suspect, to Martin's, but by mutual agreement we buy a townhouse in Wittenberg, an unspoken acknowledgement we are neither of us as healthy as we once were and there may come a time when the Lutherhaus is too much to manage.

I write to Eva to tell her of the purchase, but make light of the reasoning behind it, for to do anything else would be to accept it isn't only Martin who is old now; we all are.

You will not believe it, but we have bought the Bruno house, that we may have somewhere to live when I am too fat or too lazy to walk all the way from here to the market! It is pretty enough, and will serve our needs well when it is just we two to consider. The children are growing up so fast I fear they will have flown the nest all too soon…

When the reply arrives from Konigsberg, the handwriting unfamiliar, I know, without reading, what it will say. There can only be one reason for Basilius to write. I am still sitting on the bench by the kitchen, the letter lying open on my lap, when Martin comes home. I look up at him, my eyes stinging, as if they are full of grit.

'How can it be? She was so alive,' I say.

He plumps down on the bench beside me. 'Who, Käthe?'

I hold out the letter. 'Basilius has written to tell us that Eva…' When I say her name it is as if it opens a floodgate, the tears that eluded me coming in great, choking sobs. He turns to face me, taking both my hands in his.

'I'm sorry, Käthe, this is a heavy blow.'

'She was my oldest friend; and too young … too full of happiness to die.'

'No one is too young, Käthe, we of all people know that, and as for happy … better she had a good life with Basilius than a miserable one.'

CHAPTER THIRTY-NINE
WITTENBERG, AUGUST–SEPTEMBER 1542

It is barely a year before the jest I made in my last letter to Eva, the one she was destined never to receive, becomes a reality. Martin sends Hans, now sixteen, along with his cousin Florian, to study grammar and music at Torgau, and I wonder if I will recognise him when he returns, for he is already taller than his father and as sturdy. However much I know I will miss him, I don't protest, remembering Barbara's advice to choose battles I can win. But when Paul pleads with his father to be allowed to accompany them and Martin agrees, I do object. 'We know he is clever, that much has been obvious almost from his first words, but nine is too young to go away from home. He has no idea what it will be like. I do not think he will cope without us.'

'He will not cope without us? Or you will be bereft without him?'

'I know what it feels like to be cut off from family.'

'He will not be cloistered and will have Hans and Florian to look after him.'

'They are young men. He is still a child.'

'A child with a brain in him that should be nurtured. And he will be living in the schoolmaster's house and well looked after. Besides, Torgau isn't far. I promise you, if he is homesick he can come back at any time.'

And with that I have to be content.

It is at mealtimes I feel their absence most. Two seats at our table, that though they don't remain empty for long, for me remain peopled by ghosts. There are other ghosts too, that come at odd moments to trouble me, however hard I try to lose myself in the comfort of routine. They flit in and out of the rooms at the Lutherhaus, shadowy and insubstantial: the children we lost to fever, Barbara and Eva, my unborn child, and even Kath, who though alive, feels as far removed from me as to be as good as dead, for all the likelihood there is of a return to Wittenberg. I school myself to focus on daily activities and refrain from looking further ahead, for fear of worse to come.

Martin is at home: lecturing, writing, and holding forth at Table Talk, a new group of students and guests listening and debating and scribbling down his every word. He is not always well, suffering from bouts of dizziness, problems with his bowels, and with recurring periods of depression, when he shuts himself away, as he did when word came of Andreas Karlstadt's death. Once, when three days pass without a word between us and I am at my wit's end, I dress in mourning. He is jolted out of his silence.

'Who has died, Käthe?'

'I thought God had,' I say, 'if Martin Luther is so depressed.'

There is no explosion, only a quiet, 'Oh, Käthe.'

'Come back to us,' I say. 'We need you.'

Young Martin, at almost eleven continues to make me

feel uneasy. When I suggest to Martin I think he relishes the hunting of songbirds a little too much, he laughs at me.

'Every young boy enjoys hunting, just as every girl enjoys skipping. It is perfectly natural.'

I try to tell myself it is merely his physical resemblance to Klement that disturbs me, and it is unfair to judge him so, but the unease remains. We both delight in Paul, for the word that comes back from Torgau is he is happy and shows much promise, studying with a will, though Margarethe wanders around the Lutherhaus like a lost soul, for want of him.

'He will go far,' Martin says, 'for he has inherited both dedication and intellectual ability. The first from you, the second from me.'

It is a backhanded compliment, but I let it pass.

Magdalena is at an awkward stage, part-child, part-woman. On her good days we are the best of friends and can work together with a will. She continues to sing like an angel, a soaring soprano to my alto, harmonising naturally, without the need for a musical score. On her good days, I wish she could stay just as she is forever. On her bad days, she growls at everyone who dares to look at her and I learn to keep my distance.

Dorothea is philosophical. 'Don't worry about it. Don't you remember what it was like to be thirteen and unsure of your place in life, of what the future held for you?'

I think back to Nimbschen. At thirteen my future stretched ahead of me, safe, dull, monotonous. Every hour of every day prescribed by rules and observances, with no possibility of anything other. And difficult or not,

I'm glad she has the better portion.

The boys have been away less than a month when she complains of a sore head. At first I make light of it, for surely it is nothing more than that she has stayed out too long in the sun and will be bravely in the morning. But by the next day she is running a fever, and when Martin comes breezing into the chamber she shares with the other girls, his booming voice clearly intended to cheer her up, she winces, as if listening to him hurts.

For a week her fever rages, Dorothea and I taking turns to sit with her, but despite all our efforts, constantly wiping her down with cloths wrung out in water set to chill in the basement, we fail to reduce her temperature, her skin on fire. Martin sends word to Torgau for the boys to come home, a sure sign, though he does not say so openly, he fears for her recovery. And although it is only part way through September, the leaves on the trees outside her window curl as if they too are dying before their time.

It is at dusk, Martin and I sitting either side of the bed, when I sense a stillness creeping over her. For a moment I think it a good sign she is no longer restless, but as her eyelids flicker and her features smooth out and her chest rises one final time, her hand slides from my grip, to lie palm up on the coverlet.

Martin gathers her in his arms and cradles her against his chest, his sobs harsh and guttural as if they would tear him apart. 'I never imagined,' he says, 'parents could love their children so much... That I could.'

I retreat to the far side of the room, for I cannot bear to look at them, at her, for if I once allow myself to cry I fear I shall never be able to stop. I am still dry-eyed

381

when Dorothea opens the door, and taking the situation in at a glance, she disappears to return with Bugenhagen in tow. He kneels on the floor beside Martin, putting his arm around his shoulder, and it seems to steady him, for he begins to cry more softly, the harsh note gone.

He gestures to me to come to the bedside, but I am unable to either move or speak. I am glued to the floor, and though I am not crying on the outside, I feel as if my insides are melting away, down through my legs and out through the soles of my feet to seep through the cracks in the floor, leaving a hollow shell behind.

I know nothing of the arrangements for her funeral, nothing of what is done in my name, and I stand at the graveside, with no sense of how I got there, no awareness of the people clustered round me. The words of the committal flow over and around me, like a current, and I cling to Martin's arm for fear I will be washed away. He is urging me forward. I look down, as if through a curtain of rain, at the flower in my hand, milk-white liquid oozing from the crushed stem. As he prises my fingers apart, allowing the flower to drift down onto the coffin lid, my legs give way. I teeter on the edge of the grave, his tightened grip holding me upright, while Bugenhagen pronounces the final benediction. Afterwards, the image that haunts me is not of Magdalena, but of Margarethe, her eyes red-rimmed, stepping forward with a posy of wild flowers produced from behind her back. They are already drooping, the petals scattering, as she drops them into the grave.

We are none of us the same, however much we try. Martin is busy, as always, but his footsteps are leaden and many of his old ailments return to trouble him. As we slip towards autumn his breathing difficulties increase and he is constantly clearing his throat and spitting sputum. Once I would have been irritated by it and would have remonstrated vigorously, now I lack the energy for more than the mildest complaint, and find myself worrying instead. He talks of pains: in his ears and legs and kidneys; of dizziness and of issues with his bladder and bowel I'd prefer not to be the subject of conversation at our dinner table; and I begin to think there is little left of him functioning as it should.

When I try to make a jest of it he shrugs. 'I am an old man, Käthe, and am fortunate to have lasted as long as I have.'

I cannot deny the truth of that and it frightens me. Perhaps something of my fear shows in my face, for he continues, as if in encouragement.

'I have made a new will, with proper provision for you and the children.' There is a hint of his old autocratic self. 'I have named you guardian, for I know of no one who could do a better job. Do not let them take that away from you.'

I nod, acknowledging the affirmation, but though once it would have wrapped itself like a blanket around my soul, now it gives me less pleasure than if it had been a contract for logs he spoke of. I can barely cope with Magdalena's death, and I have no wish to think on his. My own health issues I don't share, though I suspect Dorothea has an inkling, for sometimes I surprise her watching me, and she takes on more and more of the work in the house, waving aside my protests.

Hans, Florian and Paul return to their studies at Torgau, and for a time the younger children slip about the house like wraiths, as if afraid to raise their voices, lest they invite censure. It is as if the Lutherhaus is shrouded in shadow, Martin and I also tiptoeing around each other, our conversations stilted, reduced to practicalities. And when I overhear him, his voice ragged, telling Philipp Melanchthon that Magdalena's death has torn his heart in two, it is a double blow, that he can speak thus to a friend, but not to his wife.

'He used to talk to me,' I say to Walpurga, when she calls on a pretext. 'But in this it seems we are no better than strangers.'

She catches her lip between her teeth, a gesture I have come to recognise signifies uncertainty, then, drawing in a deep breath, says, 'When we lost our firstborn, for a time Johannes would not even mention her name. When I finally had the courage to challenge him, I found his silence came, not from a desire to bury her memory, but from a fear that to talk of her would distress me. Perhaps Martin feels the same.'

It is a new perspective and one I need time to consider. 'If she had only died in the spring I would have had the garden to occupy me, but as it is...' I tail off, but she makes the leap.

'You find it hard to find a focus?'

'No focus, no energy for work, no matter how little Dorothea allows me to do.'

'The wound is still raw, Kat, for all of you, and perhaps the more so for that it was unexpected. Had she been much younger, or frail...'

384

'Like Elizabeth?'

'Yes.'

'I didn't begrudge God Elizabeth, not in my heart of hearts, for it was clear from the start she was more fitted for heaven than earth, but Magdalena...'

'Was your little songbird, and on the cusp of womanhood.'

'I wanted to see her married.' As soon as I say it, I realise it is the kernel of my loss, and I feel a fresh guilt that I should think of myself at such a time.

She leans across the table and takes both my hands in hers, her grip firm. 'It is not unusual to want to live vicariously through your children, and doubly understandable for you, for your own childhood was taken away. No one would blame you for laying your hopes on her... Kat?'

I begin to shake, the tears to flow, and she comes alongside, wrapping her arms around me. When I am done, she says, 'It is healthy to grieve, Kat, healthy to cry, but...' – she hesitates – 'healthier still if you can cry together, believe me.'

Despite Walpurga's advice, Martin and I do not cry together, and I wrestle with how to achieve that aim. We are sitting after supper, the younger children, still subdued, clustered around the stove, when I bring out Martin's lute. His first reaction is to wave it away, but I lay it in front of him and steel myself to speak. 'Play for us, Martin, please. We have neglected music lately, and all of us the losers by it. Something cheery. A folk song perhaps?'

Margarethe comes to stand beside him and rests her hand on his knee. 'Please, Vati.' The other children scramble up to surround him, echoing the request.

385

He picks up the lute and strums and we both wince at the discordant note. There is a catch in his voice. 'This has indeed lain too long.' He tunes it swiftly, then ripples up and down a scale and begins to sing, softly at first, and then with more confidence as we all join in. After the third song, I produce the hymnbook he wrote for Magdalena and place it on the table, open at her favourite hymn. His mouth tightens and I think he is going to refuse, or at least choose a different one, but Margarethe puts her hand on his arm and looks up at him, her eyes shining.

'This is Magdalena's favourite. If we sing loudly, will she hear us?'

Stroking her hair, I say, 'No need to sing loudly, poppet, heaven is only the sky away; she'll hear.'

Over her head I look at Martin, my eyes full of appeal. He takes his handkerchief and wipes at his cheeks, and with a deep breath plays the first chord.

I shut my eyes and see Magdalena, not as I last saw her, pale and weak, but dressed all in white, her auburn hair curling loose on her shoulders, her eyes sparkling. I imagine her singing along with us, her face up-tilted to a cloudless sky, her voice soaring like a lark.

Afterwards, the children abed, Martin picks up the book again and begins to play, hymn after hymn after hymn, and as we harmonise, the distance stretching between us contracts. And when finally he sets down the lute and reaches for my hand, I slip onto the floor at his feet and the tears come to us both.

CHAPTER FORTY
WITTENBERG, OCTOBER–DECEMBER 1542

We have had our share of troubles, and it seems they are not over yet. Martin stands in the doorway of the Stube, his expression grave.

'What is it?' A myriad of possibilities flash through my mind, none of them good.

He hands me a letter, which is brief and to the point.

Joachim Jonas has drowned in the Saale river. A needless accident. Justus will write more presently, but for the meantime he asks for our prayers.

I think of Kath, of how, though she would not have admitted to it, and despite, or perhaps because of his mischievous nature, she favoured Joachim.

'If only she were here, I could go to her.' Another thought. 'If Jonas had not accepted the call…'

'Jonas was but following God's leading. No one could have anticipated this would be the outcome.'

It is three days before we hear from Justus again, three days in which my mind whirls with questions – how did it happen, why, and chief among them, the question I have wrestled with since Magdalena's death: how could a good

God let these things happen. That last, a question I must argue out for myself, for I cannot disturb anyone else by my lack of faith.

Martin is at the university when the messenger arrives with Justus' second letter, and I retreat to our chamber to open it. The writing covers only half a page, the detail factual, presented without obvious emotion, yet I sense the pain in every syllable.

...the children were given strict instructions not to go down to the river, which was in flood following heavy rain. But Joachim threw a stick in at the bridge and scrambled to the bank to follow its progress downstream, apparently to see how long it would take to reach the meadow. Jost tried to stop him, and when he couldn't, he gave chase, shouting for him to come back.

There is a blot of ink on the paper, as if Justus' hand has shaken, then the stark statement: *Joachim turned around and lost his footing, and before Jost could reach him, he was swept away. My only consolation is that they say drowning is a swift death and without pain. But that helps neither Jost nor Kath. He blames himself, while she blames our move to Halle. I fear for her state of mind and for our unborn child.*

That news is unexpected, and I don't know whether to be glad or concerned, for, like me, she is over old for pregnancy, and another loss, coming so soon on the heels of this one, would be even harder to bear.

There is an honesty in his final words that almost breaks my heart, for I know how hard it must have been for him to write so.

I fear Sophie blames God, for she looks at me with eyes as hard as pebbles, and when she should say her

388

prayers, she keeps her mouth firmly shut. And most of all, I fear I find myself in sympathy with her.

When I show the letter to Martin, he reads to the end without comment, folds it up and sets it aside. After a moment I break the silence. 'What will you say to him?'

He doesn't answer immediately, instead takes my hand and turning it over traces the lines on my palm. 'We are called to weep with those that weep. And of a surety that is what is needed here. Though as you know, sympathy has never been my foremost virtue.'

In any other circumstance I would have laughed at the understatement, but not in this. He hesitates. 'Hard as this is to contemplate, Käthe, if we had not our own sorrow to bear, perhaps we could not have shared in theirs.'

Winter comes early, with biting frosts setting the roads hard and turning the verges to crackling. Martin is once again writing, his latest pamphlet, *The Jews and their Lies*, as harsh as the weather. He calls their synagogues 'dens of devils' and advocates burning them down and expelling all Jews from Saxony.

I question Bugenhagen. 'Where has this virulence come from? There are no Jews in Wittenberg to cause trouble, and when he talked of them in the past he advocated winning them over to faith by respect and kindness.'

'In the past he expected them to be convinced by his teaching that Christ was their Messiah, and he has been bitterly disappointed. And I fear he may have been infected by tales of atrocities from elsewhere: the eating of babies and the like.'

'Do you believe them?'

'Of course not. And, if Martin allowed himself to think straight, neither would he. But Magdalena's death has hit him hard, harder I suspect than any of us realise, and sometimes if we cannot rail against one thing, we find another target.'

'But what of the harm these may do if they are distributed as widely as most of his writings are?'

'Regrettable as this pamphlet is, it says little more than has been said a hundred times before and in other places. I do not think we need worry unduly about the effect.'

I hope he is right, and try to put it out of my head. The continuing cold nips at my cheeks and ice-coats the entire town, so that going to the market is like walking through a living confection. Branches of the trees gleam silver and bend under the weight, and icicles like daggers hang from rooftops and windowsills. The river is sluggish, clogged with ice flows, and there is talk of the likelihood of a frost fair come Michaelmas. The children are excited at the prospect and so am I, for their sake, and our own, for we could all do with some cheer.

I write to Kath, making four attempts before I am sufficiently satisfied to send it. I can share her sorrow, but what I cannot share is the anger she may feel, for my grief for Magdalena is not tinged with blame. I enquire of her pregnancy and express my hope all will go well, and towards the end of November, when I had almost given up hope, she replies:

...I am well enough, though my ankles swell if I walk any distance and I am dizzy at times. But the babe is growing, indeed I am almost as round as I am tall and won't be sorry to shed my load. It will be a Christmas

child, and though it will never replace the one we have lost, it will at least ensure I have no time to brood on past ills. There is talk of visiting Wittenberg in the spring, but I hardly dare hope for fear of disappointment. I have missed you sore, and trust you will forgive me for not writing before...

I share the letter with Walpurga, as we share most things nowadays. We are the only two remaining of those I counted my particular friends, and she is the more precious as a consequence. There have been so many partings: Eva, Anna, Else, Kath, Elizabeth, Muhme Lena. Dead, deserted or driven away, the effect is the same. The Melanchthons are frequent visitors in our house and our children are inseparable, but somehow Katharina and I, despite sharing our name, have never truly recovered from our period of estrangement nor achieved the closeness we might have wished.

When another letter comes it is the worst possible news. Kath Jonas is dead. Dying on Christmas Day giving birth to her seventh child. When I tell Martin, it is hard to keep the bitterness out of my voice. 'How can Justus bear it, first Joachim, now Kath? It is a heavy price to pay for a quiver-full.'

He is staring out of the window, unseeing, and I know he is thinking of our own family, our own losses. And for the first time I am thankful my own seventh pregnancy ended in miscarriage. For at least I am still here and our children not motherless.

CHAPTER FORTY-ONE
WITTENBERG, MARCH–JUNE 1543

As if in compensation for the harsh winter, spring also comes early, the air warm and still, the vegetable garden watered not by rainfall, but by heavy dews that settle on the ground each night. Despite the lengthy frosts of the past months, the soil warms quickly and sowing gets underway on the land outside the city. Whether it is the pig manure we spread in the autumn or the weather conditions, at Zulsdorf the germination levels are high. Surveying the spikes of young plants, a fresh greening carpeting the fields, it is as if I too am reborn, the difficulties of the previous year behind me.

For a time Martin too is in fine form, the university flourishing, and the students now comprising almost one-third of the population, the town is filled with an air of youthful optimism and a liveliness that cannot help but cheer us all. Besides Lucas' print-works, five other print shops have sprung up and all of them are kept busy. One-third of everything produced flows from Martin's pen, many of his earlier works going into fifth and sixth reprints, and Melanchthon's writings are also popular.

392

When Martin is away, as intermittently he still is, though generally for shorter periods than before, I am in charge of ensuring both the quality of the printings and that they are done to schedule. The men are used to me now, and though once they might have objected to the oversight of a woman, they appear to accept my competence. I come home from one such visit and express my satisfaction at the reception I have received, but Dorothea mutters, 'To your face, maybe, but I daresay it's a different story behind your back. And who knows what scurrilous rumours they might be spreading...'

Her pessimism amuses me, and when Walpurga and I meet later in the square behind the Town Church, I regale her with Dorothea's dire predictions and we laugh together. We stroll towards the market, chatting: about the children, the new lodgers in the Lutherhaus, who have not yet settled to our routine, how the waiting list for those who wish to attend Table Talk grows ever longer and how it is a constant struggle to make our income stretch to match our expenditure.

'Isn't the money you get from guests sufficient?'

I make a face. 'It would be, if Martin would allow me to gather it all in. But he is too trusting, and if someone comes crying "poor mouth" he is ever ready to waive their fee. And there are always those who spin a good yarn, however little bearing it has to the truth. We have been seriously stung more than once.' I shrug my shoulders. 'I do my best, but sometimes his generosity is frustrating, especially when I can see the story being told is as full of holes as Dutch cheese.'

Walpurga grins. 'I've never eaten Dutch cheese. Have you?'

'We were brought a present of it once. I wasn't overly impressed. It was chewy and rather bland. My preference is for a more creamy offering, or something with a bite to it.'

'Does Martin give away money as well as refuse to take it?'

'I don't give him the chance. But silverware, that's another matter. If he had his way we would have none at all, for it would all have been either gifted to people he considered worthy causes or pawned to meet our commitments.' We pause on the corner outside the Cranach print-works. 'You know we were once offered four hundred gulden a year for the rights to Martin's work? We would have been debt-free.' I sigh. 'But it proved to be something on which I couldn't move him.'

'One of the few things then.' She tucks her arm through mine and grins. 'If we are to believe the gossips…'

I flare out my skirt, laughing, in an oblique reference to the 'petticoat rule' I am accused of, and she laughs with me. But as we cross the square I look up at the Cranach house, at the window where I used to stand looking out, and memories multiply, choking my amusement.

Something must have shown in my face, for Walpurga also sobers. 'You miss Barbara.'

'How can I not? She was the first person, bar Martin, to welcome us here all those years ago. And remained a true friend throughout.' I look down at my feet, at shoes she gifted me, at the blouse, also hers, and feel the need to unburden myself. 'I cannot but feel guilty about her death, for if she hadn't been helping with the fever in the Lutherhaus she might still be here now.'

She grips my hand. 'You mustn't think like that, Kat.'

Her response is so close an echo of Martin's, I find consolation in it and manage a smile as we part.

We are none of us smiling when the first case of measles is reported in the town, for next to the plague it is the childhood disease we fear most. Though we try to keep them away from any source of infection, one by one the children in the Lutherhaus succumb, until they are all ill. This time it is Walpurga who is the godsend, brushing aside my objections to her help. She doesn't mention Barbara, but I know she is in her thoughts as she says, 'I had measles as a child and am in no danger.'

To our great relief most of the children bounce back quickly, their fever dropping and appetite returning within ten days or so, though they continue to scratch at the rash for much longer, despite our admonitions to the contrary. Margarethe, however, does not bounce back, and I sit by her bedside, day after day, and week after week, consumed by the fear we may lose her.

My prayers take on the feverish quality of the cloister, and though it makes me guilty to think of it, there are times when I wish for the comfort of the rosary. At my lowest point, when she has been ill for eight weeks and the fever still rages, Dorothea comes to sit with me. 'I love the boys,' I say, 'but she is our only remaining daughter, and I couldn't bear it if...'

Dorothea is firm. 'She is a fighter and has hung on too long to give up now. You'll see.'

Martin too is struggling, and I fear for *his* health, both physical and of the mind. When I find him writing a letter and lean over his shoulder to read it, he tries to hide the paper with his hand, but not before I catch the first sentence: *I have had enough and am worn out...*

I cover his hand with mine. 'It is no shame to be wearied. I feel it too. Who wouldn't after all this time.' I offer him the encouragement Dorothea offered me. 'While she is alive, we must not lose hope.' And to convince myself as much as him, add, 'Besides, I think her colour a little improved today, and her breathing less shallow.'

Whether it is our patience or our prayers that are rewarded, by the tenth week Margarethe is sitting up, and, though still white-faced and with arms and legs like sticks, is demanding to see Arlo. We have never allowed him in any bedchamber, but Martin carries him up the stairs and releases him at the door. He bounds in and leaps onto the bed, his stumpy tail wagging, and licks at her face. She tangles her fingers in his fur and rubs her nose against his and he wriggles his rear and yelps in his own version of ecstasy.

Her eyes are alight, and as she hugs him against her I no longer care about the inconvenience of dog hairs transferring onto the coverlet, or the damage his claws might do as he scrabbles to get comfortable. I ignore the dampness of his saliva on her cheeks and focus on her smile, the first we have seen in more than two months. She is crooning into his ear, a steady stream of what seem like nonsense words to us, but to which he reacts with an ever more vigorous wagging of his tail.

Martin is standing behind me, and heedless of the presence of Dorothea and the boys, he puts his arms around me. I can feel his heartbeat, fast, but steady, and wonder if he can also feel mine.

Margarethe has been up and about for several weeks when Bugenhagen appears. We are sitting in the garden in the early evening sunshine, enjoying a rare moment of relaxation. 'Isn't Walpurga with you?' I ask, seeking to quash my fear that, though the epidemic of measles is all but over, something may be amiss.

His excuse is unconvincing and ill prepared. 'What ... no ... she's ... busy, setting down ... beetroot, I think.'

It is so nonsensical I laugh as he flounders – for it's clear whatever else he has come to say it isn't illness brings him. 'Really? Beets? Your garden must be well ahead of ours.'

Martin is laughing too. 'Ever the horticulturalist! I take it you have some news to share.'

Bugenhagen's glance towards me is apologetic. 'News and a need for advice.'

'I'll leave you to it, then. It's time I saw to the children anyway.'

Later, as we are preparing to retire, I say, 'Was Bugenhagen here on university business?'

'No. It was a private matter, but the advice he wanted I was loath to give.'

I swing round, startled, hairbrush in hand. 'Now I *am* curious! You are not normally so reticent.'

'Maybe not. But in this I judged it best he makes up his own mind.'

There is a stillness in his face, a clear desire *not* to give any clues, but I don't want to let it rest, for had it simply been a theological matter he would not be so mysterious about it. 'Does it concern Walpurga or the children?'

He places one hand on my shoulder as if in apology. 'I shouldn't say…'

'You can't stop now, Martin. Else I will worry away at it like Arlo with a bone. And you know I will keep whatever it is to myself.'

'He has been offered the bishopric of Pomerania. It is an opportunity anyone would be foolish to turn down.'

My knowledge of geography is sketchy at best. 'Pomerania?'

'Near the island of Wollin. It would be a homecoming for him.'

I cannot conceal my dismay. 'If I lose Walpurga I will have no one left.'

He squeezes my shoulder. 'You may not have to. Bugenhagen sought my advice because he thinks of refusing.'

'Did he say why?'

'He suspects Walpurga will not wish to leave Wittenberg and is reluctant to ask her to make the sacrifice.'

'Does she know?'

'No. So you mustn't let it slip. If he refuses the offer, she will likely never know.'

Chapter Forty-Two
Wittenberg, January 1545–February 1546

The Bugenhagens stay in Wittenberg, the offer of the bishopric never mentioned in my hearing, so I presume Martin is right in his supposition Walpurga knows nothing of it. I am sorry Bugenhagen has lost a good position, but glad we are not to be parted, for increasingly in the following months Martin is required to travel all over Electoral Saxony to carry out visitations. Even when his journeys are relatively short, to Leipzig, or Halle, I fear for his health. There are those who are still vigorous at sixty, but Martin has had so many ailments, and most of them recurring problems, he has begun to look every inch his age. When I watch him as we prepare for bed at night, I cannot fail to see the slackening of the skin on his arms. It hangs loose and wrinkled over shrunken muscles, like an oversized coat, and I wonder if my skin will do likewise when I am his age. Eva thought him an old man when we first came to Wittenberg, and I cannot disagree now. Although he continues his preaching with as much fire as ever, his sermons are noticeably shorter and he no longer walks everywhere, content to be driven to church in the wagon. The change in him isn't only physical. Once fiery, he is now irascible, his attitude towards Wittenberg altered.

It has been his world since long before he renounced his vows, but now he seems disenchanted, seeing only faults, where once he would have looked for chinks of light. He is as extravagant in his condemnation of the town and its inhabitants as he has always been of the papacy, and I don't know whether to be encouraged by the vigour of his complaints or distressed by his desire to shake the dust of the town from his feet. He comes home from the university and bursts into the Stube, short of breath, his face the colour of fresh beets.

'Sit down and let me bring you a drink,' I say, afraid if he doesn't he may suffer an apoplexy.

He waves away my offer, planting himself in front of the stove.

'What has it all been for?' he says, but leaves no time for an answer. 'They are lazy, cheating, stealing, whoring, drunken, greedy and superstitious!'

'Who?'

'Wittenbergers. Who else? I detest the ungodly behaviour we suffer day after day, despite any attempts to teach otherwise.'

I take his arm, and at first he tries to pull away, but when I refuse to let go, he allows himself to be led to a chair. One battle won, I focus on calming him. 'There are many good people in this town, Martin, our friends among them. Will you condemn them also?'

His colour is subsiding as he accepts the tankard of beer I pour for him, but his acceptance of my statement is grudging at best. 'There are no more true Christians in this town than any other place. I wish I could be anywhere but here.'

His wish is granted, for throughout 1545 he continues to be called to surrounding towns to ordain pastors and sort out disputes. I can see the toll it is taking of him, but when I suggest he curtails his journeyings, he shrugs off my concerns.

'I go at the elector's command, Käthe. You know I can do no other.'

I do know, but not because the elector drives him, but rather because he drives himself. It doesn't stop me worrying, or from writing to him regularly to check how he is. And each time I write I try to include some snippet of encouraging news: of a sermon in the Town Church well received, or some charitable endeavour gaining supporters, or a student Melanchthon reports as showing particular evangelistic promise.

Whatever I have written, it is clear his discontent continues to fester, for in July he writes from Zeitz.

I have no desire to return to Wittenberg, to live out my life in a town with so little reverence for God or the gospel. It is my wish you return the Lutherhaus to the elector, sell all we have in Wittenberg, and move to Zulsdorf. If my salary can help to improve it while I am alive, it may serve you well should I die, for I fear the wolves in the city will devour you once I am gone. Tell Melanchthon and Bugenhagen of my decision, for I shall not come back to Wittenberg.

I tackle Bugenhagen first, not to pass on Martin's message, but to ask him to intervene to change Martin's mind, for he more than anyone has reason to wish us to stay, else his own refusal of a bishopric will have been

401

wasted.

Misinterpreting his hesitation, I say, 'Do *you* think we should go?'

'No. But there is perhaps another reason for Martin's reluctance to return. There was a falling out, with Philipp, and they didn't part on the best of terms.'

'I heard nothing of it.'

'Neither did I before Martin left, but Philipp has confessed it since, though not the cause. I suspect it was a trivial matter blown up by ill-considered words on both sides.'

'Can it be mended?'

'I'll speak to Philipp. And between us we'll bring Martin home.'

When they return, it seems Martin and Melanchthon are the best of friends again and nothing more is said of a move to Zulsdorf. Martin continues to suffer with asthma and catarrh, intermittent ear infections and sciatica, all of which are exacerbated by cold. Despite it, I am almost glad when winter comes, hoping it will keep him in Wittenberg, where at least I can attend to his needs. But in January, he receives a request to go to Mansfeld.

He looks up from the letter, and I see in his gaze the frustration he will not express. 'There is a dispute between the counts of Mansfeld, which we are asked to adjudicate.'

'Does it have to include you?'

'I cannot avoid my obligations, Käthe, and Mansfeld is not so far away. No doubt we will be there and back again in no time.'

'No doubt,' I say. 'The counts have always been noted for how easily they resolve their differences.'

He ignores my sarcasm. 'Sometimes it is those who have the closest family ties who struggle to live amicably together. I am a Mansfelder and therefore feel a special responsibility.'

'Can it not wait until the spring? It isn't the weather for travelling.'

'By spring they might have become so entrenched as to be irreconcilable. Besides, we are not snowbound and therefore have no excuse. But if it will set your mind at rest, Justus and Aurifaber will be with me and we will break our journey at Halle.'

I cannot overcome a feeling of dread and formulate a new plan. To my surprise he doesn't resist when I insist Martin and Paul accompany him.

'Their uncle Jacob will be glad to see them.' His hand on my shoulder feels like a benediction. 'I shall write to you as soon as we arrive.'

The first letter, dated January 25th, comes from Halle, but is far from encouraging.

We left here yesterday making for Eisleben, but found the Saale river flooded and clogged with ice floes. It had over-topped the road and the surrounding land, and threatened to re-baptise us, so we judged it safest to return. We will remain at Halle until it is safe to proceed. Which I'm sure will be soon.

It turns out Martin is right. He writes again on the 28th.

I write in haste for we will depart tomorrow. You need not fear, for the count has sent a troop of horsemen to accompany us. Paul in particular is excited at the prospect of riding in such company and will no doubt be keen to share his experience with you on our return.

When a few days later the weather closes in, I begin to regret sending the boys, fearing they might all be held at Eisleben until the spring, without even letters able to get through. My spirits lift, however, when February comes in bright and sharp, with clear, star-filled nights and glittering mornings. In the garden the apple trees are sugar-coated, and trailing branches of the soft fruits snap underfoot like kindling. Watching the younger children as they make slides in the frost on the paths between the vegetable beds, polishing them to a shine, the absence of Martin and the boys is as sharp as the air. Every morning I have to break a skim of ice in the ewer in my chamber, and I gasp with the shock of the cold as I dash the water on my face. My breath puffs silver and I dress with as much haste as if I were an Israelite preparing for the Exodus. The insides of the windows are frost-etched, the patterns like fern fronds, fine-stemmed and delicate, the sun shining through them so that they sparkle.

I write to Martin, confident that, the ground firm, the roads will be passable, and am rewarded by a speedy reply. Despite the serious content, I am reassured and chuckle at the manner in which he presents it. He begins:

Thank you for your concern, but let God worry, for he could create ten Dr Martins should the old one drown in the Saale, or burn in the oven, or perish in Seiberger's bird trap. Since you started worrying there has been a fire outside my chamber door, and when I was on the toilet, a stone, the size of a long pillow and as wide as two hands, almost fell on my head. Which, had I not jumped out of the way, would have squashed me like a mouse in a trap. If you do not stop, I fear the earth might swallow me whole!

As to health, I have a bad leg, and have to confess I am somewhat grumpy as a result, but Justus Jonas, no doubt envious of my ailment, knocked his leg against a drawer in order to keep me company.

That letter is quickly followed by another, and this time I can almost see the satisfaction on his face.

The counts are reconciled, their children friends and sledging together happily. Despite the fresh snowfalls of the past days, we hope to return home this week, for our job here is done, thank God.

I share both letters with Walpurga, and we laugh together at the image of Martin as a mouse.

Torgau: December 1552

I am so very, very cold. The covers are pulled up to my chin and tucked in tightly, as I would once have swaddled a babe, and though I know they mean well, that they hope to make me warm, I hate the thought that I am reduced again to infancy. The room is full of people and shadows. They cluster in the corners and line the walls and I put my hands over my ears to silence the cacophony of voices: young and old, strident and mocking, pompous and chilling. 'Well past her prime and not the prettiest of the pack.' '...rather too fond of her own opinions...' 'Whore ... spawn of Satan ... an abomination...' '...petticoat rule...'

I cannot stop them, but neither can I tease them out into coherence. Except for Melanchthon. He is by the window, his back to me, but the words are clear. 'Anyone but her.' It is the hardest of all to bear, for I thought his opinion of me altered, but perhaps he only pretended a change, for Martin's sake. Or perhaps I am mistaken and it isn't him after all. The others crowd towards the bed, their faces swimming into focus, huge and grotesque, spittle flying. They frighten me, as Klement's shadow pictures of goblins and dragons and wolves and bears once did, and I wish I could hide my face under the covers as I did then.

'Please,' I say, 'make them go away.'

The man by the window turns, a lit candle in his hand, and I think I recognise him.

'Paul? Is that you?'

He comes to my side, sets the candle down, and reaches for my hand. 'Of course, Mutti.' As he does so, I see a dark shape crawling towards me on the bedcover and I shrink back against

406

the pillows.

'It's only my shadow,' he says. 'There's nothing to fear.'

'What about them?' I say, gesturing.

'There's only us, Mutti.'

'Look,' I say, 'there. Philipp Reichenbach, Glatz, Clara Jessner, Chancellor Brück. I don't want them here, for they are none of them friends of mine.'

There are tears standing in his eyes, and he presses my hand, his voice soothing. 'Shut your eyes, Mutti, and I will send them away.'

Obediently I close my eyes and hear the shuffling of feet and the opening and closing of the door.

'They've gone, Mutti,' he says. 'They've gone.'

There is a knock at the outside door and muffled voices, then footsteps on the stairs.

'Friends to see you, Frau Luther.'

I nod. 'They were good friends,' I say. 'But they brought the worst of news.'

Chapter Forty-Three
Wittenberg, February 1546

I know as soon as I see them standing in the doorway of the Stube, their bonnets in their hands.

Bugenhagen steps forward. 'I'm sorry, Katharina.'

'No… He wrote of coming home … of bringing a present of trout from the Countess Anna … we were going to enjoy it together.' I collapse onto the settle and shut my eyes, willing them not to be here when I open them again, the message they bring not real. I feel a touch on my arm and force myself to look up, and they are still there, the compassion I see in their faces all the confirmation I need.

Bugenhagen proffers a letter. 'The elector has written…'

I brush away his hand, demand, 'When…? *When* did he die?'

Caspar Cruciger's tone is gentle. 'The day before yesterday. Between two and three in the morning.'

I can manage little more than a whisper. 'The boys…?'

'Were with him when he died. Along with Jonas, Augustine Schurf, the Count and Countess Albrecht, their own physician and the city pastor.' He pauses, as if to give me time to take in what he's saying, continues, 'They say he slept away, peacefully.'

'I don't understand. He was well six days ago when he last wrote... How could he be dead even before I got his letter?'

'That's all we know, Katharina.'

'Perhaps...' Bugenhagen holds out the letter again and I grasp it greedily, tear at the seal.

Dear Special One...

At any other time such an address would have warmed me. As it is I begin to shiver uncontrollably, for if the elector writes thus, there can be no mistake.

We have learned with deep sorrow that our dear, devout Martin Luther departed this life...

My eyes blur. I thrust the letter back at Bugenhagen. 'Please...'

He reads it to me, his voice steady, but the words trickle into my head and out again, like water into a bucket with a hole in it.

...the immensity of your pain ... commend him to the Lord ... ease your burden ... we will not forsake you.

Bugenhagen lays the letter on my lap. 'The elector will keep his promise.'

'It is too soon. Margarethe, Paul ... they are too young to lose a father.'

'God in His infinite wisdom...' he begins.

I look up at him with a flash of anger. 'Has forsaken me.'

Melanchthon steps forward as if to protest, but Bugenhagen halts him.

'It is too soon for all of us, Katharina, and only God knows why, but be assured, He hasn't forsaken you, and nor will we.'

There is a rush of cold air as the door opens. 'Mutti?'

Margarethe flings herself at me, beating her fists. 'It's Vati, isn't it? Why did you let him go?'

Caspar Cruciger intervenes again. 'It was your father's decision.'

She looks up at him and jerks her head at me. '*She* changed his mind a hundred times before, why not in this?'

His tone is measured, controlled. 'No one could have changed his mind in this, child. It was his calling.'

'*Was?*' She drops her hands into her lap, her shoulders slumping, anger replaced by anguish. 'He's not ill? He's never coming back?'

Bugenhagen leans down and strokes her hair, as he would one of his own children, and I know he intends it as a comfort when he says, 'Your brothers were with him when he died.'

She tosses her head as if to throw off his hand. 'But I was not.'

I reach out to hug her to me, for I want to feel the warmth of her body against mine … want to have something of his to hold onto; but she shrinks back as if my touch would burn, and scrambles to her feet, her eyes as hard as pebbles, the accusation clear.

'You weren't there either.'

'I pleaded with him not to go, Margarethe, but he wouldn't be stopped.'

The tears are cascading down both our cheeks now, and she brushes at hers with her sleeve.

I know what she is thinking: that we weren't enough to keep him here, and I wish I could say something, anything

410

to ease her pain, but I have no words to offer, for I share her thought.

'You mustn't blame yourselves,' Cruciger begins.

I look at the three of them, hovering over us, dark-cloaked, and though I know their intention is to console, they seem like crows at a carcass. 'Go away,' I say, 'please, just go away and leave us alone.'

'I want them all to go.' Dorothea is with me in the kitchen as blindly I scour and scour at an already spotless pan. 'I cannot bear to have guests here now. And what point is there? Table Talk cannot continue without Martin.'

'Guests or students, we cannot just throw them out. They will need time to find other accommodation.' She takes the pan from my hand and sets it back on the shelf. 'At least wait until after the funeral.'

She is the voice of reason, but it doesn't change what I feel.

'You don't need to be with them, I will see to everything, but we would be failing in our hospitality – and the good doctor's memory – to act hastily.'

'It was my idea to have them here.'

'Yes. But he came to value their company, and would not have wished them to be cast adrift without warning.'

'As I have been?' I am aware I sound petulant, but am past caring.

She turns me to face her, the sympathy of yesterday replaced by an uncompromising sternness. 'Self-pity does no one any good. You have a daughter that needs you to be strong, and a houseful of orphans who also looked to

Martin as a father. Are they to lose a mother as well?'

There is a moment of hesitation, of a friendship hanging in the balance, before I capitulate, recognising the affection behind her words. 'I will wait. But I cannot sit at table with them. If they talked of ordinary things it would anger me, and if they talked of Martin I do not know if I could restrain my tears.'

Further news comes from Torgau. Though there will be funeral sermons preached in Mansfeld, as custom dictates, the elector has ordered Martin be brought home, to be buried in our Castle Church, in the company of princes. I am touched by the esteem it indicates, but fear a delay. The only funeral of significance I have experience of was of our previous elector, and I think with dread of the time taken for *him* to be brought to Wittenberg. When Bugenhagen calls on the Sunday afternoon to see how I am, I ask, 'Will it delay matters?'

'No reason why it should. The coffin will already have been cast, and the service in Mansfeld is likely past. They will bring him here with all speed.'

And so they do, word sent ahead to prepare for his arrival. We gather outside the city gates, and despite the large crowd, there is a subdued air, with little more than a low murmur of voices to break the silence. Even that fades away when we hear the jingle of harness and clip-clop of hooves and know the cortège approaches. I clutch Margarethe's hand as I hear the creaking of an axle, though I don't know whether I am supporting her or the other way round. The bier is uncovered, the coffin draped in the Wettin colours. Walpurga is on one side of us, Dorothea on the other, each ready to hold us up should the need arise. As the bier rumbles to a halt, I spy

412

the boys among the horsemen and step towards them, feeling a combination of pride at their bearing and an overwhelming need to touch them. Justus Jonas forestalls me, dropping down from a wagon and coming forward to clasp my hand, his attitude formal. I have so many questions for him, but now is not the right time. Mindful of the watching crowd, and determined not to let Martin down, I curtsy and then hold myself upright beside him as around us the procession regroups.

The clergy are first, along with the younger of the students, their voices blending with those of the Castle Church choirboys, their trebles soaring high above the lyrical counterpoint of tenor and bass. They are singing one of Elizabeth Cruciger's hymns, and a favourite of Martin's, and I bite hard on my lip to stop myself crying out. Immediately in front of the bier come the sixty-horse escort from Mansfeld, Hans and Young Martin and Paul at the tail, sitting poker-straight. The horses are perfectly matched, and I think how Martin would have scorned such a detail. Our wagon is next, Justus handing me up, and as we settle on the hard bench and begin to jolt over the cobbles I wish I could walk as the men of the town do. I glance over my shoulder and see Jacob Luder and other of Martin's male relatives, some of whom I've never seen before. If Martin were a wealthy man I might think they come for a share of the spoils, but as he isn't I take comfort from knowing he was much beloved. I cannot see past them, but I know they are followed by Martin's university colleagues and the city dignitaries, led by Lucas Cranach. I wonder if he is thinking of Barbara and wishing she were here, as she has been at all the important occasions we have shared in the past. We process through the city along crowd-lined streets, and as we pass, the townsfolk flood after us, their sense of loss as tangible as my own. In the Castle Church I stand by the coffin, flanked by my children. On one side Hans and Young Martin stare straight ahead; on the other, Paul and Margarethe clasp hands, their shoulders shaking. I ache for them all and struggle to concentrate, as first Bugenhagen, then Melanchthon lead us in thanksgiving for Martin's life and offer comfort in our sorrow. There is a swell of sound as we sing a final committal hymn and it is done.

The rest of the day passes in a blur of voices and faces and endless expressions of condolence, and at the finish I have no idea who did or didn't speak to me. All I know is I will not rest until I have questioned Justus Jonas, for I need to understand how Martin died.

It is early evening when Justus is announced. The stove is blazing and I am sitting as close to it as possible, for I cannot get warm, despite the rug around my knees and the shawl over my shoulders. I gesture him to the seat opposite.

He pulls it towards me and once more takes both my hands in his. 'Everything that could be done was done for him.'

I nod. 'Thank you.'

'And you can take comfort it was a speedy passing, for it was only on his last evening he felt the tightness in his chest and retired early to bed. The doctor went to check on him in the middle of the night and found him shivering and struggling to speak. That was when we were sent for. He was wrapped in warm towels and the countess tried to revive him with a solution of the salts you sent, but to no avail.'

I am thinking of the children ... of myself. 'Did he say anything?'

As if he realises I need something to cling to, but the answer to the question might not be the one I want, his grip on my hands tightens. 'He died a good Christian, Katharina, his last words, 'Into thy hand I commit my spirit. Thou hast redeemed me, oh Lord.'

'Nothing for me?'

'You know you were always in his thoughts while he was away from home, his letters testify to that. But at the last he was looking up, Kat, to see the gates of heaven open for him. That is the picture we must seek to remember.'

His use of the diminutive of my name is my undoing, and I begin to shake, great choking sobs ripping through my chest. I sense his discomfort as the tears flood down my cheeks, but I do not know if I will ever be able to stop.

CHAPTER FORTY-FOUR
WITTENBERG, FEBRUARY–JUNE 1546

At first it seems everyone wishes me well, all the fears of how I would be treated if Martin were not here to deflect detractors seeming groundless. Expressions of sympathy and offers of practical help come from far and near, and though nothing can fill the aching void I feel inside, it is a comfort to know my children will not be left destitute. The elector offers Hans a position in the chancery, and though it means a permanent move to Torgau, I can see his suppressed excitement at the prospect and know he must take it. At almost twenty it is time he made his own way in the world, and he cannot have a better offer. The dukes of Mansfeld send two thousand gulden to be held by me in trust for the children and I am gratified both by their generosity and their faith in me to administer the gift. Other gifts of food and money pour into the Lutherhaus and compensate for the loss of Martin's salary. Some, from our particular friends, could have been anticipated, but many are not, coming from people I scarcely know.

Walpurga is helping me divide Martin's clothes into those that could be passed on to someone in need and those suitable only to be cut up for rags. It is a job I didn't want to tackle on my own and I am grateful for her support. I fear I might cry as I examine his shirts and undergarments for wear, but find, with a specific aim to focus on, I manage dry-eyed. She nods towards the pile to be saved. 'Before your marriage,' she says, 'this pile wouldn't have existed, for the good doctor wasn't noted for taking care of his attire.'

'Is it ridiculous to be proud there *are* clothes that can be handed on?'

'Not at all. It is a testament to your good management. Of the man as much as his clothes.'

I feel tears welling, and not wishing to embarrass her, I turn my head away, though clearly not quickly enough, for she says, 'I'm sorry, Kat, I didn't mean...'

'It's all right, *I* never know what might make me cry; how can I expect anyone else to? But I don't want my friends to have to walk around me as if on eggshells.'

Taking me at my word, she asks, 'Did Martin leave a will?'

'Yes. He promised he has made provision for us all, for he felt the old ways of leaving a widow at the mercy of guardians was outmoded and ungenerous and should be replaced. I believe it was witnessed by your husband and Philipp Melanchthon and Caspar Cruciger.'

'Not Chancellor Brück?'

'No.' I have an uncomfortable feeling in my stomach. 'Should it have been?'

She shrugs. 'Perhaps not, though I believe he likes to have his finger in every pie. When is it to be read?'

'The day after tomorrow. And the chancellor is to be here.'

417

'It will be all right then, I'm sure.'

'I hope so, for Brück has never been a friend of mine.'

We sit around the table in the Stube, Brück at the head, myself at the foot, the children ranged along one side, Bugenhagen, Melanchthon and Cruciger on the other. A folded paper lies in front of Philipp Melanchthon, and my stomach lurches as he lifts it and clears his throat to read.

I, Doctor Martin Luther ... to my beloved and loyal wife, Katharina, the following items as a dower...

Brück is resting his elbows on the table and at the mention of dower places his hands together and taps his mouth with his fingertips.

Philipp continues.

One, the Zulsdorf estate. Two, the house Bruno, and three, the cups and jewellery: rings, chains and medals, both gold and silver...

I have begun to relax, relief flooding me, but Brück's face darkens steadily as Philipp reads, his hands pressed ever harder together, the knuckles standing out white. Several times he opens his mouth and clamps it shut again, in deference perhaps to the convention that to interrupt the reading of such a document would be discourteous in the extreme. However, when Philipp reads, *I have full confidence she will be the best guardian for the children...* it appears he can contain himself no longer.

'This is outrageous! She must *have* a guardian, not *be* one. It is against all tradition, and illegal besides. Are we to set aside our laws in favour of this woman?'

'Perhaps,' Caspar Cruciger, always the diplomat,

418

intervenes, his tone deceptively soft, '…we should consult the elector. Herr Doctor Luther will not have written thus lightly. And there is ample evidence in the regeneration of this house of Frau Luther's capabilities.'

Brück is scathing. 'There is ample evidence of her parsimony and her acquisitive nature.'

My hands are clasped so tightly I am hurting myself.

'Come, come.' Bugenhagen half rises to his feet, but Philipp waves him down again.

'Let us deal with what is *not* contentious first, and for the remainder, no doubt the elector will oblige us with a judgement.' He shoots an apologetic glance at me. 'If we are to overturn precedence, we need higher authority than that in this room.'

Brück is on his feet leaning forward, his face close to Philipp's, his hands planted on the table in front of him. 'I am the elector's chief legal advisor; is that not enough authority for you?'

Philipp is firm. 'No one is disputing your standing, Chancellor, but this is a sufficiently unusual situation to merit taking it to the elector himself.'

Brück straightens, waves his hand as if in dismissal. 'Very well. But know this, my advice, which no doubt the elector will seek, is Frau Luther should be content to live modestly with her daughter on an electoral allowance' – his tone alters from combative to smooth, his smile manifestly false – 'which I would be pleased to recommend.'

Philipp looks for a compromise, but I am adamant. 'I do

419

not care for what he is *pleased* to recommend and I will *not* be dictated to by him. You know it is out of malice he acts, not any desire to look to either mine or the children's interests.'

'Maybe so, but he has the law on his side.'

'*Maybe so?* He may have the law, but I have the wishes of that dear, good man who lies in the Castle Church on *my* side. And who is better placed to know what his children need? I will accept the elector's ruling, and no other.'

Nothing has been settled when I hear that the Wachsdorf estate, on the other side of the Elbe, is on the market. It is the first time since Martin's death I have felt a spark of genuine interest in anything new, and I tell Walpurga, 'Martin was once offered that land but didn't buy it. A decision I have regretted ever since. And now there is another chance.'

'Do you really want to add to your work?'

'I want an inheritance for the children to ensure they will never be in need.'

'You cannot buy it without permission, surely?'

'No. More's the pity. That is why' – I meet her eyes – 'I hope you will speak for me to your husband, and in the meantime I shall ask Melanchthon for his opinion. He is nothing if not honest.'

I do ask Philipp but am not happy with his reply, for although he agrees with me Wachsdorf would be an appropriate purchase, he prevaricates, suggesting I also consult Brück before making my desire more widely known.

'Why? He will oppose the purchase, as he opposes anything I have ever sought to do, consulted or not.'

'He is a dangerous enemy, Katharina, you have ample

evidence of that. If you consult him, perhaps it will suit him to comply.'

'Nothing that suits me will suit him. I will appeal directly to the elector.'

'At least let me see the appeal before you send it.'

I cannot fault his offer, and so, when next he calls, I hand him the statement I've prepared and watch his face closely for a reaction.

'You have made a coherent case, Katharina. I will take it to the electoral council and recommend it be forwarded to the elector.'

It is a halfway house, and perhaps the best I could hope for, but I am not sure I have enough friends on the council to count on a good outcome. 'Well?' I demand when I catch up with Bugenhagen as he is crossing the square behind the Town Church towards his house. Was my appeal sent to the elector?'

He nods, but it's clear he is holding something back.

'What is it?' I say.

'The elector asked Brück for his opinion.'

'And he gave it. And no doubt not in my favour.' I cannot hide my bitterness. 'What did he say?'

'I'm not sure you want to hear it.'

'Oh, I do. I need to know my enemy to know best how to fight him.'

His reproof is gentle, but a reproof nonetheless. 'It is perhaps best not to approach Brück in such a combative manner. Much of what he said can be discounted and will be recognised as such, if you allow him to diminish his own arguments by overstatement.'

'What?'

'That the boys might leave their schools and become

country squires, for instance.'

'That *is* likely!'

'Indeed. But he made other points some will consider reasonable.'

Heedless of the fact we are in public view I grip his arm. 'Just tell me. Whatever they are will not be improved by the waiting.'

'He suggested if you were to get the estate you would do so much remodelling there would be no money left for the children. That you only want the property for yourself. That the best solution is to break up your extravagant household and send the boys back to school immediately.' He has left the worst till last. 'And that the elector should appoint separate guardians for you and the children.'

The sky begins to spin, his voice coming from far away, and I can't make out what he's saying. Someone is shaking my arm and there is a sharp scent in my nostrils. I open my eyes to see Walpurga leaning over me, and sense her relief as she turns to her husband and scolds, 'What did you say to her?'

He is defensive. 'She asked what Brück said.'

'And you told her. In great detail, I'm sure. When she was standing in the street?' It is unlike Walpurga to be so forthright, and I realise with surprise I'm sitting on an upturned crate, with no idea how I got there. When I put my hand up to brush aside what I think is a stray strand of hair, I find blood on my fingers.

Walpurga takes my arm. 'Can you stand? Let's get you inside.'

She cleans my cheek, then presses hard on my forehead.

'What happened?' I say.

422

'You fainted, and have Johannes to thank for it.'

He is shamefaced. 'I'm sorry, Katharina, I should have…'

I wave away his apology. 'Has the elector made a decision?'

'Yes. And mostly in your favour.'

Walpurga wrings out a cloth in cold water, presses it to my head again. 'If you had told her that first she wouldn't be sitting here with a bruise the size of an egg.'

'*Mostly* in my favour?'

'The elector has ratified Martin's will.'

I want to smile, but paradoxically, feel a prickling of tears. I brush my hands across my eyes as Walpurga passes me a handkerchief. She turns to Johannes. 'Everything will be all right then, won't it?'

He is hesitant. 'Despite the ratification, the council insisted on guardians and the elector has agreed. There will be separate guardians for Katharina and the children, the purchase of Wachsdorf to be decided by them. But whatever happens, there is to be one thousand gulden in trust for the children.'

Now I *am* smiling. 'With this and the two thousand gulden from the counts of Mansfeld, they will be well looked after. I shall write to the elector today to thank him. And if I must have guardians, ask that my brother, Hans, and brother-in-law, Jacob, be appointed. Family members are appropriate, are they not? They, I'm sure, will look to their nephews' interests.'

'I think,' Bugenhagen says, carefully, 'there will need to be someone from Wittenberg among them.'

'The mayor, then, or Ratzeberger. Philipp Melanchthon?' Belatedly, I realise he may feel slighted not to be included, so add, 'I imagine I cannot suggest someone like Lucas or yourself, who might be considered too close to me to be impartial?'

He nods. 'Write your letter, and we may pray all will fall into place.'

If only it were so simple. Guardians are appointed, and to my satisfaction, but the wrangling and debate continues. Round after round of proposals and counterproposals, some originating from the guardians, some with Brück. And caught between them, the elector, whose sympathy for my plight is undoubted, but who seems, to my frustration, either unable or unwilling to make a decision. I begin to despair of there ever being a resolution but am determined not to give up the fight, for the children are my priority now. We are into June when the elector finally rules Wachsdorf can be purchased in the names of the boys and the money laid aside for them be put towards the price. In the meantime, they are to remain under my authority in Wittenberg and the Lutherhaus can continue as before. It has been a hard-fought victory, and it is impossible not to feel some satisfaction. I am particularly pleased Wachsdorf is to be a knightly fiefdom, the boys' status assured, but it doesn't compensate for the hollow I have inside. Nor dry the tears I shed in private night after night.

Chapter Forty-Five
Wittenberg and Magdeburg, July— October 1546

Without Martin, we are all of us seeking a new equilibrium. I begin to take in students again, and by July the Lutherhaus is once more bustling. At mealtimes, although the table is crowded, the buzz of conversation just as it once was, all I can think of is the one missing voice. I remember when I tut-tutted at some of Martin's more outrageous comments, and the jests I considered coarse, and wish with all my heart he was still here so I could do so again. I pick at my food, serving myself ever-smaller portions in order to be able to finish what is in front of me, and hope no one else will notice. And despite the loosening of my waistband and a worrying lack of energy, I cannot force myself to eat more. I try to involve the children in everyday tasks, so that neither they nor I have much time to brood, and for them at least it seems to work.

Margarethe and I are in the garden harvesting beans, when she begins to hum softly. It is one of the hymns Martin wrote for Magdalena, and I pause and, setting the basket down, wrap my arms around my chest, swallowing to clear the lump in my throat and fighting the desire to tell her to stop.

She looks up and breaks off, flushing a deep red. 'I'm

sorry, Mutti, I…'

I manage a croaky 'We cannot be forever avoiding all memory of your father.' Drawing in a deep breath, I shut my eyes and begin to sing the hymn from the point where she left off. I have a vision of Martin strumming on his lute, with Magdalena at his shoulder singing her heart out, and for a moment I stumble over the words, but as Margarethe joins in, our voices blending, I find the confidence to go on. When we reach the end I hold out my arms and she folds herself into my chest. I feel her heart beating against mine, the words we've just sung ringing in my head. Releasing her, I lift my basket and we resume our work, and as we do I take up another tune and another, and find in the words a solace that had thus far eluded me.

As the elector suggested, Hans takes up employment at the court at Torgau, and for the sake of Young Martin and Paul, and especially Margarethe, I pretend I do not mind him going, though his absence magnifies my loss. Only to my sister-in-law do I let down my guard, for she understands what it is to be a widow and to see life stretching ahead full of increasing emptiness. I pour out my soul to her but take care no one else sees what I have written

…who could not be deeply grieved and saddened over the loss of such a dear and precious man… No words can express my heartbreak, and I can neither eat nor drink, nor even sleep…

I sign myself 'Dr Martin Luther's widow', for that is all I am now, and will ever be.

426

It is not how I would have wished to be stirred out of the despondency threatening to engulf me, but stir me it does. Philipp Melanchthon comes to call with the news, his face even longer and his expression, if that were possible, more lugubrious than usual. 'The emperor is on the move, his Imperial Army threatening territories held by the Schmalkalden League.'

'And will it touch us?'

'Johann Frederick is mustering troops and will march with others to meet them.'

'But that is rebellion. Martin always said…'

'Martin was an idealist. The elector is a realist and recognises there are times when even good Christians must oppose those in authority over them.'

'Must it be war?'

'When the alternative is to be overrun, Katharina, war is inevitable, however much we might wish it to be different. But it is the intention of the League to pin the Imperial Army on the other side of the Danube.'

'And will they succeed?'

'If all the signatories hold their nerve and if there is no treachery, perhaps. Otherwise…'

'Otherwise?'

'There are rumours … and if they prove true, we may have reason to be thankful for our recent fortifications, however inconvenient we found the building of them.'

'What rumours?'

'That Duke Maurice may support the emperor.'

'Against his own father-in-law and his cousin?'

'The inducement of the electoral crown, is, I imagine, a temptation hard to resist. And it's well known, cousin or not, he has long hated Johann Frederick and coveted his

427

crown.'

And treachery it turns out to be, for when Johann Frederick and his army are occupied in fighting the imperial troops two hundred miles away, Duke Maurice invades Electoral Saxony. He sweeps through the territory almost without opposition, moving steadily nearer to Wittenberg. Hans returns home from Torgau to participate in the defence of the city, which increasingly resembles an armed camp. There are those, Hans among them, convinced that the new fortifications will ensure we can see off any threat, but I am not so sure, and make preparations to leave if the need arises, for I will not risk the younger children's safety, should Wittenberg be overrun. Dorothea agrees with me and together we load a wagon with valuables and necessities, and leave it sitting ready for a hasty exit. All my thoughts, which have for six months been centred on Martin and the hole his death has left in my life, now turn to contingency planning should we find ourselves in danger.

It is late autumn when word reaches us Zwickau has fallen and Wittenberg is now firmly in Maurice's sights. When the university plans a move to Torgau, Hans suggests I follow suit.

'If I were Maurice, I would wish to take Torgau, and thus strike at the heart of Johann Frederick's territory. To lose Schloss Hartenfels would be a blow from which our elector would likely not recover. No. I will *not* follow the university. I will take the children to Magdeburg. I think they will be safer there.'

'What of the farms?'

'What of them? I can do no other than leave them in the hands of the men who work them, and pray God they,

428

and the stock and land, may survive the depredations of an invading army.' I inject confidence into my voice but inwardly doubt any of our hard-fought-for holdings will survive the onslaught. It is a bitter thought, but one I push to the back of my mind, for the children's safety is the most important thing now. On the night before we leave I sit with Dorothea in the kitchen, the thought of the morrow's journey lying between us, a weight that cannot be shifted.

'Am I doing the right thing?' I ask.

'You are doing what you think best. Which is all any of us can do.'

We are not wanted here and it isn't hard to see why. The streets of Magdeburg are thronging with refugees. Everywhere lines of carts and wagons piled with goods clog the routes into the city. Perched on top of them frightened children cling on, lurching from side to side as they jolt over the cobbles, the women walking beside them reaching out a restraining hand each time an ox stumbles or a child threatens to slip. We are moving at a snail's pace and I might as well be walking as attempting to drive, for the horses pulling our wagon have no option other than to plod along behind the cart in front. There is one advantage to being raised up, however, for those who walk are constantly jostled and pestered by men offering help: to lead them though the city, to find them somewhere to stay, to protect them from robbery, or worse.

One such catches my eye, as he insinuates himself in front of a young woman bent almost double under the weight of a bundle strapped to her back. She has two small children hanging onto her skirts, and her arm is looped through the leading rein of a donkey which plods beside her carrying two bulging panniers with a collection of kitchen utensils tied together with string balanced on its back. The man speaks to her and offers to take her bundle, leaning down to tousle the hair of the youngest child. At first she is hesitant, but as he smiles at her, she relinquishes her burden. He shoulders it and leaning down swings the smallest child onto his shoulders, forging a path through the crowd. She scurries to try to keep up with him, but when the way is blocked by a wagon with a damaged axle he drops back, and standing close, one hand steadying the child he carries, he urges her towards an alleyway off to the side. I am too far away to make out his words, too far away to call out a warning as, his hand on the small of her back, he cuts the string at her waist and slides her purse into his sleeve. I will not fall prey to such, but I do begin to fear I have made a wrong decision. The maid who accompanies us sits mute and white-faced; Paul and Margarethe, usually so vocal, huddle down among the goods we carry, likewise silent. Young Martin sits beside me, stiff as a washboard, and I dare not look at him, lest his obvious displeasure is released.

We struggle through the crowds to the outer edge of the city, and I find the address I have been given. It is a far cry from the Lutherhaus, the roof sagging, moss growing on the thatch, the paintwork of the window frames and doorway peeling, and the pane in the only glazed window cracked. As we climb down from the wagon, Margarethe looks at the building and turns to me in mute appeal. I make them a promise. 'We will not stay here a moment longer than we need. But better far from home and safe than in our own place and in danger.'

Young Martin stands apart, radiating annoyance. 'I should have remained with Hans.'

I try to mollify him. 'We could not journey here alone. It was too dangerous. I needed your protection.'

'Now you are here and safe, let me return. There are younger than I manning the walls.'

The words are admirable, but the tone is belligerent, and once again I am struck by his resemblance to Klement. But perhaps bullishness is what we need now. There are obvious dangers, but I don't want to admit them to Paul and particularly to Margarethe, and I struggle to think of a way to keep hold of Young Martin without frightening the others.

'And stop calling me "Young Martin". Father is dead, so there is no longer any need to distinguish between us.'

I cannot argue, however much calling him simply 'Martin' would emphasise my loss, but I must say something, so offer, 'When we are settled I will let you go, and pray God we won't be far behind you.'

CHAPTER FORTY-SIX
MAGDEBURG AND WITTENBERG,
NOVEMBER 1546–MARCH 1547

Late autumn in Magdeburg has an extra bite to it, or perhaps it is that the stove is undersized and we must eke out the coal for fear the supplies will run out. Draughts funnel around the ill-fitting shutters and under the worm-eaten doors, and it is impossible to remain warm, however much we wrap ourselves up. Margarethe, who has never felt the cold before, complains of tingling in her toes, and when I examine her feet I find them swollen and red and insist that, however uncomfortable, she wear two pairs of stockings. Paul makes regular forays to the market, but each time he returns with less than the time before, for food too is in short supply and the prices increase daily. They say the population of the city is swollen to double the normal count, and though we are not under siege, the effect is the same. The open drains fill to overflowing and there is talk of typhoid and cholera, and scaremongering or not, it frightens me. The woman who owns the house we lodge in, initially kind, becomes increasingly truculent as the weeks go by, constantly finding something new to complain about. And if Margarethe and I do venture out, people stare at us and mutter behind their hands, or spit on the ground as we go past.

'Why do they dislike us so?' Margarethe asks.

'There are too many of us. We take their food and their fuel and cause all manner of hardships. We can hardly blame them if they wish we weren't here.'

'Can't we go home?'

It is what I ask myself every day, the answer always the same. 'Not until we know Wittenberg is safe.'

'There are soldiers there to protect us.'

Even bundled up in several layers of clothes she is pretty, her figure beginning to blossom, the thought of the unwanted attentions she might receive a different kind of concern. 'From opposing forces, yes, but there are other dangers in a garrison town.'

With a perception that takes me by surprise she says, 'You needn't fear I would allow anyone to take advantage of *me*.'

I have not thought of Jerome for many years, but I think of him now, the hollow in my stomach as he looked at me, and do not know if I would have been able to resist had my virtue been tested. I force myself to look straight into her eyes. 'It is not always so easy to resist a handsome face and soft words.'

She tosses her head. 'For others maybe. Not for me.'

It is a confidence I don't share, but denting it will not accomplish anything, so I hold my peace. And as the months wear on and the atmosphere in Magdeburg becomes steadily more unpleasant, I devour every snippet of news that comes our way. In November we hear Maurice has been promised the electoral crown, and that

433

Borna, Altenburg and Torgau have surrendered to him. I cannot believe what I'm hearing. 'Torgau? How can Torgau of all places let Maurice walk in without a fight?'

There is real anger in Paul's face and a scornful edge to his voice. 'He promises to protect our faith and treat Johann Frederick with respect.'

'What kind of respect steals your cousin's crown?'

'You were right, Mutti, to bring us here.'

In December the word is Johann Frederick has returned and has liberated many of the previously captured cities. In January, that Maurice has held Leipzig, other cities negotiating with the emperor. In February, that Johann Frederick intends to avoid an outright battle and use the winter to his advantage, depending on the emperor frittering away his resources through siege.

Margarethe is bewildered. 'It cannot *all* be true?'

Paul shrugs, an old head on young shoulders. 'Truth, rumour, who knows?' He touches her cheek. 'But you are safe here.'

It is the beginning of March when we finally hear from Hans that Wittenberg has been held and, the city secure, it is safe for us to return home.

Paul holds out the letter with a smile for Margarethe, but it doesn't reach his eyes.

She is excited. 'Home! We can really go home?'

I look at our meal on the table, the half-stale bread, the cheese I cut the mould from before slicing it thinly, the watered beer. 'Yes. We will go home.'

At first sight the countryside seems unscathed, the lack

434

of colour in the fields no more than the usual dulling of vegetation after frost. But we haven't gone very far when I begin to notice there is no stock of any kind, and a general air of desolation in the farmsteads we pass. The further we travel the more featureless the landscape becomes, and it takes me some time to realise what is lacking. Where we passed forests on our outward journey, there are now swathes of scrubland pockmarked by tree stumps and a scattering of branches, bare but for a few withered leaves clinging stubbornly to the stems.

Paul pulls the wagon to a halt opposite what must have once been a prosperous farm, to judge by the arched entrance and the three-sided courtyard of outbuildings. I stare at the blackened walls and the collapsed thatch, and at the jagged remains of roof timbers standing out stark against the greying sky. It is a sobering reminder we are still in the middle of a war. 'No wonder food is scarce.'

'What happened here?' Margarethe's hand is over her mouth, her gaze fixed on a bundle of what looks like old clothes lying against a half-open door.

Paul is already part way across the yard as I put my arm around her and pull her close. 'Don't look.'

He reaches the bundle, bends down, straightens again, his face drained of colour, and casts about as if looking for something, then heads towards the furthest away building, clearly once a barn.

I call out, 'It's not safe!'

He turns, his expression uncertain. 'We can't leave...'

'We must. If any more of the roof were to fall in...'

He ignores my instruction and enters the barn, only to come out again immediately, spreading his hands wide in a gesture of despair. 'There are others ... and no tools left...'

Margarethe wrenches herself free and slips to the ground stumbling towards him, her shoulders shaking. I leap down after her and grasp her arms, turning her back to face me. 'Come away. There's nothing we can do.'

For a moment she resists, then with a shudder allows herself to be lead back to the wagon. We set off in silence and none of us look back. Much later, as Paul drives on through the darkness, his hands clenched tight on the reins, I say, 'You could not dig graves without a spade.' Margarethe slips her hand in mine and drops her head onto my shoulder. Her voice is little more than a whisper. 'Why must there be war?'

The Lutherhaus is as we left it, but for the lack of people, the corridors echoing as we head for the kitchen. Dorothea doesn't make any attempt to hide her pleasure at our return, enfolding each in an embrace that threatens to squeeze the life out of us. Even Paul is not immune, and though he attempts to wriggle free, his face is suspiciously pink as she plants a kiss on his cheek.

'You have been sorely missed.' She is bustling about laying salt fish and fresh bread on the table and a jar of pickles. 'We do not feed so well as once we did, but we are not starving yet.' Then, as if it has only just occurred to her, 'And have taken to eating here; it is warmer and more convenient. I hope...'

I slide onto the bench seat. 'It is the only sensible thing to do.' As dusk falls I cannot wait any longer. 'What of Hans and Young Martin?'

'Though we would not have wished for this, I think the responsibilities he has taken on will be the making of Hans. You can be proud of him.'

'And Martin?'

She looks down, and brushing breadcrumbs to the edge of the table, collects them in her hand. 'He has not found himself yet, but he is still young.' And then, as if to distract, she nods at Margarethe. 'But I think this young lady needs her bed.'

Margarethe tries to stifle a yawn. 'I'm not tired...'

'Tired or not, we will all benefit from a good night's sleep.'

'But we haven't seen...'

Dorothea cuts in, 'The boys are on sentry duty and won't be home tonight.'

I usher Paul and Margarethe to the door. 'Tomorrow is another day.'

I wake to birdsong drifting up from the garden and my spirits lift. It is good to be in our own place again. The boys are at the table when I come down for breakfast, Hans' smile for me wide. He leaps up and I note with surprise how much he has grown in the months we've been away and now towers over me, though still slight in build.

'Mutti! I am so glad to see you home again.' He hugs me then holds me at arm's length. 'And well; if thinner than I remember.'

'We are all thinner, you included, but perhaps none the worse for that.' I think of the farm we passed on the road.

'At least we are alive.' I step towards Martin.

His expression is wary and he darts a glance at Dorothea, as if afraid of what she might have said. 'Mutti.'

He too has grown, but in contrast to the leanness of Hans, his face is puffy, the whites of his eyes bloodshot. I am determined not to let him see my dismay. 'It is so good to have my children together again. I hope it may last.'

'Where are the others?'

'I have left them to sleep. It wasn't the easiest of journeys, for we encountered some of the ravages of war, and it was not the most pleasant of sights.'

It is clear whatever else may have changed in Wittenberg, gossip still flies fast, for Paul and Margarethe have barely finished their breakfast when Walpurga appears. Her face is drawn and pale and her clothes hang loose on her once ample figure, but her welcome is, if anything, more effusive even than Dorothea's. We head to the garden and drag a bench to a patch of sunshine by the fruit canes, ignoring the nip in the air. At first our talk is all of the children and how they do, and then of the town and those of the residents who remained, despite the dangers.

Finally she asks, 'Have you talked to Hans about the farms?'

'There has been no opportunity yet, but I hope to go myself, at least to Wachsdorf. Tomorrow perhaps.'

She sucks in her upper lip.

'Do you know how they do?'

'Johannes has been to both Wachsdorf and Zulsdorf.'

'That was kind, I could not have expected...'

'You are among our closest friends, why should we not look to your interests, when you are not here to do it

438

for yourself?'

'Because of the danger?'

'He didn't go until he judged it safe.'

She isn't smiling, so I know the news is not good. 'What did he find?'

'The lands are decimated, the stock gone, stolen likely.'

'The buildings?'

'In a poor state also. I'm sorry, Katharina.'

'Don't be. Forewarned is forearmed. I always suspected I would return to find them damaged, for they are both on well-travelled routes. The only question was how severe the damage would be.'

'Do you have money to repair them?'

'As it happens, yes. Just before we left Magdeburg a gift of fifty thalers arrived from King Christian of Denmark. It will be well spent on repairs and restocking the farms. I think even Martin would have approved.'

Her relief at my mention of his name is palpable. 'I'm sure he would. He was proud of how you managed those farms.'

'Yes. Yes, he was … in the end.'

I waste no time in putting the king's money to work, and though the price of what seed there is to be had is extortionate, I pay it without demur, for if we are to have fodder for stock to see us through the winter it must be sown now. Building materials are also in short supply, but I manage to beg and borrow sufficient to make the most urgent repairs. My days are full and each night I fall into bed exhausted, but I'm grateful, for it means I have little time to think and as a result sleep long and deep.

April comes in damp and mild, and I watch with pleasure the new shoots as they poke through the soil, at

439

first a sprinkling and then a covering of green rolled out across the fields. 'Perhaps,' I say to Walpurga, 'this is will be a better year.'

Chapter Forty-Seven
Wittenberg, April 1547–August 1548

My optimism is short-lived, for we have been home only six weeks when word comes that the emperor himself is in Saxony and is moving north along with Maurice and King Ferdinand in pursuit of Johann Frederick. It is as if the whole city is holding its breath to see what may happen.

Young Martin is full of bluster. 'We saw Maurice's threat off before. We can do so again.'

Hans is more cautious. 'If these combined forces reach Wittenberg we will not be able to hold out against them.' He doesn't need to tell me what we should do, and once more I make preparations to leave. This time it isn't only Young Martin who protests, but Margarethe also.

'Must we go to Magdeburg again?'

I choose my words carefully, for I don't wish to frighten her any more than I must, 'This time we will make for Denmark, for King Christian is our friend and will welcome us.'

She is even more horrified. 'So far? We may never get back, never see our friends here again.'

'We won't be going alone. Walpurga Bugenhagen and her children are to accompany us. And others also … If the need arises.'

She speaks primly, as if an adult before her time. 'I shall pray it does not.'

We all pray, but it seems God isn't listening, and there is a certain irony that it is on Saturday of Holy Week when news reaches us.

Hans' face radiates dismay. 'The opposing armies met at Mühlberg, and Johann Frederick's forces are routed.' He swallows. 'The elector has been captured and stripped of his position.'

I clutch the edge of the table to stop myself falling. 'He is still alive?'

'He was sentenced to death, but the sentence has been commuted to life imprisonment and exile to Worms. Maurice…' – his tone is bitter – 'is to be our new elector and we will have to bow to him. And to the emperor when he enters Wittenberg.'

'The emperor is coming here?'

So it seems.'

'I will not bow.' Margarethe tosses her head. 'He cannot make me.'

'We will none of us have to bow to him, for we will not be here.'

We start out well enough, a ribbon of wagons heading north, but this time we take few household goods with us, for we have a long way to travel, food supplies taking priority. As we leave the city, I look back at the towers of the churches standing proud against the skyline and think of Martin lying in the nave of the Castle Church and the stories told of marauding troops, of the desecration of churches, and wonder if he will be left to lie in peace.

I find this journey much more arduous than I expected. Whether it is because we have had so little time to recover from our last flight, or because it feels much more final, I don't know; only that I am wearied and unable to present an encouraging face to the children. Walpurga does her best, but it is clearly a struggle for her also. When we arrive at Gifthorn and are advised not to attempt to go further because of the hazards of travel in the region, I see my own relief reflected in her eyes.

Duke Franz, on whose advice we stop, offers us hospitality, and though we are refugees, he doesn't treat us as such, but as guests. It is a kindness that almost reduces me to tears, but he waves away our thanks. 'We owe much to your husband, Frau Luther, for without his teaching we would still be in chains. This is but a small way to repay it.'

Privately, I worry we cannot trespass on his generosity indefinitely, but Walpurga is more sanguine.

'Let us be grateful for today, Kat, for we do not know what tomorrow may bring.'

It seems she is right, for we have been there barely a month when news arrives from Wittenberg. Duke Franz scans the letter quickly then reads it aloud.

Our elector ceded the city to the emperor to save lives and not one has been lost. When he entered Wittenberg, his first port of call was the Castle Church. There were those who suggested dear Dr Luther's body be dug up and burnt and the ashes scattered...

I gasp and wrap my arms around my chest. Duke Franz looks up and smiles at me and continues.

The emperor's reply encouraged us all, for he declared he did not make war against dead men. It seems not only are Martin's remains safe, but the city also and the university too. By the time you get this letter classes may already have resumed.

I stand up. 'If the university is back we must return home, and at once.'

'So quickly, Frau Luther? Has our hospitality been so poor?'

I fail to see the glint in his eye and redden. 'Not at all, we are so very grateful, it's just...'

He interrupts me with a laugh and waves to a servant to bring wine. 'I did but jest, for this calls for a toast.' He indicates the window, through which the final rays of the setting sun slant across the floor. 'You *will* wait for morning?'

'Yes. Thank you.' As we raise our glasses to happier times ahead, although I am vexed for our elector, and hate to think of him a prisoner, the tensions of the past months begin to melt away.

We make good speed on the journey home, my mind full of thoughts of how I shall fill the Lutherhaus and make it pay. I feel more energetic than I have for months and am looking forward to visiting the farms and seeing how the new crops are doing and if we will have a good harvest. Building up our stock cannot be done in a season, but I am optimistic that in a year or two we will be back to where we were before the war started, and in God's good grace the inheritance for the children will be secure. Beside me, Margarethe betrays her excitement in an inability to sit still and a constant barrage of questions: 'Will we be able to stay at home? Will the garrison be disbanded? Will Hans remain in Wittenberg? Will he still have employment at the court in Torgau? Will Paul go back to school?'

I put my hands over my ears, laughing. 'Stop, stop. This time we will be home for good. Beyond that, I have no idea. But at least there will be peace.'

It is Paul who asks the question still troubling me. 'What of Johann Frederick?'

'We may pray that Maurice keeps his promises to him.'

I am disappointed on two counts. Despite Maurice's assurances, Johann Frederick remains a prisoner, and Philip of Hesse with him; and our farms, which only eight weeks ago had seemed on the road to recovery, have been decimated for a second time. Trees have been felled and the crops destroyed, the barns damaged and the livestock gone. It is a bitter blow, but one I am determined will not destroy me also.

Walpurga is the only person with the courage to ask, 'Do you have the means to repair and restock them a second time?'

It is a question that has preoccupied me since my first visit to Wachsdorf and one to which I have found a solution. 'Funds, no. But we still have silver.'

'Oh, Kat.'

I shrug. 'I cared deeply for it once, but war puts a different complexion on things. And perhaps it is a lesson I should have learned long ago.'

At the Lutherhaus recovery is swift, for with the return of the university there are many students requiring board and lodging, and more who remember the comfort of our rooms and the quality of our food than we can accommodate. It is hard to turn folk away, but as Walpurga says, it is a good problem to have. Several of the larger rooms are let to the university as lecture theatres, and aside from the additional income, in the absence of Table Talk, I take pleasure in seeing the corridors thronging with students and in hearing their voices raised in debate. The entire venture is so successful I plan an ambitious renovation of the whole building. The guardians are more cautious, but I manage to convince them, the house once more ringing to the sound of hammer and chisel and saw. Tools and buckets of lime lie in passageways ready to trip the unwary, and the cheerful whistling of the workmen is occasionally interrupted by an oath, hastily cut off in deference to the setting, as someone hammers a thumb instead of a nail.

Hans does not return to Torgau, Maurice having no need for his services, but Duke Albrecht provides him with a scholarship to study at Konigsberg, and though it is further away from home, I make myself happy for him. Paul has enrolled in our university and remains at home. Margarethe catches the eye of more than one of our students, but I do not think her ready for an attachment yet and so reject any overtures on her behalf.

Walpurga questions me gently, 'Is it that she is not ready? Or you are not ready to let her go?'

'Both,' I admit, 'but so far she hasn't shown a particular preference for any of her potential suitors. If she was to favour someone suitable, I would move heaven and earth for her.'

Perhaps it is my vehemence that causes her to ask, 'Forgive me, Kat, but do you ever think of him?'

'Jerome? Not for years. But watching Margarethe grow up and seeing the students interest in her has brought it all back. The hope, the longing … the almost despair. I want to spare her that.'

She nods and, as if to spare me the memories her query has evoked, steers the conversation in another direction. 'What of Hans? Do his studies suit him?'

'I believe they do, but he has ambitions to be a lawyer, and I had hopes Albrecht would sponsor him to go to Paris to finish there.'

'*Had* hopes?'

'He has refused and claims Hans is not a diligent student.'

'And you don't believe him?'

If it were Young Martin, I would, for he seems born to trouble, but the responsibilities of war settled Hans. I suspect it is the expense Albrecht thinks of. But what can I do? He will stay at Konigsberg and I suppose I should be grateful.'

The Lutherhaus is booming, but the farms are drinking money and I am forced both to pawn more of our silver and to take out a mortgage on Zulsdorf. I sign the papers in the presence of Melanchthon, and though he says nothing, I am sure it is the refurbishment of the Lutherhaus he thinks of, and how, without that expense, this one might have been avoided. Inwardly I acknowledge the truth of

447

it, and for the first time understand something of what drove my father to remarry. And though at times I am lonely, that is a solution I will not contemplate. I cannot touch Wachsdorf, nor do I wish to, and for a time, when I consider the future of the land holdings, I lurch between buoyancy and despair.

Chapter Forty-Eight
Wittenberg, September 1551– September 1552

We have had four years of peace, in our small corner of Saxony at least. In the outside world there has been turmoil aplenty, but it has not touched us. Once I would have wished to be abreast of affairs, now I am content to look no further than my own circle of family and friends. Hans' studies are satisfactorily completed and he is employed at the court in Konigsberg; Paul is training to be a doctor; and Margarethe, at seventeen, is vivacious and competent. Only Young Martin continues to give concern, unable to settle to anything productive. And although I have not the stamina I used to have, I take satisfaction from the fact our holdings are profitable once more and have begun to look forward to happier times ahead.

When the spectre of war resurfaces, with Duke Maurice apparently no longer content to be the emperor's vassal, it is a double blow. I cannot bear to think what may become of us should there once more be a sustained conflict, and there are also more immediate problems. Melanchthon, representing the guardians, comes to me with the ill news.

Maurice has levied taxes on all property to pay for his warmongering, and the drain on my resources is likely to be substantial.

'Are the demands legal?'

'That would be for the courts to decide. Without a ruling, you cannot refuse.'

'I will go to court then, for it is my future and that of my children at stake.'

To Walpurga I say, 'Maurice has the Electoral crown. What more does he want?'

She expresses the bitterness I feel. 'It seems whatever a ruler has, it is never enough.' She gestures at the court papers strewn on the table. 'Will you gain your compensation for the burden the war taxes have put on you?'

'I don't know. But even if I do, there will be other pressures, for war places burdens on us all.'

With the New Year comes a new resolution. I am swivelling my wedding ring, an unconscious action that has long become a habit, and when I look down at it, I know what I must do. Before I can change my mind, I write again to King Christian.

Since my late dear husband always considered you a most Christian king ... I humbly beseech your Royal Majesty to have mercy on this unworthy widow ... to grant me the allowance once promised to him ... I am compelled to petition you for help, since everybody else treats me as a stranger...

I do not have long to wait for a reply but am afraid to open it. It lies on the table all afternoon until Paul returns from classes. I hold my breath as he breaks the seal. His smile is enough and I grab it out of his hand. 'Thank God,'

450

I say.

'Thank King Christian, rather,' he says. 'Will this enable us to prepare and plant the fields?'

'Yes. Oh, yes.'

We are approaching the harvest, our fields shimmering white-gold in the summer heat, when Melanchthon and Bugenhagen appear, their faces wreathed in the broadest smiles I have seen for years.

'What is it?'

Bugenhagen, forgetting convention, grasps both my hands. 'Good news, Katharina. The Convention of Passau guarantees freedom of evangelical faith and worship throughout our territory. We will finally have peace throughout Germany.'

'And best of all,' Melanchthon interrupts him, as if he cannot wait a moment to tell me, 'Johann Frederick is free.'

'Will he return home?'

'He is already on his way. And well received by the people, for the affection they hold for him has never wavered.'

'He will not get back his crown?'

'Maurice remains the elector, but the word is Johann Frederick will establish a court for himself at Weimar and be joined there by his wife and sons.'

'I wish them joy. I wish us all joy.'

Bugenhagen gives my hands a final squeeze. 'Amen to that.'

'I wonder if Johann Frederick thinks longingly of

451

Hartenfels or his castle here,' I say to the Bugenhagens, as we share a supper together.

Walpurga pauses as she pours me a glass of wine. 'It would be surprising if he does not.'

Bugenhagen sets down his knife. 'You would think so, but it seems he is concentrating on looking forward, not back. You know he has renamed the hunting lodge at Wolfersdorf, where he was reunited with his family, as Schloss Froehliche Wiederkunft.'

'Palace of Happy Returning. I like that. It is an example to us all.'

We gather in a harvest that will see us well through the winter. Initially, due to the prolonged dry weather, I worry about the brook serving the Heffner land, but it continues to flow. Wachsdorf is also in good shape, and by early September I think we too have turned a corner. I share my optimism with Dorothea. 'The boys' inheritance is secure, and in a year or two I may be able to redeem the mortgage on Zulsdorf, which should ensure Margarethe's future.'

It is hard to believe it is six years since my dear Martin's death, though sometimes when I think of all that has happened since, I wonder it isn't longer. They say time heals, and it is true the pain is dulled, but I still miss him, though the Lutherhaus and the farms and especially the children and their concerns take all my attention.

With no further need of protection for the city, the garrison withdraws, to the general relief of all those with daughters of a certain age, including me. A relief short-lived when their legacy becomes apparent, as plague once more stalks the city. When the university decamps en masse to Torgau, Melanchthon and Bugenhagen try to persuade me to go with them, but I have twice, through absence, lost almost all we had, and I don't wish to risk it a third time.

'I shall go if the plague reaches the Lutherhaus, but not before,' I say. 'And you may consider that a concession, for we have ridden out the storm of the plague twice before and no doubt could again.'

For a week or two, isolated as we are at the extreme end of the Collegienstrasse, it looks as if we may escape. I should have known our good fortune wouldn't last.

The first case is one of the servants, who, breaking the embargo on visiting within the town, brings the plague to us. Dorothea tends to her, swathed from head to toe and with a mask over her face, and despite my protests, she forbids me entrance. 'You made a promise,' she says. 'Now go, and take Paul and Margarethe with you. I am old and childless, and if I succumb it is little loss.'

As we travel alongside the Elbe, heading for Torgau, I pause the wagon and look back at Wittenberg. It is very much as I first saw it, a jumble of roofs filling the skyline, smoke spiralling from a hundred chimneys. Dominating the view, the twin towers of the Town Church in the centre and the spire of the Castle Church at the far end: fingerposts pointing to heaven. It represented freedom to me then, and it is my town now. As I leave it for the third time, I pray it will not be for long. The road is in a bad state, the hard-packed mud pockmarked with potholes, another legacy of war. It is impossible to avoid them all and each jolt jars my spine.

'We will be black and blue by the time we get there,' I

453

say, when a front wheel hits a particularly deep hole with an ominous creak. 'If indeed we get there at all.'

Paul is encouraging. 'It is not far now, and at least we will be safe from the plague.'

I smile for him. 'And you will be able to resume your studies without any fear of what is happening at home.'

The city is in sight, the ribbon of waterways surrounding it glinting in the sunshine as I steer the wagon onto the main track leading to the city gate.

'Where will we stay?' Margarethe asks.

I half turn to answer her and inadvertently jerk on the reins, causing the horses to break their stride and the wagon to lurch sideways. The edge of the track is crumbling, and in an effort to avoid the wheels slipping into soft soil, I pull hard the other way to drag the horses round. We lurch to the other side of the track, the front horse throwing his head up and baring his teeth, resisting my control. He pushes back, baulking, his front legs stretched out straight, the second horse ramming into him from behind, the wagon swaying. Afraid it may topple, I shout a warning and leap down. As I reach out to grasp the bridle of the leading horse, he rears above me, hooves flailing. I take a step backwards and stumble, my foot catching on the edge of the ditch; the last thing I know is a sharp pain in my side as I fall, and unable to stop myself, I roll sideways, twisting my head to avoid swallowing the muddy water swirling upwards to meet me.

Torgau: December 1552

One half of the room is flooded with light, the other cloaked in shadow. In the distance I can hear singing, a swell of sound, rich and full, the medley of voices blending in harmony so perfect I cannot help but cry. I want to join them, but someone is grasping my hand, holding me back.

I turn my head to see who it is, and find Margarethe, with Paul behind her, and I think they must be able to hear the singing too, for they also are crying.

'Isn't it beautiful?' I say, as I try to slip my hand free.

Her grip tightens, and she drops to her knees beside the bed and lays her head on my chest. 'Don't go, Mutti, please don't go.'

I reach out with my other hand to touch her face, to capture her tears, and smile. 'I must. It is my time ... to go home.'

'We will take you home soon, Mutti.' Paul's voice is cracking.

I shake my head. 'Not to Wittenberg.' I look towards the light and feel the warmth penetrating the bedcovers. It pours over me and into me, dispelling the cold. The singing is closer now, rising to a crescendo, the words becoming clear.

'Holy, holy, holy, is the Lord God Almighty, who was and is, and is to come...'

They are all there. Magdalena and Martin, Muhme Lena and Kath Jonas, Elizabeth Cruciger, Eva and Barbara. And the children, clustered around their feet, baby Lizzie in Magdalena's arms. Andreas Karlstadt is there too, beside Martin, an arm draped around his shoulder. 'Look!' I say to Paul. 'They are reconciled at last. Anna would be so pleased.'

'Mutti.' I hear the anguish in his voice and feel Margarethe's tears on my hand. I stroke her hair. 'Don't cry, please. I'm not afraid, and you must not be either. I cannot stay, but you both have so much left to live for.'

'You have us.'

'And you were … are a joy.'

I feel her tremor. 'But not enough.'

It is so close an echo of her pain when Martin died, that I know I must offer some last words of comfort before I go. I reach out my other hand for Paul and he falls on his knees beside me and I gather them both close. Looking beyond them to the light, I say, 'I can see heaven opened, and in the midst of the great throng I hear your father's tenor voice ringing out, "Worthy is the lamb who was slain…" and soaring above it Magdalena's soprano, "…to receive power and wealth and wisdom and strength…"'

I think of the chantress at Brehna as she placed her fist against my stomach, and remember her exhortation, 'Breathe from here, Linnet,' and I stretch upwards. For the first time in months my voice is strong and true, filling the room to overflowing with music as I join in the song's climax, '…and honour and glory and praise.' As the notes die away, I see a path opening through the crowd. I see a throne, and Jesus, standing, his arms spread wide. And I hear a voice, calling, 'The Spirit and the Bride say, "Come".'

Glossary

German terms

-chen – suffix attached to a name, or shortened name, as a
   form of endearment
Damen – a collective term for a group of women
Hans – shortened form of Johannes
Hanschen – diminutive for Johannes
Haus – house
Lenchen – diminutive for Magdalena
Liebchen – a generic term of endearment
Rathaus – town hall
Schloss – castle / palace
Shaube – overcoat
Slub – raised imperfection in the weave of cloth
-strasse – suffix meaning street
Stube – heated parlour
Tailclout - nappy
Wirtschaft – formal church ceremony to solemnise a
   marriage

Author's Note:

For the last three months of her life Katharina von Bora was bedridden following a fall while trying to stop their horses bolting and potentially overturning their wagon. Although it isn't known the exact cause of her death, it is likely she broke either her pelvis or her hip in the fall. This may have led to pneumonia, which in turn, if untreated, can cause delirium and ultimately death. This is the progression I have chosen to follow here. She was buried in the Town Church at Torgau in December 1552.

Her marriage to Martin Luther was seized on by Catholic opponents as the fulfilment of the myth that the Antichrist would be the offspring of the union of a renegade monk and nun, and also opposed by many of Luther's closest friends and fellow reformers. A marriage of convenience on both sides, which blossomed into an enduring love, it became a paradigm for clerical marriage, then and since.

Their married life was eventful. She handled the pressures and stresses with courage, resourcefulness and resilience. These included death threats, Luther's illnesses and bouts of depression, running their very large household as a boarding house while financially constrained, and moderating Luther's overly generous impulses.

She managed their farm and brewery, organised the printing of much of Luther's writings, and challenged his characteristic outspokenness. She coped with miscarriage, the deaths of two children, several outbreaks of plague, and the devastating effects of war. Following Luther's death, she had to fight to retain her inheritance, her independence, and provide for and protect her children from the continuing conflicts and outbreaks of plague, one of which ultimately led to her flight to Torgau and her own death.

Only eight of her letters remain, and the only genuinely personal comment is in a letter to her sister-in-law following Martin's death. I have included phrases from it here. Her letter to King Christian of Denmark is also documented. Many letters from Martin to Katharina do exist. I have relied heavily on various translations of them and, in occasional cases, slightly paraphrased them in my own words, while retaining the sense. The few other letters as presented here, for example to her friends, are fictional in terms of text, but are set against the context of real events.

The verses quoted from Proverbs Chapter 31 which introduce the book are a selection chosen to reflect documented aspects of Katharina's life. They illustrate the qualities mentioned. The words of the song and the voice quoted in the final section of the book are also found in the Bible – Revelation chapter 4 verse 8; chapter 5 verse 12; and chapter 22 verse 17, respectively. (New International Version)

This is a work of fiction and, though based on extensive research, the Katharina depicted here is my own interpretation. I hope I have done both her, and the faith she professed, justice.

Acknowledgements

As with *Katharina: Deliverance* this book is based on the research trip carried out in Saxony in 2017, and again I want to thank the many folk there who gave so generously of their time and expertise to answer my questions and to show me around, particularly Bettina Brett, Daniel Leis, Anja Ulrich, Hennie Döbert, Adrian Harte, Helgard Rutte, Cornelia Stegner, Ursula Heinz, Kathrin Niese, Anja Bauermeister and Peter Ehrhardt. My research trip would have been so much less productive without your help. (My apologies if I have missed anyone out, or spelled any names wrongly.)

I am indebted to my editor, Richard Sheehan, meticulous, as always, to Marjorie Blake, who again read the unedited text, and to my husband, David, who gave me the time and space to write.

Also by Margaret Skea:

Katharina: Deliverance

Runner-up Historical Novel Society Novel Award 2018

The first book in the series, charting the early life of Katharina von Bora, the renegade nun who became Martin Luther's wife.

> *'It is very shameful that children,*
> *especially defenceless young girls,*
> *are pushed into the nunneries.*
> *Shame on the unmerciful parents*
> *who treat their own so cruelly.*
> Martin Luther

Germany 1505. Five-year-old Katharina is placed in a convent at Brehna. She will never see her father again.

Sixty-five miles away at Erfurt, Martin Luder, a promising young law student turns his back on a lucrative career to become a monk. The consequences of their meeting in 1523 will reverberate down the centuries and throughout the Christian world.

A compelling portrait of Katharina von Bora, set against the turmoil of the Peasants' War and the German Reformation and the controversial priest at its heart.

Praise for *Katharina: Deliverance*

'Assured, evocative, immersive, a fascinating read.'
Catherine Cho, Lead Judge HNS Award.

The Munro Series (Scottish historical fiction) follows the fortunes of a fictional family trapped in an historic and long-running feud between two clans, later dubbed the Montagues and Capulets of Ayrshire.

Turn of the Tide

Scotland *1586*. The 150-year-old feud between the Cunninghames and the Montgomeries is at its height. In the bloody aftermath of an ambush Munro must choose between age-old obligations and his growing friendship with the opposing clan.

A tale of love and loss, loyalty and betrayal, amid the turmoil of 16th century Scotland.

A House Divided

Scotland 1597. The truce between the Cunninghame and Montgomerie clans is fragile. And for the Munro family, living in hiding, under assumed names, these are dangerous times.

A sweeping tale of compassion and cruelty, treachery and sacrifice, set against the backdrop of a religious war, feuding clans and the Great Scottish Witch Hunt of 1597.

'Gripping from the get-go, with drama and intrigue woven throughout the tale, Skea's novel avoids the clichés that often plague this genre. For lovers of historical fiction this is a great read.'
Scottish Field.

By Sword and Storm

1598. The French Wars of Religion are drawing to a close, the Edict of Nantes establishing religious freedom in all but Paris.

For the exiled Adam and Kate Munro, the child she carries symbolises a life free from past troubles, but Paris holds dangers as well as delights. For the Munros and Montgomeries alike, these are troubled times.

'From first to last page this is indeed a 'you are there' experience. A great finale.'
Between the Lines